PAUL CARSON
BETRAYAL

arrow books

Published in the United Kingdom by Arrow Books in 2006

1 3 5 7 9 10 8 6 4 2

First published in the United Kingdom in 2005 by William Heinemann

Arrow Books
The Random House Group Limited
20 Vauxhall Bridge Road, London SW1V 2SA

Random House Australia (Pty) Limited
20 Alfred Street, Milsons Point, Sydney, New South Wales 2061, Australia

Random House New Zealand Limited
18 Poland Road, Glenfield
Auckland 10, New Zealand

Random House (Pty) Limited
Isle of Houghton, Corner of Boundary Road & Carse O'Gowrie
Houghton 2198 South Africa

Random House Group Limited Reg. No. 954009
www.randomhouse.co.uk

A CIP catalogue record for this book is
available from the British Library

Papers used by Random House are natural, recyclable products made from
wood grown in sustainable forests. The manufacturing processes conform
to the environmental regulations of the country of origin

ISBN 9780099469292 (from Jan 2007)
ISBN 0 09 946929 4

Typeset by Palimpsest Book Production Limited,
Polmont, Stirlingshire
Printed and bound in Great Britain by Bookmarque Ltd, Croydon, Surrey

To Jean, Emily and David

1

The ringing tone finally penetrated my sleeping brain. I groped in the dark and found the receiver, succeeding only in knocking it off my bedside locker, and somewhere in the distance a tinny voice called out. Reaching over the edge of the bed I found the coiled wire and slowly dragged the phone upwards. The red digits on my alarm clock flicked to 3.30 and I sensed immediately whoever was calling wasn't bringing good news.

'Yeah?'

'Dr Ryan?'

'Yeah.'

'Sorry to disturb you but we need you at the prison right away.'

I groaned, not tonight of all nights. It was 12 February and freezing outside. For the previous four days Arctic gales had buffeted the east coast of Ireland, icing roads and leaving snow on high ground. The wind chill made it even more dangerous along Dublin's dark and wet streets and the met office was advising against unnecessary journeys. So I was in no mood to be dragged out at such an ungodly hour, especially as I was very comfortable curled up beside my girlfriend Lisa. I could feel her stir as I pulled myself into an upright position and arched away from her body.

'What's up?' I was whispering so quietly I wondered could I be heard.

'We've had a suicide.'

Dammit, not another. Now I was wide awake and trying to get my thoughts in order. This was the fourth at Harmon jail in six months. The media would have a field day. 'What happened?'

'Convict in J-wing found hanged about an hour ago.'

'Any more details?' I was half out of the bed and feeling for my boxers. My hand brushed against Lisa's naked backside and for a delicious moment I left it there before rummaging at the bottom of the duvet. I discovered them and Lisa's panties at the same time and had to block out some very carnal images.

'Not much. I think it's a young guy in on an assault charge. He was only processed today.'

I kept the phone pressed to my ear with a shoulder and flicked on a side light. Now I could see my clothes, scattered to the corners of the room where I'd dropped them in a lustful hurry to get into bed. Lisa had already been there, wearing a half-smile and little else. 'Just a minute.' I had one leg inside my trousers and was skipping to connect with the other. And my mind was racing. The caller said the dead man was found in J-wing but J-wing had been closed for the past week for refits. Also, he was 'a young guy in on an assault charge'. Not true, I thought. Newly processed prisoners are never put into J-wing because it harbours dangerous recidivists. Moving this group of psychos to another centre while the repair work was going on had been a national emergency. Army, air force and armed police had escorted the convoy of murderers as it trundled to a hastily commandeered barracks outside the city. 'Where is he now?'

'I'm sorry, I don't know that.' I tried to link the voice to a face but it wouldn't come. It was male, sounded youngish, maybe thirty or forty, but there was no accent to give me a clue. I pulled a vest, then a heavy sweater over my head and buckled my belt.

'I mean, is he still in the cell? Did anyone touch him?' There were specific guidelines for prison suicides including resuscitation procedures, and as sole doctor to the facility my life was made a lot easier in subsequent inquiries by such attention to detail. Resuscitation efforts often leave marks on the body that can be mistaken for assault injuries. Equally, leaving a corpse as discovered helps in murder cases. In Harmon Penitentiary it wasn't uncommon for feuds to be settled with a contrived self-hanging. Usually the efforts were clumsy and required little more than common sense and basic forensic skills to know the man dangling from his window bars had first been throttled, then dragged to the cell and strung up. Getting witnesses was the problem. Despite forty-four prisoners to a block nobody ever saw anything. So as I slipped on my overcoat I was trying to get as many facts as possible. But the line went dead, leaving me listening to a dialling tone. Then, about two seconds later, I heard a distinct click and I stared at the receiver, puzzled.

A husky voice interrupted my thoughts. 'What's wrong, Frank? Why are you dressed?' Lisa cocked an eye at me from behind the safety of a pillow.

I leaned over and kissed her lightly on the forehead and warm fingertips caressed the back of my neck, making my skin tingle. 'I have to go out.'

Lisa squinted at the digital clock. 'At this hour?' The duvet slipped down from her breasts, distracting me totally.

I sat on the edge of the bed and stroked her long blonde hair, coiling a tress between my fingers and brushing it against her face making her crinkle her nose. But I was in a rush and decided this was not the time to explain the significance of prison suicides. 'I've had a call,' I offered, searching for the right lie. 'One of the inmates is throwing up and they want to know should he be moved out of his cell. They're worried he could start an epidemic.' It was as good as I could come up with considering the time and my need to flee. And, as always, I was trying to shield Lisa from the darker side of my work. But in the back of my head worrying thoughts niggled. Was someone listening in on that conversation? Then, have the newspapers been tipped off? If so I would face a barrage of cameras when I arrived at the massive steel gates in front of the jail.

'I hate that job you do.' Lisa pulled the duvet over her shoulders and pouted. 'Why don't you get a proper hospital position like every other doctor?'

'This conversation is going nowhere,' I said as I reached for my Gladstone bag. I flicked open the lock and checked I had a full complement of emergency drugs, needles and syringes. The patient who awaited me wouldn't need medical attention but from past experience I knew it looked good to arrive fully prepared. So into the bag went my stethoscope, auriscope and compact sphygmomanometer. I made sure everything was in place including a nine-millimetre Beretta handgun. Without removing it from the Gladstone I snapped a full magazine into position and checked the safety catch. Fortunately Lisa didn't hear the ratchet of metal against metal, the gun issue really freaked her out. 'I work at Harmon because that's where the pathology is.' I stuffed a stun grenade into my right pocket and a can of Mace into the left. 'Where else can I see patients with Aids, hepatitis B and C and a multitude of other infections all under one roof?' I closed the lock on the Gladstone and stood up. 'They're human beings just like you and me and don't deserve to be abandoned like dogs. I treat them and at the same time further my research. Now that's the last time I'm going to defend this.'

Lisa put on her hurt look, a cross between a frown and a come-on, and I had to steel myself from crawling back in beside her. 'Hurry back,' she cooed. 'We could have breakfast in bed.' She fluttered her eyelashes provocatively and blew me a kiss. 'Afterwards.' For a daft moment I almost said, After what?

The front door to my apartment is bulletproof. There is a quarter-inch of steel plate bolted to the heavy-duty wooden frame and five separate locks for added protection, including a three-minute time-delay mechanism. I slid the top and bottom bolts free and then turned keys in the two Chubbs and waited. I yawned and scratched my stubble and pressed a switch to my right. Seconds later a TV monitor fixed to the wall flickered and then glowed. The digital-sharp colour CCTV image showed puddles rippling in the wind and sheets of rain but the front entry to the complex was clear with no suspicious movements or shadows. Recently I'd become a failed expert on shadows after calling out an armed response unit when I spotted dodgy shading on the ground underneath my car. It turned out to be an oil leak and this discovery did little for my credibility. Still, the Justice Department insisted on strict security precautions including firearms training, wearing a Combo SPV stab-proof vest when on duty and living in an apartment structured like a fortress. Harmon Penitentiary was run by the prisoners and solely for the prisoners' benefit. To the cell-block bosses the governor and warders were no more than peripheral figureheads. And while the position of Penitentiary Chief Medical Officer sounded grand in reality it was the job from hell. My immediate predecessor had been brutally murdered in front of his family because he'd refused to smuggle heroin into the jail for a notorious drugs baron. The word along the wings was the system had to be taught a lesson. Before that, four other doctors had packed their medical kits and quit after a few months, unable to handle the intimidation and harassment. One found he was being shadowed by a Glasgow hit man while another had bullets sent to him through the post. The other two resigned when they discovered their children were being tailed to and from school. So in many ways that's why I was an ideal candidate for the vacancy when it was advertised. I was a tall and strong single thirty-year-old. I did have a beautiful girlfriend but she was showing no signs of settling into a permanent relationship and was not considered a risk. In addition, as an Australian national with no family ties in Ireland, I didn't have siblings or parents for the crime lords to target. More importantly, I was genuinely interested in prisoner health issues, especially the scourges of HIV and hepatitis, and wanted to carry out a research project where the subjects would stay in the same place. In Harmon few of the inmates were going anywhere, many on life stretches.

The facility was a Victorian dump with the dubious reputation as Europe's most dangerous prison. Built in castellated style, the ten-acre site resembled a razor-wire stronghold from the outside. The perimeter walls were sixty feet high and fifteen feet wide with viewing towers every hundred yards. The five holding wings shot out like spokes on a wheel with upper and lower levels. The design allowed end-to-end observation of all cell blocks from a central HQ, which was a semicircle bulletproof glass unit with a battery of CCTV and listening devices. Solid-lock steel doors, multiple rolls of razor wire and crash bollards protected the entrance. In a country that took great pride in having an unarmed police force, this high-security institution was its sole exception. After a series of hostage-taking scares, knife attacks on warders and two cell-block riots, the authorities were forced to adopt a harsher regime, including the use of fire-arms with live ammunition. The measures reduced the number of violent incidents but didn't enhance the prison's standing. A visiting committee of human-rights lawyers described it as a diseased and drug-ridden nightmare and after twelve months working there I found it hard to disagree with them. There had been a number of attempts to escape over the years, including a recent daring helicopter drop into the exercise yard. However, no one had actually succeeded and the remains of the heli-copter is on show somewhere as a reminder of what can happen when seven Uzi sub-machine guns let rip at the same target at the same time. Inside, the blocks were strictly segregated with separate eating and exercise regimes. Wings A and B detained terrorists and increasingly this meant Islamic extre-mists caught with bomb-making equipment and literature linking them to Al Qaeda. There was also a small quota of diehard IRA volunteers determined to shoot Ireland free from British oppression. Blocks C and D were the lock-ups for murderers, serial killers and arsonists while wings E and F kept violent sex offenders. The row of cells on landings G and H were reserved for less physically vicious types such as counterfeiters, fraudsters, con men and Internet child-porn perverts. There was also a women's wing but no woman doctor so I visited that unit twice a week. J-wing, where I was headed, was the most dangerous division of all.

I changed CCTV camera angles and inspected the immediate corridor outside which seemed clear. Then I surveyed the well-lit stairwell and street-level halls. They were deserted with the audio links silent, not even a draught picked up by the hidden microphones. A separate button activated halogen lights on all sides of the apartment building and I switched to outside views. The small car park was empty apart from three cars and driving rain. The six-year-old badly dented Saab belonged to me while the other two I recognised as owned by a couple living on the ground floor. I don't much care for cars, unlike some doctors who spend much of their time coveting top-of-the-range Mercs and BMWs and Porsches. I prefer public transport but Harmon Penitentiary is five miles away through narrow streets and busy roads so my beloved but neglected Saab kept me mobile. I clipped my personal alarm pager onto my belt and tested the batteries. Then I turned the Yale lock, stepped outside and waited until the door shut behind me. For a moment I stood still and tried to collect my thoughts. The click on the telephone line still bothered me and I considered going back to check that the message had actually come from the prison. Then the clunk of bolts self-engaging echoed along the passage. I knew the time-delay mechanism had also reconnected. The hallway was freezing and I was anxious to get the call over with so I pressed ahead.

I was halfway down the stairs when the niggling doubts became major worries. The J-wing mistake jarred, its significance too important for a simple error. Shifting the recidivist inmates had caused a major stir, not easily forgotten. Why didn't I read the caller ID? And the click on the line, was someone listening in? I stopped in my tracks, my heart thumping in my chest. Relax, I told myself, this could still be an error. It could be a genuine request with the warder just getting the blocks mixed up. Then the lights went out, plunging the building into darkness. I felt ice course up and down my spine.

I pressed the silent alarm mode on my pager and flicked open the Gladstone. The Beretta fitted my grip perfectly. I checked my watch, the luminous dial glowing in the dark. If my worst fears were realised then split-second moves were vital. The

alarm was connected to sensors around the apartment complex and when activated the cry for help
was carried to two police units in the immediate
area. Practice drills had shown an emergency-
response team could be with me within five minutes,
authorised to carry a small arsenal of light firearms.
A paramedic squad was also primed to react. It
was now coming up to four. With good fortune and
empty streets the assist squad might make it in less
than five minutes. I briefly considered crawling
back to the sanctuary of the apartment but just as
quickly dismissed the notion. If some gang were
after me it would only draw them to Lisa. I put
the Gladstone down, desperate not to make a noise,
and set the stun grenade beside me, ready for use.
Then I crouched and tried to hold my breath, by
now frantic with fear and dread.

Where are they? Who are they? Am I overreact-
ing? I slowly unbuttoned my overcoat, slipped it off
and laid it on the step. I sensed movement at the
top of the stairs. I was now at the middle level
with no escape backwards. My mouth was dry,
my pulse so rapid I felt dizzy. Which way to go?
Think, Ryan, think. What did they say at training
exercises? I couldn't remember. No matter how
much I mentally banged my forehead my brain
was too frightened to function. My instructor had
seen action in Bosnia, Lebanon and Liberia and
had fought his way out of many tough spots but

his wise words were wasted at this frenzied moment.

Suddenly, no more than ten feet away in the gloom below, a tall shape became obvious. 'Put the gun down, Ryan.' It was the man on the telephone, I recognised his voice immediately. The call *had* been a ruse to lure me out of my fortress and I'd fallen for it. How did he know I had a gun? 'Put the fucking gun down, Ryan. Do you want us to blow your brains out and leave you like a dog?' This time the snarled order came from behind and I spun to find two large shapes at the top of the stairs. How did they get there? They must have been hiding in a recess at the end of the corridor. And there are three of them. I'll be dead before help arrives. I'm six foot one and weigh two hundred pounds with little flab and am no slouch when it comes to self-defence. My coach says I handle myself well in training but I knew immediately hand-to-hand combat was not an option here. I held up my overcoat as cover and feinted to one side, then rolled in a ball and flung the stun grenade upwards. As soon as I heard it thump on the floor I started shooting downwards. The explosion almost deafened me and echoed round the building. I couldn't see whether my bullets had hit, as the area was black and smelling of cordite. My head bounced off the edge of a step but I kept rolling, one hand gripping my Beretta, the other protecting my fall. I discharged another four rounds, aiming wildly and hoping at least one would knock a target. I realised I was at the bottom of the stairs and scrambled to my feet. The entrance was only a few paces away and could be burst open with an almighty shove. If I reached the car park I could put distance between the thugs and myself, maybe even take cover behind the Saab and shoot it out. The emergency-response unit would be with me by then and I'd be safe. Suddenly a high-powered light flashed into my face, momentarily blinding me. I pulled my gun hand up to shield my eyes and immediately a boot caught me by the ankles, tumbling me to the tiled floor. I dropped like a stone, the force winding me.

'You bastard, Ryan. That fucking grenade nearly killed me.' I couldn't see where the menacing voice was coming from and as I twisted a punch bounced viciously off my left ear. 'Try another stunt like that and I'll tear you apart.' The light went out and I sensed two bulky shapes at my sides, strong hands gripping my arms. I could feel warm breath and smell whiskey.

'Let go,' I shouted, wriggling right and left. 'My bodyguards are outside, you'll never get away.'

Something very hard hit me on the side of the head, stunning me instantly, and the Beretta slipped from my grasp. Now I was completely defenceless, the can of Mace left in the pocket of my overcoat. My feet were lifted from under me and through a dazed fog I realised I was being carried. The front door shattered and splintered as the lock was kicked out and suddenly I was in driving rain. 'Come on, shift it,' a new voice with a strange accent called and I sensed urgency.

An image flashed in my mind, a crime-scene photo of my predecessor lying on the ground after being assassinated. His head lolled like a doll, his body slumped against a wall. His face was unrecognisable, the flesh and bone and cartilage destroyed in a hail of bullets. He was covered in blood. Now it was my turn, but not without a fight. I went limp, the effect forcing the two heavies at my arms to stumble, and there was an angry grunt followed by a string of oaths. 'For Chrissake hold the bastard,' the man gripping my feet shouted. I felt one of them skid on the wet tarmac and bent my knees, drew my legs back with all my strength and tried to spin my body. A savage grip slipped away leaving my head dangling inches from the ground. There was another angry exchange of oaths and then a boot connected with my ribs. I recoiled in pain and started shouting. Suddenly I was lying on my back, the rain drilling against my face as the wind swirled like a mini tornado. I tried to roll to one side but a heel found my groin and stayed there, twisting and grinding. I gagged as a sickening ache filled my belly. Another blow came from somewhere, landing on my shoulder, and I curled myself into a protective ball and wrapped both hands around my head.

I was soaked and terrified and aching and desperate to keep conscious. Where is that fucking emergency-response team? Then I heard the unmistakable sound of a gun being cocked and I froze. This is it. If they can't take me away they'll finish me off. I worm-wriggled furiously and jerked my head back just as the first bullet thudded into the tarmac, inches from my right ear. Then I squirmed again, this time in the opposite direction. A second round seared my scalp and I felt warm blood spurt down my neck. A vicious kick caught me in the back and then one skimmed off my left thigh. I was beginning to sink, the pain and blows taking their toll. But I had to keep going; if I stopped fighting I knew they'd kill me. Through a mountain of pain I lashed out with my right foot but only hit air. Then I rolled onto my side and flailed blindly with hands and feet but didn't connect. The rain was now driving in sheets and the icy wind stung my battered skin. I sensed scuffling beside me. 'Stand back, I'm gonna blow the fucker's head off.' I heard a heavy-duty weapon being cocked and forced my eyes open against the squall. A sawn-off double-barrelled shotgun was being

16

pointed straight at me. I splayed my arms and legs crucifix-style, and waited. Two more boots connected with my head as the barrels flashed and my world went dark.

2

I awoke screaming. I was dead; I had to be because there was so much intense light. My head felt as if it was in a vice, the pain excruciating. I darted my eyes from side to side but saw only phosphorous flare brightness, multicoloured and dazzling and confusing. Where am I? I closed my eyes and immediately the image of a double-barrelled shotgun flooded my brain. I screamed and tried to move but the throbbing in my temples was so severe I collapsed back in a heap, moaning and panting in short bursts. My head hurt, my ribs ached, my back and shoulders and legs were sore. There was a sharp rawness coursing in a straight line at the back of my scalp. My groin was furnace hot. I was a writhing, struggling bundle of extreme pain. I desperately wanted to speak but the effort was more than I could handle and I heard myself grunt and whimper and sob.

*

'It's OK, Mr Ryan. Everything's fine.' A man's voice came at me from the left and I turned towards it but neck spasm made me wince and catch my breath. 'I'm going to give you something to make you comfortable.' Then I heard another voice, this time female and reassuring. A warm hand curled around my own and squeezed it gently and I squeezed back, desperate for any form of human contact. I overheard a snatch of conversation and almost cried with relief. It was real people talking with normal-sounding voices. I wasn't dead. Suddenly I felt a sting in my backside and heard the word morphine whispered. The warm hand was now stroking my forearm while another brushed at my hair. My mind drifted and the hurt began to ease. I kept my eyes closed and pushed a hand beneath my body and felt damp sheets, then a mattress. I pressed my neck against the softness holding me up. The mattress started to move and I floated to the outside lane of a slow-moving traffic circle. Now I could hear car horns and people babbling and the hum of stalled vehicles. I sniffed, expecting to smell diesel fumes, but only got a hint of Hibiscrub antiseptic. I'm in hospital. Please God, let me be in hospital. Then my senses fogged over and mercifully I fell asleep.

'Where am I?' I was propped up in bed on a bank of pillows, awake but this time not so fearful. My eyes took in the space, its clinical white walls and ceiling with a dark blue door almost directly in front. Crossword-puzzle-patterned privacy curtains were half drawn on each side, immediately reminding me of a hospital recovery unit. The room was about thirty foot square with a tight-pile industrial-strength beige carpet. Another blue door opened into a grey-tiled side cubicle that looked like a bathroom. There were two chunky and narrow panelled ripple windows unusually high up on the walls. They offered little light compared to the harsh fluoro tubes above me. I was underneath faded yellow linen with a red logo machine-stitched to the corners. A drip was attached to a vein in the back of my left hand and through a blur I read '5% Dextrose' on the fluid bag. Another bag hung from a stand and I wondered what had coursed through my veins while I was unconscious. Pushed into a corner was the apparatus of resuscitation. There was oxygen tubing with plastic face masks; suction piping and a collection bottle; an anaesthetic trolley with syringes, ampoules, stainless-steel artery clips and needle holders, scissors, bandages and swabs. Rust-red endotracheal tubes rested beside a shiny stainless-steel laryngoscope. There was a cardiac monitor at eye level and I watched with simple fascination as my heart rhythm flickered across the blue screen. I was relieved to see the red lines zig-zag in the correct mode, the impulses carried from three electrodes stuck to my chest. Whatever had happened during the assault, my heart was still in perfect working order. A pretty young nurse in green fatigues leaned over me. 'How are you feeling, Mr Ryan?' She lifted my right hand and stroked the skin. She was smiling at me and I knew it wasn't a false smile because her eyes smiled too and I felt reassured.

'Where am I?' I tried to sit up but couldn't as a fresh wave of pain swept over and I felt light-headed and sick. The blood must have drained from my face as the nurse's expression changed immediately. She gently eased me into the support of the pillows and pressed a buzzer on the wall. A red light glowed on the tip of the buzzer and if my guesswork was correct somewhere outside another red light would flick into ON mode, alert-ing medical staff. I lay back and waited for the dizziness to pass and when I looked up again a female doctor was frowning at me. She was wear-ing Islamic headdress and clothes, her skin sallow. There was no name tag to help me identify her country of origin and so I plumped for Egypt. There were a lot of Egyptian medics working in Dublin.

'You must take it easy, Mr Ryan, and please do not move without help,' she admonished. 'You have been in another world altogether for the past twenty-four hours and you are very weak.' She paused to inspect a chart and then adjusted the drip rate. It gave me a few seconds to absorb what she'd said. I've been out for a whole day! What did those bastards do to me? The doctor returned her attention. 'Fortunately, you have not broken any bones or damaged internal organs but you were severely beaten.' She forced a medical panic alarm into my right hand, turning it so my thumb rested on the button. 'From now on if you need help, press that. If you want to use the toilet, press that. If you feel a change in your condition, press that. If you feel you are getting cold or too warm, press that. If you—'

By now I'd heard enough. 'Yeah, yeah,' I snapped. 'I'll press the fucking button. Now tell me, where am I?'

The doctor's expression switched from frown to disapproval and I silently cursed my bad temper. This was as much a cultural mistake as ill manners. 'You are in hospital and you will stay here until they decide it is safe for you to leave.' This time her tone was neutral, as if she was reading from a prepared statement.

'Which hospital?' Suddenly I didn't give a damn that I'd annoyed her, I was the one in the bed in no man's land. 'Is it Beaumont or the Mater? Maybe St Vincent's or St James's?' I threw out a list of Dublin hospitals within a five-mile radius of my apartment. I had to be in one of them.

'I am sorry. I am not permitted to tell you.' The doctor scribbled a note on the chart and turned on her heel. I struggled to sit up and challenge the dismissive answer but the furnace in my groin suddenly became an agony and I called out. The faintness and nausea started to crawl back into every pore and I needed to throw up. I dry retched, the spasms draining the strength from my body, and I had to hold my ribs and gasp in between gags. Then another sting hit my bottom and I slipped back into the traffic queue. This time in my trance I really thought I could smell diesel. And I couldn't stop giggling, convinced I was hallucinating. Everyone here spoke with an English accent. Even the lady from Egypt.

'Lisa, where's Lisa? Oh, my God, did anything happen to Lisa?' A terrible sense of dread washed over me.

'Who is Lisa?' The friendly nurse was holding my hand again while one of her colleagues sponged me down. Minutes earlier I had woken as warm soapy water hit my thighs and I had had to stifle a cry of indignation. I must have wet myself in the drug-induced sleep, the ultimate humiliation.

'My girlfriend. She was in my apartment when I was attacked. Is she OK? Did they go after her?' I heard the fear in my own voice.

23

'We have no information on anyone called Lisa and you are the only patient we're dealing with.'

Oh, the relief. They can't have got to her. 'Can I see her? Can you call her and let me speak with her?'

'I'm sorry, Mr Ryan. No one is allowed to see you.'

'I just want to talk to her.'

'Or talk to you.' Friendly face had shifted to cautious information-giver. 'They are taking this seriously and have given strict instructions not to allow visitors or telephone calls.'

'Fuck them,' I snapped. I wasn't going to be dictated to by the Justice Department. Hell, I was their prize catch. 'I want to talk to Lisa. I want to hear from her that she's all right.' Even swearing hurt me and I had to grit my teeth against the pain. 'Who's in charge around here?'

The nurse made a face and her eyes darted towards a corner of the room. She moved the privacy curtains so I could see. An armed detective spilled out of a soft chair, a half-smile flickering as he caught my astonished stare. I could see a revolver on a side table and a Heckler and Koch MP-5 machine pistol rested against his shoulder. Underneath his unbuttoned and unfamiliar-looking black uniform he was wearing a bulletproof vest. They *are* taking this seriously. I looked at the nurse. 'Where am I?' She glanced at the officer and I saw him shake his head. He stood up and came closer.

'You're in hospital, Mr Ryan. Just take it easy and stop asking so many questions.' He pointed his gun at the blue door. 'There are two more armed policemen outside.'

My head was spinning from this new information and I half wondered was the morphine still in my system. The nurse lifted my head and plumped the pillows, then she smiled at me; but this time her eyes didn't smile and I wasn't reassured.

My nurse's name was Helen, she finally told me after I had badgered her for hours. She was a Bristol-trained SRN with loads of experience, including a stint at Cook County Hospital ER in Chicago, the busiest emergency unit in North America. 'I'm impressed,' I told her as she fussed over a bandage stuck to my scalp where a bullet had ploughed a deep furrow. The laceration was now protected by stitches. She was soaking caked blood away with a warm antiseptic solution and it stung, but not enough to complain. 'You must have seen a lot of action.' Now she was cutting at hair beyond my field of vision.

'Yes, big time. Gunshot wounds, knife wounds, crowbar wounds. All sorts of different injuries came through those swing doors. Then there were the usual casualties such as traffic accidents, road falls and things like that. I really enjoyed my time there. I got a lot of experience, the work was challenging and I was never bored.' A gloved finger probed at my gash.

'Then managing me one-to-one must be a real bummer,' I said.

She stopped what she was doing and looked straight at me, her expression a confusion of concern and hesitation. 'No, absolutely not. I've been working the p—' She suddenly cut short and her face disappeared from view. When it reappeared I could see she was flustered. 'I've been doing this and that for some time, just for variety.'

I knew she was lying but I couldn't understand why. And I knew that she knew that I knew she was lying and I knew that she knew I was trying to understand why. The whole place was a mixture of contradictions. For a hospital it was unusually quiet. I hadn't heard a bedpan drop, a telephone ring or a shower run since I'd regained consciousness. Nor had the frantic klaxon of an ambulance in full throttle reached my ears. And, apart from my own foul mouth, there wasn't the hint of bad language. This was not the norm in any hospital I'd worked. Where am I?

'There was a man with you on the day I recovered. I distinctly remember a male voice. Who was he?' Nobody was answering my questions fully, not Helen, not the armed policeman, not the Egyptian doctor. Every response was evasive, controlled or changed halfway. I decided on a different approach. 'I don't remember seeing him again.'

Helen nibbled at her lower lip, her eyes avoiding mine. 'That was Dr Mills, the trauma specialist. They insisted he oversee your management until you recovered.'

That sounded reasonable, to a point. 'Will he check in on me again?'

'Em, I'm not too sure but I'll ask if you like.' Helen was writing on a fluid-balance chart at the end of my bed, still avoiding my gaze.

'Who are "they", Helen? Every time I ask a question all I'm offered is "they" ordered this, or "they" won't allow this. What "they" is everyone talking about? Is it the Justice Department?'

She deliberately glanced at her watch. 'It's past six, Mr Ryan. I'd better ring for your dinner or you'll miss out altogether.' She gave a nervous laugh. 'And that wouldn't do, would it?' She was out of the unit quicker than I could reply, leaving me alone with my thoughts. As the door clunked behind her I realised there were significant bolts keeping it shut. Much the same sound came from the door to my own apartment. I waited a few minutes and then examined the fluid-balance chart. There was only a child-like squiggle at the bottom of the page. There were no words or medical shorthand notes.

★

I worked on Helen. I was now in my fourth day in the single and rather lonely recovery room and she was the one constant figure during my waking hours. She'd disconnected the IV line when I started to keep down fluids. She brought my meals and cleared the tray away afterwards. She checked vital signs every four hours, administered painkillers when I asked for them and chatted to me regularly, trying to keep my spirits up. She changed the bedlinen, plumped my pillows and held my floppy arms as I took my first unsteady steps. She washed me from head to toe and didn't even blush when she inspected the bruising around my groin. From her expression and nibble on her lower lip I gathered the sight wasn't pleasant. But as my strength returned and the pains abated I could stir with more freedom. So I watched her every move, which was no great hardship as she was easy on the eye. When she smiled she lit up the room, so I teased her to make her smile. 'I think I need another bed bath.' That was about fifteen minutes after the previous one. I was enjoying the sensation of warm soapy water against my skin. 'Will you take my temperature, I feel feverish.' I wasn't, but it was as good an excuse as I could come up with to keep her in the room and pump her for information. Slowly we became friends and she was more relaxed in my company. I believed she was becoming sympathetic to my plight.

*

After lunch I asked for a television or radio to relieve the boredom but the police bodyguard said it was impossible to get reception in this room. He ignored my disbelieving stare. When I asked for a newspaper he told me there wasn't a recent one about the place.

I inspected my battered face in the mirror. I had two black eyes, bluish to purple bruises on my left cheek and much the same on my right ear. My left ear was swollen and red and my forehead showed gravel marks where the skin had skimmed the ground. I also had a thick growth of stubble and it itched like hell. I undid the white hospital-issue gown and let it fall from my shoulders and groaned as I saw the welts and contusions on my chest and sides. I touched the back of my scalp gingerly, careful not to disturb the stitches. My testicles were normal and undamaged even though my scrotum was swollen. My penis was black and blue as if I'd spent a month's work experience in a whorehouse. How did they not break any bones? They certainly didn't hold back with their boots and fists and whatever else used to subdue me. And how did they miss with that shotgun? It was pointing straight at me. Nothing made sense.

'Are you ready?' Helen had a green plastic beaker full of foamed soap and when I nodded she started lathering my chin and side locks. We were in the ensuite bathroom and out of the corner of my eye I could see her examine me in the mirror. 'You've lost a lot of weight,' she said as she dabbed on a shaving brush of lather.

I looked at my chest again, noticing the ribs straining at the skin. 'You're right,' I muttered, 'I used to carry much more flesh.'

My face was covered in foam and I watched as Helen produced a cut-throat and sized me up. 'Where will I start?'

I turned my head from side to side; relieved the bruising was covered, if only for a few minutes. 'It's your call,' I said. 'From where I'm sitting, even if you start slashing instead of shaving it won't make me look any worse.'

She laughed and our eyes met in the mirror but she averted her gaze. She put one hand on my forehead to steady and started a gentle sweep from chin to cheek. I could hear the bristle rasp as the blade sliced through. She continued along the neckline, then switched attention to my sideburns and didn't nick the skin once. I have a good head of jet-black hair that needs attention every three weeks but right then it looked a mess, as if I'd been in a wind tunnel. What the hell, I wasn't entering any beauty competitions.

'I'd say you're quite a handsome man underneath all those bruises.' Helen had finished and was wiping away surplus foam. She held a hot towel against my face allowing me just enough space to see. The same red machine-stitched logo was on the towel as the bedlinen. The steam had misted up the mirror and I had nowhere to look to distract myself.

'Where am I, Helen?' I asked. I was sitting on a swivel stool and turned so I had her full attention. I took her hands in mine and squeezed them, just as she had done to me three days earlier. She chewed her lower lip and looked past me, scuffing her toe at the floor. I felt she wanted to tell me something.

'You're in hospital,' she said, louder than necessary. She stretched past me and started writing in the misted mirror. As the letters appeared she continued speaking. 'And you're making excellent progress.' THE ROOMS . . . 'The doctors say you might be able to go home soon.' . . . ARE . . . 'But maybe we'll keep an eye on you for a bit longer.' . . . BUGGED.

I stared at the words, my mind doing yet another somersault. What the hell is going on? Why would the Justice Department bug me? I looked up at Helen and she shrugged and shifted the face towel to my neck. Then she wiped the letters away, careful not to leave even a trace.

Alone in my room I sat at the side of the bed and played with the food in front of me. My nursing,

31

medical and police minders had taken time out for a meeting. Or so they said. On a tray was a plastic bowl of grapefruit segments as a starter, then roast beef with gravy, boiled potatoes and green peas. This was served on a paper plate. There was a plastic glass of water to wash the food down and when I'd finished I could enjoy jelly and ice cream out of a sealed plastic container. The utensils to help me eat were standard aeroplane plastic, supplied as attack- and suicide-proof. When I turned the jelly-and-ice-cream container upside down, underneath were the letters HMP. I padded to the blue door and tried the handle. It moved but the door didn't. I squinted at the tiny gap between the door edge and its frame and counted four bolts, all of them significant. I stood underneath the narrow windows with their thick glass and inspected the shadows behind. They were iron bars, I was sure of it. I lifted the jelly-and-ice-cream container again and ran a finger along the indents of the letters HMP. Now the logo on the sheets and towels made sense; the machine stitch-ing was tight but when I looked closely the letters HMP could be seen. I concluded that the linen I used and the food I ate were supplied by Her Majesty's Prison service. The room I was in was heavily secured and had barred windows. My protec-tors all spoke with English accents. There was only one explanation. I was in jail. In England.

3

I couldn't find even a twilight zone of peace. Nowhere in the late night or early morning did my brain shut down and allow me undisturbed sleep. I tossed and turned, moaned and sighed and fought for total rest, escape from the torment of irrational thoughts and desperate attempts to understand my situation. What is happening? Why am I in an English jail? Why was I beaten unconscious and then spirited out of the country? During the day no one offered explanations that made sense; still everyone avoided my increasing torrent of questions. So my imagination roller-coasted in a convulsion of panic and fear and lack of understanding. Right up to day six.

'Get up, Ryan. You're out of here.'

I rolled over and arched a hand against the glaring light. 'What time is it?'

'Coming up on seven. You've got thirty minutes to wash and dress.'

I finally located the voice; it was my police body-guard with two burly colleagues towering over me. They were in full uniform and armed, handguns hanging low on their hips. Their faces were grim and unfriendly, as if taking me to an interrogation.

'Where am I going?' I started to climb out of the warmth of my bed, for once reluctant to leave its comfort. Out of the corner of an eye I could just about make out the slim ankles of a female and squinted past the bodies to find Helen in the background. She ducked my questioning stare. 'What's the rush anyway?'

Three pairs of rough hands grabbed me by the upper arms and physically lifted me into the air, then bustled me towards the bathroom. 'You've got ten minutes to wash. When you're finished come out naked. We don't want a towel or face cloth covering any part of your body. The door stays open while you're in there. Gottit?' The tone was belligerent and threatening.

The coldness of the tiles on my feet caught my breath and I danced into the shower cubicle, groping for the power panel. At last hot water cascaded over my body, making the skin tingle and ripple. I let the spray run even hotter until it began to sting my bruises and contusions. And I wondered at the sudden turnaround in attitude. My protectors had become snarling guard dogs, snapping angrily at my heels and hurrying me from sleep. I shampooed and soaped my body liberally, more a delaying tactic than attention to hygiene. What the hell is going on now?

A shadowy figure filled the door-frame, watching every move. 'C'me on, speed it up.'

I dried and dropped the towel and edged out into the main room, any sense of shame or embarrassment abandoned. If they wanted me naked then that's the way they would find me. Battered, beaten, kicked and thumped into a mass of black-and-blue welts. Surely not a pretty sight.

'Turn around in a full circle.' The order was barked from my right and I shuffled in a three-hundred-and-sixty-degree angle, both hands hanging at my sides. Now I was fully alert and could see clearly. Apart from the heavies inspecting me from head to toe and my nurse confidante there was another man leaning against the door-frame. The light still dazzled and I didn't let my gaze rest on him for long but in that time our eyes locked.

'OK, dress him. Hold out every stitch of clothing before he puts it on.'

Helen was beside me with a pair of boxers. She turned them inside out and waited for a grunted approval before offering. I stepped into both openings and pulled them to my waist. They fitted snugly, too snugly considering how much weight

I'd lost. I decided I'd been measured while I was asleep. Next came socks and T-shirt, again each item closely inspected before I was allowed pull it on. Now Helen showed a pair of tracksuit bottoms, navy blue with elasticised ankles and waistband. The pockets were pulled out, and then pushed back. For a black moment I felt I was in some conjuring show with Helen the pretty assistant to me, the magician. I get into trousers with empty pockets and, hey presto, seconds later I pull two white doves from the seams. But more scowls and barked orders immediately dismissed such fanciful thoughts and the ritual continued until I was fully dressed, each piece of clothing cleared before being nodded through. They all fitted neatly, no sleeve too short and each vest allowing just enough free movement. Then I heard the jangle of chains and within seconds my ankles were encased in steel.

'For your own protection,' one of the bodyguards offered as he shoved me towards the door. 'Follow the leader.' I started to protest but the words stuck in my throat. What was the point?

'Wait.' The line was brought to a sudden halt as Helen grabbed my sleeve. 'Sit down.' She motioned to the side of the bed. I glanced at the henchmen but none of them seemed put out. 'I'm going to give him paracetamol to keep him comfortable,' she explained as she filled a plastic glass from a plastic beaker of water. 'He's still in a lot of pain.' I wasn't but if Helen said I was I wasn't starting an argument. She rustled in a side pocket and made a show of punching out two white capsules and placing them in my left hand. 'Swallow these in one go.' I tipped the tablets onto the back of my tongue and took a deep gulp of water. As I set the glass back I felt her fingers slip inside my right pocket. Then she ruffled my hair and forced a smile. 'Good luck,' she said and then busied herself tidying the bedlinen.

'Thanks,' I muttered, wondering why I needed good wishes. I also wondered what she'd stuck in my trousers, why I was wearing leg irons and who was the face at the door? Then my hands were linked behind my back with plastic ties and I had something else to think about.

There was no one outside, no extra minders as promised on the first day I came to. When the heavy bolts finally unlocked and the door swung open I was met by a blast of ice-cold air and found myself standing in a narrow and dimly lit corridor. There was only one room along the passageway and I had just come out of it; now it looked even less like a hospital recovery unit. I glanced above, noting no red-light warning button for emergencies and wondered where Helen had connected to when she pressed the alarm buzzer. And there was a complete absence of tables or chairs suggesting no one had stood guard the previous days. A hand gripped the back of my tracksuit top and I was frogmarched towards an iron-barred gateway twenty yards ahead.

'What day is it?' I asked.

'Christmas Day for all I care. Keep moving or we'll drag you by the heels.'

'Where are you taking me?'

'Don't know.'

I shuffled as fast as my chains would allow, desperately trying to make sense of this rapidly changing situation. I struggled for composure, scared witless but damned if I was going to let the bastards see white fear. Further along, strange faces peered at me as other steel gates were swung open, heavy-duty locks turning against heavy-duty keys jangling on wide circular loops. Everywhere the accents were English with regional variations here and there. Scouse, then Brummie and an occasional cockney. There wasn't a soft brogue to be heard anywhere and in the chill of the morning every breath frosted.

The steel doors became thicker, the locks stronger and the guards more questioning as I was marshalled from one corridor to the next. 'Prisoner's name and date of birth? Who is the officer in charge?' Whatever answers were offered were out of earshot and I was processed quickly. The walls were now natural brick and solid and at head height there was the occasional trace of dried blood. I hoped this was from someone staggering against the blocks, for no one could possibly escape from here. Then again, maybe the aggression I sensed all around came to a boil along these passageways. Accidents could happen; people could stumble or be pushed and not be able to protect themselves if their hands were restrained. Just as mine were now. What did I do so wrong to be treated like this? I'm a doctor, not some mass murderer. But I kept my mouth shut, knowing I was being worked to someone else's agenda.

'Sign for him.' A tall and mean-faced officer in navy-blue fatigues and peaked cap was staring at me. In his hand he held a clipboard that was passed behind. I heard a biro click into action, a short scrawl and a page torn away. All the time I stared defiantly into the middle distance, trying not to let the intimidating glares get to me. I adopted the attitude of my prisoner patients at Harmon jail: mean and surly and embittered. But it was all bravado for I hadn't a clue what was going on or where I was being taken. And I knew better than to ask.

Now I could see natural light ahead, weak and grey and unwelcoming. Through an open corridor of bars and steel doors I sensed feverish activity. Men in faded brown fatigues were being moved from one part of the facility to another, their shouts and banter loud to my ears after so many days in relative silence. The whiff of disinfectant couldn't mask the background reek of body odour and unwashed socks and for a brief moment I turned to look but a hand grabbed me by the neck, twisting my head forward. The grip stayed there, fierce and deliberately overtight for maximum pain but I refused to wince or protest, that would only suggest weakness. But in my split-second sideways glance I recognised the attire and demeanour of prisoners on the move, reinforcing my sense of place. It also reinforced my sense of bewilderment. The clamour of the institution soon became babble with keys jangling, feet shuffling and orders being barked. Now I could hear the noise of cutlery and crockery and the hint of freshly cooked breakfast. I smelt bacon and sausages and burnt toast and it made my belly rumble with hunger. But these sensations quickly disappeared when I was prodded around yet another corner and up to a solid wooden door reinforced with rivets. Three sets of keys turned locks and an intercom was activated before it slowly opened, hinges grinding and protesting. Now I was in a high arched atrium with uniformed officers milling around, faces set grim with whatever tasks they were at, only an occasional sense of banter detected. There were CCTV cameras and a bank of TV screens on which constant movement could be seen. A high-decked reception desk had a group of men and women wearing different uniforms working at PCs, their eyes darting up from the keyboards only occasionally. Paperwork was being thrust in front of them, snagged and jammed into various trays. There was the soft murmur of conversation and the atmosphere was more office than penitentiary, the air cleaner and fresh from good ventilation.

From behind someone pulled me to a halt. 'Wait here.' With my ankles shackled and my hands tied it was unlikely I was going to have a leisurely stroll around the prison, checking the medical facilities and doing quick physicals.

'Sure,' I said politely, bottling the anger struggling to break through. Now I could observe the setting without the threat of grip burns on my neck. This had to be the front hall of the jail; its architecture and relatively laid-back security suggested a zero-level risk zone. It reminded me of the Harmon Penitentiary reception area for visitors: sterile, non-threatening and businesslike. And it suggested I could be on my way out. But to where? Any sense of elation at the thought of freedom was dampened by the uncertainty of what lay ahead. And Helen's touch in my pocket still intrigued. Even though the bulge was barely noticeable against my skin it seemed like a white-hot coal, scorching and irritating.

'Frank Ryan?' I turned and found the face at the door I'd seen earlier. I couldn't figure out what it was but something seemed familiar about him.

'Yes.'

'My name is Noel Dempsey and I'm responsible for your transfer.' Having a name to this face didn't help me make a connection until I suddenly realised I'd heard his voice before.

'Where are you taking me?'

'Shortly the chains will be removed. I'll give you a few minutes to loosen up and then we're leaving.'

'Where are you taking me?'

'There's a security van waiting outside for the journey. You will be put into the rear and placed in seat restraints. These are for your own protection and it would be easier all round if you cooperated fully. The journey isn't that far so you won't be uncomfortable for too long.'

'Where are you taking me?'

'You ask too many questions.'

It was a large van with Unit 4 logos in bold red on the side and rear panels, backed up to the entrance so I could be moved directly inside. In charge was a two-man black crew in khaki outfits carrying nightsticks, handcuffs and cans of Mace. They took control immediately, bored and indifferent to my plight, and before the doors slammed shut I saw rain and felt a slice of bitterly cold air. Inside I looked around, my now-handcuffed hands feeling the bodywork. It was solid, as solid as the four narrow tinted windows high up on each side. I was strapped to a padded seat with locked restrainers at waist and ankles but there was enough length on my wrist chains to allow me to scratch my nose if I reached up and bent my head down at the same time. A deep rumble beneath my feet told me the engine was being gunned alive, then a jolt as the van moved. I swayed as it swerved and bumped, my head bouncing off the padded headrest. Inside this fluorescent-bathed chamber with only my thoughts to keep me company I wondered for the hundredth time what was going on. And I was angry. The aches and pains and bruises had healed to a degree of comfort and my strength had returned. The weight loss had stabilised and I felt I'd gained a few pounds. I flexed my biceps, watching them knot and bulge underneath the layers of clothes. Then I clenched and unclenched my fists, running the knuckles along my tracksuit seams until they reddened and became warm. I tightened my quads, first the left leg, then the right. I kept doing that until the muscles ached.

Then I remembered Helen's package. It was deep inside the pocket on the right side and almost impossible to retrieve. I leaned as far as I could to one side to make the pocket gape, then tried to flex my chained hands downwards. My fingers stopped an agonising inch above the bulge. Now I slid downwards until the waist restraints dug into my belly and tried twisting from side to side. The bulge swivelled off the seat edge and now I could rub my leg repeatedly up and down until I sensed it dislodge and shift. I sat back in the seat, exhausted from the effort. Sweat was forming on my brow and a drop began a long journey from neckline to chest. I took a deep breath and turned again so the pocket peaked and now my desperate fingers finally touched off the bulge. It felt soft and I was scared I would push it deeper and out of reach. At last I managed two fingers around an edge and slowly, tantalisingly teased the mystery bump free. It was a crumpled tissue, as if balled and squeezed there as a joke. I stared at it for maybe three minutes, unsure what it might contain, if anything. Then I saw black ink lettering. With sweaty fingers I pulled the hankie out from each corner and flattened it gently against my knee. The movement of the van combined with the few minutes of Houdini efforts had left my legs trembling and I had difficulty reading the letters. As I looked down beads of sweat dropped onto the tissue and were quickly absorbed, further blurring the ink. But I managed to read Helen's message before it was lost. U WR SDTD ND NTRGTD.

The carrier must have taken a hump-backed

bridge at some speed as suddenly I felt my stomach sink and my legs turn to jelly. Perspiration dripped down my face and my hands shook. I began to hyperventilate and had to concentrate hard not to psyche myself into a panic. Then I tried rational medical analysis. Six or so days ago I was a normal individual doing a normal job, even if it was in an extraordinary institution. Then I was attacked and beaten up in Dublin. Five or so days ago I woke in a unit, supposedly a hospital room but in fact a prison cell in England. And for the rest of the time I was lied to by a considerable group of people including policemen, doctors and nurses. Lied to about time, about place and about circumstances. Now I learned I'd also been sedated and interrogated. My life held no secrets so what was there to learn? What could I possibly have that demanded such outrageous questioning techniques? By now I was fit to kill and managed to wipe my forehead with the tissue, relieved the ink smudged beyond recognition. I dropped it onto the floor and ground it into pieces with the thick ribbed soles on the trainers I'd been issued. I started jiggling my knees for exercise and worked at every muscle I could move without restraint, all the time my mind in overdrive. By the time I felt the van come to a halt I had made some careful calculations based on the half-life of morphine and standard anaesthetic agents. I combined that with

my understanding of the moment of unconsciousness and finally coming to. There were twelve hours
missing. What happened to me during that spell?
What information did 'they' think I had that could
only be learned through a sedated interrogation?
The tornado of questions left me like a caged lion,
ready to rip my captors apart.

'Out.' Noel Dempsey was trying to stand upright
against heavy winds blowing across deserted and
flat countryside. The rear doors to the Unit 4 security van were open and the crew had unfastened
the restraints. Only my hands remained cuffed.

I sat defiantly in the seat and scowled out at
them. 'Fuck off.' Daring combined with anger was
emboldening me.

'Oh, for Chrissake, Ryan, get out. If I have to
go in after you someone's going to get hurt and
it won't be me.' Dempsey was wearing a heavy
overcoat with lapels up to the neck. Against the
gusts he had his head buried deep for protection.
Squalls of rain drilled against the wide tarmac
beneath his feet and the van rocked slightly with
each flurry. The two black men were looking in at
me, their expressions a mixture of contempt and
loathing. Their khaki uniforms were getting soaked
and they were shivering. I could almost hear their
thoughts. If you don't shift it, man, we're gonna
take lumps outta you.

'Take the handcuffs off,' I shouted against the background racket. 'My wrists are bleeding.' And they were, I'd spent the past ten minutes deliberately chafing them against the connecting chains to the point where the skin broke and split. It hurt like hell but I persevered until I had enough blood dripping along my hands and onto my tracksuit bottoms. It looked good from my point of view.

Dempsey leaned slightly into the van to have a closer look and I sized him up. He was an inch or so above six feet, lean and hungry looking with pinched features. His hair, now blown in all directions, was mousy brown and thinning. He had a hawk nose, like a beak and prominent. I put him somewhere around his early forties. His inspection lasted no more than seconds. 'Take them off,' he growled, 'and then get him out of there.'

Now I was in the full force of the gale and felt the chill cut to my bones. Spats of rain bounced off my face and I turned towards the airflow and let it catch me full on. The shock heightened my senses and I felt my heart pound as I took in the setting. We were at some remote and almost deserted airstrip, fields on all sides and only one access road. An attempt had been made to screen the flight path with chain-link fencing but it had rusted and fallen down in places, leaving gaps like missing teeth. The wind and rain were strengthening and in the distance I could see an orange wind-sock flapping wildly. There was a cluster of single-storey out-buildings that I presumed were the control tower cum waiting area. I'd once done a spell in the Flying Doctor Service in Australia and was familiar with bush airstrips offering the most basic landing and take-off facilities. About five hundred yards ahead a small aeroplane was slowly edging towards the beginning of what looked like a runway. Against the storm I could just about hear the growl of its engines. The Unit 4 crew linked arms with mine and pressed me behind Dempsey as he struggled to make headway against the elements. The bite of the wind and sting of the rain forced everyone's head downwards and I deliberately kept the pace to my own speed. At first I entertained thoughts of escape but as I took in the bleak and exposed terrain I knew I wouldn't get far. And I wanted to get closer to Dempsey as I had a feeling where I'd heard his voice before.

We were within twenty feet of the aeroplane, a white Cessna 340 with blue trim and ID markings D416HJ on the fuselage and underneath both wings. It looked about a tenth the size of a commercial jet and when its retractable hull door opened inside I could see leather seating for four. In the cockpit a pilot and co-pilot wearing headphones craned their necks to see what was coming their way.

Dempsey turned to me. 'OK, Ryan, you're on the move again. I want you to get inside the plane and sit in the seat to the immediate left of the door. Understand?'

'Where are you taking me?' I put menace into my voice.

'Up in the air.' Dempsey matched me, menace for menace.

'Cut the shit. Where are you taking me?'

'Up in the air.' Now his menace was tempered with indifference.

'Where you taking me?'

'Fuck off.'

My arms were still linked to the Unit 4 crew and they tightened their grips, sensing confrontation, but I loosened up and they relaxed slightly.

I finally sat inside the hull, held back by strong seatbelts. My eyes acknowledged the two in the cockpit but not a word was spoken as they waited until Dempsey secured his place directly opposite. I massaged my bloodstained wrists, exaggerating the discomfort, but Dempsey paid no attention to me and turned away when the door slammed shut.

Now the engines roared and the Cessna jerked slightly, then moved slowly into position for take-off. The crosswinds buffeted the bodywork and there was a hairy moment as the tail jumped slightly, caught in a fierce updraught. The intercom crack-led into life.

'Control, this is December four one six Harry Juliet.'

'Go ahead, Harry Juliet.'

'Ready for take-off.'

'Read you.'

The surge of power from the propellers shook the bodywork and the aeroplane moved forward, gathering speed rapidly. As the throttle was opened and the control column pulled back the craft tilted slightly, then bumped back onto the tarmac before the nose again lifted into the air. I felt my insides move in a queasy motion and gripped the side rests tightly, my knuckles whitening as the plane fought against crosswinds. Then we were high in the air and minutes later banked to forty-five degrees off central and below I could see tiny cars rushing along narrow lanes, small houses and hedgerows. Then rain filled the porthole windows, obscuring the view as the plane continued its ascent, occasionally hitting tur-bulence and making Dempsey's face turn grey. He studiously avoided eye contact, all the time staring ahead as a thick bank of dark clouds surrounded the craft. I slowly and stealthily undid my seat-belt but kept the buckles in front in both hands. I sensed the Cessna level out, the passage begin to smooth, and we were above cloud. The pilot glanced behind and I forced a smile.

'I know you, don't I?' I asked Dempsey.

He turned towards me and I knew by his eyes whatever he said was going to be a lie. And I was pretty pissed off by lies.

'Not that I'm aware of,' he said with ill-disguised contempt, 'and I doubt we mix in the same circles.'

Yes, now I knew where I'd heard him before. His big nose offered a slight nasal intonation that was only too recognisable.

I waited until we hit another patch of turbulence and he was off guard.

'You rang me about six days ago, didn't you?'

Dempsey's features twisted in forced puzzlement. 'What are you talking about?'

'Yeah, you did. I recognise your voice. You told me to come to the prison, that some young guy on an assault charge had hanged himself. Come on, you must remember?' I eased my restraints looser. Dempsey's eyes darted towards my hands, still caked with dry blood. 'You're talking shite, Ryan.' He started fumbling with his seat-belt, his alarm now obvious. 'I've never seen you before in my life.'

I leaned across the narrow aisle so my face was only inches from his beaked nose. 'Yes, you have, you bastard. And you pointed a shotgun at me while I lay half-conscious on the ground.'

He darted for my throat but I warded his grip away. I sensed commotion in the cockpit and the

51

Cessna lurched as it hit another sudden air pocket. Then I head-butted Dempsey right in the middle of his face, flattening his nose and chipping his upper teeth. There was blood everywhere.

It took the pilot almost ten minutes to restore order and even then we nearly crashed into a lake.

4

'What the hell's going on, Frank? As if you're not in enough shit already I hear you nearly brought that aeroplane down.' Bill O'Hara was head of the prison service and had put a lot of effort into recruiting me. He glared at me from the other side of the large teak desk in his offices at the Justice Department. 'What were you thinking? Have you lost the plot?'

I returned the glare and kept it fixed. 'You tell me, Bill. I'd like to know what the hell's going on too.'

'Look at your face. Have you seen yourself in the mirror?'

'What do you think I've been doing? Apart from a nurse the mirror was almost my only companion. I know every bruise and swelling like they're my best friends. And you haven't seen my body. Or perhaps you've heard about it?' I pushed myself back in the soft chair and waited. Maybe now I'd get the explanations I deserved.

O'Hara's face creased in dismay. 'I think all that hammering has damaged your brain. Maybe that's why you hit Dempsey.'

This was most certainly the wrong approach as far as I was concerned and I spluttered with outrage. 'I hit Dempsey because he and his gang nearly kicked the life out of me. When four of them couldn't hold me down he tried to blow my head off.' I switched to self-righteous mode; something I don't often get a chance to indulge and wanted to dole it out in spades. 'So don't give me the Dempsey hard-done-by line. He's lucky I didn't throw him out of that plane.'

It was the evening of 18 February and twelve hours since I'd been dragged unceremoniously out of my prison bed. The flight from the remote airstrip to Dublin (where I eventually learned I was being taken) lasted an hour longer than necessary after I put darkness between Noel Dempsey's ears and a lot of his blood on my tracksuit. The pilot spent considerable time calming things while his partner struggled to keep the light plane under control in the swirling air currents over the Irish Sea. But I was still in a foul temper when we eventually touched down at a military airport north of Dublin. Bill O'Hara was first to get a tongue-lashing, although it wasn't having the desired effect. 'Noel

Dempsey is one of our top officers,' he snapped. 'He's been used in prisoner transfer duty for years and no one's attacked him until now. Frank, you're way out of order on this.'

This was not the script I was expecting. I had anticipated apologies, embarrassed clarifications and offers of recompense. 'What are you talking about? Since when did I become a prisoner? And what the hell was I doing in an English jail? What's going on, Bill? I deserve straight answers.'

O'Hara sat back in his chair and studied me. When he spoke again his voice was hard. 'Frank, is there something you want to get off your chest? We could resolve any issues right here and now if you care to open up. However, I'm warning, this bluster will get you nowhere.'

For a split second I almost wished I was back in the prison room and being comforted by Helen. Despite her half-truths and evasive answers I believed I would make sense of the nightmare eventually. But the way this conversation was going I was starting to have serious doubts. 'What are you talking about? Do you have any idea what I've been through? I was beaten to within an inch of my life and had a shotgun forced into my face. I was sure I was going to be killed. And when I eventually came to I thought I was dead.' I held his stare defiantly. 'You know all this, don't you?'

O'Hara sighed like a man with a ton of problems

resting on his narrow shoulders. He started drumming his fingers on the leather-topped surface. 'Frank Ryan, I knew when I hired you I'd bought into a tough nut. That's what Harmon Penitentiary needed. I liked the way you deliberately sought out difficult postgraduate work and preferred exciting challenges rather than boring career-enhancing moves. Bush doctor in Australia, army doctor in Kosovo, medical investigator for Amnesty International. None of these I ever found on any other CV. So I liked you a lot before we even met. But this baloney you're spewing at me is making me rethink that first appraisal. So for the record let me put you straight on what actually happened.' He pulled out a drawer and slapped a manila folder on the desktop, then started flicking through pages inside. From where I sat there was a bunch of typed notes being sifted. Finally a single sheet was fingered and lifted free and he began reading, offering the gist of its contents.

'On 12 February around three in the morning you were arrested by police in the Tottenham area of London while involved in a brawl outside a nightclub.'

I started forward in my chair, stunned by his words, but he immediately held up a hand not to interrupt.

'As the officers tried to calm the mêlée you hit one on the shoulder forcing him to draw his truncheon. You continued to lash out until it became necessary to subdue you with force. At this point you collapsed and went unconscious. You were taken to the nearest Accident and Emergency unit but when you came round and started swinging punches they removed you to a local police station. There you head-butted an officer and had to be clubbed into submission a second time. At this point it was decided to shift you to a secure detention centre. You apparently lapsed into unconsciousness and finally came to in a resuscitation room at Wandsworth jail.' He paused and scowled at me over his half-moon glasses. 'Now do you recall these events?'

My mouth opened and stayed open. I leaned forward in my chair, the air disappearing out of my lungs at a rapid rate. I felt breathless and had to gulp in gasps to stop myself keeling over. Whatever craziness I thought I was going through in the prison recovery room seemed quite rational compared to what was being thrown at me now. I looked down at my hands and found they were shaking; the dried blood still caked to fingers and underneath nails. With Noel Dempsey's gore stuck to the front of my tracksuit I knew I must have appeared like a criminal but image and reality are two very different things.

'Bill,' I heard myself croak, 'what are you on about? Where did you get that parcel of lies?' For some reason Noel Dempsey's face flashed in my mind and I suspected him immediately. Then more thoughts flooded and I was utterly confused. Why would Dempsey concoct such a tale? What's in it for him? But then, what's in it for O'Hara? 'You seriously aren't offering me that as an explanation for all that's happened?'

O'Hara leaned across the desk and fixed on me with eye contact that bored right through my head. 'I most seriously am. And while you may prefer your own cock-and-bull story there are a lot of official signatures to each statement in here.' He flapped the pages in the air for my benefit. 'The summary skips the finer details. Dempsey read the full report and warned me it was brutally embarrassing, especially for a doctor. So if you want to continue in denial that's your call. But it's not going to help me persuade the minister to keep you in your position. He's already sent a letter of apology on our behalf to the UK authorities and that nearly choked him. He's a Republican to the core.' He shook his head, muttering under his breath. Then he loosened his top shirt button and ran a finger around the collar for relief. 'The amount of alcohol in your system may explain some of your behaviour but it certainly doesn't excuse it.'

I sat in my seat bewildered, my brain in yet another tailspin. I couldn't believe what was on offer as the facts of my ordeal. My usual alcohol consumption borders on teetotal by Irish standards and I hadn't been in London for weeks, the last time a lustful few days with Lisa. Lisa, I suddenly thought, she'll put them right. 'Bill,' I came back strongly, 'on the night in question I was in bed in my apartment in Donnybrook with my girlfriend Lisa Duggan. She'll remember the prison call asking me to attend there urgently. She must have heard the commotion in the corridor and couldn't have missed a stun-grenade explosion. Have you spoken to her?' I sat back, a sense of relief washing over me.

'As a matter of fact I did,' countered O'Hara just as confidently and my reprieve disappeared as fast as the nervous smile ghosting my lips. He flicked through the paperwork until he found the sheet he wanted. 'Statement from Lisa Duggan taken 14 February, the day after we were notified by London Metropolitan Police you were being detained at one of Her Majesty's prisons.' He lip-read the words, mumbling out loud the relevant bits. ' "I've known Dr Frank Ryan for three months" . . . blah, blah, blah . . . "been dating for two months" . . . blah, blah, blah . . . "saw him on 10 February after a meal and night out in Dublin".' I almost missed the rest of the drone. Lisa and I had been sharing the same bed for nine months, sometimes at her place but more often than not at mine. What is O'Hara talking about, this isn't correct? I kept my cool and listened. ' "Last contact was at Dublin airport at six fifteen on the evening of 11 February where Dr Ryan was getting a flight to London to attend a medical conference on prison health issues." '

O'Hara set the statement down and leaned back. 'Can I add something else?' I nodded, my thoughts still roller-coasting.

'Your apartment was checked thoroughly by my men. The government-issue Beretta, stun grenades and cans of Mace are intact and untouched. For that I am truly thankful. God knows what would have happened if you'd been carrying that sort of hardware when you were arrested.'

I felt my world disintegrating, my mind turning to sand and slipping through an hourglass. Soon I would have no brain tissue left and could end up in some institution for the insane, babbling and rambling. For the first time I began to seriously question my recall of events on the morning of 12 February. Certainly Bill O'Hara's version sounded much more mundane and un-extraordinary. A drunken brawl and arrest made sense compared to the dramatics of my version. I scrambled to collect my composure, knowing I had to come back strongly, that any confusion would give O'Hara too much ammunition. 'Bill, I'm not quite sure what's happening. For the past few days I've had a sense of being driven to someone else's agenda. I had an armed guard in the prison recovery room and all of the staff claimed everything being done was for my own protection and that "they", whoever the hell "they" are, were taking my assault very seriously. Can you help me out on these facts, Bill? Don't tell me I dreamed those up too.'

O'Hara was originally from the border area of Ireland and had a strong Cavan accent. His years of working in Dublin had given that brogue a harder edge. It was common knowledge in the prison system that his rural roots burst to the fore when he was angry and now as spittle frothed his lips I could almost tell what street in the county he came from. 'You were under guard in a safe room because we insisted. Putting a prison doctor among common criminals is not a wise decision. And the "they" you wonder about was in fact me. I was worried someone connected with your work at Harmon Penitentiary provoked the assault. But we were reassured on that. The crowd you squared up to were no more than local drunks and bully-boys. Not the sort of company I'd expect you to keep.'

I'd never seen O'Hara so angry. His red face was now glowing as if his blood pressure was sky high. His flecked lips were flush with his teeth and his eyes looked like blue bullets aimed at my forehead. But still the offered facts were grossly at odds with my truth. I know how to handle myself and rarely, if ever, get so drunk I'd become involved in a row. I was not in London at a medical conference; hell, I hate such functions. Prima-donna medics vying for attention while they bore the pants of their audience is not my idea of education. So even though my legs were weak and my senses reeling I knew I could sort out this appalling confusion.

'Can I use your phone?' A call to Lisa would clear these contradictions. Now I forced my hands steady as O'Hara slid the phone across. I punched in Lisa's mobile number. It didn't ring. I smiled weakly and mumbled something about wrong digits. O'Hara didn't smile back. I started praying as I jabbed again at the touch-tone buttons, my fingers frantic with haste. Come on, Lisa, please answer. Somewhere in satellite land a monotone voice told me the number I was dialling was no longer in use. I placed the handset back on its cradle and avoided eye contact across the table. 'Can I read my girlfriend's statement? I'd like to see the signature.' The pages were passed over. I skipped the text and focused on the handwriting at the bottom of the page. It was her scrawl; there was no doubt about it. Frank Ryan, I warned myself silently. Either you've lost your mind and been hallucinating or this agenda is bigger than you thought. And right now, Ryan, err on the side of the big boys, they've built a considerable case against you. Back off confrontation.

I deliberately allowed my shoulders to shrug and my body slump. I leaned forward and rested both elbows on the desk and let my head drop onto cupped and blood-caked hands. I sighed deeply. 'Bill,' I mumbled, 'I'm very confused. And I'm tired and still sore from the attack.' I paused, rocked my head from side to side and then corrected myself. 'Or brawl or whatever happened.' I stared at the manila folder in front, out of the corner of an eye trying to read the text upside down. O'Hara must have seen this for suddenly the pages were tidied together and shoved back in the drawer. I let my head slip slightly, as if in defeat, and offered the demeanour of a man totally crushed. All the time I was thinking furiously, fast-tracking thoughts and observations and queries that had done loop the loop for days. Especially I wanted to know why my room was bugged, why I was sedated and interrogated, but decided not to bring these matters up. One, it would compromise Helen and she at least had shown kindness, sympathy and enlightenment. And two, I knew damned fine O'Hara would have a story up his sleeve to make them seem like yet more aberrations of recall. I imagined myself in a fifteen-round heavyweight boxing contest. I'd definitely lost the first two rounds, the assault and imprisonment.

And I was on the ropes and being counted down in this, the third. But that still left twelve mini-bouts of counter-attack. I decided to wait for the bell and retreat to the corner. I needed space to think, time to regain my confidence and seek counsel on tactics. I'd taken a battering but I wasn't on the floor.

'Can I go back to my apartment and take a few days off? I don't know what's come over me and I'm definitely not thinking straight.' I wasn't exaggerating. 'I need to be on my own.' I glanced over and for a split second caught O'Hara off guard. He was looking at me with a strange expression, what I took to be a mixture of regret, deceit, compassion and self-loathing. He averted his gaze immediately, coughed to distract and fiddled with the top button on his shirt.

'I'll call a driver. I have to discuss this with the minister first thing tomorrow and I'll ring you as soon as I have something to report.'

Alone in the back seat of a squad car I watched the people of Dublin go about their uncomplicated lives. It was close to ten o'clock and the streets were busy with late-night shoppers clutching bags, pub-crawlers spilling outside hostelries to have a smoke, lovers holding hands and window-shopping. Everyone seemed to have a normal life but me. I, Dr Frank Ryan MD, medical adventurer and explorer of the darkest recesses of human experience, was caught in a bear trap. The car sped along St Stephen's Green, the oasis and consumer centre of the sprawling Irish capital. It zigzagged through stalled traffic close to a Luas tram line before gathering speed, ignoring lane discipline around the tightly policed zone. Lights were glowing in the Shelbourne Hotel and inside I could see people gathered at a meeting, heads together and drinks in hand. Normal folks doing normal things. We broke two red lights and amber-gambled others and soon were speeding along the Georgian splendour of Fitzwilliam Square in the Dublin 4 district. A solitary hooker was touting for business. Around 10.30 the driver dropped me outside my apartment, into a cold but dry night with no clouds and glittering stars. I stood for a moment in the darkened car park, shivering and unsure of myself. Then I gradually became aware of the emptiness of the complex. There were no cars outside the building. Where's my Saab? Where are the blue Nissan Primera and the silver Renault Clio belonging to my neighbours in the flat below? Galvanised into action I darted along the tarmac, trying to recall where I was lying when Dempsey had me at the wrong end of a shotgun. The air chill numbed my fingers yet I was on my knees and feeling the ground but it seemed sound, certainly I could detect no indents where bullets might have burrowed into the surface. I opened the front door with a spare set of keys O'Hara had offered ('your own set is in some police station in Tottenham') and flicked on lights in the hallway. The silence almost overwhelmed and I made to knock on the door of the couple that rented the apartment on street level but no lights came from their windows or underneath their front door. And their cars were gone, suggesting they were out. Which was strange as the one thing I knew about them was their carefully controlled lifestyles. I couldn't ever recall them coming in late. Once and once only had I overheard them talking but it was in a foreign language, or at least foreign to me. Then again, being brought up in South Australia had isolated me from many cultures and most languages. In Adelaide the whole world is a distant land.

A wave of exhaustion swept over my body and one half of my brain screamed sleep. But the other half wanted answers and I flicked on every light at ground level. Then I ran up the same stairs I'd tumbled down six days before, jabbing every control I could see. Now the complex was fully lit with barely a shadow. I stood outside my apartment with my back to the door and looked around. This is where the stun grenade exploded; surely the blast caused scorch damage? I tortoise-crawled my way along the path I'd taken in the early hours of 12 February, inspecting every inch of wall and floor.

It was clear. And it wasn't fresh clear, as if newly painted or touched up. The muddy grey walls seemed as usual, scuffed here and there and flaking at higher levels. The linoleum flooring was dirt free but I couldn't convince myself it was overly clean. There were occasional blemishes and coffee stains, just as I remembered when I spilled a latte-to-go some months previously and forgot to wipe it up. I inched forward on my hunkers, eyes just above the steel-ridged edging. They were unsoiled with no hair or blood where I'd banged my head. Surely that sudden and violent contact would have left a trace? But hard as I looked nothing showed. And since I'd never before inspected the stairwell with such intensity I couldn't be sure this was its usual state. Overseas workers from Romania or some other Eastern European country cleaned the complex. Again I wasn't good on languages other than English, preferably as spoken between Burra and Broken Hill. Possibly they had been in over the past week and done an exceptionally good job because I was getting nothing from my minute search. When I ran the flat of my hand along the floor very little grime stuck. Now I was at the front door, where it had been crashed open. I felt the woodwork and checked the steel bar and wire-strengthened half-window. If I allowed my imagination run wild I could convince myself everything was new but again the wood and paintwork and especially the door-frame didn't appear damaged or repaired or replaced. By now my physical reserves were at a low ebb, the initial adrenalin rush drained to near zero.

Inside the apartment and with all lights on I allowed my gaze take in the scene. The rooms were tidy to show-house standard, unlike the usual mess of my lifestyle. In the kitchen the draining board at the sink was spotless and not cluttered with dirty and washed crockery mixed together, as is my usual unfortunate habit. The waste bins were empty. Light switches had been wiped clean of finger marks, the gloss at hand height on doors now fresh and unspoiled. I knew O'Hara's team had checked for my government-issue Beretta, stun grenades and Mace but he didn't mention they were house-proud.

In the bedroom I focused on the in-built wardrobes, doors closed and handles grime free. Inside should be my clothes and Lisa's overnight collection, which had increasingly become significant the more she stayed. I gripped one knob but didn't pull, wondering what I'd find. My heart was doing somersaults and I felt jittery. Please, Lisa, don't let them have got to you. Please be here for me, if only through that awful blue dress I told you I liked but secretly detested. I took deep breaths to calm my overactive imagination and slow my racing pulse. When I open this door, I thought, I will see high-heeled shoes, runners and flat walking footwear. I will also discover a cosmetic case, sanitary towels and washbag, plus a range of morning, noon and evening wear. With any luck I might find Lisa, hiding from me and waiting to jump out. 'Hi, Frank, what have you been up to?' Then I'd wrap my arms around her slim body, smell the perfumed soap off her hair that I used to sink into with such sensual delight. I'd catch her long blonde tresses and coil some into a ball and brush it against my face. Then I'd lift her onto the bed and smother her with kisses, feeling her hands respond to my lust, grope for grope.

For a few seconds I closed my eyes and indulged these fantasies but when I opened them I found the door agape in my grip and the wardrobe neatly arranged. I pulled at suits and shirts and sweaters frantically, my wild eyes searching for a silk sleeve or narrow leather belt. My fingers skimmed bare high shelves and flung empty drawers to all corners. I forced suitcase locks, nails breaking as I fought with fiddly latches. My hands shook as I threw out the last item. There was not a trace of Lisa Duggan, not a lipstick, tube of badly squeezed toothpaste or strand of hair. She might never have existed except in my mind. I slumped onto the floor and forced my trembling body under control. It's one thing cleaning my apartment and securing government-issue hardware, but it's another matter altogether removing my girlfriend's personal effects.

Exhausted and tormented, with my body begging for sleep, I continued the inspection but it offered no clues other than the faint smell of cleaning fluid. Finally I stood at the door and went through the checks I'd done on the early morning of 12 February, before I left. I flicked the switch to my right but no image glowed back at me from the TV monitor fixed to the wall. The CCTV cameras had been disconnected. Minutes later and I was staring into an empty cupboard where the CCTV tapes were stored. Someone had plundered the 12 February cartridge and everything going back for thirty days.

I jabbed at the button that activated halogen lights around the complex and ran to the windows and looked out. The car park was still in darkness. I almost tripped over a rug as I sprinted from room to room, frantically squinting outside for signs of light. But only gloom surrounded the building. Every security device the Justice Department had installed to protect me had been deactivated.

I forced my brain quiet under the sting of a cold shower and vigorously towelled myself dry. At last I collapsed into bed, dragged the duvet around my shoulders and fought for sleep. But too many images forced their way into my teeming thoughts and I tossed and turned, restless legs searching for a warm spot. Now I began to wonder about Harmon Penitentiary and my inmate patients. Who had looked after them over the previous days while I was out of action? In particular, who dealt with their addiction crises? Without heroin or its prescribed substitute, methadone, whole wings of the jail would be simmering and seething jungles of strung-out junkies.

I was dozing, my body twitching and my breathing laboured, when the notion struck me. At first I resisted the urge to leap up and start running. I was deadbeat and moving still-aching limbs was a major effort. Yet the idea was so strong I knew I wouldn't have peace without checking. And as soon as the resistance collapsed I was fighting with the locks on the front door, cursing the time-delay mechanism. At least they hadn't disconnected that. Suddenly the bolts gave and I dragged the door open, making sure to jam it ajar before haring towards the stairs. Stark naked and caring not a damn I skipped steps, tumbling and stumbling until at last I was at the front entrance.

In better days each time I left the complex I went through a security routine. First I scrutinised every outside corner I could see and then the roof.

The angle is such that I could never see far enough but right now that wasn't important. For weeks I'd been following the creation of an intricate spider's web in cracked joints above the door-frame. It was something I kept to myself, knowing how much Lisa hated spiders. I tracked the spread of the web, admiring the creature's attention to detail. The foreign cleaners' cloths and dusters had never reached this crevice and I'd never drawn their attention to it. Now, with lights blazing and the hallway fully lit I stood in the same spot and squinted upwards. My heart rocked inside my chest and I felt short of breath. At first my eyes couldn't focus and I had to rub at them repeatedly to clear the bleariness. Where are you, Mrs Spider? Come on, where is that magnificent web you spent so many careful hours creating? It was gone.

I went back to bed but not to sleep. Someone had done a remarkable clean-up. Yet not so perfect that deliberate scuff marks and stains weren't reproduced. But they'd slipped up by removing the spider's web and cracks above the door-frame. There was fresh plasterwork in that spot which hadn't dried completely.

As I waited for dawn to claw its murky grey fingers along the city skyline I was sitting up in bed, propped on a bank of pillows. I had moved on physically, from prison room in London to apartment in Dublin. But mentally I was still in no man's land, confused and unsure of the rules of engagement.

5

Harmon Penitentiary erupted that same day. The riot started in C-wing, the section for murderers, serial killers and arsonists, and an area where trouble was always expected. Drug dependence along these cell blocks was rampant with many prisoners controlled by methadone. But after a scandal in which paramedics were caught siphoning the drug for personal consumption new rules were enforced. Now only a registered doctor could deal with addiction prescribing and as I was out of action nothing was being dispensed. I heard the news as it broke on the radio during the six-thirty bulletin.

Police in riot gear have been called to Harmon Penitentiary after disturbances in one wing spread to two other divisions. In what the governor described as a well-planned manoeuvre, around two a.m. inmates in six cells set fire to their mattresses and shouted to be taken out. Warders rushed to the scene and began evacuation procedures but were attacked and overpowered. Keys taken from one officer were used to open the rest of the cells, setting the prisoners free. Up to an hour ago disturbances were still continuing within these wings with a number of warders held hostage. One unconfirmed report says syringes filled with HIV-infected blood are being held against the throats of two officers. When contacted earlier a spokeswoman for the Prisoners' Rights Organisation said the Justice Department has known for some time the institution is a powder keg waiting to explode. With heroin and other drugs widely available many inmates have severe psychological as well as physical illnesses. When illicit drug stocks run low addicts rely totally on methadone, a medically approved heroin substitute. However, the current CMO to Harmon Penitentiary has been away for the past week and the Justice Department has been unable to recruit a locum.

There was a pause and pages could be heard shuffling.

Our reporter at the scene says smoke can now be seen coming from behind the prison walls and extra police are being drafted in.

I turned down the radio and lay back in bed, at last able to smile. I reached over and checked the phone, listening to the dialling tone, and then unplugged it from the wall. Would Bill O'Hara come looking for me? Despite everything he claimed had happened he still needed me. But I'd spent the night teasing out his version of events and found many inaccuracies, inconsistencies and riddles. The bruising on my body and face reflected the beating I remembered so vividly and didn't match a street brawl and baton thumping. The wound to my scalp was too straight and deep for anything other than a bullet track. Suspects, violent or otherwise, are first detained after arrest in a local police station and rarely moved straight to a major prison. The clean-up of my apartment was way too good by any standards and suggested it had been pulled apart and then rearranged. What were they looking for? The statement taken from Lisa was dated 14 February, 'the day after we were notified by London Metropolitan Police you were being detained at one of Her Majesty's prisons'. That was Bill O'Hara's version. But there was an armed detective guarding me by then, even though O'Hara claimed the special protection was ordered after notification from the UK authorities. He was twenty-four hours out in that part of his concocted story. And where was Lisa? Why wasn't her mobile phone connecting? How the hell had they got to her? And why remove all her personal effects? Why was I sedated and interrogated and my recovery room bugged? What was I doing in a jail in England?

There were more questions than answers and as I fought to pull these bizarre events together I came to one conclusion. Something was going on at Harmon Penitentiary bigger than any riot. The breaking news didn't surprise, for the institution was indeed a powder keg of addiction. The Justice Department would now be desperate for my services and I'd go back if asked but this time I'd be more wary. It would have been nice to have a mate or close male friend to confide my problems with but I was a loner used to keeping my counsel to myself. It's an outback thing; you grow up being taught self-reliance and independence. Solve your own problems. Now I sensed I'd have to draw on skills learned and an inner strength forged by years of working the bush.

Life in South Australia wasn't easy. There were five of us, me and my two younger sisters and my parents. I was the only male so it was drilled into me I would be the man of the house should anything happen to Dad. This is not an easy concept to grasp when you're only five years old. We lived in a sandstone-and-slate house with a galvanised-iron roof two hundred miles north of Adelaide, the state capital. The stone and slate were recovered from nearby creeks and held with wet mud that dried hard and cemented fast. The iron roof was laid on original cedar shingles and when it rained the noise was like machine-gun fire. The station was over a hundred thousand acres of barren scrubland holding mainly sheep, five horses, some cattle and a wildlife of kangaroos, emus, eagles, possums and wombats. Rain was infrequent, the state the driest and hottest in Australia.

When I wasn't at school I went everywhere with Dad, collecting water, building dams and hand digging courses to divert rainfall into huge galvanised-iron containers. My early life included back-breaking fence mending, driving trail bikes to check water levels and keeping dangerous brown snakes away from the homestead. I learned to shoot at nine and how to skin rabbits by age ten. I took over the station when Dad went into hospital to have his appendix out. At the time I'd just turned fourteen and he was about thirty-eight. He moaned and groaned for days and only relented when he couldn't walk with the pain. My mother drove our battered and grime-streaked Holden ute over pot-filled roads while I watched the colour drain from Dad's face at each bump. The nearest town was one hundred miles south and there the doctor didn't even examine him; he knew it was Ned Ryan and Ned Ryan didn't like doctors and therefore his belly-ache must be serious.

'I'd say you've got yourself a dirty appendix, Ned.'

The sun beat down on the truck and sweat was dripping along my father's face, his bedraggled and thinning fringe stuck to his forehead. Blowflies buzzed at his eyes but he hadn't the strength to swat them away. 'Nah, it's probably some virus,' he mumbled, the words forced and laboured. 'She'll be right. Give me a course of strong antibiotics and I'll be fine.'

The doctor was about to say something when Dad passed out. It was another hundred miles to Adelaide and the big hospitals there but by the time we'd stopped twice for petrol, changed a puncture and topped up the radiator his appendix burst. So while he spent a month in hospital recovering from peritonitis I took over the day-to-day running of the station. It was shearing time, the most intensive and demanding stretch of the year when almost ninety per cent of all income is earned. The shearers arrived with their usual entourage of cutters, wool handlers, boss men and cooks, and stayed for three weeks. I rounded sheep on motorbike and drove them across dustbowl paddocks to compounds at the back of the house. My mother and sisters struggled to keep the animals from scattering and rode their horses bare-back from pen to pen to keep control.

It took my father six months to get over his sick-ness, what with the considerable weight loss, slow-healing wound and repeated doses of antibiotics. In that time we became close friends, the relation-ship more than a son-and-father bond. He sprawled out from an old horsehair sofa in the slate veranda at the front of the house, issuing orders and telling me when I was going wrong.

We bought a bigger bike and I delighted in scorching flat strap over the slate-covered hilly terrain, the sun in my face and the wind keeping me cool. I checked galvanised tanks, mended fences and herded stock from barren ground to irrigated pastures. With kangaroos and cockatoos, emus and eagles keeping me company I ruled my world. The stillness and shimmering heat suited my mood and like some Aboriginal tracker I came to understand the oft-troubled harmony between man and the elements. Inspecting dirt marks I could see where a lamb had been taken down and dragged away. I scanned cloud formations for signs of heavy rains and the likelihood of dry ravines becoming raging torrents within an hour. I learned how to let a snake slither past my boots while I stood rock still and how far to let it move on before letting a breath out. The snakes had no eyesight but their heat sensors picked up vibrations. Bird flight patterns warned of thunderstorms hours before we heard the first rumble.

My muscles developed as fast as my body and by eighteen I was tall and strong and, according to my mother, 'a handsome young man'. Despite years of sun exposure my dark hair didn't bleach and with my weather-beaten features, at the age of eighteen I stood out among the crowd of medical students at Adelaide University. Most came from privileged urban backgrounds and were caught up in money and clothes while I still fretted over blocked dams and burst water pipes two hundred miles away. Friends went to the cinema and pubs but I held on to my money because there wasn't enough. South Australia was in the fifth year of drought and our stocks were depleting. Wool prices had collapsed so every cent counted. To avoid the embarrassment of being seen to scrimp and save I avoided college social events, concentrating on studies and waiting on tables for cash. Without realising it I had become a stereotype, a tall, dark and handsome, silent and brooding student. I mightn't have experienced much culture but I had a lot of girlfriends.

Big trouble came to the station one spring, when I was twenty-four and in my final year at med school. I was home to help with mustering and my sister Sue had taken a trail bike to the north and nearest side of the property to check water levels. She left after breakfast, advising how long it usually took to reach the boundary.

'It's gone eight,' she said as she inspected the ancient mahogany grandfather clock in the hallway. 'It'll take two hours to get there, half an hour to look around, then two hours back. See ya around one.'

Sue was a tall, willowy eighteen-year-old then, a good-looker like my mam but tough as old boots like my dad. The younger Ryans had inherited handsome features and stoic personalities, taking most things in their stride and rarely losing their tempers. Living in such isolation and with a mountain of work to do didn't allow for sulks or tantrums or ego trips. Sue took a water bottle and an emergency bag for punctures and falls and then was off, waving her sun hat and disappearing round a bend in a cloud of dust. But she didn't take her mobile phone. And she didn't return at one.

'She'll be right,' said Dad over lunch as my mum began to worry. The front door was open and she was drying pots with a cloth as she kept vigil behind the fly screen. Outside, the sky was cloudless blue and the countryside greening after recent steady rains. Even the vegetable patch looked as though it might turn good and bright red petals on Sturt's Desert Pea were opening.

'Maybe she's trying to pull some fence together,' I offered to lighten the mood. But secretly I wasn't happy with her no-show. We'd been warned of the outback and its dangers and knew not to delay anywhere unnecessarily, especially when no one could tell if there was a problem. I ate dessert with little relish, my eyes darting out a side window and the foreground ahead. A single trail led to the front of the station and all movement was through a rusted iron gate bolted to a cross-wire fence. Sue could only return that way but she hadn't done by three. Or four. By six Dad and I had full tanks in our motor bikes, mobile phones charged and extra medical supplies. Grim faced we set off in different directions so we could approach the northern boundary from separate routes. The sun was sinking to my left, casting an intense red and orange glow that bathed the landscape and created bizarre shadows behind rock outcrops.

Two hours later I found my sister lying unconscious in the dip of a hill no more than a mile from the homestead. Her badly damaged bike was pushed to one side, my headlights picking out its twisted spokes. The territory was scrub with saltbush, gum trees and an occasional Blackwood wattle. Nearby a goanna lizard stared at me, hissing and backtracking. Tiny eyes glowed as possums kept watch from the safety of tree stumps. I turned my bike so the beam was fixed on Sue and examined her as best I could. She was on her side and coiled up in the foetal position. The water bottle was empty and still clutched in her right hand. She wasn't moving and her denims were ripped and soaked with congealed blood. When I turned the headlights to another angle I saw for the first time the distinct whiteness of bone poking through cloth and clusters of blowflies gorging on exposed flesh. On my hunkers in the gloom I spotted the predatory tracks of a wild dog.

Sue was breathing but it was laboured. I had enough medical experience to know she was badly injured and when I moved her she whimpered and opened her eyes but they were glazed and rolling. Her lips were parched and I immediately trickled fresh water over them, trying desperately to force some into her mouth. But she was too weak. I called Dad on the mobile and waited. By now the sun had gone and the night chill was settling. The countryside was alive with the wildness of the Australian bush yet it seemed to me as deserted and lonely as the far side of the moon.

In Dublin I was brought to the moment by a news flash; even with the radio at low volume it caught my attention:

A helicopter is now circling Harmon Penitentiary and directing officers are on the ground. Two fire crews are on standby outside the prison but have not been allowed inside the compound. Smoke can be seen billowing from C- and D-wings but the governor has issued a statement saying riot police have regained control of E-wing. However, four warders are still being held captive with two under threat of attack. In the last thirty minutes a line of communication has been opened between one of the prisoners and a specialised hostage negotiator. We'll update this story as it breaks throughout the morning.

I glanced at the digital clock. It was 7.05 a.m. I gave them no more than another hour, and then they'd have to call for me.

While I waited for Dad to make his way to the crash site I examined Sue as best I could. Then I called the Royal Adelaide Hospital on my mobile and tracked down the duty trauma surgeon. He familiarised himself with the circumstances.

'Where are you?'

'About a mile from the house. We're two hundred miles from you, though.'

'Have you any obs?'

'Yeah.' I always brought my med school kitbagwith me wherever I went on the station, hoping I'd never have to use it. 'Her blood pressure's low at ninety over fifty and she's got a tachycardia of one forty.'

'Any obvious injuries?'

'Left compound tib and fib with considerable blood loss. The bleeding had stopped by the time I found her. I think her right shoulder's gone too and she has a depressed left-sided skull fracture.'

'Jeez, that's pretty bad. Is she conscious?'

'Nah, she responds to painful stimuli but not to the spoken word. Her pupils are equal and reacting, though.' Basically Sue had multiple fractures with a serious head injury that had left her unconscious. The reaction to pain was consoling but only a little. I reckoned she'd been lying in a heap for at least four hours, allowing for travelling time to and from the northern boundary. She was close to home when she came off the bike, probably knocked over by a wild animal leaping straight into her path. Sue was an experienced bush woman and well able to look after herself. But kangaroos have a habit of bounding out from behind scrub or rock at the wrong time.

Dad finally tracked us an hour later after I gave him directions. The headlights of a four-wheel-drive Subaru station wagon momentarily dazzled as it ground to a halt yards from where I stood. I was shivering and stripped to my boxers, every other strip of clothing wrapped around my sister to protect her body temperature. I took control immediately, explaining the severity of Sue's injuries and the urgent need to get her to hospital. It might have been a total stranger lying there the way I spoke, yet every word was accurate and to the point. There was no time for emotion; Sue's survival depended on action and not sobs. First we manoeuvred her onto a mattress in the back of the station wagon and threw blankets over her. It took us an hour to make it back to base, me wrapped in a sheet for warmth and Dad driving as slowly as I dictated while I kept watch. The homestead was lit up and my mother anxiously pacing the veranda when we rounded a corner and entered the front stretch. The house dogs barked and circled the car as it came to a halt and my mother looked on in horror as her daughter was eased out. By then the helicopter ambulance was well on its way from Adelaide.

We built a bonfire of scrub and wood and ragged clothes and old furniture, then soaked it in petrol and set it alight. The flames jumped thirty or more feet into the night sky and Dad kept it under control while my other sister ran around dousing any falling sparks. We didn't want to create a bushfire to add to our problems. Ninety minutes later we heard the steady drone of the rescue chopper and made contact by mobile. Up in the air they told us they could see the fire clearly where it stood out like glowing embers in an immense darkness. The roar of the engines as the helicopter set down scared wildlife, and where all light ended and an infinity of shadows began I could see the shapes of retreating kangaroos. Wolves howled and crows fffarked while under a sky with a million stars Sue was transferred to a stretcher. There wasn't room for passengers and searchlights picked out the farmhouse as the giant steel bird climbed into the night sky and headed south. We stood in silence, me praying and hoping and dreading and wishing we hadn't let her go out on her own. As the red and amber warning beacons banked to the left we gathered closer to the fire for warmth. It was cold and now eerily quiet in the bush. I glanced around and saw my younger sister clinging to my mother, both sobbing.

Dad never moved, his eyes tracking the chopper until it became no more than a blip in the distance. Then he hugged me fiercely and I could feel his big chest heaving with suppressed sobs. 'Well done, son. You did good back there. We'd better look after your mam and sister now and not show any weakness. It's a tough bloody life out here but it's a good one too. You're your own boss and master of your destiny.' He draped one arm over my shoulder and shifted my body so we faced the blackness of the outback. 'No better place in the world, if you ask me. God's own country.' But I knew it was bravado, a show of spirit for my benefit. Hell, so your sister's gone and bashed her head in. You can't buckle because of that. This is Australia and things happen that just have to be dealt with. This is where character is formed. We're made of strong stuff so quit whingeing and throw another log on the fire.

Sue came home three months later. She was partially paralysed down her right-hand side and needed a stick to walk. Her speech slurred and her healed leg had a significant deformity making it look like a bulge underneath the skin. Her personality changed too, from the Aussie bush girl's easygoing and 'no worries, mate' philosophy to an anxious worrier. A year later the property and its stock were sold and the family moved closer to Adelaide. My mother had had enough of the isolation and dangers of countryside as harsh and barren as the top of South Australia. Her days of shooting brown snakes when they came within six feet of the house finally ended and she didn't look one bit unhappy when Dad finally closed the rusted iron gates at the front paddock. Not long after, I started my world travels as an adventurer, seeking out trouble spots to use my unique and dynamic combination of medical and outback know-how. I loosened up, no longer the penniless loner. I was an open and carefree spirit anxious to explore new countries and savour whatever the world threw at me. I wanted to look into the darkest caves of the mind, investigate the other side of medicine from what my colleagues were studying.

I took everyone at face value until proved otherwise and offered an open and caring attitude to my patients.

I came to Harmon Penitentiary five years later after a spell as an army doctor in Kosovo (where I was responsible for the health of thousands of soldiers) and medical investigator with Amnesty International. Both posts carried me headlong into the poisoned politics of the Balkans conflicts and challenged my thinking. Nowhere in Australia would I have had to stand at the side of mass graves, nor would I have had to collect evidence on appalling atrocities inflicted on defenceless women and children during ethnic cleansing. When I eventually moved on to Dublin I wanted to research the health effects of long-term confinement and drug addiction. By then I was battle hardened and emotionally weary and actually believed the CMO role would be relatively trouble free. I hadn't reckoned on the deviousness of Ireland.

I reconnected the phone around eight o'clock and seconds later its shrill tone rang. I let the call run until the answering machine kicked in. 'Frank, this is Bill O'Hara. Answer the bloody phone.' I waited. 'OK, Frank, we're coming to collect you.' He was in a rage by the sound of his voice. 'Make sure you're dressed and ready to go. The prison's in an uproar.' CLICK. I wanted to gloat but couldn't. I wanted to tell O'Hara to fuck off but wouldn't. I showered quickly, dressed and waited.

The door to my apartment nearly came off its hinges at eight thirty. From outside came muffled shouts and pounding fists, the noise levels dulled by the steel reinforced wood. The latest radio bulletin suggested a worsening of the situation at the jail with more smoke and at least one fire engine now inside the compound. The hostage negotiator wasn't having any success and two prison officers were still being held under the threat of syringes filled with HIV-infected blood at their throats. This was every warden's nightmare and every prisoner's deadliest weapon, almost considered more dangerous than a switchblade or handgun. Better a quick end with a slit throat or a bullet to the head than the slow lingering death of Aids. I undid the bolts and waited for the time-delay mechanism to tick through. Then I swung the door open to find two youngish-looking policemen waiting. Both did double takes when they saw my bruised and still slightly swollen face but quickly collected their wits. 'Dr Ryan?'

I nodded.

'We need you at the prison right away.'

I slipped my house keys into a side pocket and pulled the door after me. 'Let's go.'

There was a squad car waiting in the car park, its engine running and exhaust billowing into the early-morning chill. In the rear Bill O'Hara scowled out at me, his features twisted in the frustration of the moment. Less than twelve hours earlier he'd given me a rollicking and sent me home with my tail between my legs. Or so he might have thought. Now he needed me more than ever. He needed my medical skills and experience; he needed my strength, both physical and mental. Most of all he needed my unflinching courage. Handling rampaging mentally disturbed and drug-addicted murderers holding their own prisoners isn't detailed in any medical text. I would have to think on my feet and prepare for the worst scenario.

I climbed into the back seat, studiously ignoring O'Hara's glower and forced an exaggerated yawn. Then I stretched my long legs as far as they would go and turned slightly. 'I guess the minister gave you the nod,' I remarked as casually as I could force.

'Fuck off,' O'Hara snapped as the car jerked forward, then spun in a half-circle before scorching away.

Out of the corner of my eye I noticed my Saab back in its usual place. But the blue Nissan Primera and the silver Renault Clio of my apartment neighbours were still absent. I settled into the seat, crossed my arms and stared straight ahead, my mind in overdrive. Whatever about the situation at Harmon Penitentiary, I needed to get back to work. I had a lot of scores to settle.

6

We sped through the city's teeming streets behind two police motorcycle outriders, their sirens blaring and blue sidelights flashing. Cars, vans and buses parted before us and when they couldn't our driver mounted the pavement or scorched through oncoming traffic on one-way streets. Pedestrians stopped to watch and heads shook or came closer as Dubliners wondered what was amiss that the Highway Code had to be flaunted so aggressively. Along the quays a two-carriage cattle transporter had to divert suddenly to let us by and nearly mowed down a queue waiting at a taxi rank. Fists were shaken and horns sounded angrily as our entourage forced its way west, cutting under canal bridges and flyovers and even rat running housing estates to take the quickest route. Children weighed down with schoolbags cheered us on, waving and jumping at the excitement of the moment.

Three minutes after nine we pulled up outside Harmon Penitentiary to find a media scrum waiting. TV crews were fighting for position with print photographers who were snapping at anything that moved. There was jostling and cursing and flying hands and jabbing elbows. As the cortège screeched to a halt journalists immediately surrounded the car while sound engineers thrust booms overhead. Cameras were shoved in our faces and questions rat-a-tat-tatted from screaming mouths. How many prison officers are being held hostage? Is the jail on fire? Have any inmates managed to escape? Will the army be called to break up the riot? As I struggled to get past this mob everything seemed a blur, the faces, the questions and the movements melded into one enormous blob of seething and raucous humanity. We no-commented our way through a cordon of blue uniforms and then rushed to the front of the penitentiary. I kept my head down, trying to assess the mood and also to protect my battered face from that evening's TV screens. If this was flashed across the world I didn't want my family in Australia to see me in this state.

For the first time since I'd worked in the prison the outside crash bollards were down and the entrance wide open, its steel-strengthened doors hauled apart. Inside, a fire crew was working flat out pumping water towards a smoke cloud billowing into the morning air. Armed police with helmets and visors up shuffled edgily around, their demeanour suggesting uncertainty and agitation. I hoped their trigger guards were in place. The air smelt of smoke and burning rubber and fear. Bill O'Hara was barking orders to anyone who looked in his direction and soon four henchmen in body armour and carrying batons surrounded us. I'm over six feet but felt dwarfed by this crew as they guided us past rolls of razor wire towards the next entrance and inside the walls.

The prison governor was a tall, lean and bald man called Don Campbell and he was waiting for me at the administration annex. He glanced quizzically at my face but then focused on the matters to hand. Bill O'Hara cupped one hand to his ear as the powerful blades of a helicopter suddenly swept overhead. 'We're going up to C-wing,' Campbell shouted. 'Where the hostages are being held. D-wing is under control again after we pumped CS gas inside. The roof is still on fire but holding.'

I waited until the chopper noise abated. 'What happened to the prisoners?' I dreaded to think how any bunch of homicidal drug addicts would cope with lungs full of irritating gas.

'They've been taken to a military hospital under

armed escort.' Campbell then waved to one in a group gathered nervously round a CCTV screen. 'Get this man body armour,' he pointed at me, 'and a hip belt of Mace.'

The errand boy returned within minutes and soon I was secured inside a protective suit that was stab-, needle- and fist-proof. I didn't ask if it withstood bullets, hoping no one was trigger-happy. I refused the Mace. 'It'll only provoke more trouble,' I explained as I fiddled with a zip fastener on my leggings.

'That's your call,' said Campbell, 'but I'm noting it for the record.'

I shrugged. It was my call. We moved to the bank of CCTV cameras and there could just about make out moving shapes on one screen. The rest were smudged beyond usefulness.

'They've thrown crap at the lenses and there's few visuals. I have a team working on thermal imaging from the roof. The place is a cesspool and two of my men are on the floor with syringes at their throats. Another two are tied to railings.' Campbell reached for a cigarette. 'They're strung out as hell. We handed over two hundred Valium to gain time and they disappeared in minutes. I told them you were coming to sort things out.'

I did a double take at this, then pulled the protective gloves tighter on my fingers. 'I need to see for myself.' I strode ahead; my expression fixed in a scowl but my guts in knots. I felt sweat bead under my armpits. Common sense shouted back off, this is not your problem. You're a doctor and you're not trained in prison disturbances. And what about last week? What about the lies and deceit and beating? Why not quit and call a press conference and expose the conspiracy? But there was no turning back, if only because it was my duty to look after the inmates. Their health was my responsibility and that included withdrawal symptoms causing murderous intent. And I had my own agenda to maintain links to the detention centre. Surely in here was the answer to the riddle of my recent hell.

We hurried past riot police and a crew of paramedics, their white uniforms and Red Cross bags in stark contrast to the sea of blackness filling the compound. 'How many men are inside C-wing?'

'Seventy-two,' Campbell came back immediately.

'Are they all addicts?' I may have been the CMO but my knowledge of every inmate wasn't complete. Also, since many lied about their habits it was a nightmare trying to decide who was really in trouble or maybe just collecting extra for the division.

'I'd say fifty are full-time dependent with another twelve coming down on the methadone programme.' We took a short flight of steps two at a time and now the smell of smoke became stronger.

'I need eighty ampoules of diamorphine, thirty

milligrams strength. I also need four boxes of five-millilitre syringes and two boxes of thirteen-gauge needles. I need antiseptic wipes, tourniquets and a large sharp-disposal box.' I was still thinking what else I might need when out of the corner of my eye I noticed the governor's questioning stare.

'Diamorphine,' I repeated, and then added, 'better known as heroin. I'm not going up there with nothing to offer.'

Campbell's faltering composure now collapsed. 'Where am I going to get eighty ampoules of heroin?'

'Hospice supplies. They keep stores for terminally ill patients. Raid their coffers and explain the reasons later.' I had my hand on a stair rail when I added another item to my list. 'Oh, I also need eighty ampoules of Maxolon to mix with the heroin so we don't have them vomiting.'

Bill O'Hara's red face went suddenly rather grey and Don Campbell's Adam's apple bobbed up and down as he scribbled my orders into a notebook. By now his cigarette was just a glowing butt.

C-wing was up three long flights of barred and gated stairs and at every tenth step warders stood guard, keys swinging in wide circular steel loops and batons drawn. Everyone was grim faced and the sense of heightened tension was palpable. There was a sub-dued murmur of anxious conversation as we moved through the levels until gradually the shouts and yells and oaths of confined and agitated men reached my ears. Yet another gate was opened and as I stepped through I felt a hand on my right shoulder. O'Hara had decided he'd gone far enough and briefly our eyes met but just as quickly I turned away. Don Campbell kept with me, pace for pace as we swung into a foul-smelling tight corridor cramped with riot police and marksmen with sniper rifles. A steel-barred gate was closed and faced against it was the hostage negotiator. He had a handkerchief over his nose and mouth as I squeezed in. Campbell made brief introductions and I learned the mediator's name was something Douglas. Against the background din hearing clearly wasn't easy. 'This is a nightmare,' he hollered. 'It's impossible to bargain with junkies.'

My immediate difficulty was seeing past a pile of broken bunk-beds pushed against the gate. To one side, weapons of twisted metal and splintered lengths of wood were stacked for quick access. Burnt and still-smouldering mattresses lay outside cells, the smoke further impairing any view. It took me ten few minutes to appraise the set-up. The scorched and blackened cell block ran sixty by forty feet with twelve cells on each side, all with their doors opened inwards. Here at the top level natural light struggled past a dirty grey fog collecting underneath an arched opaque glass roof. Iron bars ran along at six-inch gaps. The singed flooring was made of plastic tiling with a wide central gap between opposing rows of cells railed to chest height and supported underneath by toughened mesh to prevent suicide and homicide attempts.

At the far end of this railing two warders were forced onto the bars by wrist ties. Their trousers had been pulled to their ankles and belts used to hold their legs together at the knees. I couldn't see their faces. Faeces and urine had been tipped onto the floor, smeared on walls and allowed to drip to lower levels. The stench of human waste and smouldering mattress filling was almost overwhelming and I had to stop myself gagging.

In this section prisoners wore their own clothes, an almost universal code of denim and dirty T-shirts and trainers. Tattoos dotted flesh and the flesh was of every size and shape, tall and small, fat and thin. I spotted a group of four crowded at the entrance to one cell, shouting and whooping at something going on inside. I shuddered to think what was entertaining them. Others milled around aimlessly, yelping and bellowing and kicking at small fires. One man in boxers and T-shirt was banging his head against a wall and blood streamed down his face. An enormous and tall black man I knew to be Nigerian was crouched in one corner, his body shaking and shuddering. In the past year there'd been a sharp increase in black and Asian convicts, usually on narcotics charges. Beside the Nigerian a pot-bellied and older inmate was doing some provocative dance, as if trying to stir the flames of racial hatred. The Nigerian appeared too disturbed to care.

As the brownish-grey cloud shifted I saw five other prisoners in another corner chatting as if this was a normal recreation break. Beyond my full range of view but with legs sticking out, I located where the hostages were being restrained. I had no idea how many detainees were holding them down or whether blood-filled syringes were being held at their throats. But this was Europe's most dangerous prison and I had no doubt such tactics were being used. On the other side of the bars were murderers, serial killers and arsonists, violent men with little hope of freedom and nothing to lose. For some, whether they lived or died was no more important than getting a fix. Without heroin there was no life. Then, as I squinted past the makeshift barricade, the mangled and bloodied body of a prisoner was dragged onto the landing while onlookers tried to shield the view. To crazed shrieks of delight the victim was thrown over the railings and caught by the steel mesh. Behind I heard a string of oaths as one of the marksmen watched this killing through a long-range lens.

'Who runs this block?' I asked.

'Dan Steele,' said Campbell. 'This is his level and nothing happens without his say-so.'

'Where is he?'

'Sixth cell along on the right.'

I counted out the doors. Number six was open but no one was going in or out. 'Has he been talking?'

'One conversation only. Said this was not of his doing. Said the scag heads were too far gone and he couldn't control them.'

'Do you believe him?'

'No. He's a malicious bastard who manipulates everyone around him. He's covering himself from the fallout.'

By now it was impossible to know where each inmate was and how many were actively involved in the disturbances. Campbell had offered a head count of seventy-two but that had already been reduced by one. I was going to have to work around a figure of fifty addicts who hadn't had a fix for days. And they had four warders hostage, two at the wrong end of HIV-contaminated needles. Pumping CS gas would seal their fate; they'd either be strangled or injected and right then I couldn't decide which was worse. Shooting one or two as an example would stir similar problems. Storming the block equally didn't seem a wise option. Reasoning with the men, pleading and cajoling was the only sensible strategy but the negotiator wasn't succeeding. Only I had the goods to satisfy the hunger. But I needed a leader to deal with.

'Steele,' I shouted. 'Dan Steele, come out here.'

Inside the wing some prisoners stopped and turned towards me. The headbanger paused for maybe a moment before returning his attention to the wall, while the Nigerian barely looked up. But I did manage to make eye contact with one inmate. 'You, get Dan Steele immediately.'

His lower lip curled in a sneer and he gave me a V-sign. I knew a barrage of abuse would follow so I forced the pace. 'If you want a fix I can do it.' Now I had instant attention and new faces appeared at doors. 'I've got one hundred per cent heaven. I've even got clean needles. But nobody gets anything until Dan Steele meets me.'

Instead of coming closer the inmates retreated to the far end of the landing, some fucking me off and others making abusive gestures. A smouldering mattress was kicked to encourage the flames but it only disintegrated into a charred mess. Despite the cold I was sweating. And trying to calculate how long it would take to get all the diamorphine I needed from the nearest hospice. If I couldn't convince the junkies I had the readies there'd be instant retribution.

Dan Steele came with a formidable reputation. From canteen gossip I knew he'd spent twenty of his fifty-six years behind bars on charges ranging from hand-bag snatching as a youngster to murder at age twenty.

He'd grown up in a downtown area notorious for breeding criminals. His father died in a gangland shoot-out while two of his uncles ended their lives in penitentiaries in other jurisdictions. His sister was currently an inmate in the women's wing after killing her baby by overdosing him with methadone. Apparently the kid was crying too much and she gave him a double spoonful of the heroin substitute to soothe. The infant was dead for forty-eight hours before she knew.

Steele's current stretch was twenty-five years for the brutal homicide of two drug couriers who had double-crossed him on a deal. Steele hunted the duo around Europe, from Holland through to France and Germany, until they ran out of funds and headed back to Ireland. He finally tracked them to a dingy motel in Cork, the southernmost city of the country. According to trial evidence the gangster tortured the couple for three days before shooting them in the backs of their heads. He then attempted to destroy the evidence by burning the bodies in a bath soaked with petrol. Unfortunately for him the inferno he created spread rapidly and the fire brigade doused the flames before the victims were charred beyond recognition. In court the killer smirked and joked knowing he had an outside team working on the jury. When news of the intimidation broke his case was taken before an all-judge bench and he was found guilty. At sentencing he gave vent to his fury with an outburst of threats and terror against the judiciary. For this an extra eighteen months' penalty was added.

I had another angry shout in my throat when Steele stepped out from cell six and faced towards me. Through a gap in broken bunk-beds I inspected the killer. He looked an inch or so over six feet, broad shouldered and carrying little surplus weight. He had a good head of greying hair slicked back and showing off his wide forehead. Bushy brows hooded his eyes and even at a distance I could see a scar running from his left ear to his chin. He was smoking a cheroot, drawing deeply and making an exaggerated puff back into the smog. He was in navy trousers and crewneck sweater, his attire at odds with his fellow inmates. Then he started slow and deliberate steps towards the gate, his eyes fixed on me through a gap in the barricade. He stopped about ten feet away, kicked at a broken plank and waited until his cigar was finished, maintaining eye contact. Despite the appalling stench making me want to throw up I managed to keep his stare. Up closer I could see him better, thick lips and sallow skin and nicotine-stained nails chewed to the quick. He had a pugilist's nose and coiled around his neck was a tattoo of a snake, the creation suggesting a tightened noose. He was in scuffed, pointed black shoes that might have been fashionable in the 1950s. He ground the cheroot under a heel and walked the last few paces, stepping carefully past an upturned slop bucket.

I waved my support crew to retreat and finally there were only Steele and me eyeballing one another through iron bars. The mind game was stacked heavily in his favour. He was on the side where the warders were being held. A nod from him and their lives could be ended or spared. He inspected my bruised face and a smile flickered. 'I heard you were in a brawl.'

I swallowed hard, struggling for composure. He's fishing, don't give him any information.

'And it looks as if you didn't do so well.' The voice was deep and throaty, as expected from a man drowned in a life of booze and cigarettes.

'I walked into a door.'

He thought this over in mock pretence. 'How many times?'

'Enough.'

'Looks like it, too.'

I shrugged. We were communicating and that was a start. There was at least one convict not strung out. 'I need help.' Steele was a criminal monster but no fool. I'd decided on honesty and straight talking. Trying to patronise or cajole more likely than not would be met with cynical indifference.

'Shouting isn't gonna get you anywhere. Where's your manners?'

'I needed to get your attention. It's not like I was going to send you a letter.'

He fiddled in his pockets until he found another cheroot and lit up. 'So what's your problem?'

'Everything going on behind you.'

'I can't see behind me. I don't have eyes in the back of my head.'

'Don't fuck with me, Steele, I'm really not into playtime. I need help and I need it now.'

He pulled a face to let me know he was considering my situation.

'This can only end in one of two ways,' I continued. 'The guys here fill the block with CS gas and start shooting. Then they force their way inside and keep shooting until they get to the hostages. But by then I reckon they'll be dead or have syringes sticking out of their necks and wishing they were dead.'

Steele shifted position, all the time keeping me in his line of vision.

'That's a lot of dead bodies with no gain.'

Closer along the landing a straggle of inmates strained to hear the exchanges. They were edgy and obviously distressed, arms wrapped tightly around their bodies. It wouldn't take much aggro to set one off on a killing spree.

'What's the other option?'

'I give you what you all want.'

'What the fuck would you know what we want?' he sneered. He waved a hand to show off his living quarters, a smoke-damaged, sewage-strewn and death-ridden prison landing. 'This is home for us, Dr Ryan. For you the worst that can happen is a fight with a door and even then you lose. Your needs are in a different world.' In my peripheral vision I sensed more prisoners on the walkway. The noise had abated, though; there was less shouting and futile jeering.

'We're not talking my needs. I could quit and not lose face and be declared a hero for getting involved. I'm a doctor, remember? I check your blood pressure and listen to your heart and then go home and lead my own life. I don't need this aggravation and I certainly don't need lectures.' I started peeling off the protective gloves. 'I am the only sensible choice. I have enough heroin to make everyone happy. Let's face it; this block isn't agitating for better pay and conditions. They want a hit and they want it badly. Well, I can do hits, big time. But not under threat.'

Steele looked towards the back of the landing. When he spoke again his voice was hard and intimidating. 'I have no control over the junkies. What they do is their affair and if it causes more shit to rain down then that's your problem. But I do know this, doctor-who-can't-open-a-door-without-getting-his-face-kicked-in. If anything does happen we're not dealing with martyrs. Those mongrel warders have pulled some nasty stunts in their time. They make life in here even more of a hell than it already is.' He took a drag of his cheroot and puffed the smoke into my face. I didn't blink. And at least the smell of his cigar masked the other sickening odours. I knew Steele was aware the governor was listening to every word. Bad-mouthing the officers was his way of preparing the ultimate settlement. By deflecting blame to the authorities he was trying to minimise the inevitable retribution.

'Give me names and issues and I'll see they are dealt with,' I offered. 'This has to end sometime, then we'll have inquiries.'

Steele was unimpressed. 'You're only the doctor, remember? You shovel tablets to pill poppers and think you've done a day's work.'

That annoyed me. 'I do more good in one hour than you'll ever do in all your miserable existence. We're wasting time and I can sense itchy trigger fingers behind me.'

Steele flicked ash onto the floor and then slowly walked away. He summoned a group together and the gang disappeared into a cell. On the landing the Nigerian was on his side and curled up in a ball, his tormentor fled to another corner. The headbanger had slumped onto the floor, face bloodied and fingers trailing through pools of urine. There was more activity beyond my full field of view and I saw ankles and trainers and faces darting back and forth. A plate was flung in my direction but it smashed harmlessly on the tiles. Somewhere a tinny voice started singing a Rolling Stones number and soon there was a chorus of 'can't get no satisfaction' complaints.

'I have conditions.' Dan Steele was back again, no cheroot but a scrawl of writing on a tattered piece of paper.

This could be the breakthrough, I thought as I tried to calm my heart speeding from palpitation to fibrillation. 'If it's within my power to agree to any conditions I will,' I said.

'I'm not asking for an audience with the Pope, just basics.'

'Call them out.' I turned so I was sure the governor was able to hear. He nodded to me to go ahead. Then in the distance the swirling blades of the police helicopter could be heard, coming closer.

'Twenty crates of Jameson whiskey,' Steele began.

'Done.'

'Nah, make that forty.' Steele was grinning at me; delighting in the game he'd created.

'Fuck off, I'm not agreeing to one item only for you to keep doubling until the distillery runs dry,' I shouted against the overhead beat of the helicopter. 'Name an item and let's see how it runs.' Agitated calls from the police marksmen distracted me and I waved a hand for them to shush.

'Skin mags,' yelled Steele against the dum, dum, dum of overhead rotor blades. 'I want lots of them, and no soft porn.'

I gestured a yes. The outside furore was now deafening.

'A thousand cigs split into—' Suddenly somewhere glass shattered loudly and everyone froze. 'What the—' Steele mouthed and spun away. The ceiling inside the cell block was blasted in a wide circle, collapsing a single unit in a cascade of shards. Shadowy figures appeared at the gaping hole and started dropping objects into the landing. Then came the distinct thud of stun and smoke grenades. I dropped to the ground and covered my head. I heard the gate forced opened and the barricades kicked down. The passageway echoed to curses and rushing feet trampled over me, heels digging into my sore ribs. Now came more glass breaking and gunfire. I frantically curled further into a protective ball and tried wriggling my body away from harm.

7

PRISON RIOT ENDS IN BLOODBATH.

CARNAGE AT STATE PRISON.

4 DEAD, 6 INJURED AS ELITE FORCE STORMS
PRISON.

The media feasted on the events at Harmon
Penitentiary. Morning and evening papers carried
eyewitness accounts with anonymous sources nam-
ing the main players. Bill O'Hara from the Justice
Department was the 'mastermind' behind the attack
that effectively ended the standoff between convicts
and police. Prison governor Don Campbell was the
'hero' who stood up to the 'drug-crazed' inmates
and kept them talking while his officers were under
threat. Douglas, the negotiator, was identified as the
battle-hardened mediator who shuffled the conflicting demands until the crack army unit made its
move. Many cameras captured the final moments

of the confrontation and the images were beamed across the world.

The Minister for Justice, a staunch Republican named Patrick Halloran, called a press conference after he allowed reporters to follow him through Dublin's City Hospital, consoling and glad-handing the warders who'd been held captive. None of the men was seriously harmed and all escaped the needle-in-the-throat nightmare. Two were caught in friendly fire and one sustained a broken leg in the frantic scramble. The five dead were prisoners while another three sustained non-life-threatening bulletwounds. Halloran called the riot a 'violent and despicable act by desperate men, hell-bent on destroying the usual calm atmosphere of the penal complex'.

The names of the dead and injured convicts were made public along with their crimes. When I read the list side by side I knew there would be little public sympathy. One of the victims had strangled two teenagers and attacked another four during a ten-week killing spree. Two others were arsonists, one causing the deaths of three children in a carefully prepared petrol-bomb attack. The fourth had bludgeoned his wife to death in a row over a TV programme while the final fatality occurred with a Muslim terrorist transferred to C-wing only ten days before. For the man and woman in the street these losses were almost welcome and the call for a public inquiry by opposition politicians was greeted with cynical indifference.

Using language that reflected his 'hanging judge' reputation, Halloran repeated his reasons for denying an inquest. 'Murder is murder is murder. We're dealing here with convicted murderers and the length of their sentences reflects how seriously the judiciary viewed their appalling crimes. I'm sure law-abiding citizens everywhere will join with me in thanking God none of our forces were killed. We owe an enormous debt to the brave men who freed the hostages.' He announced a review of security at the penitentiary and vowed to prosecute those involved in the disturbances. Four army doctors were assigned to deal with the immediate drug-addiction crisis. 'I'm sure,' he ended the briefing, 'society will take a serious view of how these thugs treated the very officers entrusted with their well-being and protection.' His words were recounted verbatim and without challenge by most commentators and to anyone with an ounce of compassion it made for very depressing reading.

Dr Frank Ryan MD was not mentioned anywhere, not in print or radio or television coverage. After all that had happened to me in the previous week I could half understand why O'Hara would want to keep me from the media. And I was quietly pleased as reports of my involvement would have reached Adelaide and worried my family. A quick lying e-mail reassured them all was well.

I analysed the situation further as I inspected my Saab in the apartment forecourt. The weather was still bitterly cold with easterly winds that cut to the bone and I was in denims and roll-top sweater over winter thermals. Dark rain clouds were gathering overhead and an occasional wet fat splat bounced off my forehead. The car looked as I remembered it, battered and dented in the same places, front and left side panels with scratches along paintwork on the boot. Inside, the carpet was worn at the driver's feet and scuffed beneath the passenger seat. Grime and dust covered most surfaces and the windscreen wipers needed replacing, as before. I never kept an eye on the mileage and couldn't convince myself the odometer had changed significantly. I spent almost an hour going through the engine and boot, taking out the spare wheel and jack and tyre-change tools. I even emptied the windscreen fluid container. My hands were blue and fingertips numb as I inspected the wheels and exhaust with a torch. I was searching for any tracking device to follow my movements but if there was one hidden I couldn't find it.

And all the time I wondered about the dramatic changes in my life over the period of seven days. I speculated again about Helen's messages, the misted mirror warning the rooms were bugged and her rolled-up tissue scrawl U WR SDTD ND NTRGTD. From inside the Saab I stared at the empty tarmac spaces where usually the blue Nissan Primera and silver Renault Clio were parked. I hadn't seen them or their owners since I'd been returned to Dublin. I was mulling that over too when for some reason one of Dan Steele's passing comments flashed in my brain. 'I heard you were in a brawl.' Was that no more than a trawling exercise or did the cell-block king know something? I immediately dismissed the idea as fanciful. How on earth could he gain access to the inner workings of the Justice Department? I opened the glove compartments but found only tissues, a half-packet of mints, chewing gum and an AA manual. Still the notion niggled and while I fiddled to unscrew the interior light fittings conspiracy theories raged in my imagination. I rubbed my hands together, feeling the fingers glow and tingle as warm blood rushed through. Now I linked Steele to some bizarre plot contrived by Bill O'Hara to test the state's prison system. Maybe, I rationalised as I felt along the padded headrests, Steele is in the hands of the authorities and deliberately provoked the riot to achieve ends as yet unknown. This didn't stand up to scrutiny; Steele was no friend of the state and unlikely to be recruited as an insider. I admitted defeat trying to explain why his name wasn't leaked to the media just as I admitted defeat in proving my Saab contained a concealed tracker. I parked the issue in my mind for the moment. There was other groundwork I needed to complete. But not until the cloudburst flooding the forecourt cleared.

'Hi, I'd like to speak to Lisa Duggan.' In a dripping-wet public call-box in Donnybrook village, about a quarter of a mile from where I lived, I rang Lisa. I chose an outside land-line in case my home and mobile phones were bugged. Lisa worked in Americabank, an investment institution based in a glass-and-steel high-rise in Dublin's financial district along the River Liffey. Often on a date waiting for her to finish work I followed the river commerce, especially Guinness barges ferrying kegs of stout to foreign ports. Rivers fascinate me. So much water flowing aimlessly towards the sea, while back home it would be diverted and urged along dust-bowl paddocks to nurture the parched red earth.

I leaned further into the booth to shield my ears from a tailback struggling along the main artery into the city. As the operator connected I listened to a corporate sales pitch. 'Sorry, sir,' she interrupted my drifting attention, 'what was the name again?'

I held my temper. 'Lisa Duggan.' I stomped my feet to stop the creeping freeze and read a business card stuck on the perspex window. An Asian Beauty offered intimate services at 'home or hotel' as long as I had a valid credit card. I switched interest to dialling codes for European numbers. I glanced at my watch, noting the call was now into its fourth minute. Usually I'd be connected within thirty seconds. The worry I dreaded was soon confirmed.

'I'm sorry, sir, there's no Lisa Duggan here.'

I almost blurted that she must be mistaken, to try again. 'Perhaps I've got the wrong name.' I forced my voice as normal as I could control it. 'Could you put me through to Foreign Exchange anyway? That's where she used to work.'

There was an ill-tempered 'one moment' and the Americabank sales pitch returned.

'Foreign Exchange, Jim Patterson speaking.'

Thank God, a voice I recognised and a name I knew. Patterson worked in the same division as Lisa. 'Hi, Jim, it's Frank Ryan here. Do you remember me? I'm dating Lisa Duggan.' I took a deep breath and waited.

'Hello, Frank, how are things?' I let my breath out. Patterson sounded normal and engaging as he continued. 'I was looking out for you in that prison siege. Do you still work at Harmon?' I wanted to squeeze through the cable and shake the man's hand. This was the first level conversation I'd had with another human being for over a week. 'They kept me away from the action,' I lied.

'I'm a doctor, not a hero.' I heard a short laugh. Suddenly horns started blaring close by. Two drivers were exchanging road-rage curses as one car was squared up to another. A red light one hundred yards further along was playing up and offering a stop-to-go system that bordered on comedy. 'Jim, I'm trying to speak with Lisa. You wouldn't happen to know where she is, would you? The operator told me there's no one at the bank with that name.'

I sensed a hand cupping the mouthpiece at the other end and a muffled interruption. Then Patterson was back. 'Sorry about that. Someone was asking about Euro exchange rates.' He cleared his throat. 'Lisa left here five days ago. She said there was some family crisis and she had to take time out. For some reason she emptied everything from her desk. Didn't she call you?'

The handpiece was almost glued to my ear and I managed to mumble some reply as the broker now tried engaging me in banter. But the words were automaton and my mind started spilling through the hourglass again. Lisa had quit her job. Lisa had signed a false statement. Lisa could not be contacted on her mobile phone. Lisa's personal effects had been cleared from my apartment. 'I gotta go, Jim,' I lied. 'Someone's at the door.' I set the phone back on its rest and stared at the Asian Beauty advertisement and wondered had Lisa been caught up in my nightmare too? Images of our days and nights together rushed into my tortured senses. Lisa and I holding hands while we strolled along Merrion Square, the garden showpiece in the heart of the city. Lisa choosing lingerie while I looked on, urging her towards the more racy brands. Lisa and I making love, her softness and wetness and little cries of pleasure. Lisa listening to my stories of the outback, her eyes getting larger with each tale of daring and hardship. My head slumped and I fought for control, totally at sea and bewildered and frightened. Bill O'Hara's devious face flipped into my imagination and I punched the perspex weather shield. 'You lying bastard,' I shouted out loud as my fist crashed again. A sharp tap on my shoulder brought me to my senses and I turned, cheeks glowing with embarrassment, to find an elderly lady waiting. 'Behave yourself, young man,' she snapped and pushed past me. 'This is a nice area, you know.'

Knock, knock. I rapped my knuckles against the door of the apartment underneath mine, stood back and tried to act nonchalant. I twisted my features into what I considered a bored and in-different expression, and then tried hiding it with one hand when I remembered the bruises. I gave it three minutes and knocked again, this time with some force. But the thuds on the wood only died in the emptiness of the corridor. No one answered. Twenty paces took me to the front of the complex and I stared out as yet another shower swept over Dublin. The forecourt was dark and wet and layered with puddles that rippled in the squall. My Saab stood on its own, its state reflecting my own situation. Miserable, abandoned and depressed. Where have my neighbours gone? Was it co-incidence or something more sinister that they disappeared just as I began my nightmare? I wanted to believe coincidence but my head was now so full of conspiracy I decided on the sinister option. I had to find out more about them but wasn't sure where to start.

I caught a cab into the city centre and tried to block out the driver's moans about the government, the weather, the cost of petrol, Ireland's chances in the next World Cup and his own indifferent health. By the time he dropped me outside the Westbury Hotel, off Grafton Street, I knew about his stomach ulcer, late-onset diabetes and 'terrible corns'. The man was a walking pathology textbook but I was in no mood to speculate on his long-term outlook.

The showers had passed over the east coast but thick grey clouds still clung defiantly to the skyline making the daylight gloomy and the streets dark. Pedestrians hurried for shelter and smokers shivered outside offices, drawing on their cigarettes for heat. I hurried along Dawson Street, dodging wheel splash and avoiding Romanian beggars. Then I paused to inspect the windows of Hodges Figgis bookshop, filled with promotional posters for the latest Tom Clancy blockbuster. On Nassau Street the traffic was at a standstill as a large tour bus fought its way across the middle of road. There was much horn blaring and many sour-faced drivers. I entered Trinity College, Ireland's premier university, through the Lincoln Place entrance and made my way towards the med school buildings. The campus playing pitches were windswept, muddy and deserted with only a soggy rugby ball suggesting an abandoned game and early shower. Students hurried along the walkways, wrapped tight against the cold. The contrast between academic attire in Dublin and Adelaide was marked. In the South Australian capital it was mainly T-shirts and denims and tracksuits. The warm and sunny climate encouraged jaunty steps and smiling features. Here, in the most westerly island before the Atlantic, the weather was so fickle and cold in winter that chins were buried hard against chests and faces red-raw.

Six months earlier I'd obtained a reader's card allowing me to use the med school library and there I had scoured heavy texts on infectious disease patterns. One of my medical interests at Harmon jail was the effect of Hepatitis C and HIV diseases in the same patient. Did chronic liver damage accelerate the spread of the HIV virus throughout the body? I had collected a significant body of research material from the inmates at the prison with this unfortunate combination and was making solid progress on management protocols.

Now as I edged past the narrow desks in the library, trying not to disturb students poring over *Gray's Anatomy* and similar tomes, my mind was elsewhere. In a side room was stored a collection of recent newspapers, usually dating back three weeks. There was the *Irish Times*, the *Irish Independent*, the *Examiner* and even the tabloid *Sun*, the last much admired by male undergraduates for its page three girls. I grabbed a handful dated 12 February and onwards and squeezed into a corner. There was no account in any paper of an incident in or near my apartment complex in Donnybrook. Reporting was confined to old favourites such as Iraq and a general disorder throughout the Middle East. Islamic terrorists were making renewed threats against American multinationals and the US State Department was issuing its millionth warning to citizens abroad to be alert. In the sports pages doping scandals grabbed the headlines with rioting soccer hooligans coming second. But it was the home news pages I focused on intently. I scanned every paragraph and photo for even a remote suggestion of something having happened to Dr Frank Ryan MD, physician to Harmon Penitentiary. My name did not appear until the riot erupted and then only in the context as 'sole medic trained in prisoner substance-abuse treatments'. I was portrayed as an Australian adventurer on work experience in Dublin and probably using the job as CMO to enhance my career. I couldn't fault that observation. But apart from that there was no hint the media were aware of my abduction and transfer to a London jail. Indeed, the only relevant account, apart from the riot, was the evacuation of J-wing on 5 February to allow a revamp of the sanitary facilities. Photographs of the armed cortège transferring the murderous inmates to another detention centre accompanied the text. This I knew already, although at the time I wasn't convinced about the sudden attention to hygiene. The whole prison was a health hazard with in-cell plastic buckets as toilets and 'slopping out' the only method of disposing of human waste. It was degrading, disgusting and against international rules on basic prison standards. But the Victorian facility was too expensive to replace and stood steadfast as the main high-security detention centre in the country.

I looked up to see a podgy girl staring at me and for a paranoid moment I wondered whether she was spying. Then I remembered my battered and bruised face and felt sure she was concerned some brawler had gained entry to the reading room. I grinned and saw immediately that my winning smile disarmed her. She grinned back and I buried my head in newsprint, afraid my harmless gesture might be misconstrued. I was in no mood to pick up girls, podgy or otherwise. I glanced over an article from the *Irish Times* overseas bureau on the hunt for Milos Bracchovis, an East European gangster wanted for gun running, murder, rape and narcotics offences. According to the report Bracchovis was hiding out in Zagreb and protected by a small group of henchmen. I skipped the rest of the account and returned my attention to anything, no matter how vague, that would hint at Frank Ryan and his life.

But after an hour I gave up and slumped back in my seat. In the reading room next door there was the shuffling and sniffling and whispers of students at work. I allowed some self-indulgent nostalgia, recalling less troubled days sheltering from the baking heat of an Adelaide summer around exam time. I could almost smell gum trees and hear the screeches of cockatoos as I drifted towards hotter climes. Then a clap of thunder and the rattling of window frames brought me to the moment. The outside gloom darkened even further and I stared at a window as its six panes were pounded with hailstones, drilling against the glass with a storm-driven fury. While the heavens opened over Dublin I teased out my many conversations with Lisa. She was always so interested in me. 'What did you do then, Frank?' I could see her face, scrunched in dismay as I told of the horrors of Kosovo or chairing some Amnesty investigation. But was it really dismay? I asked myself now. And what do you know about her? She gradually learned everything about me, knew my parents' names and my sisters' whereabouts. Lisa Duggan familiarised herself with all things Frank Ryan. On the other hand, Frank Ryan was so besotted and bedazzled by her beauty that he barely paid attention to the lack of background offered in return. Lisa had two brothers 'working in banking in the City of London'. Lisa came from 'down the country'.

'Whereabouts?' I remembered asking.

'Oh, Frank, it doesn't matter. It's so tiny compared to the wide-open spaces where you grew up. It doesn't even make the map in Ireland.' Fool that I was I let that roll unchallenged.

'Any sisters?'

'No. Kiss me, Frank.' I did and that ended that Q&A.

'Do your parents ever come to Dublin?'

'Let me feel you, Frank. Just let me feel you again.' Another simple query deflected by preying on my sexual weaknesses. God, but I was so hot for that girl.

'I'd like to see where you grew up, Lisa. Can we go there some weekend?'

'Of course. Any time you say.'

'What about this weekend?'

Pouting face. 'No, not this weekend. Everyone's away at a wedding.'

'Marry me, Lisa. Marry me and I promise you I'll make you the unhappiest woman in the world.' I laughed as I said the words but I was deadly serious.

'Is that a proposal, Dr Ryan?' Flickering eye-lashes and sideways glance that always drove me wild.

'If it is will you say yes?'

'No.'

'Why not?'

'Because it's too risky, Frank. It's too risky.' She unbuttoned her blouse slowly, then stopped and offered me to finish the row. When I entered her she was still whispering, 'It's too risky.'

What was so risky? Was there some scandalous family secret Lisa was frightened I might find out? Was there another man? Oh God, don't let it be another man, I silently pleaded. Give me a family secret and scandal any day, not someone else more special to her than me.

I was feeling very sorry for myself when

another clap of thunder rattled the window frames. Minutes later a ribbon of torrential rain rushed across the college lands, wasting itself on already soaked earth.

8

'We're offering a severance package.' In his Justice Department office Bill O'Hara swivelled in a worn green leather chair, a handful of fingers drilling at the desk in front. While his body moved his eyes never left me. 'Your contract runs for two years and it's now closing in on the first twelve months. The minister will pay the second-year salary in full with pension and social welfare rights.'

'In return for?'

'In return for you leaving on 31 March, by which time we should have our new recruit in place.'

My eyebrows arched. A new recruit so quickly? How did they swing that one? They had difficulties hiring me as CMO and even that was from a short-list of one. 'I'm delighted you headhunted another doctor so quickly,' I lied. 'Who is he?'

'I'm sorry, Frank, but we have been instructed not to release details, for security reasons. All I can tell you is your successor is a forty-two-year-old Canadian with wide experience of penal systems in a number of countries.'

A yes-man, I immediately decided. Another stooge in the Justice Department's collection of stooges. 'I wish him luck,' I continued my deceit. 'He has his work cut out for him. Harmon's no easy ride.'

O'Hara stopped swivelling. 'We're also introducing a range of prison reforms to make medical supervision easier.'

'And I'm not good enough to enjoy those changes?' I pretended spite but really couldn't give a damn.

'You are a liability,' O'Hara spat the words. 'Your recent behaviour has marked you as unstable. In that hellhole institution we can't afford unsound staff members. There was a government meeting last night and Patrick Halloran demanded your resignation. No one challenged him.'

I watched O'Hara as he offered these latest half-truths. The words came easy but the body language suggested a man ill at ease. In the short time I'd been in Ireland I had become reasonably friendly with him and sensed he had little appetite for this message.

'What if I refuse?'

'That would be silly.'

'Why?'

'Halloran would crush you. He spent years

131

harassing paramilitaries until they retreated so far they disappeared from sight. You know how he forced anti-terrorist legislation through parliament with bullying tactics that almost split the administration.'

I nodded, having heard many times how the fiery Justice Minister used every underhand manoeuvre he could think of in a controversial vote. He demanded mandatory life sentences without parole for anyone found guilty of subversive activity. And the burden of proof wasn't onerous; the sworn word of three senior policemen would clinch a verdict. Prominent lawyers threatened to take him to the European Court of Justice to have these draconian powers blocked but Halloran counter-attacked, accusing them of being soft on terrorism. The Irish people, sickened by years of subversive violence, rounded on the lawyers so angrily their offensive collapsed. Having subdued his fiercest critics the Justice supremo made intelligence-gathering a top priority in police tactics. Within twenty-four hours of legislation over two hundred non-nationals were detained for questioning and twenty-five charged with various offences ranging from false passports to owning seditious material. Like his US counterparts he saw Islamic fundamentalists up every tree.

'So he's too tough to challenge?'

O'Hara's eyes narrowed to warning slits. 'Exactly. If you want to keep your CV unblemished I'd take the deal and run. And thank God for it. Halloran could just as easily go public with your recent transgressions and that wouldn't look good in medical circles.'

I nodded agreement. Certainly with such a well-planned abduction and cover-up it would be pretty much impossible to convince outside authorities of my side of the story. 'You're right, Bill, it is time to move on.'

I dropped my chin as if in defeat but kept O'Hara in my upper visual field. He was staring at me intently, eyes boring into my forehead. He's scared stiff, I thought. This is not how malign doctors are dismissed. Hell, their demeanours are announced in a flurry of revelations and the unfortunates then castigated in public. O'Hara is hoping I'll back down and quit. Now I offered a rueful smile. 'I do miss the sunshine,' I said, 'and Ceduna beach and surf. And I miss cold Fosters on a really hot day. I'll take the package.'

O'Hara's shoulders relaxed. 'I'll make sure we give you a glowing reference and offer every facility at our disposal in any new position you choose.'

'Thanks, Bill. That would be a big help.' I was all meek and humble. But we were playing games. I knew that he knew this was not how Frank Ryan handled challenges. And I knew he knew my demeanour was for show. And we both knew neither of us would change these tactics. They wanted rid of me and were trying to ease me out without a fuss. I would co-operate. In the short term. And yet I really wanted to shake O'Hara's hand and say, C'mon, Bill, this nonsense has gone on long enough. Why don't we have a beer and you tell me what the hell is really happening and then I'll disappear into the outback? Waddye say? And how about a final word with Lisa? Lisa, I'd say, you were the only woman I ever met who made me happy, fully happy. Forget the sex, it was great but there was more to us than all that bedroom stuff. Lisa Duggan, you weren't just a beautiful girlfriend, you were everything I wanted in life. We have the same impish sense of humour, argue furiously over cinema and theatre and devour Asian food. If you've left me then I'm a broken man. Sure, I'll pick myself up again and find another girl eventually but it'll be very hard to reach the peaks of love I touched with you. You're a very special woman, Lisa Duggan. How about arranging all that, Bill?

But I knew it was impossible. O'Hara had a story for any query, a rock-solid defence. I decided to run with the deal and let them think, as much as they'd believe, that I was beaten. I did have one question. 'Bill, why don't I just quit now? There's not much point in me hanging around here for another five or six weeks. If I make it home soon I'll catch the end of summer, when the stifling heat is slackening. I could take a break and start looking for another job pretty much immediately.'

O'Hara leaned across the desk. 'That's not an option. Your replacement can't start until the end of next month and we can't run the prison without a CMO. The army doctors are refusing point blank to continue to provide cover.'

In my head I was calculating how long it would take to unravel the mystery of recent events. From my mouth came the words I knew O'Hara wanted to hear. 'Sure, Bill. That's OK by me. I'll go in again tomorrow.'

As I left the room I could almost feel his suspicious eyes boring into my back.

In Dublin Corporation planning offices I completed my query form and paid the fee for a property-title search. I watched as my application was passed from one, then another official and finally to a young woman yawning in front of a PC. Her fingers danced along the keyboard and her head tilted as she inspected the screen. Fifteen minutes later I was handed a single page with the information I sought. Now I knew that the block I lived in was owned by the Justice Department. Bill O'Hara's men ran the complex and Bill O'Hara's men must also have known my street-level neighbours. Whoever they were, in my estimation they became an integral part of the conspiracy. For days I'd wondered how my abductors had gained entry to the apartments. The front door was fitted with secure bolts and trip alarms. As I stood in a freezing gale trying to flag a taxi I decided the gang had hidden out below and made their move when I was in a deep sleep and most vulnerable. Squeezed into a corner of the back of a cab I stared out at the grey skies above the city and plotted my next move.

In another wet and graffiti-scarred phone booth I called Conor Mason, crime correspondent of a major daily tabloid. Mason had a formidable reputation in the trade as a news breaker and sometimes a news maker. His front-page exclusives on corruption profits gripped the nation and made him public enemy number one for the felons involved. In revenge for these disclosures his house was petrol bombed and his car tailed. There were numerous death threats and he was the only reporter allowed to carry a handgun. Mason had contacted me a few times in the past for inside information on the convicts and their crimes at Harmon Penitentiary but I was pledged to secrecy by my contract. We'd met once in a coffee shop just off the quays but he quickly realised I was of little use and quit after fifteen minutes, leaving me staring into the dregs of a cappuccino. Now I no longer felt bound by the rules of my employers.

'Mason here.'

'Conor, it's Frank Ryan. Remember me? CMO to Harmon?'

There was a short pause followed by a suspicious 'yes'.

'Any chance we could have a chat in private?'

There was another cautious pause. 'Is there anything in particular you'd like to talk about?'

'Maybe.'

'Like to tempt me with a hint?'

'Not over this line. But it'll be worth your time.'

We met in the same coffee shop, tucked into a busy laneway and with good views of fellow customers and outside pedestrians. I arrived first and secured a table at the rear. As I sipped on a mug of strong black filter I jotted a few thoughts on a paper napkin.

Mason squeezed in beside me twenty minutes later. He was carrying an *Irish Times*, folded neatly in two. As he set the paper down I spotted a micro-cassette player poorly hidden between the pages. A small red light glowing on its casing warned me a tape was already running. We made small talk until Mason's latte was nearly finished; in particular I hedged the reasons behind my bruised features. Then he glanced around, his ferret eyes taking in the room and its occupants. I followed his inspection and couldn't see anything unusual. Two or three groups huddled close to the window, conversation flowing. The solo customers were too far away to overhear anything we said while our waitress was distracted by steam spouts. Even so he checked under the table for listening devices, smiling at me as his lips mouthed meaningless words. Mason was a forty-year-old bull of a man, heavy set with jowls that reminded me of a lion feasting on prey. Heavy smoking had taken its toll on his skin, now rough and coarse with yellowing eyebrows. He was in bulging trousers and ill-fitting sweater. His reddish hair was wet from his walk and he ran a hand through it as we spoke.

'So what's up?'

'I need information,' I said.

Mason's eyebrows nearly disappeared into his hairline. 'I'm the journalist. You're supposed to offer me intelligence.'

'We can trade.' I tried to keep the urgency out of my voice. 'I'll give you background on the prison riot if you tell me everything you know about two men.'

Mason rested his chin on upturned knuckles. 'What about that security contract you were so concerned about?'

'It's null and void.' I held up a hand. 'No questions, we're working under the same rules as my bruises.'

Mason shrugged. 'I can live with that. Tell me about the siege. I need to know what's on offer.'

So I told him. I spilled everything on my involvement and my attempts to calm the murderous atmosphere with pledges of heroin for the addicts.

Mason listened intently; repeatedly checking the cassette was engaged.

He interrupted at one stage. 'Where the hell were you going to get so much heroin?' I explained that side of my plan. The reporter's gaze stayed fixed on me as the story spun out. He cut through a few times to clarify facts and names and made notes in the margin of the newspaper. Within ten minutes he had another exclusive and I could see a glint in his eyes as he plotted the account in his mind. Then he slumped back in his chair, uncertainty etched on his face.

'How come they were left so long without a fix? Why weren't you looking after them?'

'I was otherwise engaged.' I drew an imaginary circle round my face, then shook my head at his questioning look.

He frowned and shifted in his chair. 'Do you think you were being used to buy time?'

'Possibly. I wasn't there for long but maybe it was enough for their plans.'

'How do you feel about that?'

'How I feel doesn't matter a damn. The Justice Department runs Harmon Penitentiary like some experimental penal colony. They pay no attention to prisoner health issues.'

Mason gave a hollow laugh. 'You say you're naive but don't let me think you're stupid as well. Prisoner rights are foreign territory in this jurisdiction.

Prisoner health issues are something that happens in other institutions, certainly not Harmon jail. You are CMO to some of the most dangerous and vicious criminals in this state and any other for that matter. If they all died of bubonic plague tomorrow morning there wouldn't be one tear shed. Wise up, doc. CMO in Irish prisons is a rung above trustee. You're dirt to the inmates and dirt to the authorities.'

I listened but Mason wasn't telling me anything I hadn't already worked out. I let him have his say, if only to appear taken aback by his superior knowledge and insights.

'Well, I've had enough of it. I'm quitting.'

Now he looked surprised. 'Why?'

'Time to move on. I can't stand the weather here and the pay and conditions aren't sufficient to make me hang in any longer. That riot was the final straw. I don't want to be the next hostage at the end of HIV-infected needles.'

'You knew that risk when you took the job.'

'It's different being aware of a risk and seeing it up front. And it's not every day you get to see a man beaten to death and thrown about like a sack of potatoes.'

'He was a snitch.'

My eyes widened. This was news. 'How do you know?'

Mason held up his hands in mock defence. 'I have my sources. He was a drug dealer turned

140

mole due early release in exchange for inside information.'

'He mustn't have been much good. How come they didn't know about the riot before it happened?'

'Maybe they did,' said Mason and I nearly fell off my chair. 'Maybe they let things run as long as they wanted before intervening. I find it strange no warder got seriously hurt in the exchanges while the inmates were shot like dogs. Makes you think, doesn't it?'

It did and I was thinking furiously. Mason slid a cigarette into his mouth and drew on the filter. 'I'm trying to give them up,' he explained. 'I find it easier to pretend than go cold turkey.' He ordered another two coffees, ignoring the give-me-a-break look from the waitress when he offered a fifty-euro note. 'Did you know C-wing is back in action?'

My head jerked with surprise. 'No, I've been kept away since the siege.'

'They had a gang of workmen in there within hours of prisoner evacuations. Steam hoses cleaned up the mess and then the damaged areas were replastered and painted. New bunk-beds bolted to floor and walls. A temporary roof was lowered into place next day. D-wing is also getting fast-track repairs despite roof collapse. Does that all not sound unusual?'

Unusual wasn't a strong enough word for Mason's snippets and for the next few seconds we stared at

141

one another, eyes wide with shared disbelief. Then the reporter snapped off his cassette and leaned forward. 'What you've told me is good. There's enough material for a major scoop and the info could have come from a number of sources other than you. But there's more to the riot, I'm convinced of that.' He shuffled in his chair so he had a better view of the café and spoke to me out of the corner of his mouth. 'The prison system is bursting at the seams and to lose one block means worse overcrowding somewhere else. Even so, I still can't get my head around the speed with which that wing was restored.' He drew on his unlit cigarette and blew imaginary smoke into the air, then turned towards me. 'I'm running background checks on the prisoners shot dead.'

I cut in, uncertain of Mason's train of thought. 'Why?'

'Were they targeted? Was this riot really a disaster waiting to happen or was it set up to cleanse the system? I don't know, I'm only asking the hard questions to see if we get answers.'

'Those guys hadn't had a fix for a week,' I said. 'They were severely strung out.'

'I know,' he countered, 'but three of the four killed were not addicts, that I have on good authority.'

This set me back on my heels and I had to double think my responses. 'There was a lot of gunfire.

From where I was lying I think anybody could have been hit.'

'Exactly my point,' Mason pressed, his eyelids flickering as he thought out loud. 'Anybody, yes, but why those three? I'm not convinced by the Justice Minister's explanation. He's refused all inquiries. The squad that stormed the wing disappeared as soon as the prisoners were back under control. No one saw their faces and all information relating to them is restricted, for operational reasons. Maybe I see scheming where none exists but I'm in this business too long not to have a healthy suspicion index.'

As I listened I desperately wanted to share my own conspiracy theories but held back. Mason and I worked to different agendas and the journalist would use and dump me as quickly as Bill O'Hara. I knew to keep my thoughts to myself.

'And J-wing is still empty.' He threw out that nugget for my reaction.

'Is it?' was all I offered.

'Yeah. Doesn't that make everything else even more dubious? J-wing holds the most dangerous recidivists in the system and they're now enjoying relative freedom in an army base. Yet C-wing is re-paired within forty-eight hours. It doesn't add up, Frank. Why is it so vital to have one block back in order quicker than it takes paint to dry while another division is still undergoing sanitary refurbishment almost three weeks later?'

'I don't know.' Across the table Mason's face creased in disbelief. 'And I'm not holding anything back,' I pleaded. 'You're ahead of me on most of this and I'm just trying to make sense of it all. And I agree, the official explanations sound less and less believable.'

We stared into the middle distance for some time, each to our own thoughts. Far from helping me understand my plight, Mason's words only confused me further. If I told him all that had happened to me he would have another dramatic scoop. But I would be no closer to finding the truth, for media revelation or not I was confident Bill O'Hara would deny everything and have the proof to make me out as a common liar. I knew that was not the way to go.

Mason interrupted my reverie. 'What's your side of this?'

'Two names. Dan Steele and Noel Dempsey. I want every press cutting you can access on Steele going back ten years and anything new you have on him.'

Another scribble filled the diminishing blank spaces along the *Irish Times* margins. 'OK,' he said. 'That's no big deal. Most of Steele's activities are on public record.' He glanced over. 'Who's Noel Dempsey?'

'I don't know. All I can tell you is he's with the Justice Department.'

'What'd he do?' Mason's eyes darted at my bruises.

'I'm not sure.'

'Ah, for Christ's sake, Frank, open up. How can I help you if I don't know where you're going?'

I leaned into my chair and gripped the edge of the table, arching my fingers to ease the spasms building up. I'd been clenching and unclenching my fists for days and the muscles were beginning to ache. Finally I looked over at Mason. 'I don't know where I'm going. And that's the honest truth.'

Mason stared at me for maybe a minute and then collected his bits and pieces. He stood up, dropped his unlit cigarette into his coffee and leaned closer so he couldn't be heard. 'You'd better find out soon, Frank. Your face suggests another exclusive.'

I almost stepped on the envelope as I opened the ground-level door of my apartment. It was long and business brown with FRANK scrawled on the front and sealed carefully with Sellotape. The tape had been hastily stuck down and was twisted and rippled. Inside was a single white A4 page with two sentences: BE VERY CAREFUL FRANK AND STAY OUT OF THIS. I LOVE YOU, PLEASE BELIEVE ME. LISA.

I held that page for hours afterwards, reading

and rereading the simple message. The words were written by Lisa, of that there was little doubt. Her spidery scribble was very recognisable. But had she delivered the note or used an intermediary? I didn't know and cared little. She loved me and that was all I wanted to hear. Maybe there really was some family calamity that had taken her away but that now seemed unlikely in light of her warning. *Stay out of this*. But what was 'this'? And where was she? And the hell I was going to stay out of it, I wanted her back.

9

My bruises were healing fast. The welts had gone through the changes of a sick rainbow, from purple to brown and now a faint yellow. The bullet track along my scalp was a keloid scar, tough and thick. My ribs and limbs ached less though I grimaced when shaving: there was one shoulder muscle still holding out. At least I didn't draw so many stares when I walked the streets. Confidence in my appearance was restoring itself, and that was important when presenting for duty at Harmon Penitentiary. It's not good for standards when the doctor looks worse than his patients. Back home I could fall off a trail bike, get rope burns on my hands or face blisters from sun exposure and it didn't bother me. Hugo Boss hadn't reached the Australian outback, nor Calvin Klein or Giorgio Armani. Image didn't rule, existence reigned supreme. The only time I made a fuss of myself was on a date and even then I had hours to prepare. My girlfriends were often from neighbouring properties, separated by miles of scrub and hills. What with unsealed roads and rampaging kangaroos it often took an hour to drive ten miles. What awaited me then was a lifetime away from what I was dealing with now in the jail's only examination room.

'H'w'm I doin'?'

It was 25 February and six days since the prison riot. I was grudgingly accepted back as CMO, the prisoners hearing how the governor set me up. I even sensed some sympathy for my plight. Before answering the h'w'm I doin'? I ran an eye over the liver-enzyme report on the desk in front. Bilirubin was up, ALT was up, AST was up, albumin was down. In fact, everything was either up or down, abnormal as hell. Then again, my patient was a heroin addict with end-stage liver disease so I shouldn't have expected different.

'You're OK, Mallet. No significant change since last time.' Across the table a toothless grin spread across Art 'Mallet' Murphy's face. In Harmon every prisoner had a nickname, rarely was anyone addressed by his or her official title. It worked easier for me when I followed this convention and so I used a range of identities. Patch, Gutser, Baldy, Nipper, Boyla, Crowbar (after his murder weapon), Ferret, Foxy, Blackie, Blob, Blondie and, my favourite, Volcano. Commonly an 'o' was tagged on at the end of first names, so the landings had dozens of Davos, Antos, Deccos and Rickos. In the women's wing such tags weren't as widespread but they were often more vicious. Bitch was the least offensive.

Mallet was in on a serious assault charge after clubbing an elderly lady for her handbag. 'I never see'd the oul' wan, all I see'd was her handbag,' he tried explaining when we first met. For twenty euro he almost ended one ageing woman's life and secured his third eight-year conviction. Mallet was forty-two but I didn't think he'd celebrate his forty-third birthday. He was wasted to seven stone, down five from his usual weight. His teeth were gone, his mind wandering, his skin yellow and liver grossly swollen. He was so jaundiced fellow prisoners shunned him as if he was carrying some contagious bug that flew through the air. I didn't offer any insight into his dismal outlook; I just kept saying things were stable. His life was bad enough without grinding him into the dirt. Mallet left with a bottle of vitamins that I knew he'd pass off as uppers somewhere along the misery chain outside.

My next five charges were depressingly similar to the first: heroin addicts with hepatitis, three of whom were also HIV positive. Any treatments were doomed to failure with this group as they shot up with shared needles whenever a hit was possible. Drug smuggling was an art form, ranging from small lots thrown over the perimeter wall during exercise to internal concealment. Rectal and vaginal examinations were almost routine and soft fruit forbidden after one inmate arranged for his oranges to be injected with heroin. He ate four during visiting hours and spent the next day in an opiate coma. Drugs were also the main prison currency. Dust (tobacco), draw (cannabis), scag (heroin), coke (cocaine), uppers (amphetamines) and downers (hypnotics and tranquillisers) were accepted as payment for most things. Equally skin (porno) mags or just a left hook would also work in certain situations.

Grudges were settled with a viciousness that sometimes took my breath. Snooker balls in socks, blades embedded in toothbrushes, and sharpened mop handles were typical weapons. Most attacks occurred when the cell doors were opened in the morning, surprise being the essence of success. Stairwells, exercise yards and the gym were preferred battlefields. Despite blood and flesh flying nobody ever saw anything and there was little value in me asking what happened as I sutured the wounds or bandaged the cuts. My work at the prison was a holding assignment and nothing more. The doctor–patient relationship was based on loathing and distrust. The convicts thought me part of the system while I found it safer not to become friendly with any one inmate.

The women's prison was even more difficult terri-tory. I was young, strong and handsome and my patients young, weak-willed and desperate. I was offered a range of intimacies in exchange for uppers, downers, heroin or crack cocaine. Occasionally there was the honest and simple request to relieve sexual frustration. I could have got laid ten times an hour twice a week if I'd wanted but I'd rather have fought my way out of a snake pit. My pre-decessor had been gunned down because he refused to smuggle narcotics into the prison. However, he'd indulged his sexual fantasies in the women's wing and thus became compromised and soon black-mailed. Apparently he did act as a mule for some time but caved in when the scores became too frequent. That's when the prisoners decided on payback. The man who ordered the hit was my next patient.

'You're looking better, doc.'

I leaned back and watched Dan Steele try and get comfortable in the rickety chair opposite. He squirmed and wriggled his bottom and then settled.

'Did the nurse get your medical details?' I asked.

'Yup. Everything from migraine to arthritis.' He made a fist. His knuckles were swollen and deformed. 'Somebody's face did that,' he said. 'And it still throbs in the cold weather.'

I ignored the brag. 'What's so special you have to see me?' It was standard practice for the prison nurse to screen patients. So many lied just to get out of their cells it could take all day to plough through a waiting list.

'My headaches are acting up.'

'Uh-huh. Anything else?'

'Isn't that a start? Don't you take notes or something? What sort of a fucking doctor are you anyway?' The words were angry but the body language didn't match. Steele didn't seem the sort who visited doctors.

'I always write my reports after I see the patient.'

'Well, I can't sleep with these damn headaches,' he growled and cricked his neck for effect, then massaged his temples. 'Maybe I've got a brain tumour or something. I think I should get an X-ray.'

'X-rays are like gold dust,' I said. 'The last two inmates sent to hospital tried to escape. One had three accomplices who attacked the radiology staff, the other arranged for a CS-gas container to be left for him. He cleared the ground floor inside twenty minutes once the fumes started spreading.'

'I heard about that,' Steele snapped. 'Didn't do them much good.' It didn't. Both escape attempts failed when police officers in plain clothes produced handguns and batons. The Justice Department crowed over these minor victories but a doctors' union forced a four-week block on radiology services in protest. They even clubbed together to buy a portable machine for use inside Harmon but it crashed within a week and was currently idle and awaiting spare parts.

I continued. 'You know the system. Health is not a priority. I have six psychiatrically disturbed men I cannot transfer because of bed shortages in the criminal mental hospital. So I have to keep them sedated in padded cells. It's barbaric but all I can do.' Steele listened impassively. Whether he was paying attention was another matter but I felt I had to get my side of the story out. Telling him was as good as writing it up in the prison newspaper. 'If you need an X-ray I have to complete forms for the radiologist and the prison governor and then personally plead your case.'

'Jeez, I'll be dead before those bastards make a decision.' I agreed but didn't say so. I took out a small patient card and scribbled MIGRAINE on one corner. I looked up again. 'How long have you been troubled with migraine?'

'Long enough.'

'Long enough isn't good enough. I need to know the timescale.'

I was about to launch into a lecture when Steele double palmed me to hold. Then he floored me with a simple sentence. 'You're being followed.'

I felt as though he'd planted his gnarled fist between my eyes and I sat bolt upright in the chair. For a moment I didn't speak, just held his hard gaze. He was in a T-shirt and I could see the snake-around-the-neck tattoo more clearly. In the flash of a stupid second I almost asked where he'd had the artwork done. Then I collected my wits. 'I don't know what you're talking about. If you're only here to stir trouble maybe you'd better quit now so I can deal with the really sick inmates.'

He stood up and edged towards the door, checking no one was listening. The room was cramped but reasonably soundproof, being at the end of a solid concrete unit. All inmates were frisked before entering and an armed warder stood outside in case of trouble. There were two panic buttons for emergencies. Unless specifically demanded by the treating physician, medical complaints were dealt with confidentially.

'Everyone's sick in this place.' Steele squirmed back into his seat. Outside I could hear muffled shouts, followed by the clanging of upturned cutlery. 'Nobody gets priority unless they're having a heart attack and even then they need to be in a coma. Sick isn't the issue.'

'What is the issue?' I pretended vague interest but inside my alarm antennae were humming.

'You.'

I tried to smile to protect my slipping mask but it wouldn't come. Steele was staring at me like he knew a ton of stuff. And like he knew I didn't know half of what he knew and he would use that information for his own good.

'Where's your gun?' The question was unexpected and threw me. When I returned to work I was refused permission to carry my Justice Department issue Beretta or use Mace for protection. When I queried this a letter from Bill O'Hara was shown by way of explanation. In it, O'Hara's directives were precise and abrupt. Dr Frank Ryan must not be given firearms. He may carry Mace, but only while visiting red zones. Red zones are the most dangerous landings in the penitentiary.

I decided not to answer Steele's question, wondering whether silence would tease more out of him. It did. 'I hear your arms certificate has been withdrawn.'

'I'm sure you hear a lot of things in here. Not much else to do but talk and gossip.'

Steele grinned and the long scar on the left side of his face wrinkled to an inverted V. 'This isn't gossip, Dr Ryan. This is fact. While I may be stuck behind bars twenty-four hours a day I like to know what's going on in the world, especially when it might impact on me. So I keep tabs on you, have been since you started working here.'

Inside, I froze. Steele has been monitoring me since I arrived in Ireland? 'And what have you learned in that time?' I asked, not sure I wanted to hear the answer.

'You're OK. You're not like some of the other stooges sent here to spy on us. The word along the landings is you're the genuine article, a doctor interested in prisoners.'

'You're not here to give me a reference. What's your angle?'

'Listen up,' he growled, his whiskey voice deepening. 'You might learn something for your own good. I know everything about you, where you came from, where you worked last and where you live. I know about that Lisa tart you were shacked up with and I know about you getting the shit kicked out of you.' My mind went into the hourglass again, control slipping as fast as grains of sand. 'What I don't know is what happened to you after that. You disappeared off my radar for days and only turned up again when I heard you nearly took the head off that bastard Dempsey.' He stood up and leaned across the table. 'I know even more than that, doc. I'll tell you the rest after you arrange my X-ray.' He was out of the door before I could draw breath.

I sat in my chair for maybe five minutes, heart fluttering and hands shaking. I found it hard to concentrate, so many new images and fears forcing their way into my consciousness. Dan Steele has had me shadowed since I arrived in Ireland. Dan Steele knows everything about me, including my relationship with Lisa. More disconcerting,

Dan Steele knows about the attack at the apartment and how I went missing. And, dammit, Steele knows Noel Dempsey. Just what the hell is going on? I offer the Justice Department a good service and they drag me into some shadowy conspiracy. And all the time career criminal Dan Steele has inside knowledge. He knows more than I do and I'm the one in the eye of the storm. What do they think I'm made of? Do 'they' really think they can get away with this? Whatever 'this' is.

Let them feast, I thought. Let them fill their bellies and then strike. In this fifteen-round heavyweight contest I was still losing. I was KO'd in the first two, the assault and imprisonment. Again I'd lost on points in the third with Bill O'Hara's concocted story. I'd called it wrong and was only saved by the bell at the prison siege in the fourth. And now I was back on the ropes, outwitted and outpunched. It was time for a tactical change.

My mind was distracted years back to a string of sheep kills on the station at home. For days Dad and I searched the scrub and valleys for signs of dingoes, the most likely marauders. Eagles could take young or weak lambs but usually left feathers at the scene. But with these kills we saw only scuff tracks. Our stock was protected by a dog fence, a man-made barrier stretching about four thousand miles from Queensland across New South Wales and the tip of South Australia to the Great Australian Bight. North of the fence you could run cattle, south only sheep but occasionally floods would damage the screen and allow dingoes through. When we lost twenty sheep in three days we went hunting. Dad went west while I took up position a mile south of the homestead under a large gum tree, my body wedged deep into its huge knotted roots. It was mid-July, winter in Australia, and mercifully thick cloud blocked the sun. It had rained steadily for a week so the dams and water levels were good. I waited for six hours in drizzle, and then took a break for dry clothes. I went back for another ten-hour vigil and headed home again.

It was on my third watch that the pack showed up, four hungry and mangy wild dogs sniffing and pawing the damp earth as they emerged from cover. I could've clipped one with a decent shot but that would've frightened the other three away and we'd still be looking. There was no time to call for help; by the time Dad caught up the dogs would have scattered. I followed the troop, hunching and dodging, hiding behind rocks and bush vegetation. I knew the dingoes would seek out the nearest waterhole and maul the sheep crowded there. I followed them for the best part of a mile, maybe a mile and a half, before I saw them settle in for another attack. The huddle of sheep split widely as the dogs circled, barking and snarling, sharp teeth snapping. Finally they brought down two of the slowest beasts and started ripping flesh. I gave them enough time to fill their bellies and become engrossed in the feast. The steady bleating from a distant paddock masked the crack from my rifle as I picked them off, one by one. That's all it takes with brutes of low intelligence, cunning and patience and decent hardware.

Now, as I sat in my worn and chipped chair in the medical room of Harmon Penitentiary I decided to use similar strategies. Dan Steele was a brute but an intelligent one. The Justice Department was also a brute, but massive and clever with infinite resources. I had cunning and patience, if a limited time, left in Ireland. I had no hardware and would somehow have to overcome that problem. In the meantime I would wait, learn a little more, and wait again.

Clinic over, I walked the landings with two warders, trying to make small talk. A severely disturbed inmate had become unusually subdued overnight and they wanted him checked. If they knew about my dismissal they weren't letting on and the conversation was terse and curt with little banter. It was lock-up time and the blocks seethed with an air of tension you could almost touch. The atmosphere at Harmon was always poisoned but since the riot the pent-up anger and resentment had heightened. The cells were overcrowded, often four men squeezed into a two-man unit. Allowing for food and exercise breaks the inmates were kept in the cells eighteen hours a day.

Little wonder so many relied on illicit pharmaceuticals. Little wonder there was so much violence.

'I hear C-wing is back in action.' I threw the comment as a hook for information.

'Yeah, full to the rafters. D-wing should be ready in a couple of days.' That was the only response despite a few other leading queries.

'What about J-wing? Is that still being refurbished?'

There was no reply and I sensed the duo deliberately ease their steps so they were inches behind. I kept walking. A door was opened with three sets of keys and it swung heavily on its hinges. We were now in a small corridor of padded chambers for convicts showing obvious psychiatric symptoms. The steady boom of fists pounding a door at the furthest end greeted us. The warders, big strong men with specialist training, prepared to open the first cell.

'Got your stab-proof vests?' I checked.

'Yes.'

'Yep.'

'Mace?'

A can was flashed for my scrutiny.

'OK, let's go.'

I waited until I heard the locks give and then gestured the holding officer to stop. Two sets of questioning eyes drilled into me.

'If J-wing is still empty, maybe we could transfer a few up there. All that spare space and natural light would help their mental state.'

I knew by the immediate gaze aversion I'd touched on a sensitive area. 'Then maybe again not,' I mumbled and slipped on a pair of protective gloves.

When the door was finally dragged wide my first patient was curled up in a corner, arms hugging drawn-up knees. I didn't need to examine him to know he was dead.

10

'He was dead two hours, maybe more. Padded-cell prisoners are on ten-minute supervision but since the riot many staff are redeployed. I don't think he was checked before we went in.' I was briefing crime correspondent Conor Mason on the latest tragedy at Harmon Penitentiary. The tape in his micro-cassette player was spinning, the red light glowing in ON mode. The journalist eyed me closely, as though I might suddenly run away if he didn't keep watch.

'How do you mean you don't think?'

'There's a roster on the landing which wardens tick when they've checked a prisoner. It's like time sheets in toilets where the cleaner scratches his signature every half-hour to look like he's a good boy. All the while he's out the back smoking and reading the paper.'

'And is that what happened?'

'I can't be sure but it's a reasonable assumption. Everything was marked as if he'd been properly observed but his body heat was significantly down. I don't have the autopsy report but I'd guess he was dead two hours.'

Mason leaned into his chair, pulled a cigarette from a full packet and flicked it onto his lips. He drew hungrily on the unlit filter. All around in the open-plan offices came the clamour of a busy newspaper, phones ringing, fingers typing, orders barked. Editorial staff rushed from cubicle to cubicle looking for hard copy, checking deadlines and demanding rewrites. I'd chosen Mason's workplace in case I was being followed. Dan Steele's warning had got to me but I reckoned it unlikely anyone would tail me all the way to this floor.

'Let me get something down.' Mason opened a new file on his PC and began typing. He spoke to me out of the corner of his mouth, cigarette hanging from lower lip. He identified the file as PADDED CELL DEATHS and added a few lines of introduction. 'OK, run the gist by me again.'

I waited while a young woman leaned into the booth with fresh coffee. She glanced at me and our eyes met briefly. I could tell she'd be back with more for as long as I stayed.

'There's a major problem at Harmon . . . hell,

there's a long list of problems but this is the most recent. Drug abuse is rampant and can precipitate psychosis.'

Mason's eyebrows shot up.

'The prisoners go mad,' I explained in lay terms. 'They mix cocktails of heroin and cocaine, even adding amphetamines and tranquillisers. Some are injected, others swallowed. The mind becomes swamped by a surge of chemicals and can overload. Overload produces deranged and disturbed thinking including hallucinations and paranoia.' Mason kept up with me, drilling the keyboard at a hundred miles an hour. I watched as he followed the words on the PC terminal, his face scrunched with concentration. He nodded to me to go ahead. 'Also, inmates can develop psychiatric symptoms within weeks of incarceration. This is especially true of teenagers. When they come down from the initial shock of sentence and realise where they're locked up their brains go to frogspawn. I see a lot of depression, agitated depression, anxiety and agitated anxiety. If the conviction is for narcotics there can be withdrawal symptoms, as bad as the horrors in alcoholics. Good-looking youngsters get targeted sexually and most can't handle that. This is no different to many penal colonies with the exception that this is Europe and such primitive conditions should not exist. Primitive extends to the medical services, or lack of medical services. I can't shift my psychiatric patients to the main criminal mental hospital because it's full. So I bung the worst into padded cells and sedate them.'

'What do you think happened here?'

'Hard to say. Maybe he hoarded his medication and took it all in one go. Maybe someone smuggled other drugs to him and they inter-reacted. The post-mortem will give us that answer but won't change the system. A front-page story in a major tabloid might.'

Mason finished typing and turned to me. 'What's in this for you? This is the second scoop in four days. Before that you were a clam. What opened you up?' The cigarette on his lower lip was soggy and unravelling and he dropped it into a trash can.

'I need more information.'

'About what?'

'A lot of things.'

Mason pulled a face. 'For Jesus' sake, come out with it. All this cloak-and-dagger stuff is doing my head in. Are you in trouble?'

I swirled the dregs of my coffee and inspected the black grains. How much should I tell? How much would he believe? How much would he use and to hell with me? How far can I trust him? His phone rang; a merciful distraction and I flashed all the events over the past two weeks through the rational side of my brain. Then I reworked the same through my irrational thought and came up with scary scenarios. Scary to me but probably crazy to an outsider. As the call continued I scanned the office to make sure we wouldn't be interrupted. The coffee-jug girl was eyeing me from a distance but I avoided her gaze. Two stalls along, a group were hunched over a PC terminal, fingers pointing to the screen and heads nodding. I shifted my chair to block any intrusion.

'You think there's a lot more to that riot,' I said as fast as the receiver hit the cradle. 'The blocks were repaired quicker than made sense. Then you wondered whether the dead prisoners were targeted? This is conjecture and nothing more, you can't write an exclusive without facts. Let me offer snippets.'

Mason was now so close we could've been engaged. I told him about Dan Steele's visit, leaving out his request for an X-ray. That was something I was mulling over myself. I added how Steele revealed he'd been following my every move since I came to Ireland. I mentioned Lisa, but only in the context as an ex-girlfriend, which wasn't that deceitful. I decided not to tell that Steele also knew about the attack and my disappearance. That would have been difficult to swallow, even for a journalist. And I finished with the criminal's caution that I was being followed.

Mason's pupils slowly widened until they were as big as saucers, his lower jaw limp. 'Jesus,' was all he said when I finished. He turned to his PC and started to type, then stopped. He back-spaced the words and typed again, paused, bent his head deep in thought and finally closed the file. 'You're going to have to let me in on this, Frank. I have no way of checking what you're saying. What *is* in this for you?' This time his tone warned that he wouldn't tolerate fudge. 'And who beat you up?'

I said, 'There is something strange going on in Harmon. I don't know what but whoever's behind it is using me. I'm being shifted around for strategic gains without knowing motives. I was attacked and pummelled unconscious . . .' Mason made a so-that's-what-happened face. 'I've lost my girl-friend, I've been told to quit by the end of March and they think I'm going to disappear without knowing the answers to a lot of questions. Now that really pisses me off.' Mason made to interrupt but I flashed my eyes no. I was in full flow and didn't want to lose my train of thought. Also, I needed to be careful how much I offered, some details might be useful later. 'J-wing is closed for "refurbish-ment",' I signed inverted commas, 'but C- and D-wings are in use again. Any time I ask about J-wing I'm stonewalled. Conclusion: whatever's happening has nothing to do with plumbing.' Mason dismissed an over-the-shoulder query with an irritable wave. 'Dan Steele is priming me for some move, inside or out. I checked medical records and he's never shown at any clinic before. Now maybe there is something genuinely wrong, even killers get sick.' I noticed a cynical smile flicker on Mason's lips. 'But I suspect his visit had less to do with medicine than feeling my collar. I anticipate he'll be even more unwell in the coming weeks.'

'Is he planning an escape?'

'That's one angle. He has a sister in the women's wing so he could be pushing for help for her. Equally, he could be setting me up to carry drugs. The possibilities are endless.'

About twenty feet away a sudden commotion distracted us. Two young men were squaring up and being held back by staff. There was a lot of shouting and swearing. Mason grinned. 'Sports section,' he explained. 'There's only one ticket for the soccer international next week and both want it. They can't stand one another at the best of times and this tipped the scales.'

I watched for a moment until the pugilists separated and drifted away, angry gestures flailing in the air.

'Wankers,' Mason chuckled. He beckoned the coffee girl and she was with us in a flash. I gave her my widest smile and she went modest for a second before offering a come-on. I went limp wrist and she nearly dropped the jug. I was suddenly quite pleased with myself; my sense of humour was back.

Mason cut through the charade. 'What's your next move?'

'Get as much information as I can. This is where you and I help each other. You need dirt on the prison system and I have that in spadefuls. I need background on the main players and wouldn't know where to start looking. You have researchers. Let's trade.'

Mason stood up and pretended to stretch, then swivelled his body from side to side. I could see his ferret eyes inspect the offices. He sat down again and pulled himself flush with the PC terminal. His left hand typed while his right hand dragged a dossier from a drawer. 'Hide that. It's everything I could get on Steele.' I wrapped my coat around the bulky file, adjusting until I felt sure it wouldn't drop. 'Whoever Noel Dempsey is he's well protected. I've made calls and felt like I was checking Osama Bin Laden. Stony silence each time. I'll keep on it but I can't guarantee anything.'

'Dempsey is important,' I said, realising I was becoming obsessive. 'Find out more about him, we might have a better idea what's going on.' I noticed I was using 'we' now, enveloping Mason into the plot. Still, it helped to have someone to talk with. My Aussie reserve was making me too introspective.

Outside, I varied my routine. First I caught a cab from the newspaper building on Burgh Quay and alighted after half a mile, dropping a twenty-euro note onto the passenger seat. Then I scurried through Clerys department store on O'Connell Street, Dublin's main thoroughfare. I took a lift to menswear, then stairs to household furniture and finally a fire escape to a narrow alley. I hoofed it from there, crossing streets with traffic queues and small parks plagued with beggars. If anyone were following me they'd have one helluva job keeping up. I entered a bank in Talbot Street and picked up a pamphlet on deposit accounts while scanning every face that came in. No one looked suspicious and I slipped out of a rear exit. Crossing the Liffey I hurried to the front of Trinity College and made my way to the med school reading rooms. Here, among students a bit younger than myself, I felt safe. Any tracker would have difficulty gaining access and, I hoped, would stick out. I settled into my favourite corner and began sifting through the considerable file on Dan Steele.

The dossier was mainly accounts in Irish newspapers with extra from AP and Reuters. There were also translated clippings from dailies in Spain, Germany and Italy where Steele's criminality had made its mark. He'd hung out in the south of Spain for two years while police in Ireland and Britain sought extradition. Then he disappeared only to resurface in Germany (bank heist) and Italy (refugee smuggling). Each time his name was linked with local hoodlums but the Irishman hadn't been arrested. The bulk of the coverage related to the recent trial with pages of evidence incorporating police, forensic and witness statements. After conviction the press set out his criminal career, listing all known offences. Robbery, GBH, running brothels and living off immoral earnings, narcotics, smuggling, jury intimidation, witness intimidation, illegal betting and, of course, murder. When arrested, Steele was found to have six passports, three describing him as an Irish citizen but each with different names and personal details. There were also two British and one South African ID. The forgeries carried multiple port-of-entry stamps, some genuine and others false. A forensic scrutiny concluded Steele had actually visited countries as far away as Sierra Leone in West Africa and Ukraine in the former USSR. Investigating officers could get nothing from him about these trips and there was considerable speculation about drug and people smuggling. One unconfirmed account suggested a special detective unit was tracing Steele's international profile for evidence of a list of unsolved crimes. Prosecutors in Britain,

Germany, Italy and South Africa applied for the killer's extradition but he was locked up in Harmon and unlikely to see freedom for many years. Officers from these countries had come to Dublin to interview him but the rumour was they'd left none the wiser. Dan Steele was tight as a drum.

I took a large atlas from the shelves and pored over the places mentioned, hoping to tease out the link between them and Steele. Narcotics were the obvious explanation, especially since his final bust was linked to drug smuggling. Shifting illegal aliens from Africa to Europe was another possibility and that was also on his CV. I immediately rejected this option. There wasn't enough money in human trafficking and the risk of detection was high. Narcotics made more sense but I couldn't quite square Sierra Leone and Ukraine. Every other country he'd visited made sense and there were official files on his criminality. But these two very different nations needed closer attention. I went back to the dossier and sifted every page. Two hours later I felt I knew Dan Steele like I knew my own family. And I was glad we weren't related.

I logged onto the Internet at a computer station and searched for Sierra Leone. It didn't make for pleasant reading, almost as depressing as Steele's life story. Few places in the world had seen such brutal carnage as Sierra Leone with tens of thousands of civilians killed and mutilated in a ten-year civil war. The madness in the country reached horrifying proportions in January 1999 during a three-week siege of the capital Freetown. Then more than four thousand people were slaughtered as rebel forces took control of the city. Women were raped and children conscripted into the offensive. Eventually the largest UN peacekeeping force ever assembled was sent in to restore some degree of normality. I stopped reading and let my head drop into my hands. What was Dan Steele doing in that appalling place? Fringeing the North Atlantic Ocean, Sierra Leone was poor and debt ridden, rife with crime and violence. A white man would have stood out among the predominately black faces. And the communication barrier would have been significant; a form of pidgin English occasionally used but ethnic languages more common. He would have needed a middleman. But as I continued reading the idea of Steele visiting Sierra Leone became even more ridiculous. The population of six million had low life expectancy and an HIV rate of around seven per cent. The climate was inhospitable, tropical hot with dust storms and explosive thunderstorms in the rainy season. If Harmon Penitentiary was hell on earth, Sierra

Leone was close behind. But one fact did catch my eye. Diamonds were the main hard currency. My heart skipped a beat and I sensed I might be getting closer to the truth.

Even though my belly was rumbling and my bladder irritating I continued the search until Ukraine came up. On the crossroads between Europe and Asia and with the Black Sea at its lowest border, Ukraine was another planet compared to Sierra Leone. Around the size of Texas it had a population of forty-eight million, decent infrastructure and rich natural resources. It was blessed with a temperate climate, warm summers and not drastically cold winters. The country lagged behind Europe in growth and development after years inside the Soviet bloc but was making progress. Sex trafficking in Ukrainian women was a significant problem but that aside I doubted there'd be opportunity to muscle in on the existing underworld. So what was Dan Steele doing there? Here was another puzzle in a long line of puzzles about the man. Could his activities in Sierra Leone be linked elsewhere to his criminality? Ireland or Britain? Germany or Italy? Ukraine? Maybe these were solo operations with no connections; was he moving all the time to keep ahead of the chase? Everything was a maybe or could be or that's a possibility, speculation as wild as my imagination.

Again I caught myself short and asked the hard question. Why are you checking Dan Steele's careers? Cut and run before you find yourself totally snagged in this web of danger and deceit. Yet again I knew the answer. Frank Ryan does not cut and run.

I dined at the Khyber Tandoori, a Pakistani restaurant on South William Street. I started with oven-baked chicken pieces, then moved to lamb korma and boiled rice as a main course. I drank half a bottle of New Zealand sauvignon blanc, savouring the wine as much as I relished the food. Outside it was cold and dreary, the rain holding off after a morning of heavy showers. Ideal weather conditions for spicy food. I lingered over my lunch and even treated myself to a small brandy. As I sipped I allowed my gaze to drift. The packed restaurant had tiered floors with white-linen-covered tables. The chairs were padded and straight backed with good legroom. There was a hint of incense in the air. Conversations buzzed, glasses tinkled and plates clattered. The lunch-time crowd was mainly in groups and I didn't notice any other single diners. My paranoia and suspicion eased, the alcohol and food dulling my senses. But what was fast becoming a habit soon kicked in. I left fifty euros under a plate for payment, made my way to the toilets and squeezed out a back window. Three blocks later I bought two pay-as-you-go throwaway mobile phones. I paid in cash and with an extra thirty euro arranged for one to be couriered to Conor Mason.

11

I never wanted it this way. Life was good and I was enjoying work at Harmon. Sure, it was no easy ride but it was exciting with a sense of living on the edge. And that was something I was used to, what with my outback upbringing and frequent confrontations with nature and the elements. And I was in love. Lisa Duggan had me at the end of a line she'd spun with locks from her honey-blonde hair. When I wasn't with her I thought about her and when I was with her I couldn't stop admiring her.

'Frank Ryan,' she often scolded, 'is that lust I see in your eyes?' Frequently it was but as we came to know each other and shared days as well as nights, the desire softened. 'Frank Ryan, are you becoming all mushy with me?'

I was. With her voice: soft and feminine, giggly and bubbly. With her body: tall and slim with gentle sloping curves that hugged her jeans and filled out her blouses and T-shirts. With her temper: volatile and unpredictable but which I calmed with my arms and strength, then my lips and passion. With her mind: sharp and alert, intelligent and canny with insights that occasionally pulled me up short.

'You're a teddy bear, Frank Ryan. The Aussie macho is for public consumption. I bet you cry when you're alone.'

This is true. I struggled with tears during excavations at gravesides in the Balkans when decaying bodies of children were exhumed. I held in sobs as I gripped the heaving shoulders of peasant women wailing as their loved ones were slowly dragged from under the rotting limbs and torsos of other victims. United in death, the corpses seemed unwilling to part company. The misery, like the stench, swamped my senses. I saw caved, cracked and split-open skulls, faces mutilated by blows, bones shattered by shrapnel. I detested the thugs who'd pillaged villages, raping women and killing children. Most of the men had already been murdered or interred, leaving homes and families undefended. So my eight months in Kosovo carried me screaming and protesting into the northern hemisphere and the explosive politics of the Balkans. It toughened me up, though; there were too many bodies and too much carnage. Compassion fatigue crept in and my emotions dulled. By the time I moved to Amnesty

International I was battle hardened and grief weary. But I found it impossible to block the image of small bodies hauled from wet, clinging mud as if the earth begrudged its plunder. Even in my dreams I heard laments.

'Yes, I do cry. Not often, maybe only for special events.' That was my way of covering tracks but Lisa listened carefully; taking it all in and spinning it round in her head. She was evaluating the real Frank Ryan. As our relationship deepened the lovemaking was more gentle, slow and tender, prolonged for hours rather than rushed in hunger.

'You don't rip my clothes off the way you used to, Frank,' she teased from the passenger seat of my Saab one warm Sunday afternoon the previous September. We were driving in the Wicklow hills, Lisa showing off the green and rolling countryside and me silently comparing it to the red and parched earth of South Australia. She hiked her skirt to allow my gaze to take in her long legs and painted toenails. I pretended to ignore, all the time scanning the roads for quiet lanes. 'How about a bit of fire from those loins.' She knew how to work me. I suddenly swerved up a country trail, gripping the steering wheel to keep the car straight. 'Where are we going?' I didn't answer. I found a field with high grass and squeezed the Saab hard against a ditch to allow passing traffic. Then I lifted Lisa and carried her struggling and giggling into the middle of the field. 'Don't you dare, Frank Ryan. Put me down this minute.' The protests were half-hearted, the words more taunt than threat. 'I'm warning you, Frank. I'll scream at the top of my voice.' Her legs kicked, her skirt hiked further, my left hand caught a bare buttock. I bounced her in my arms and pressed her to me, our lips meeting in a long wet kiss.

'Go on,' I whispered as our tongues slipped free. 'Scream.' She pulled my hair hard until we both tumbled into the grass, rolling and groping, panting and aroused.

'Help,' she moaned, 'help, somebody please.' I had her skirt over her belly. 'Help.'

Later, in a coffee shop in the picturesque village of Enniskerry south of Dublin, she was still grinning at me. Grass clung to her hair; her clothes as tousled as when she'd hurriedly slipped them back on. 'That was good, Dr Ryan. Really good.' Her voice was husky, her gaze shameless. 'Did they teach you that in med school?'

Now, so many months later, I sat in that same café. Unlike my last visit when I'd made love under a warm autumn sun, today it was grey and damp with rain clouds blustering from the west. I had a window seat and gazed out at traffic and shoppers, everyone in a rush to escape the next deluge. I would never have wished it this way. I didn't want the three-day exclusives by Conor Mason that so stunned and shamed the nation the Justice Minister was forced to explain himself to a hostile parliament. HARMON HELL. WE TELL THE SHOCKING TRUTH. Mason had called it like he'd heard it. DRUGS, AIDS AND NOT ENOUGH DOCS. He spilled the truth about addiction and the abysmal health system with an 'inside special' on the psychiatric patient's sudden death. I was named as sole CMO and struggling with the workload. RIOT DEATHS OUTRAGE: MUSLIM PRISONER TARGETED. He was out on a limb on this one, staking his reputation on how the authorities decided to defend the accusation. HARMON CMO QUITS. Not that my departure would matter a damn, but it added to the sense of despair surrounding the institution. Bill O'Hara from the Justice Department no-commented his way out of queries put to him by the newspaper, as did Don Campbell, the prison governor. The government was caught off guard by the revelations and embarrassed by the litany of human and medical failures throughout the penal system. The media feasted on official discomfiture. But I could get no pleasure from their setback. Everyone was taking a hit and only Conor Mason seemed to be winning. Questioning glances followed me everywhere while I went about my prison duties. Hard looks, penetrating stares that screamed, Is this all coming from you?

*

The heavens opened, rain drilling off pavements and forcing pedestrians to shelter. I comforted my depression with another mug of sweet black coffee. I couldn't get Lisa Duggan out of my head. How is she involved in 'this', whatever 'this' is? And how the hell did Dan Steele find out about us? Think, Frank, think. Go back over everything and tease out the clues. She must have let her guard down sometime, said something out of the ordinary. Dammit man, get past her body and focus on her mind. What was she up to?

The café was almost empty, only another group of three and myself hiding out from the downpour filling gutters and creating rivers in gulleys. A middle-aged couple hurried inside, faces as angry as the skies, muttering and complaining in some strange dialect. They slipped off their rain gear and left it dripping from a coat stand, sat down and pointed at the menu. Minutes later they ordered, what I don't know. '*Kaffee bitte und zwei Stuck Kuchen.*' I tried to make sense but apart from the German word for coffee I was lost. But their conversation triggered something about Lisa. She spoke four languages: French, German, Spanish and Italian. Once over dinner I'd asked about this, wondering why she chose banking. 'You could have a high-paid overseas position in industry,' I suggested in between spoonfuls of sticky pudding. 'With respect, banking isn't that exciting.' She polished off a huge dessert of chocolate fudge cake with ice cream, ignoring my comment. That girl could have eaten for Ireland in any Olympic competition. But she was still ignoring the snipe as we took liqueurs and I worried I'd insulted her.

Jim Patterson, Lisa's colleague in the foreign-exchange division of Americabank, agreed to meet me in his offices. Again I picked a location where I couldn't be tailed, though by now I wasn't convinced of Dan Steele's warning. I'd set traps for would-be shadows, jumping on and off public transport, chasing up and down stairwells and then waiting for the rush of footsteps. So far no one appeared suspicious or out of place. Either there was no tail or they were very good.

Patterson was mid-thirties and dressed soberly in pinstriped suit, white shirt and dark tie. For twenty-four hours there'd been a run on sterling after currency speculation. The markets were frantic with high trading volumes. It wasn't a good day to side-track the broker but he obliged anyway, offering fifteen minutes max. I jumped at the opportunity. Patterson was a decent man with a good sense of humour and a long line of jokes. The dealing room buzzed with activity, the background of phones and shouts making conversation difficult.

Initially we made small talk, him quizzing me about events at Harmon. 'Did they really take out that Muslim?' This was Conor Mason's most damning accusation and it was already causing diplomatic ripples. Emal Abdul Sadiq was an English-speaking Afghan Muslim arrested at Dublin docks en route to Britain with a Land Rover packed with explosives, detonators and grenades. Literature seized from the car suggested he was an Al Qaeda operative on a mission to bomb the City, London's financial heartland. Subsequent investigations linked him with dissident IRA members who supplied the explosives and hardware. According to inside sources, they even gave the terrorist a street map of the UK capital and arranged for a guided tour of the targets before and after the blast.

In his second year in the red zone of Harmon Penitentiary the Muslim became a high-profile nuisance to the authorities. He'd refused to share a cell with non-Muslims, insisted on praying five times a day whether or not there was a search or exercise or meals being served. His plight had agitated other non-Christians and the government came under pressure to comply with the rights of a number of religions. Soon lawyers for prisoners who'd probably never seen the inside of a church issued writs seeking spiritual facilities. The problem was still going through the courts when the riot erupted and Sadiq was shot dead. Conor Mason's source believed he'd been targeted as a troublemaker and executed to put down a marker for the rest. The readers were informed Sadiq had been moved to C-wing only ten days previously, thus fuelling speculation about a contrived disturbance. The charge rocked the political powerhouse and threatened to bring down the government. And I had contributed significantly to this climate of distrust and condemnation.

'I really don't know, Jim.' I'd already told Patterson I was nowhere near the siege and didn't want to let slip my dishonesty. 'From what I heard the shooting was indiscriminate and could have gone anywhere. The landing was chaotic with smoke confusing the marksmen. If they targeted anyone successfully then they were bloody good.'

Patterson was hunched forward at his desk, jacket now hanging off the back of his chair. Out of the corner of an eye he followed the changing international financial scene, scrolling and switching screens. 'What took you to such a dump anyway?'

I sighed and pretended deep regrets. And Patterson didn't know the half of what was going on. 'Medicine is tightly structured,' I explained. 'You start as junior doctor and progress slowly through the ranks until you reach the top. By then you're too old to enjoy the success, and deep in debt. I decided on a different path. I wanted excitement, action and the chance to use my clinical skills. So I worked as a bush medic in Australia and East Africa before moving to Europe. Harmon was just another challenge.' Even as I said the words I realised how crazy the venture now seemed. Harmon was more than a challenge; it was a devious and dangerous nightmare.

'So what's up today? Lisa Duggan, I suppose?'

'Yeah. Lisa. She disappeared, leaving a ton of personal belongings at my apartment.' The lie came easy. 'Have you any idea where she is?'

'At home, I suppose. She said she had to deal with some family crisis.'

'I haven't heard from her and can't track her down.'

'Did you talk to her relations?'

'I don't know the first thing about them.'

Patterson did a double take. 'C'me on, Frank. You two were hot for each other but you can't have spent all the time in bed.'

I grinned; half embarrassed Patterson was so aware of our intimacies. Then I realised we hadn't exactly hid our desires, even being caught up against the wall in the underground car park. Sure as hell that little snippet would have spread throughout the bank pretty quickly. 'Were we that indiscreet?'

Patterson glanced around the office to make sure we wouldn't be interrupted. There was a sense of heightened tension in the air, as if sterling was about to be devalued. I couldn't help but wonder how the dealers would handle a real crisis, like a riot at Harmon Penitentiary. 'Frank, all of us wanted Lisa. She was hot. Every red-blooded male in here, and a few other places as well, spent considerable drinking time discussing the two of you. And I can tell you some of the jealous darts would have made you blush.' He flicked at the keyboard to change the on-screen data. 'How did you meet?'

I rested my chin on my knuckles. 'Believe it or not, she came on to me.'

Patterson looked surprised, then annoyed. 'Why the hell didn't she come on to me?'

I inspected the other man. He was handsome and personable, good sense of humour and pleasant smile. Looking at him from a single woman's point of view I reckoned he was an attractive option.

'I was at a medical conference in the Radisson Hotel and she was at the bar on her own. I left the lecture hall for a break and ended up beside her. She just turned and started talking to me like we were buddies.'

Lisa had been wearing an off-white cotton blouse with three buttons open offering more than a hint of cleavage. Her denims hugged her bottom. Her hair was pulled into a pony-tail showing off her face. And what a face. High forehead, high cheekbones, full lips and long dark eyelashes. There was a z-shaped scar mid-forehead from a childhood fall but otherwise her skin was clear. The whites of her eyes set off speckled blue irises.

When she smiled I thought I'd died and gone to heaven. 'You seem lost.'

I forced myself from ogling and coughed to hide my discomfort. I was caught off guard and without a line to offer. 'Well . . . ah . . . I'm . . . ah . . . oh, what the hell. I'm at some boring doctors' conference and desperate to escape.'

'Are you a doctor?'

An opener, I thought. Go for it, make an impression. 'Yeah. I'm the wild-colonial-boy type. Australian come to Ireland but not seeking his roots.'

She deliberately allowed her gaze to wander the full length of my body and I felt distinctly self-conscious. Then, brazen that she was she stood up, collected her handbag and turned to me. 'Why don't we go somewhere? Then you can tell me about yourself.' It's hard to say no to that sort of invitation.

I gave Patterson an edited version and he groaned with jealousy. 'Maybe it's the doctor bit,' he wondered out loud. 'Bankers don't make easy conversation with other bankers, we usually end up discussing government bonds or euro exchange rates.'

I couldn't resist butting in. 'I've heard that's a real turn-on for some girls.'

'If you know any, pass my name on.' He waved me quiet for a moment and called to a colleague, issuing orders on dollar trading.

I changed the subject. The office was now chaotic with dealers shouting and arguing and I felt I wouldn't get too much more of Patterson's time. 'Did she have friends here she might have confided in?'

The broker didn't have to think. 'She kept to herself. Sure, she was polite and cordial but distant. It's as if she didn't want anyone getting too close.' A quizzical eyebrow shot up, the unsaid question screaming. How did you manage it? Patterson then asked, 'Did you check her apartment?'

'Yeah. Empty and no forwarding address.' This was one of my first missions when I learned Lisa had fled Americabank. 'And her neighbours had nothing to offer.'

Patterson's face tightened, as if he was suddenly seeing a problem he didn't really want to get involved in. 'That's strange.'

I ignored the comment. 'When did she start here?'

'Maybe a week or so before you came on the scene.'

I hid my surprise. Lisa had led me to believe she'd been with Americabank for at least a year before we met. 'Was she in any other division before that?'

'Not that I know of.'

'I wonder where she worked before here, maybe she was headhunted back.'

Patterson's expression changed, as if he was trying to stifle his next comment. Then he collected himself. 'Yeah, maybe you're right. She was headhunted.'

I knew he was hiding something. 'Don't bullshit me, Jim. What's bugging you?'

'How can I put this? Eh, let me think.' He pursed his lips, rolled his eyes and eased his body away from his desk. 'OK, here's the truth and you're not to take offence.'

'Why would I take offence?'

'You and she were so close. I don't want to annoy anyone.'

'Call it.'

'Lisa didn't know banking from a hole in the ground. The gossip here suggested she was daughter of one of the directors, or girlfriend or mistress or something. She had to be here for some reason other than exchange dealing. Banker she most certainly was not. She couldn't balance a cash sheet, often couldn't remember whether it was US or Canadian dollars we were trading, wouldn't know a ledger from a shelf. OK, she was bright and intelligent and picked up what was happening. In fact, she was making a pretty good fist of things recently. But as far as I could tell she had no financial background.'

This was news; Lisa had made herself out as one of the institution's top brokers. 'Did she make mistakes, anything big that would have caused a supervisor to look closer?'

'Nah, Lisa was too clever. She used her good looks to charm the guys and they covered up for her. Our assistant manager did keep checks so she couldn't have got the run of herself and defraud millions. Lisa was a pretty face and little else.'

A much older man in a suit so loud it almost screamed entered the offices and was walking the aisles between cubicles. 'I gotta go, Frank. The boss is on patrol.'

I stood up and looked for an easy exit. I'd only taken a few paces when Patterson shouted, 'And she was never off the telephone. All overseas calls and none to financial institutions. Quite the linguist, isn't she?'

Yes, I thought, quite the linguist. Quite the mystery woman altogether. I offered a silent plea. If you love me, Lisa Duggan, please make contact. I'm dying here.

12

'So, tell me what you know about Lisa Duggan.'

Dan Steele sprawled opposite me in the prison examination room as if he owned the place. The rickety patient chair was tilted so he could lean back, toes bouncing off the floor. He had both hands behind his head, tattooed muscles bulging.

'She's the girl you were hitched up with.' His response was matter-of-fact and I sighed out loud, trying to rein in my frustration. Steele's inside information was unsettling.

'Yes, but do you know anything about her?'

A puzzled look clouded his features; real or forced I couldn't decide. 'Why are you asking me? You were shacked up with her, you should know.' He lifted his eyes to heaven, wherever heaven was through the overhead concrete, then switched subject. 'You're all over the papers, doc. Shouldn't you be giving interviews?'

The published autopsy report on the dead psychiatric prisoner suggested a drug overdose. Toxicology revealed he had high levels of antidepressants, antipsychotics, cocaine and methadone in his system, and television pundits speculated the combination had inter-reacted, causing cardiac arrest. Reporters were on the hunt for me but I'd been warned off by Bill O'Hara. To buy time I told him I wouldn't break my contract confidentiality. Now in my role as CMO to Harmon Penitentiary I found Steele sixth in line in today's clinic. I challenged him immediately but quickly sensed he was playing games and changed tactics.

'You've never visited a doctor before . . .'

He held up a hand. 'Not true. The guy who worked before you didn't behave so I called to give him friendly advice. He didn't listen and someone took the hump and blew his head off.'

'You ordered that hit.'

Steele tut-tutted like a man with a proud reputation to protect. 'That's gossip, doc. You shouldn't listen to what people ramble about in here; most of them are no-hopers who'd tell you anything you want to hear. They say I ordered a hit, who cares? The guy was screwing all the pretty girls in the women's wing and thinking life couldn't get better. He was bringing in lingerie, leathers and poppers. He walked himself to the grave. You don't fuck prisoners unless you give something back. He didn't keep his side of the bargain and got scared. He had to go. There was a long queue to whack him. Why blame me?'

'Because you were looking for drugs.'

'I deal drugs, I don't use them. Drugs are for misfits, down-and-outs and the rich but stupid. First rule in this game, don't use your own products.'

'So now I'm getting a lecture on best business practice?'

'Pay attention. I'm no angel but I've been around enough to have learned a thing or two.'

'Like what?'

'Like you're too trusting. Like you can't see when someone has you by the balls and squeezing. Like you think working here is just another job. Like you get used by everyone around you and don't know.'

I almost reacted but held back. And I wanted him to keep talking.

'The Justice Department has you going round in circles, Bill O'Hara keeps a tail on you twenty-four hours a day. Wise up, doc. If you don't get your act together you'll be on the next flight out of Dublin, broke and broken.'

There wasn't one word that wasn't true. I was being used. My bank balance, never healthy at the best of times, was closing in on red. And I was nearing the end of my tether, my patience running out. It was difficult to get a straight answer out of anyone. And even straight answers led to even harder questions.

'I'm not being followed. I've checked and there's no—'

'Or a very good tail,' he cut through. 'These guys aren't going to hunt you round streets or shops, jump on and off trams while you wear yourself out chasing shadows. They don't need to do that, they know exactly where you go. They have contacts everywhere. All they're interested in is what you're up to and will you make trouble.'

They, they, they. Again the 'they' was being thrown at me and my mind flashed to the London prison and my nurse Helen trying to evade probing questions. 'They' wouldn't allow this, 'they' said do that, 'they' were calling the shots. Bill O'Hara had claimed 'they' were the Justice Department but I was now having serious doubts. Dan Steele's inside knowledge was unsettling.

'Who are "they"?'

Steele glanced around as if there was someone behind. A babble of voices came from the corridor outside and I recognised my warder guard shouting at someone. I gestured to Steele to hurry on. 'There's more than one,' he said, 'and my contact thinks it's a group of four. Who they are and where they've come from I don't know yet but I'm working on it. I'm pretty sure your boss is in on it.'

Now I was back with the Justice Department.

But could I believe Steele? He might just as easily be spinning me a line to keep me interested. He needed me for some reason.

'In on what? What the hell's going on?'

'That you will know when I'm sure you're cooperating.'

'So you want to use me. Is that it?'

'Of course. Try thinking like a prisoner,' he said. The racket along the line of patients waiting for my services had settled and the whiskey growl softened. 'What do we do all day but dream of being on the outside? OK, some guys are so far soaked in heroin they can't think beyond their next fix, but for the rest of us this place is hell. We want to walk the streets, breathe clean air and not the stench that fills the landings. We want good food, drink and regular sex. Simple things, nothing too complicated. I don't pass the day wondering could I live in a big house and drive fancy cars, no, I do not. That's for the losers. I'd sleep in a tenement as long as I could hike the Dublin mountains. There's not as much as a blade of grass in here.'

I sidetracked the conversation to give myself time to think. 'How many people have you killed?'

Steele let the chair slip forward, steadying himself with both hands on the desk between us. His eyes were hard but not threatening, as if he'd been brought to reality by the question.

'Enough.'

'How many is enough? One, two, twenty, one hundred? More than one hundred?'

'As many as crossed me. Nobody got hurt unless they crossed me. Remember that, doc.'

It was my turn to get tough. 'Is that a threat?'

'Only if you think it should be.'

We stared at one another, as in who's going to blink first. 'You still haven't answered. How many have you killed?'

He didn't have to think. 'Thirteen by my own hands. More if you count contracts. The first was a kid about nineteen that tried cheating on a deal on smuggled cigarettes. The second was a woman in her fifties who snitched on me.'

'What'd you do?'

'Slit her throat and left her sitting up in the front room watching television.'

I was unfazed; this report was detailed in his file. 'I suppose you thought that made you a hard man?'

'I didn't. I was actually sorry for her and her family. But they had to be taught a lesson.'

I knew Steele was holding back on previous activities; the dossier suggested he'd murdered at least eight other criminal contacts throughout Europe. His law of the jungle was hard to stomach so I dropped that side of the inquisition to dig elsewhere. 'What were you doing in Sierra Leone?'

Now it was my turn to catch him with a left

hook of surprise and he visibly flinched. 'I haven't a clue what you're talking about.' The voice was as granite as the stare.

'And the Ukraine?' I pressed. 'How many languages do you speak that you can cross so many frontiers?'

'Don't go there, doc. I can help you if you help me but not if you probe too deep.'

Sore spot, I decided. I'd come back to that later. 'What can we do for each other?'

'Quit rushing. Right now you're the one with his arse on fire and full of questions.'

'And you know the answers?'

'More than you think. I make it my business to know what's going on. I could tell you where the governor goes on holiday. If I wanted I could have him strangled in his Paris apartment.'

'I'm not impressed.'

'And I know you're spilling your guts to Conor Mason.'

Now I was impressed but tried not show it. 'How do you know?'

'Who else saw that riot up close? Who else has a grudge against the government? You're the chief suspect, doc.'

'There were a lot of people on that landing, any one of them could've gone to the press.'

'But only one did,' Steele came back. 'And I can tell you the Justice Department is planning to silence you. You've created a lot of ripples. These reports about deliberate targeting are causing panic. And when panic creeps in anything can happen.'

'Do you think they deliberately shot the Muslim?' I asked. Steele was in the thick of the action and must know what happened.

'Yes.'

'And were the other victims heroin addicts?'

'No. They were mad and bad but didn't shoot up. My guess is the governor decided to clear a little space along the wings. *And* take out a few troublemakers.'

'Is this you bullshitting or for real?'

'For real. Why bullshit? What's in it for me?'

I couldn't spot any immediate advantage for Steele; other than that it portrayed him as being vulnerable. The governor could start another riot if he decided. 'How do you know this?'

'I have contacts.'

'Where?'

He tapped the side of his nose. 'Ask me no questions . . .'

'C'me on, Steele, if you're so fucking smart prove it.'

He was smiling again. By now I had a feel for a real or forced smile by the shape of the scar on his face. It went V-shaped when he was relaxed, stayed straight when uptight. 'I don't have to prove nothing. You're the one with problems. I'm tight in jail and no one can reach me.'

'That's not what I hear.' I was chancing my arm but felt I had to call his ruse.

'What you hear is shit. What you hear comes from Conor Mason and he also has you on a lead. Mason's bankrolled by a northside gang. He says nothing about them and they pay his laundry bills.'

My eyebrows shot up. 'Laundry bills?'

'Cash,' he explained wearily. 'Small-denomination notes neatly packed into brown-paper bags, like a politician's handout. He also writes about every criminal outfit around the country they give the dirt on. One of these days it'll be his last word. My friends on the street tell me they think he should go. If I say so he goes.'

My heart sank. If Steele wasn't lying then Conor Mason, my confidant, was as big a crook as the thugs he reported. Maybe, I thought in a flash of insight, that's why he hasn't been killed or injured. Maybe the threats and attacks were set up so he could keep the front of investigative journalist and get hold of a legal handgun. Maybe Mason was using me more than I knew. Maybe Steele was right, I am naive and trusting. My stomach churned with these thoughts.

'Why are you involved?' I asked. 'What can Mason do to hurt you?'

He tapped the side of his nose again and I

decided he was bluff boasting, making himself as strong inside the walls as outside.

'So what's the deal?'

'As soon as I tell you you're in, understand that.'

I said nothing, rolling his words around my head and remembering how many the monster had killed. His claim that victims were only taken out because they double-crossed him cut no ice. I knew he would slit my throat quick as look at me. But I also sensed he had me in his sights as a potential, if reluctant, partner. 'Before I hear your side,' I said, 'what's in it for me?'

'Information.'

'Is that all? No money, no secret bank accounts in Switzerland?'

The scar V-shaped. 'Wise up, doc. You're not interested in money.'

'What makes you think that?'

'Because you work here.'

He had a point and I acknowledged so with a shrug. 'Maybe.'

'Maybe, my arse.' Now Steele was eager and leaned forward on the desk. As I watched the snake tattoo bobble with his Adam's apple, I wondered how much time we had left. Most convicts were in and out of the examination room within five minutes. We were now fifteen minutes into our exchanges. 'Let's set the ground rules. You want to know who kicked the shit out of you. You want to know about

Noel Dempsey. You want to know what the hell's going on. And you want to know where Lisa Duggan is.' He paused to wipe spittle flecking on his lips. 'How'm I going so far?'

Steele had more or less summed up all my desperate queries. But I couldn't let him know that. 'I'm leaving Ireland in a few weeks,' I said. 'Next month I plan to surf, swim and wash the filth of this country from my body and mind. Sure, I'd like the answers to a few questions before I go but I'm not going to get killed in the effort.'

The V-scar went taut. 'You're lying, doc. And lying isn't going to solve our problems. If I answer one question you're in and can't go back.' He fixed on me. 'Choose your words carefully.'

By now I was acutely aware this appointment was running over and the warders would be wondering what was going on. I signalled Steele to the examination couch and he sat at the edge, feet dangling inches from the floor. I slipped a blood-pressure cuff around his left arm and went through the motions of a physical. Almost on cue there was a tap on the door and a head peered in. I waved that everything was OK and the door closed again. I could hear my own heart beating with an adrenalin rush but Steele seemed unruffled. He stared ahead like any good patient while I ran my fingers along his neck glands. This close I could see how pale his skin was from lack of natural light. His bushy eyebrows were greying like his hair and his chewed nails almost brown from cigarettes. Goose bumps blotched his forearms in the chill of the room. With repairs still ongoing in two landings the heating was kept off for long periods each day. The cells were like ice vaults.

'What's going on in J-wing?' I asked.

The pierce of his look zapped my body like an electric shock.

'It has a single inmate,' he said.

The way Steele said it I knew he wasn't referring to the average criminal. And he'd used the word 'inmate' instead of 'prisoner', suggesting whoever it was might not be incarcerated against his will. But was that enough to ask another question and drag me into this killer's murky and explosively dangerous underworld? Despite all that had happened so far I was still alive. Going with Steele's plans might not guarantee my life at the end. Now he grinned as he watched me weigh these conflicting emotions. Should I run for safety or jump into the unknown?

'What do you mean by inmate?'

The grin disappeared. 'You're in?'

There was really no contest. 'I'm in.'

The scar went V-shaped. 'This place is more than a prison, it's a marketplace,' he said. 'You can buy almost anything if you've got the readies or something to trade. You want a drink I can get you drink. I can get you any drug you so want, even prescription powders, inside twenty-four hours. You want a lawyer we've got three doing time. And there's two doctors on fraud charges. Nothing happens along the landings that doesn't filter through. And if I need extra I go outside. I have family who do favours, keep business going and sort problems. They watch out, put feelers on who's doing what and where. Harmon is a cesspool of gossip and rumours and dirty deals.'

'So what's hot this week?'

'J-wing. To make way for one unknown, forty-four prisoners were moved. Official version: upgrading sanitation. But if you look around you won't see any plumbers.'

'Who is he?'

'Find that out and you're close to the truth behind your troubles.'

'Do you know?'

'Yes.'

'Why make life hard for me? Let me in on the secret.'

'That's not part of the deal. You'll have to do your own groundwork.'

I sighed. More trickery. 'What's my side of this package?'

'Get me out of here.'

'How?'

'Get me an X-ray. You don't have to risk anything.

Set up an appointment for a hospital X-ray and I'll take care of the rest.'

'Will anyone get hurt?'

'Not if they stay out of the action.'

'How can I believe you?'

'You can't. That's what's so sweet about this. You can't trust me and I don't trust you. I can help you but not unless I'm sure you're gonna help me.'

'Just an X-ray?'

'That's it, doc. An X-ray.'

'Why X-ray? Why not a blood test or a cardiograph or an allergy test?'

'Because the City takes Harmon prisoners for X-ray. And I have contacts in the City who make things happen.'

The City Hospital on Dublin's Northside was the closest facility to the prison. For over one hundred years the institution provided health services for inmates. Any request passed by the medical and prison authorities would guarantee a half-day there for Steele. He'd be under armed guard with a covert team back-up in case of an escape bid. But Steele would have factored this into his plan, whatever the plan was. All he needed was an ally, a medical ally, to falsify documents to force through an X-ray request. I was in on the deal already and there was no turning back. It was time for answers to a lot of questions.

'Why didn't they kill me that night?' The issue

that still tormented me burst through. 'I was on the ground and they had a shotgun in my face. Why didn't they pull the trigger?'

'They had to find out if you were involved.'

Involved? What was he talking about? 'Involved in what? What the hell's going on?' I couldn't keep the exasperation out of my voice.

Steele stood up. His large frame almost towered over me, and I'm no midget. He looked down, scanning my face, and there was nearly a sense of pity in his eyes. 'Doc, you're a nice guy. Too nice, if you want my opinion, and too nice to be working here. Harmon isn't just for criminals; it holds madmen, religious fanatics and political lunatics. You talked yourself into a job amongst the most dangerous and twisted convicts anywhere. What's going on is bigger than drugs or murder or money laundering or robbery. In fact, it's best you don't know everything. Take one piece of advice from someone who's been down every dirty ditch and track. Don't ask too many questions. One day you'll find the truth but hopefully you'll be far away by then.'

This was bullshit and I knew it. And I told him so. He glanced towards the door, a signal we should cut our losses and regroup another time. 'What I hear you'll hear. What I know you'll know. But not until I'm sure you're in with me.' He moved to leave.

'What do I do?' I asked.

'Room 129, Jury's Hotel in Ballsbridge. Tomorrow night at ten exactly. Be there.'

'Why?'

'You'll meet two friends who'll tell you what's happening.'

I committed details to memory. Steele's eyes darted nervously towards the door. 'Now what do I do?'

'Keep complaining about headaches,' I said. 'Say they hurt worse when you cough or sneeze. Say you're getting double vision. Say this only to your mates; eventually it'll get to the warders on your landing. Ask to see me in four days. That morning get sick, and I mean vomit.'

He grinned and he had a grip on the door handle.

'One thing,' I shot at him. 'Who is Noel Dempsey?'

He turned the knob. 'He's the most dangerous of all.'

I had just gunned the engine alive in my Saab when a tap on the window jolted me. Bill O'Hara was scowling in. 'What's wrong with Dan Steele? That's his second visit inside a week.'

By rights, I should have told O'Hara to back off, that Steele's medical problems were confidential. However, I knew he'd already have scanned my patient notes. And I wanted to draw him into the plan. I put on my puzzled doctor's face. 'Not quite sure, Bill. He's getting troublesome headaches that keep him awake at night. I checked him thoroughly and couldn't convince myself there was anything sinister. I may have to get an X-ray if the headaches persist.' With that I explained the overlong consultation and put O'Hara on notice about a possible hospital visit.

He scrutinised me as though I had two heads, suspicion oozing from his stare. 'Watch him,' he warned. 'He put the contract on your previous colleague and you know what happened.'

I grimaced as if the memory shook me. 'I'm getting out of here in a few weeks, Bill. And I plan to leave with all my limbs working and brain functioning. Steele won't get one over me. Equally, I'm not having his henchmen follow me round the world just because I missed some important diagnosis and the bastard died. I'll do what I have to from a medical perspective and nothing more.'

O'Hara's glower stayed fixed for another five seconds and then he turned away.

'Bill,' I shouted after him, 'how's my friend Noel Dempsey? Does his nose still hurt?'

O'Hara's faced twisted in undisguised fury. In the bitter cold his cheeks were purple, the veins like tiny threads under the skin. A sudden squall blew dust in the air and he twisted to protect himself. In that instant I pressed the accelerator and scorched towards the afternoon traffic. And I wondered what O'Hara was doing at the jail, his office miles away in the downtown area. Dan Steele's words echoed in my head. 'Bill O'Hara keeps a tail on you twenty-four hours a day.'

Maybe the monster was right.

13

I stood outside room 129, Jury's Hotel, and wondered for the hundredth time if I had taken leave of my senses. By Dan Steele's ruthless blood-brother rules I was now his ally, a partner in crime. And his dossier told tales of how he shot, bludgeoned, stabbed and burned to death many previous contacts. In my mind I sensed I'd made a pact with the devil and was hurtling towards the gates of hell. But there was still time to get out, still time to run and hide and put Harmon Penitentiary and Dan Steele and Lisa Duggan and Noel Dempsey out of my mind.

Australia's a big country. I could go underground in some small outback town and lead a normal existence as family doctor with a special interest in liver disease. I would find a local girl, uncomplicated and loving and who would bear me children. I would watch my kids grow and fill out, like my parents had done with their offspring. I would teach them how to ride trail bikes, how to handle dangerous snakes and shoot only if threatened. I would explain weather patterns, bird flight formations and hailstorm warnings. I would enjoy deep blue skies and warm, orange sunsets. I would swim in surf, delighting in the sting of salt water against my skin, and roll with the waves.

I could do all that and more if I walked away from room 129. I would live, whereas if I stepped inside I was putting my life at risk. Run, Frank, run, I heard my wise brain scream. Run like you've never run before. Stay, Frank, stay, I heard Lisa plead. I couldn't get that woman out of my system and I knew there would be no peace until I found the truth behind her disappearance. Dammit, I was still in love with her; dammit, I couldn't get her out of my dreams, out of my confused thinking. Where are you, Lisa?

My knuckles almost rat-a-tatted the wood but stopped inches away. My hands were shaking, my heart racing, and I felt my forehead moisten. The deserted corridor wasn't overly warm, the heating adequate rather than oppressive. Why am I such a mess? I knew the answer. I'd always be a mess until I saw this through.

Knock, knock.

There were two men in the room. One was a

stocky and swarthy individual with suspicious and cruel-looking brown eyes. I pitched him at forty plus, maybe forty-three. He sat in an armchair by the window, the drapes pulled closed. He was in casual trousers and roll-neck sweater. He'd made a tumbler into an ashtray and it was half full of crushed butts. The smell of French cigarettes poisoned the air.

'Dr Ryan, good to meet you.' Leaning against a chest of drawers pushed into a corner, the second man smiled at me. As false and distrustful a smile as ever I'd seen. And recently I'd seen a lot. 'My name is Roger Nixon. Dan Steele says we should talk.'

Roger Nixon was not his real name, of that I was sure. But I was expecting lies and deceit and this guess didn't bother me. Nixon's smooth features suggested a young man, maybe in his late thirties. He was about five eight, slim build and wearing neatly pressed dark trousers, open-neck shirt under a cream tight-knit sweater. He had the air of a killer, his voice oily and insincere and out of town. Compared to most crooks I'd met, the accent wasn't loutish or inner city, more English with a hint of Manchester. He motioned to the man in the armchair.

'This is Ratko.' Ratko's brown eyes darted nervously at this and I concluded his name really was Ratko. Either that or he was a very good actor.

Anything was possible; I was mixing with underworld figures where the rules of engagement were decided on the spur of the moment.

'Ratko doesn't speak English,' Nixon explained as he watched me take stock. I was standing at the door, one hand behind my back gripping the handle for quick escape. 'But he knows everything about you and is pleased to meet you even if his scowl doesn't suggest that.'

Nixon's smile was patronising and falsely comforting. It provoked an overwhelming desire in me to plant my fist onto his narrow chin.

'Why don't you relax? It's not easy to do business with someone who looks as if he's about to take off. You're among friends here.'

I'd met a lot of different and difficult people in the past few weeks but none had me as worried as my new friends. For a start Ratko had a handgun resting on his lap, the butt within easy grab of his left hand. Nixon's sweater, which I now noticed carried a golf logo, bulged on his right side over what I presumed was a shoulder-holstered revolver. I checked the room. It was basic hotel standard: double bed, lockers, freestanding lights, two chests of drawers, nondescript wallpaper and a few rural watercolours to hide the bare look. Another door led to an ensuite bathroom. We were on the first floor and it was quiet even though the downstairs lobby bustled with activity. I let go the handle and sat on the edge of the bed, my gaze flitting from one to the other.

Nixon's false smile deepened. 'Lighten up, you're too nervous. All that's going to happen is a polite conversation, we discuss your involvement and set out basic requirements.'

'What's with the guns, then?'

Ratko jerked his head upwards. '*Sta je rekao?*' ['What did he say?']

I didn't understand one word and followed Nixon. ['He's worried about the guns.']

My eyes switched to Ratko. He lifted his handgun by the barrel and laid it on the ground. '*U redu je, vidis. Ne mogu to dobaviti.*' ['It's OK, see? I cannot reach it.']

Again I didn't understand a word but got the gist of the message. And I was trying to place the language. I felt sure I'd heard the dialect before, but where?

'Ignore the guns, Dr Ryan,' said Nixon. 'In this business you need to prepare for every situation. For all we know you might have arrived with police.'

I knew that was a lie; for sure I'd been followed as soon as I was spotted. For sure there were others guarding the floor and watching the lobby for just such a double-cross. That's what I would have done and I'm no fool. Ratko and Nixon didn't look like fools either.

'Well, I didn't,' I said, putting as much indignation into my voice as my dry mouth would allow. 'I'm here to find out what you're planning and if I'm going to help.'

Ratko was leaning forward, straining to understand. Nixon explained and Ratko suddenly turned to me, eyes like red-hot coals. '*Naravno da ces pomoci.*' ['Of course you are going to help.'] The snarl was sudden and startled me.

Nixon palmed Ratko to calm down. There was considerable muttering and rolling of eyes. Then he turned to me. The smile had gone. 'Ratko cannot understand why you say *if* you're going to help. We understood you had agreed.'

I shook my head. 'There was no agreement. My part of the deal is to get Dan Steele out of Harmon Penitentiary to have an X-ray. What happens after he leaves the gates of the prison is not my concern and I don't want to know about it.' This was translated.

'And what do you expect in return?'

'Information. That's all I want. I don't want money or drugs or anything like that. I just want to know what's going on.'

Nixon's eyebrows shot up in surprise. 'Information?' Before I could respond he offered this to Ratko and Ratko laughed.

'*Budala.*' ['The fool.']

Nixon looked at me, his eyes searching my face

for treachery or lunacy, I couldn't decide which. Finally he spoke. 'Information can be dangerous, Dr Ryan. When you know too much you can become part of the problem you're trying to solve. Remember that.'

By now I seriously wanted to kick Nixon in the balls. Then I wanted to wrap Ratko's thick neck in the drape cords and throttle him until he went blue. But neither action was an option so I offered a surprised face. 'Since I don't know what I'm dealing with, your concerns are of no interest. All I know is what has happened. Events and circumstances involved me yet left me confused and ignorant. I don't think a few simple explanations will bring the house down. Once I grasp the agenda I'm leaving this accursed country, never to return again.'

'Indeed.' Nixon's smile was back, more unnerving than before. 'That would be wise. Europe is a dangerous place, full of madmen and terrorists and criminals. Australia is so much safer.'

I didn't quite like the way he said that; there seemed a hidden threat. I shrugged, hoping he'd go on. Just as in my conversations with Dan Steele I was working on the basis that this sort liked to talk. From my months in Harmon I knew most felons rambled and boasted. Given the chance many would hang themselves with the dirt they revealed in conversation.

Nixon folded his arms across his chest and spoke to Ratko, the words rapid and emphatic. Ratko gesticulated and babbled in response. Occasionally the suspicious brown eyes darted towards me. What is that language? My thoughts were interrupted.

'Have you a date arranged?'

'No. I have to plan this carefully or the authorities will get suspicious and block the move. Steele has to act sick for a week, maybe more. Then I examine him, probably with a nurse sitting in to make my conclusions sound real. She'll be interrogated, I'm sure of that, so it's better to have her believing. Then I telephone the hospital and explain my worries and ask for an X-ray. I also have to fill out an assessment form for the radiologist with a copy to the prison governor.'

Nixon interrupted. 'What if they deny the request?'

'They won't,' I came back strongly. I wanted to show these bastards what I was made of; right now they had me firmly under their control. 'That's my side of the deal, to swing this. If Steele does what he's told and I fake the medical notes they can't refuse a basic investigation.' Out of the corner of my eye I could see Ratko sitting forward on his seat, face twisted in uncertainty.

'Then what happens?'

'On the day, Steele will be taken in an armour-plated van to hospital. He will sit in the back, handcuffed and wearing ankle restraints. There will probably be a chain around his waist padlocked to the framework. I would imagine four armed warders will accompany him, and that's not counting the two in the front cabin. When he gets to the X-ray unit this retinue will tag along. I think there will be armed undercover police already there and prepared for any escape bid. How you spring him from that crowd beats me. But then, that's your problem, not mine.' I was actually smiling now and I could see this annoyed the hell out of Nixon. He gave me a dirty look and then spent a laboured few minutes translating.

'It is a problem, but not insurmountable.'

'Good,' I said. Bad, I thought. 'Now, I want something in return.'

Nixon's eyebrows arched.

'For every step I take Dan Steele towards freedom I want something back.'

Nixon shrugged. 'OK.'

This was the most difficult part of the strategy and I had spent hours mulling it over. What question was the most important? What information was vital and would unravel the mystery? What should be held back, even deduced by rational thought? My heart wanted to know about Lisa, my body cried out for her. My head warned she was not priority. Dan Steele said the identity of the inmate in J-wing would lead me closer to the truth. He also said Noel Dempsey was the most dangerous of them all. There were so many questions and instinctively I knew answers would be drip-fed to keep me on a leash. There was little chance this duo would explain everything, wrapped up nicely in an easy-to-understand package. No, they would keep me interested and on side. But once Steele was free, God knows what plans they had for me. Tonight I believed I'd only get the answer to one, maybe two queries. And tonight I didn't think either would crack the code. I decided on a cautious approach.

'Who is Noel Dempsey?'

'Noel Dempsey,' Nixon repeated, brows furrowed in deep thought.

'Dempsey,' snarled Ratko as he lit up another cigarette. One puff later and a cloud of smoke wafted over my head.

There was a nervous silence, Nixon and Ratko exchanging glances. Then Ratko shrugged and muttered something, Nixon made a so-so face. Ratko took a deep drag of his cigarette, exhaled into the air and continued his rant. Nixon listened intently. I listened intently but was completely lost. I gave up trying to place the language. It would come, probably too late to be helpful. I checked the time. It was closing in on ten thirty and there was sweat under my watchband. Still I felt calm, almost relaxed as I let the two argue. My question must have caused some disquiet for the exchanges became heated. For a brief second the image of Noel Dempsey flashed in my head. Tall, lean and hungry looking with pinched face. Thinning mousy hair and prominent beaked nose. Or had until I head-butted him right on target.

'We don't know anything about this man.' Nixon was waving a haze of smoke away.

'That's a lie,' I challenged. 'You know everything about Dempsey. You've just spent the past few minutes arguing about him.'

A slight smile flickered and then disappeared on Nixon's lips. 'Let me put it another way. This is not the time to tell you about Dempsey. When we are confident of your commitment, then you will learn about him.'

I had the next question ready, half expecting fudging from Nixon. I put on my vague but mildly interested voice. 'Where is Ratko from? I'm trying to place his dialect.'

'*Sta je rekao?*' ['What did he say?'] said Ratko.

Nixon translated and Ratko's eyes lit up. '*Nemoj mu nista reci. Reci mu da odjebe i da gleda svoja posla.*' ['Tell him to fuck off and mind his own business.'] He glared at me throughout this diatribe and I sensed another negative reply.

'Ratko is not on your wish list, Dr Ryan,' said Nixon, choosing his words carefully.

'Who he is and where he comes from is not your business.'

Ratko now became an integral part of the secrecy in my eyes and I needed another combatant like a hole in the head. The conspiracy was widening to include non-nationals. Maybe he's Ukrainian, I thought in a burst of inspiration. Maybe Ratko is Dan Steele's international criminal companion. More twists to my corkscrew nightmare. I switched subject, very aware of Ratko's hostile stares.

'Where is Lisa Duggan?' Now my heart was in my mouth. If these thugs knew Lisa then she had to be involved somehow in this whole mess. Ratko looked at Nixon and Nixon shrugged. They launched into another discussion and I heard the surname Duggan at least three times. There was less arguing this time, though.

'This was your girlfriend?' Nixon looked straight at me.

'Yes. But she's disappeared and I'm trying to find out where she's gone.'

'She works for the United Nations.'

United Nations? 'Did you say United Nations?' My chin dropped, my mind went into the hourglass again. My Lisa? The international financier who couldn't balance a cash sheet? 'What the hell is she doing in the United Nations?'

'*Sta je rekao?*' ['What did he say?'] Ratko cut through and Nixon translated.

'*Nemoj mu nista vise reci. To je dovoljno.*' ['Tell him no more. That is enough.']

'It is, eh . . .' Nixon was struggling to get the right word, '*wiser* that you hear no more from us. Tonight we have met and now you know us and we know you. More will follow when we can trust you. Dan Steele is too long in that stinking prison.'

'What the hell are you talking about?' I made to stand, my anger obvious. 'You've told me nothing. If you want help you'd better put a lot more on the line.' I slapped a fist into an open palm. 'Or Steele can rot to his death in jail.'

Out of the corner of my eye I spotted that Ratko had his revolver in his left hand, the barrel pointing straight at me. Nixon hadn't budged but had tensed, as if preparing for a fight.

'You're a novice in this game, Ryan. Steele said as much and now I understand what he meant. This is not hide-and-seek, it is much more dangerous.' The voice was level and unemotional. But I sensed a veiled warning. 'We have to plan how to take Steele from his minders. That gives you time to prepare your departure and get a grip on life. Be patient, it will save you a lot of trouble.'

Nixon motioned to his sidekick and Ratko ground his cigarette into the tumbler. He slipped the handgun under his belt and dragged his sweater over the butt. Minutes later I was on my own, staring along an eerily quiet and dimly lit corridor.

Having a flat tyre didn't improve my stressed-out spirits. I cursed and swore as I struggled in the gloom of the hotel car park to jack the Saab, find the change tools and switch tyres. Forty minutes later I was driving through damp and dark streets, the traffic mercifully light. I checked in the rear-vision mirror if I was being followed. Then again, Dan Steele warned I wouldn't be chased in any ordinary way. If the Justice Department wanted to keep an eye on me it could use any number of tails. Police, undercover agents, paid informers, doormen, receptionists, taxi-drivers, the list was endless. I forced myself to relax, speaking to my seething brain as if it were sitting beside me in the passenger seat. Who is Ratko? Where does he come from? How does he fit in with everything else? Why is it so important to shield his identity? What the hell does Lisa Duggan have to do with the United Nations? Or is this a lie to keep me in line? Maybe they know nothing about her but offered the scrap to keep me quiet. Questions, questions with run-around answers. What an appalling life. No one should have to suffer like this. I swung off Merrion Road onto Shrewsbury and cut through side streets until I was at my apartment complex in Donnybrook. I fixed the brake, switched off the engine and sighed. Another bloody awful day. It was only when I looked up that I noticed lights burning in my rooms.

I took the stairs two at a time, cursing and swearing and squeezing my fists into tight balls. I'd had enough; no one was going to fuck with me tonight. I fumbled with the door locks, screaming at the wood while I waited for the time lock to give. Three minutes later I was rushing through the hallway, shouting threats and roaring warnings. My heart was pounding, sweat streaming down my face and neck. I snatched a long-bladed knife from a kitchen drawer and held it high in my right hand. I kicked open the door into the living room and jumped inside, waving the blade in an arc. There was no one. Back into the lobby I swished wildly, hoping to catch flesh. I hit only air.

Finally I stopped outside my bedroom, panting and drenched in sweat. No light came from underneath the door. I willed my pounding heart silent, and strained to hear. Nothing. I slowly turned the handle and then kicked the door open and the hallway light flooded in. I could see the corner of my bed, the wardrobe and a single chair. I smelt cigarettes, French cigarettes, like from Ratko's collection. I darted fingers round the corner and hit the switch, then rolled in a ball along the floor until I reached the far wall. I was on my feet and screaming and flailing the knife, my wild eyes searching for the enemy. There was none.

The room was empty; only smoke wisps from a ground-out butt that had scorched the wooden surface of my bedside locker. And beside the butt was a padded bag. I darted through every room again, this time less frightened, less scared. When I finally took up the padded bag it felt light but with something inside. I ran my fingers along the surface and then the inner bulk; all the time checking over my shoulder no one was coming at me. Perspiration dripped from my forehead and my hands shook as I teased out the contents.

I stared numbly at the photograph envelope from a commercial laboratory. Then I read the company name, Adelaide Fastprint Labs, and knew immediately it was from South Australia. With wet and trembling fingers I sifted the prints. The first photo was of a town street I recognised. It had traditional stone shop fronts with tin roofs and slate verandas. The stores were bathed in bright sunshine and any shadows were straight and deep. They were side by side: Delange Real Estate, Cowper Bakery (fly screen open and one customer going in), McKenna Hardware (GIANT CLEAROUT SALE sign in front window). This was the main avenue in Balgawroo, the small settlement my folks moved to when they quit the outback.

My fingers struggled to drag out the rest of the prints, some spilling onto the floor. I snatched at them. I almost vomited when I turned up one shot showing my father resting in a wicker chair on the front lawn of our new house. In a separate clip my mother was talking to him, one hand on a hip, another dragging at her hair, a familiar stance. Then came one of Sue, my brain-damaged sister who used a cane to walk. I knew the photo was recent as Sue was leaning on an Irish blackthorn stick I'd sent her for Christmas, three months previously.

By now my belly griped and my legs felt so unsteady I had to sit on the edge of the bed. The final glossy snap chilled me to the bone and I almost cried out in distress. Ratko was posing beside a road sign to Balgawroo, right hand resting on the pole. A sniper's rifle was slung over a shoulder and he was smoking a cigarette. He was smiling at the camera and it was the triumphant smile of a killer.

I slumped onto my knees, mind reeling, and breathing laboured. I felt dizzy and nauseous and groped my way to the bathroom. My guts were heaving as I knelt in front of the toilet bowl, holding my belly. Dan Steele had me trapped. Dan Steele could do what he liked with me. I felt my bladder empty and warm urine flooded my legs and trousers. I didn't care. My stomach finally gave up and I vomited, gasped, spat and vomited again. The room went dark and I saw shooting stars. I dry retched for maybe five minutes. Then I slumped beside the bowl and started to sob.

14

'I want two guns, a Glock 19 handgun and an M-76 sniper rifle. I know you can get them so don't give me that surprised look.' I was in an underground car park north of Dublin and sitting in Conor Mason's ten-year-old Volkswagen. Like its owner, the car was scruffy and untidy, as if it hadn't been washed in years. Chocolate wrappers littered the dash and side wells, beer cans lay on the back seat. The upholstery smelt like a brewery and so did Mason. Somewhere above us, hidden by three levels of concrete, a weak spring sun was struggling for attention through a bank of grey clouds. The day was blustery but mild, the recent biting winds were now over Scandinavia and replaced by warmer southerly breezes. To me it made little difference whether it was snowing or scorching; I was distraught and consumed with revenge. They'd crossed the world to seek out my family and showed they would kill if I did not cooperate. Well, fuck them, now it was my turn to start punching.

'Are you rambling?' Mason's cheeks were flushed and his eyes bloodshot as though he was nursing a massive hangover. 'How would I know anything about that sort of hardware?'

'From your minders, the gang who look after your financial affairs and pass on information on the lowlifes of this miserable little state.'

'And who gave you that bullshit?' The rebuttal seemed half-hearted.

'Dan Steele.' This was as good as an upper-cut and Mason's head jerked on his big shoulders. 'He offered a lot more, like how much you're being paid, the names of the main players and where you hide the money.' None of this was true but by Mason's strangled expression I knew I was getting to him. 'And Steele plans to kill you,' I threw in for good measure and watched the blood drain from the journalist's face. Even the whites of his eyes cleared. 'But I've warned him off. He wants my cooperation on a deal and I've agreed. Part of the arrangement is he stays away from us.'

Mason gulped. 'What's the deal?'

'I'm springing him from jail and then we both quit the country. You stay alive and write an international exclusive.'

'Don't do this, Frank. That bastard will chew you up and spit you out. He's the most dangerous criminal in that bloody prison. Mean, bad and cunning. Whatever you've agreed, back off before it's too late. Go to Australia and hide out. Go to the North Pole if you have to but stay away from Dan Steele.' Spittle flecked Mason's lips and the smell of last night's beer filled the car. But his warnings fell on deaf ears; I was past the point of taking advice and being spun like a top at everyone's whim. I told him that, and told him about discovering the photos and of Ratko's killer smile. That shook him even more and he shifted in his seat and stared at the windscreen. 'Jesus,' was all he muttered. 'This is much bigger than I thought.'

'They let down a tyre to delay me and somehow got into the apartment. How the Justice Department didn't see them beats me. I was sure they watched my rooms day and night.'

'Jesus,' Mason muttered again, 'what the hell *is* going on?'

'Can you get me the guns? And ammunition?'

For the next five minutes Mason pleaded denials of gang involvement. He knew nothing about northside mobs bankrolling him, or about writing selected and slanted articles. But when he saw my disbelieving look and got extra comments about Steele's insights he quit pleading and owned up. And started believing.

'Since when did you become a marksman?'

'While in Kosovo,' I said. 'To pass the time I

had shooting competitions with US Marines. I was used to basic rifle training and the soldiers tried to impress me with their weapons. Within a month or so I was pretty useful with most artillery. Also I had small-firearms instruction here in Dublin before I set foot in Harmon. I never thought all this would ever come in useful.'

'I bet you didn't,' growled Mason. He slipped a stick of gum in his mouth and started chewing furiously, as if he wanted to grind the gum to nothing. 'Tell me again what you want?'

I told him, adding that the Glock would be easy to source in the Dublin underworld. The sniper rifle could be a problem and his contacts might have to go looking.

'Where?'

'How the hell do I know? This is my first criminal act. But from what I've learned in jail nothing's impossible. If you wanted a Sherman tank it wouldn't surprise me if DHL delivered within forty-eight hours.' I offered some angles to speed up my order. 'Terrorist contacts would have access. Police and army marksmen can be bought if you know their needs or deviancies or addictions. A rifle could easily go missing and return when I'm finished the job.'

'What job? Jesus, Frank, what are you planning?'

'To hurt a few people. When this is over they'll know they shouldn't have gone after my family. I have big strong shoulders and can take whatever's thrown at me. But now that they've targeted my folks they've got something coming.'

There was a moment's silence, Mason's eyes darting from side to side as he inspected me and the car park. I could see the big man was confused and frightened, like myself; gradually realising he'd stumbled headlong into something sinister and dangerous. He stuck the gum on the dash and searched his pockets. Soon he had a packet of cigarettes open, popped one into his mouth and lit it with the car lighter. He drew hungrily, coughed and wound down the window to spit. He wiped his lips and took another drag, sighing with contentment. 'This is no time to deny life's pleasures.'

I opened my window, snuggling into my clothes as cold air groped in. I waited until Mason's nicotine addiction settled. 'Have you anything for me?'

He turned on the engine and fiddled with the heat control to get warm air at our ankles. 'There is a Caucasian foreign national in J-wing, identity and country of origin unknown. He's guarded night and day, two armed officers at each end of the landing. He eats in his cell, the food brought directly to him. They have contrived some sort of toilet and washing facilities so he doesn't have to leave the block. He is brought to the exercise yard on his own and allowed to walk for an hour. They vary the times but it's always at night, whether it's raining or not.'

I listened as if my life depended on it, which for all I knew was true. And at last something had filtered down from the landings.

'He's been there over three weeks now. He has a visitor, also Caucasian, once a week, and the two go into his closed cell. The visitor stays an hour, maybe two. My source says he carries a briefcase and looks troubled, head down and muttering, big scowl on his face. He gets in and out through a back entrance reserved for the governor and uses fire escapes to avoid direct contact with most of the warders.'

'The government is in on this,' I interrupted.

Mason nodded. 'Has to be.'

'Any idea who he is?'

Mason sucked on his cigarette, coughed and spat more phlegm out the window. 'No, and my source is too scared to dig. He says there's never been anything like this at Harmon. The prison is a fortress full of homicidal maniacs. If this man is so valuable it's a helluva risk putting him in there.'

'Or a very good idea,' I wondered out loud. 'The last place on earth anyone would go looking for him and the last place they're likely to get at him.'

'Maybe,' Mason conceded. He rubbed his eyes and scratched his scalp. The cigarette butt was tossed outside. A car swung into a space two lanes up from us and instinctively we both ducked. A young woman in a tracksuit and carrying shopping bags got out, checked her parking and then disappeared from view behind a concrete pillar. Mason let out a deep breath. 'Jesus, I'll be a nervous wreck by the time this is finished.'

When will it finish? I kept my thoughts to myself. And how will it finish? Ratko's killer smile flashed and my guts tightened. Who are you, you bastard?

'I need more information,' I said.

'Like what?'

'Lisa Duggan, my girlfriend, works with the United Nations.'

'You told me she was in banking,' said Mason. 'Since when did she move to the UN?'

'This one I'm not sure of,' I admitted and explained why. 'But it's an angle I need checked.'

'OK, leave it with me. When I know I'll call.' Now Mason squared in his seat so he had me in full view. 'If Dan Steele wants me dead he'll get his way. You've gotta help me out on this one, Frank. You owe me.' There was despair in his voice.

'Leave Steele to me,' I came back. 'He needs me more than I need him.' This was a barefaced lie but I hoped it would calm Mason and push his information gathering into top gear. 'He has to do what I tell him until he's out of that jail.'

'And then what?'

'And then he gets what's coming to him.'

Mason groaned. 'Jesus, I don't like the sound

of this. This is no street mugger you're dealing with. He has contacts everywhere . . .'

'Tell me about it.' Ratko's cruel eyes stared at me.

'. . . and if he can't do the business he'll pass the job on. You're challenging one of the biggest criminal networks in Europe, Frank. Remember that.'

There was another strained silence. I kept vigil on the level by the side mirror, watching cars pull in and out, listening to tyre squeals and revving engines. Conversations and shouts became loud and then died, one-sided mobile phone calls frequent. The zone was busy and that suited me. I thought it less likely someone would take a shot at us here.

'Noel Dempsey,' Mason spoke again, 'is as mysterious as our J-wing inmate. He doesn't work for Justice, that I'm sure of. I've run background checks with three different contacts. One knew the name but cut me short. The most he would offer is Dempsey is an important government official. All this suggests covert, undercover, top secret, call it what you want. But he's no pen pusher.'

Somehow this didn't surprise me. Then again, nothing surprised me any more. 'One thought that struck me,' Mason continued, 'is he could be a government official assigned to an outside agency.'

'Like what?'

'There are Irish advisers, government and non-government, working overseas on different projects. I know a few with the World Bank, others with the European Commission in Brussels, an old girl-friend of mine heads up a multinational aid agency in Sudan. That sort of thing.'

Somehow I couldn't imagine Conor Mason with a girl. As I looked at him now it was hard to believe he'd ever been younger or slimmer or attractive in any way. His belly strained his trousers and shirt, two buttons opened at his midriff for comfort. His red hair was dishevelled, his skin coarse and ageing. But his mind was alert and ticking and his notion suddenly appealed to me. Maybe that's how Dempsey came to be the one who dragged me out of the London prison. But why lure me from my apartment and almost kick the life out of me? Questions and no sensible answers. What happened that night after I went unconscious? Lisa must have seen and heard everything; the CCTV cameras would have picked up even shadows. I needed to go back to the apartment and revisit the nightmare.

'So what do we do?' Mason cut through my reverie.

'Keep trying for more on Dempsey, I still think he's a key player. Steele says he's dangerous. Dangerous to him or dangerous to me I don't know but we need to find out. Also push for infor-mation about the J-wing inmate. Steele claims he knows the inside there too but I'm damned if I can figure how.'

'Steele has so many contacts, Frank. He has police, judges, and government officials and customs officers on his payroll. If he wants news he doesn't read the papers, his network tells him.'

There was little doubting Mason's grasp of the situation; Steele had already floored me with comments proving he had informants with considerable classified knowledge.

'He's told me Justice knows I'm the source for your exclusives,' I said.

'Well, that didn't come from me,' Mason protested. 'I owe those bastards no favours and they can't stand the sight of me.'

'Yeah, but is it bothering them enough to muzzle you? Your claim they orchestrated that riot might be true. And if it is they're capable of anything.'

Mason frowned. 'Maybe we're getting too close for comfort.'

That was something I was actively considering but dared not say.

'Maybe,' continued Mason, 'the government has both of us in their sights.'

I opened the passenger side door and climbed out. Before I left I leaned across and whispered, 'It's not the government I'm worried about.' But I wasn't totally sure that was right.

*

The return trip through Dublin was difficult. Roadworks, tramline upgrades, roundabout regrading and cable laying suggested the city was being dug up with no real plan what to do next. Car queues stretched to and from the M50 motorway that ringed the western fringes. I zigzagged backstreets and narrow lanes until one hour later I was sitting in my front room. I showered and made a snack, idly watching the television. Sky News had a breaking story about a suicide bomber in south Baghdad who'd infiltrated an international oil company complex. There were dozens of casualties, and clips from shaky cameras showed mangled bodies carried aloft by screaming and terrified Iraqis. Another shot presented a local hospital with casualties in its forecourt and paramedics struggling to insert IV lines and bandage wounds. The studio cut to a correspondent in battle fatigues reporting breathlessly from the scene. One hand over her left ear and the other clutching a microphone she was shouting, panting and sweating, and darting worried glances over her shoulder as screaming sirens scorched past. There are likely to be 'many deaths', she believed, and 'countless injured and maimed'. Then came background images of distraught and wailing relatives rambling aimlessly amid rubble and dust, shocked and beating their chests. Close-ups caught the distraught faces of women struggling to hold the bloodied bodies of their children.

Fuck you, George Bush, I thought. Why don't you ask them how liberated they feel right now?

In the Sky studio a sombre anchorman read from a bulletin. 'There are unconfirmed reports of foreign casualties among the dead,' he announced. 'I must stress these are very much initial accounts and it will take time to clarify. But it would appear a number of non-Iraqi civilians did take the brunt of this explosion. Reuters is saying there are at least four non-nationals still in that mound of rubble you saw on your television screens a moment ago. We'll update this and other stories right after the break.'

I flicked the OFF button and stared at the wall.

I went outside. It was coming up to five o'clock and the evening gloom was settling. In my mind I retraced the events of 12 February, when I was dragged into the car park and kicked unconscious. My Saab was where it was every time I parked, in the third lane to the left. The street-level apartment was still unoccupied so the extra spaces were unused. That night two cars belonging to my mysterious and now disappeared neighbours were in place. They too must have heard the racket, must have seen what was going on. And they too, I was sure, were in on the abduction.

I stood in the middle of the forecourt and panned my gaze. With both feet together I inched my way in a full circle, looking from the tips of my shoes to the top of every building. First I noticed the roof CCTV cameras that had once protected my flat were gone. It wasn't enough just to disconnect them, I thought. No, the bastards had to physically take them away as if to rub my nose in it. The red-brick complex was built on an in-fill site and surrounded by a cluster of buildings. To my left with my back to the door it was mainly residential, to my right an old office block with communication antennae. Straight ahead was the sole entrance, a single lane of tarmac that led to another narrow road that in turn fed traffic onto a major artery.

There was a light breeze as I retraced my positions, where I suspected I'd fallen, how far I'd managed to roll away before the shotgun was discharged. Then I walked the fifty or so yards to the next street and looked up and down. Despite the darkness and passing headlights I could still make out the doors and windows and rooftops of the terrace. It took me some time but I finally spotted what I was praying I might see. Less than twenty yards to my left there was a triple CCTV unit fixed to the side of an office block, one lens pointing in my direction. I studied the camera from a number of different angles before deciding it might have the data I needed. Despite the time, now after six, and the fact that staff were leaving their workplace I knocked, introduced myself and asked to speak with the security head, a small black man with white staring eyes.

'Are you poollliiice? Cos if you're not am warned to say nuthin.' He folded his arms together over his chest and locked onto my gaze. 'So waddye want to do?'

My phone rang at three the next morning, while I was in a fitful sleep. I counted six rings and waited after it went dead. Conor Mason had suggested a contact routine, believing the land-line to be bugged. Thirty seconds later the phone rang again, this time for three cycles before cutting out. I followed the time on the digital clock. Exactly ninety seconds later the phone kick started and stopped almost immediately. I pressed my mobile into action and went into the shower and began running water. I turned on hot and cold taps in the basin and flushed the toilet. Then I called Mason.

'What's up?'

'One of Steele's henchmen was killed in Baghdad yesterday. Guy named Declan Tierney.'

Baghdad?

Mason continued, speaking rapidly. 'Tierney was one of four security men working for Brokins, a London company dealing in bodyguards for executives in trouble spots.'

'And they hired one of Steele's gang?'

'Uh-huh. And he wasn't even the worst. The

news coming out says three others were killed. Tierney plus two South Africans and a Serb.'

My head was reeling and the steam from the shower getting to my lungs. Still I didn't want this conversation overheard by any of O'Hara's listeners.

'Brokins is refusing to comment and issued a fax confirming four of its operatives were killed while protecting essential staff at one of Iraq's major oil refineries. They're not offering identities or backgrounds. All the networks are reporting on the scandal of employing criminals and mercenaries in Iraq. It's big stuff and paints the coalition administration in a bad light.' Mason paused as if to catch his breath. Before I could get a word in he came back. 'The South Africans have history and the Serb is wanted for war crimes.' The line crackled and Mason's voice faded and then came back. '. . . ted Nations . . . maybe . . . resea . . . anyway, that's something to think about.'

'You're breaking up on me, Conor.' I tried not to shout but the noise of running water and the bad line conspired against me.

'What?'

'You're breaking up.'

'. . . morning . . . ret . . . bast . . . got . . . mation . . .'

'Conor, can you hear me?' The line went dead.

★

I paced the floor, trying to rationalise this new information. One of Dan Steele's henchmen sidelines in the lucrative mercenary market. I'd read of ex-cons and hardened killers being recruited by at-risk firms in the Middle East. But nowhere in Steele's dossier did it hint any of his cronies was mad enough to work as a hired gun in Iraq. I sent a text to Mason asking for another meeting. And I still had the security guard's information to consider.

15

Mason was right, the Baghdad story was big. IRAQ'S
SECRET ARMY ran a banner headline in the London
Times, 6 March edition. SUICIDE BOMB KILLS
MERCENARIES was the sub-text in a faxed copy that
arrived at my workstation later that morning.
According to the report, four of the twelve casualties of yesterday's suicide bomb were henchmen
employed by an international oil company to protect senior executives. One of the South African
dead was Deon Hulter, a member of Koevoet, a
notorious counter-insurgency unit that operated in
Namibia in the 1980s. Koevoet was an out-of-
control troop responsible for killing up to five
hundred people a year, mainly SWAPO guerrillas,
POWs routinely shot after interrogation, and civilians. The other South African casualty was Frans
Norte, a member of the infamous Vlakplaas death
squad operating inside the country. According to

The Times, Norte received amnesty from the Truth and Reconciliation Commission in return for details of his murderous criminal activities.

The Serb victim was Goran Mujkic: the International War Crimes Tribunal in The Hague wanted him for crimes against humanity, particularly 'the collection and mistreatment, including murder and rape, of civilians within and outside the Omarska camp'.

The Irish mercenary, Declan Tierney, was an equally infamous thug with a long record of criminality. The report hinted at a link with Dan Steele, 'considered Ireland's most ruthless career felon, now behind bars in Harmon Penitentiary.' There was an outline of Steele's past with further analysis of Tierney's association. Murder, extortion, kidnapping, narcotic trading and people smuggling cropped up repeatedly. The article went on to detail the background to unsavoury security personnel in Iraq.

There are an estimated 1,500 South Africans employed by American and British contractors, many using the experience they gained as mercenaries during Apartheid to bolster their credentials. But not only Apartheid-era terrorists have found opportunities. Prior to the US-led war, Saddam Hussein hired over a dozen Serb air-defence specialists, many of whom were wanted for paramilitary activity during the Balkan wars. When Iraq fell, some of these Serbs stayed behind selling their services to the highest bidders, usually defence firms. Hardened campaigners from other conflicts, especially Afghanistan, soon joined them.

I poured a strong black coffee, added three level teaspoons of sugar and considered the story. Iraq was certainly the most violent and dangerous country in the world, thanks to George Bush, Tony Blair and my prime minister, John Howard. Sure, the companies charged with rebuilding the nation were coming under enormous pressure from various militias hell-bent on maintaining chaos. And where there is strife, gangsters often follow, trying to make a fast buck with deadly know-how. But what was one of Dan Steele's men doing there? My understanding of Steele and his crew was that they avoided trouble spots to concentrate on making money. Selling drugs. Selling people. Exploiting women for prostitution. Illegal gambling, racketeering and whatever else criminals spend their spare time scheming. I concluded that Declan Tierney was freelancing. Probably he no longer had links to Steele and was ploughing his own miserable lowlife furrow. Probably he was fleeing the trans-European police dragnet looking for him, hoping to hide out in Iraq until Interpol got fed up. But the more I thought of it the more I sensed I was wrong. Steele's gang members tended to stick together and there were few freelancers. Whatever Declan Tierney was up to, Steele almost certainly knew about it.

'What was he doing in Iraq?' I asked Conor Mason later that day.

'Waddye mean, what was he doing in Iraq? He was an experienced gun for hire, that's what he was doing.' Mason looked at me with wide-eyed astonishment, as if I was a slow learner annoying the teacher with basic questions.

'I understand that bit, but what I don't get is one of Steele's cronies working as a mercenary. It doesn't fit with their usual activities. They like to use guns but they're not soldiers, they don't like being shot at.'

Mason didn't give this much thought. 'You're all over the place on this, Frank. Try thinking straight for a change. Tierney was a dangerous criminal. Tierney had an international arrest warrant on his head and probably wanted to lie low but still make money. So he signs up for protection duty in Iraq. Let's face it, he was an ideal conscript. Reuters is saying the security firms out there hire anyone who can tote a pistol. They're not worried about background; hell, the more criminal the better.'

We were back in the same underground car

park; both of us huddled in the front seats of Mason's Volkswagen. It still stank like a brewery and I ran a finger over the dust-covered dash and inspected the result.

'So what are you now,' Mason snapped, 'a car valet?' He rubbed a sleeve over the rest of the grimy dashboard. 'Happy?'

'Have you anything more on the J-wing inmate?' I was watching a black BMW that had swung into a parking spot two lines ahead. The driver hadn't got out and it was now coming up for five minutes.

'He's in a witness-protection programme,' Mason actually whispered the answer.

I twisted in my seat so I had a better view and forced quiet a surge of questions. 'What sort of witness protection?' A thought flashed, maybe the inmate has crucial evidence in some mobster case coming before the courts. 'Is it a local trial?'

'I doubt it. Whoever it is doesn't speak English.'

Now I was totally focused. Dan Steele claimed the identity of the J-wing inmate held the clue to my troubles. Whatever notions I'd entertained about this man were now shot to pieces. A foreigner in a witness-protection programme had not been factored into my thinking. 'How do you know?'

'I have one source working the landings and he gets cash in exchange for information. I've used him for years but I've never seen him so wound up. He's scared that anything he gives me will be traced back. He's warned this is the last he's offering.'

The driver of the BMW still hadn't surfaced. I sensed we were being watched but didn't dare break the flow of conversation. 'So we have a foreigner in a witness programme but no local involvement,' I said. 'Who is he giving evidence against? And why is he in an Irish prison?' Silently, I also wondered how Dan Steele knew about him.

Mason said, 'I don't know, and by the vibes I'm getting I'm not likely to find out. But whatever's going on has government involvement at the highest level.'

I lapsed into silence, keeping an eye on the lanes ahead. As I watched for signs of movement from the stationary car I wondered about this fresh news. The inmate is in Ireland, I decided, to keep him at a safe distance from those he's going to give evidence against. Conclusion, this is not an Irish problem. Yet the Irish government is going to extraordinary lengths to protect his identity. One, they've transferred dangerous recidivists to an army camp to keep J-wing secure. Two, they have a tight control on information coming out of the jail. Three, this man is protected by armed guards twenty-four hours a day.

I turned to Mason. 'Dan Steele warned me the Justice Department was planning to shut me up, maybe even planning to silence you. But no one has come near me.' I glanced quizzically at Mason and he shook his head.

'Me neither,' he said.

'So what,' I continued, my thoughts spilling faster than my tongue would allow, 'is so important about this man that the prison system has to be compromised?'

Mason was staring at me strangely. 'And how the hell do you fit into all this?'

I ignored his question. 'You were saying something when you rang but I couldn't make it out, your mobile was breaking up.'

Mason's brow furrowed and then an 'ah yes, I remember' look crossed his features. 'Your girlfriend, what's her name?'

My heart plummeted. What was coming? 'Lisa.'

'Yeah, Lisa Duggan. She is attached to the UN. Works as translator and investigator in the east European division dealing with war criminals, gun runners, people traffickers, that sort of thing.'

I swallowed hard, uncertain I'd heard correctly. 'Are you sure?'

'Sure as can be, she's certainly no mystery. The UN is like an open book and it was easy to get details. And here's the funny bit.' Mason slipped a roll of chewing gum into his mouth and started hammering it with his teeth.

What's the funny bit? I almost screamed. Don't make this any worse for me.

'She's not based here, she works out of Belgrade.'

Belgrade? That had to be wrong. Lisa was rarely out of Dublin for as long as we were dating. Or was she? My mind went into the hourglass again as snatches of past conversations and excuses I'd never challenged now surfaced. I struggled to keep my composure.

'What does she do?'

'She's attached to the Office of the Prosecutor.'

'What?' The sand stuck in the hourglass.

'She deals with prosecution of human-rights abuses. She's in charge of collecting evidence, identifying witnesses and exhuming mass graves. Then she prepares indictments for tribunal judges.'

This was so dramatic I physically grasped Mason's arm to stop. My expression must have reflected my confusion and distress as Mason leaned back in his seat to get a better look at me. 'You OK, Frank?'

'No, no. I'm fine,' I lied. Lisa was leading a secret life. Dammit, why did she lead me on? She knew I was in love with her, why didn't she share this with me? I would have been so supportive; in fact, I would have been proud of her work. I was doing much the same with Amnesty. And then the penny dropped. Maybe Lisa wasn't allowed, or thought it too dangerous to say anything. Whatever she was dealing with she had to keep me out of it. Or perhaps she knew of my involvement with war crimes evidence in Kosovo and was ordered to keep her distance and maintain her silence. Now I felt myself go suddenly cold. Maybe they didn't want me that night. Maybe they came for Lisa. I started shivering. Oh, Jesus, they've got Lisa and this is all a cover-up to keep me away.

'Frank, I think you should go home. You look dreadful. You're shaking like a leaf.'

I was shivering uncontrollably and I pulled down the passenger-side vanity mirror and inspected my face. My eyes were bloodshot and bleary, my forehead and cheeks an accordion of wrinkles as I struggled for composure. My upper lip was quivering. I wanted to share my fears with Mason but I'd already kept most of these details from him. And, in the depths of my soul, I didn't trust him. Dan Steele's comment had destroyed my confidence in the journalist's integrity. That and his admission that a local gang was bankrolling him.

'Did you bring a gun?' I managed to croak.

'Yeah.'

'Where is it?' I forced my hands between my thighs to stop them shaking.

'On ground level you'll find a rubbish bin twenty yards to the left of the lift as you're looking at it. It's taped up with a scrawled sign saying DO NOT USE. Peel the tape off and the top comes away

252

easily. You'll find a Glock 19 and two boxes of ammunition.'

'What about the sniper rifle?'

'They're working on that for me. Give me another few days.'

I looked straight at Mason, my mind in another whirlwind of fear and dread. 'Conor, whatever you do don't double-cross me.' I held up a hand to stop his protest. 'I don't know what's going on but the more I dig the more worrying it gets. I've enough enemies as it is and I wouldn't like to suddenly discover you're another.'

Mason's features hardened. 'Dr Ryan, maybe you should get out of this country while you still can.' This was the first time Mason had ever addressed me as doctor and I knew my comment had hurt. 'You think you're running a one-man squeaky-clean investigation bureau. Well, let me put you wise. You're a walking time bomb, stumbling into dangerous and treacherous territory, mixing with the most vicious criminals on earth. And you think you're going to save the world with a frigging stethoscope. I'm no angel and I accept that. But I know when to play the opposition to stay alive. You, you . . .' His anger was so white hot he stumbled over the words, 'you just can't stop finding new battles to fight.' He reached past me and opened the passenger door. 'Why don't you fuck off home to your mother before you get hurt.'

It was then that I noticed the shadow coming at me from the rear. In the same split second I realised the black BMW was now behind us. 'Get down, get down,' I screamed and grabbed Mason by the collar. Our heads collided as we ducked, my left hand scrambling for the side lock.

'Jeez, you guys are real touchy. Did I interrupt a heavy-petting session?'

I looked up to find a thirty-something in glasses and suit staring at me in disgust. 'I only came to tell you you'd left your lights on.' He started back-pedalling. 'This is a public space, you know.' He climbed into his car and drove off, head shaking.

I kept the passenger door open and took deep breaths of clear air. My heart was thumping and I felt empty to the pit of my stomach. I started to climb out but fell back when my legs wouldn't take my weight. I slumped in the seat, breathing heavily and wondering why my world was collapsing in around me again. When I looked over, Mason's face was white and he was fumbling to light a cigarette. I gave him time to flick the lighter on.

'How did you find out about Lisa?'

He finally got the tobacco glowing and inhaled deeply. 'Contact in the UN.'

'Can I speak to him?'

'No. Contacts like to stay anonymous. They don't talk to every Tom, Dick or Harry.'

'What about Noel Dempsey?'

Another drag. 'Still nothing.'

I had something on Dempsey but I wasn't offering it to Mason. I'd cross-reference information he offered if it ever came.

'Was there anything else you said last night I might have missed?' My heart was still pounding and my body shaking. 'The last I heard was the Serb and some war-crimes connection.'

Mason was puffing so strongly the car filled with smoke and I had difficulty seeing. He took another drag, spat a corner of filter away and then squashed the butt into the ashtray. 'Is it possible these four have links other than hired guns?' he asked. 'Check out that angle.' He gunned the engine alive and switched the gears to reverse. 'Then again, maybe we should get out of this before we both get killed.'

The Glock was perfect. Whoever planted it knew what he was doing. The gun was wrapped in three layers of white cotton, then sealed inside tinfoil. Over that was a long roll of thick plastic, followed by a final cover of dirty rag. The rag smelt of dung and looked as if it had flecks of dung, guaranteed to deter the casual explorer. Two unopened boxes of ammunition were similarly wrapped. Folded neatly beside them was a heavy-duty paper bag from a hardware chain. As I hailed a cab I looked like an everyday shopper, though probably with a deeper frown than most. When I finally got space to inspect the handgun I was relieved to see it was the genuine article and not from Taiwan. The Glock logo and number 19 with Austria and 9x19 were on the left side of the slide. The Glock logo was on the grip with the serial number clearly marked under the barrel. It was oiled and clean. It was light and easy to handle. There was plenty of ammunition. I was ready for action.

I fled the M50 motorway where it fed traffic onto countryside north of Dublin and drove here and there until I came across a deserted forest trail. By now, coming up to three in the afternoon, the light was fading and the evening chill creeping in. I was wearing a leather jacket over a woollen sweater, the leather zipped to the throat. I pinned a crude dartboard-design cardboard target to a tree and paced five metres back. As I took aim my mind was filled with conflicting images and thoughts. My folks in South Australia were fine, I called them after I discovered Ratko's photos and made sure they were safe without giving away my concerns. BANG. My attackers may not have come for me that night. BANG. They probably came for Lisa. BANG. What is Lisa working at that is so sensitive that a huge conspiracy of deceit and treachery has to be created? BANG. Why Belgrade? BANG. And why did Noel Dempsey confiscate the CCTV images from the office block on the road alongside my apartment? The security guard had described Dempsey to a tee, the clinch being the prominent beaked nose and nasal voice. But Dempsey didn't know there was a back-up system and copies of the films. BANG. Which I had sight of for five hundred euros in cash.

I took down the target and inspected my marksmanship. The six shots fell within a decent three-inch radius of the bull's eye. Indeed, all but one was in a more impressive two-inch radius, just to the left of the aim point. Certainly good enough for workable skirmish activity. I loaded ten rounds into the magazine and prepared for rapid fire drill.

BANG, BANG, BANG. Noel Dempsey was easily identified in the films, at one point talking with a group of three others. Two could be seen carrying significant-looking firepower, probably AK47s. And this before they entered the apartment complex at 2.30, as shown by the clock on the films. BANG, BANG, BANG. Two police cars scorched towards the development at 4.05 exactly. This would have fitted in with response time after my alarm was activated. At 4.07 a paramedic van rushed in the same direction. The same three patrols drove out at a more relaxed pace thirty minutes later. BANG, BANG, BANG. Two smaller cars, which I forced myself to recognise as my neighbours' Nissan Primera and Renault Clio, edged out, stopped and then drove off in separate directions. BANG. Now what the hell was all that about?

The ten rounds hit home within a two-inch radius suggesting the six-round test was good because of my shooting rather than the gun's accuracy. Most rounds fell off the aim point, which made me think the rear sight was slightly off. That could easily be addressed. I clipped in another eight bullets. BANG, BANG. An SUV of some description had pulled into the apartment complex at 4.15. It re-appeared on the street and into the CCTV images twenty minutes later. Close scrutiny (another two hundred euros) showed the SUV had two occupants going in but three coming out. The extra passenger was a slightly built individual sitting in the rear. As enlarged and enhanced as the security guard could offer for another fifty euros (I was broke), we both concluded this was a female. I knew it was Lisa. BANG, BANG, BANG, BANG. In my sights I had the cardboard target. In my mind I had Noel Dempsey. BANG, BANG. As the last two rounds shredded the mark I almost believed I could see the shots pepper the bastard's arrogant face.

Just before six that evening I called in to the prison for a late clinic. I specifically asked to see Dan Steele on the pretext of assessing his condition.

With events developing so fast it was a useful exercise in keeping the crime boss's medical status in the open. He looked surprised when he was brought down from the landings and studiously avoided my gaze as his handcuffs were released. As soon as the treatment-room door was closed I gave vent to my fury.

'That was a dangerous mistake, Steele,' I spat through gritted teeth. 'You shouldn't have targeted my family. I've spoken with them and they haven't an inkling they are under threat and that's the way I plan to keep it.'

He shrugged.

'Call your mongrels off. If any of my folk topple from a ridge, or get knocked down by some hit-and-run driver, or end up in the river, then I'll rip you apart limb from limb.' I gripped the desk between us for support and to calm my shaking hands. I felt spittle form at my lips and quickly wiped it away.

Steele inspected some spot to the right of my vision, his face a mask of disinterest.

'You'll get your fucking X-ray, I'll see to that.'

'Good,' the crime boss spoke at last. 'Now nobody will get hurt.'

Steele's reassurance didn't ease my conscience but I was at his mercy and he knew it.

'If you want out of here you'll do what I say,' I came back, my anger still surging.

Finally he locked onto my gaze. 'No, doc, you'll do what I say. I keep control and we all get to stay alive. It's simple really.' He quit before I could say another word.

16

I don't believe in God. Haven't done since about age fifteen, and nothing I've seen or heard or read since has convinced me this lack of belief is mistaken. If anything, what I've seen and heard supports atheism. I was brought up Presbyterian, and Sunday service was conducted in a stone church about twenty miles from the homestead in a village called Sandy Creek. Sandy Creek was no more than a line of shops straddling the highway from Broken Hill in the far north to Adelaide along the south coast. It had a pub, called the Hotel (even though it couldn't take guests), and a general store selling everything from shotgun cartridges to ice cream. At the side was a petrol pump that did good business, it being the only fuel stop for fifty miles in either direction. There was also a dental surgery ('hours 10–12 on Mon and Weds and Fri'), a part-time pharmacy, a part-time bakery and occasional butcher. There was no beautician, doctor, estate agent, dry-cleaners or furniture outlet; for such things you travelled to the nearest decent-sized town, one hundred miles south. A husband-and-wife team, Frank and Terri, ran the main shop but since Frank was more often in the bar than behind the counter it fell to Terri to keep the shutters open and business ticking over.

The clergyman who preached from the village pulpit was a tall and slim God-fearing man called Sanders and he knew how to whip up a good sermon. When I was young I'd come home from church quaking about everlasting damnation and roasting in the fires of hell. Such penalties, Sanders claimed, should be expected for stealing even an apple or a soda. Being Presbyterian I was also warned against Catholics and popery. There was a Catholic chapel somewhere to the north but it may as well have been on the moon for all I saw of it. To my folks the chapel was as sinful as a drinking den, the priest as dodgy as bedamned. Around then, reports had surfaced of sexual abuse by Irish Christian Brothers running orphanages for the state. The accounts were appalling and a shocking indictment of the Brothers and their religion. As Dad read the newspapers it pumped up his dislike for Catholics. All priests became potential paedophiles, and nuns vicious and frustrated clergywomen. But worse was to come. The Reverend Sanders (fifty-eight if he was a day) ran off with Terri (forty on each of her last three birthdays) from the Sandy Creek store, the rumours suggesting they'd made a honey nest on the east coast. There was talk of a love child.

I was coming up to fifteen then and already a sceptic, but this forced a serious rethink of all things religious. Those who preach loudest, I decided, are usually untrustworthy. In my eyes this was confirmed by stories of how the most devious and depraved Brothers were often those posing as the most virtuous. Righteousness was in inverse proportion to their prayers and supplication. Good was not necessarily the opposite of evil, they sometimes came hand in hand and hidden by a black soutane. When officers of the churches became no more reliable than snake salesmen I believed the institutions to be equally unstable. I quit attending service at sixteen except for big occasions like Easter and Christmas. At seventeen I passed on God altogether, much to my mother's displeasure. By then I think Dad was only a Sunday Christian and hadn't much time for clergy of any denomination. Despite his tacit approval, I still felt my conscience challenged and often asked the hard questions.

But I kept going back to basics. If God is so bloody good it's time he cleared up a lot of the confusion. Do I pray to Jesus or Buddha or Allah? Do I pray at all? Is anyone listening? Nobody, was my final conclusion. Yet I recognised how important religion was to many people, particularly during personal crises, and in later years saw the comfort of belief for the dying. But then I also saw unpunished wickedness and found it beyond my comprehension to reconcile this with a loving deity. I continued to opt out. So I can't say whether the events before midnight on 6 March were heaven sent or just good luck. Or maybe Bill O'Hara's bad luck. One way or the other, there was little godliness around when I opened my apartment door at eleven thirty.

'Why don't you answer your fucking phone?' O'Hara was in a foul mood, his face as twisted as a corkscrew.

'I didn't hear it,' I lied.

He stormed into the living room, picked up the receiver and checked the dialling tone.

'Seems all right to me.'

'I was in bed. The one on my locker has the bell turned off.' Considering I was fully dressed this was obvious deceit. Still, I managed to keep my face straight, delighting in the other man's discomfiture. I hadn't moved from the front door, wondering why two armed police officers were hanging around the hallway.

'Get your coat,' O'Hara snarled, 'we need you at the jail.'

Uh-oh, I thought. Here we go again. 'Why?'

'I have a very sick prisoner.'

Since when does Bill O'Hara, top civil servant

in the Department of Justice, come calling for the prison doctor? My suspicion must have been obvious. 'It's genuine, so for Christ's sake, move. We haven't got all night.'

'What's wrong?' I didn't budge. *It's genuine.* With these words O'Hara admitted the truth about the night I was attacked and abducted.

'I don't know, that's why we need you. He's having a heart attack or an asthma attack or some fucking thing. Quit standing there like a useless prick, grab whatever bits and pieces you need and get downstairs.' It was unusual street language from the Justice man.

'Should I take my own car?'

'No, we haven't time.'

Heart attacks and severe asthma attacks required hospital attention and O'Hara knew that. 'Did you order an ambulance?' I shouted from the bedroom as I checked my Gladstone bag.

'No.'

'Why not? If this guy's really sick I'll—'

'Quit mouthing and hurry.' O'Hara's face was purple from frustration. 'I don't care what's wrong with him but he can't leave the prison.'

I had a gut feeling about where I was headed.

I was ushered into Harmon through the governor's entrance, a first in itself. Usually I made my way to the medical quarters via a steel-strengthened staff door that ran into a warren of underground corridors and finally a spiral staircase to street level. At the beginning of the century three inmates escaped through this route after attacking a warder and stealing his keys. Now, as I waited for doors to be unbolted, I tried to get a feel for the emergency.

'Who is he?' No answer. Keys jangled on circular steel loops, as another barred gate was swung open and then closed. I was taken through a different barrier I'd never seen before.

'What age is he?' No answer. Now I found myself on the fire escape, an iron stairwell sealed in by razor wire. Detainees could escape from flames but they couldn't escape from the prison.

'Any medical history?' No answer. Another mortise was attacked and I was in a corridor I'd never used before, a spy passage that overlooked the prison workrooms. There were slatted openings in the ancient granite allowing observation of activities below.

Then, as we turned a corner, the familiar smell of the institution became obvious. It was a mixture of decay, cigarettes, toilet fumes from slop buckets, body odour and unwashed socks, food and disinfectant. Shouts came from distant landings as convicts tried to pass the night hours. Other and angrier responses suggested not everyone was up to a late discussion. Steel against steel, rattled locks, hurried footsteps and the clunking of heels on iron-work. Here massive and recent gates slowed our progress; each requiring six separate catches to turn before we passed through.

O'Hara was ahead of me, panting at the hurried pace while the same armed officers stayed close to my back. I kept to the middle and offered the demeanour of a routine visit, knowing it was not. Now I recognised the terrain; we'd entered the red zone, the most dangerous area of Harmon. In this division security was suffocating with more warders per criminal than anywhere else. Stab-proof vests were compulsory, cans of Mace standard. Stun guns and CS gas were stored in heavily protected safes. Offenders exited their cells singly or not at all and exercised at separate times from other landings to reduce the risk of violence. Often these recidivists were heckled: psychos, looney tunes and lunatics the most common tags. And with in-house tension running high it didn't take much to start a brawl. Stopping the affray was a different matter and often warders would let a scrap run its course, whatever the likely outcome, rather than intervene. They knew fights could be faked to draw them in and then get turned on them with vicious retribution. Punch-ups could also be started to distract from other devious or dangerous affairs. An escape bid, a murder plot, a chance to distribute drugs, the schemes were as many and varied as the thugs who plotted them.

O'Hara stopped at J-wing. I wasn't sure what to expect; the mystery of the sole inmate had been preying on my mind for days. I took deep breaths to calm my pounding heart and gripped the Gladstone tightly. This is it, Ryan. You're getting closer to the truth, are you ready? Can you handle whatever pans out? Despite the armed back-up I felt vulnerable, as if I was going to be shoved into a group of homicidal madmen.

'Follow me.' O'Hara's voice dropped an octave. Radically unusual for this landing, the main entrance of half steel plate and upper iron bars was open. Fluorescent lights glared from recessed fittings, throwing shadows about a small group crowded round a cell in the middle of the landing. The division was eerily empty with every door ajar. In normal times it would be full of edgy and often strung-out inmates, smoking and talking or shooting up. At the first sight of authority there'd be sullen looks, jeers and a retreat to privacy. On one awful occasion I chanced upon one convict injecting heroin into the neck of another. Now all I could hear was laboured breathing and mumbled voices, then a foreign accent cajoling or pleading, I couldn't decide which. Two armed policemen stood to one side; their handguns holstered and assault rifles leaning against a wall. Their nervous glances worried me. What is going on?

Don Campbell, the prison governor, was waiting, his bald head bobbing above the others. His face flooded with relief when he saw me. 'Thank Christ,' he couldn't contain himself, 'I thought we'd lost him.'

Harmon Penitentiary cells are small, only thirteen feet by seven. The walls are solid with a skim plaster surface usually adorned with pictures of naked women, often in pornographic poses. Now and then there is a personal card or photograph but this is less likely in J-wing where lifers can be abandoned by relatives. The cell into which I was ushered was noticeably stark with only a single bed on which lay a man. In the gloom it was hard to be accurate but I put him at fifty, maybe slightly older. He had a thick growth of grey hair that matched his bushy eyebrows. He was in a checked shirt, unbuttoned to the waist and pulled open. There wasn't much flab. His chest was smooth apart from a distinct scar under the right clavicle that looked like a bullet-entry wound. He was wearing denims that were too clean by prison standards. His hands were by his sides, shaky fingers picking lint off the blanket on which he lay. I calculated he was three inches short of six feet by the way his toes almost touched the bed frame. An oxygen cylinder was by his side and someone had strapped a face mask on.

Over a background hiss there was strangled breathing, his neck muscles straining to draw air into his lungs. I noticed his tracheal windpipe tugged inwards with each breath. His lips were blue as were his ear lobes, his skin an unhealthy dusky colour.

'Waddye think?' Bill O'Hara was hovering anxiously at my shoulder, now joined by a stranger.

Before I could answer the stranger leaned past me. '*To je doktor.*' ['It's the doctor,'] he nodded towards the man on the bed.

My head swivelled at the shoulders. That accent again. The last time I heard that tone was two nights ago. Then it was my tormentor Ratko speaking. However, despite an overwhelming urge to solve every pressing question my first responsibility was to the distressed patient.

He had difficulty getting the words out. '*Reci mu . . . da ne mogu . . . da disem.*' ['Tell him . . . I can't . . . breathe.'] I strained to understand but was at sea.

'What'd he say?' I asked.

'He cannot take a breath,' the stranger-turned-translator replied. He was a small, stocky man with pale skin and thinning dark hair, wearing a black leather overcoat.

'Can I get a name?' I was sitting on the bedside, my fingers feeling for a pulse.

'No.' This from O'Hara.

I folded a cuff around a limp arm and checked

blood pressure, my mind racing as how to handle the situation. If I pushed too hard O'Hara might call for an outside medical team. If I did nothing I'd learn nothing and I wasn't going home no wiser than I came in. Dan Steele claimed the identity of the inmate in J-wing was vital to my understanding. I decided on a softly-softly approach. Demanding explanations might backfire.

'Are there prison notes?' It was a try, if nothing else. New inmates are entered into the system in a fashion that hasn't changed much over a century. Full name and last known address; crime and sentence; court and county in which convicted; date of conviction; age and height and colour of hair and eyes; complexion and distinctive markings (it is often impossible to fully describe many tattoos); religion and contacts for emergencies. In recent years nationality became yet another important vital statistic.

'He's not in the system.'

I glanced up as if this was a big surprise. 'And you don't need to know why,' O'Hara clipped.

My patient was now puffing, froth gathering on his lips. I leaned across and turned the oxygen to full, my eyes searching for vital clues as to the illness. With my stethoscope I listened to his chest, noting there was air entry into both lungs despite the laboured breathing. This ruled out collapsed alveoli. The bases were clear, ruling out infection, effusion and oedema fluid. His heart rate was rapid but the pulse strong and regular, blood pressure acceptable, and when I checked he wasn't feverish. Over my shoulder I called the position. 'Bill, if you want this man to live you're going to have to open up or bring him to the City Hospital where they've got the machines to make a diagnosis.'

'Do *you* know what's wrong?'

'I think so. But I'm not working in the dark. I need to know who this man is, his nationality and past medical history. I also need to know if he's on any medication and whether he's been taking it as prescribed. In addition—'

'His name is Sefik Barisik and he is from the village of Vukovar in Croatia.' I turned to the interpreter. He was forcing O'Hara outside to stop him interfering. 'He is fifty-one years old and has a history of asthma. What else do you need?'

Vukovar in Croatia. What the hell is the Irish government doing with a witness-protection detainee from Croatia? Suddenly the accent clicked and a million images from Balkan killing fields flooded my brain. That's where I'd heard the language before, while excavating mass graves along the Croat–Serb border. My mind screamed for explanations but I held my control and asked, 'When did he develop asthma?'

'Perhaps six months ago.' The English was excellent, if heavily accented.

I checked the patient's chest again, noting few wheezy sounds in either lung. Still the windpipe tugged; still there was an unhealthy colour to the skin. His eyes met mine and I could see terror. He thinks he's going to die. I flashed a reassuring smile, then started rummaging in my Gladstone. One minute later I had a small butterfly needle in a vein in the crook of his left elbow. I drew blood and emptied it into a couple of bottles for lab analysis. The blood was a deeper blue than normal reflecting a low oxygen saturation that in turn reflected impaired breathing.

'Has he ever had sinus problems or nose polyps? Ever complain of things like that?' There was a pause, then a considered no.

'Is he on medication? Inhalers, tablets or anything?' The tug at the throat was becoming more pronounced, the gasping more laboured.

'Yes.' A washbag was passed for my inspection. Inside was the usual paraphernalia associated with asthma sufferers: inhalers, steroid tablets, theophylline tablets, anti-allergy tablets.

I looked straight at my patient. 'Have you taken your medication today?'

His eyes darted to his companion and my question was translated.

'*Da*.' ['Yes.'] He managed to nod so I understood.

'He took one slow-release theophylline this morning and at ten tonight. He's been taking too much of his relieving medicine and not enough of the preventative inhaler. I warned him but he wouldn't listen. He is very distressed.'

I listened carefully. In the medical information was a nugget. 'Is he under pressure?'

'Pressure? A weight? A heavy weight, maybe this word I do not understand.'

'Stress,' I explained.

My patient's pulse had increased by ten beats a minute and his colour was disimproving. His fingers plucked at the lint, his body moved restlessly on the bed. His chest rose and fell but not in any usual pattern and the movement seemed twitchy.

'Stress? Yes, yes. He is having a number of stress.'

I sensed Bill O'Hara edge inside and draw the translator away. I tried to catch his mumble.

'When the doctors diagnosed asthma was he very stressed then?'

I heard my words passed around and Bill O'Hara trying to rephrase them.

'Yes.'

'What was happening?'

O'Hara cut through. 'Is this necessary? What's so important about his life history?'

Without turning I put everyone on notice. 'Do you want to call an ambulance and let somebody else take over? I don't need this aggro, I can walk away. So if you don't mind I'll ask the questions.'

'*Sta . . . on kaze?*' ['What . . . is he saying?'] My patient croaked and I waited while this was interpreted.

'*Reci mu . . . da ne dopusti da umrem.*' ['Tell him . . . don't let me die.'] Whatever was said came from a very frightened man. He grabbed my hand, his grip surprisingly strong considering his condition. I felt his nails dig into my skin.

'Sefik,' I said out loud. 'I'm going to give you an injection.'

I waited until this was explained, Sefik's blood-shot and terror-stricken eyes darting from me to his partner.

'*Da, da. Vi cete mi pomoci da se oporavim?*' ['Yes, yes. You will make me better?']

This was deciphered as I searched the bag. At last I found the right vial. 'I'm going to make him better but he must do what I say.' As words flowed to and fro I recognised more of Ratko's language. I felt there was a good chance he was also Croatian and wondered if there was a link between him and my patient.

I broke off the top of the ampoule and drew up a clear fluid.

'What are you giving him?' O'Hara's fretting was beginning to annoy me.

'Why don't you go outside until I'm finished?'

'I don't trust you, Ryan. Show me that vial.' He was making no effort to hide his anger.

I flushed the last drops of fluid into the syringe and turned to pass the ampoule, dropping it before his grasping fingers could meet. The glass shattered on the tiled floor. 'Sorry, Bill.' I shook my head in mock disappointment. 'And that was my last one.' I could see the Justice man wanted to strangle me there and then.

'Sefik, you must relax. As I inject this medicine you're going to feel the tightening around your neck ease. I want you to close your eyes and focus on your throat.' I squirted three millilitres of fluid into his vein. Sefik was straining to sit up but I gently eased him back. 'Relax, relax.'

As the instructions were spelled out our eyes met again. Help, please help. I don't want to die. He let his head drop onto the pillow and fixed on the ceiling.

I waited a few minutes and pressed the syringe plunger again. 'Let those throat muscles go loose.' Translated. 'Focus on your throat, Sefik. Try and imagine it is a blocked pipe. You can make that blockage go away. But you have to let go, *you* have to make it happen.' Translated.

He mumbled something.

O'Hara mumbled something.

On the outside landing not a word was spoken, everyone gripped by the drama inside cell twelve,

J-wing. Where recidivist murderers usually stayed incarcerated, one man from a foreign country was fighting for his life.

Sefik's chest slowly, agonisingly eased and the strained breathing began to relax. His minder was whispering, probably encouragement, and the Croatian murmured a response.

'You're doing well.' I gave him the thumbs-up and for the first time saw a smile flicker. 'I'm giving you the rest of the medicine.' I nodded to the minder to translate, then: 'Keep thinking about that blockage in your throat. *You* can make it clear.'

Sefik's eyelids flickered for a few seconds and then closed tightly. The ropelike neck muscles were loosening and the tug at the throat less obvious. The twitchy and laboured noisy breathing was abating to a more relaxed up-and-down pattern. The duskiness around his ear lobes was fading, his lips becoming a healthy pink. I checked his vitals. The pulse rate was still fast but I put that down to overdosing on his anti-asthma medicine. Relieving drugs can speed up the heart if too much is taken and by all accounts he'd been drawing on the stuff all day without relief. Another clue to the real condition. I busied myself taking basic observations. Sefik's blood pressure and temperature were still within normal limits and his lungs clear with better expansion. I took more blood samples, noting the colour had improved there too.

'*Hvala, doktore.*'

I shrugged. 'I don't understand.'

'He said thank you.' The minder deciphered and I grinned at Sefik. He even managed to grin back before his body was racked with a fit of coughing. My heart flipped as I watched him go a sudden and dramatic purple, then clear a wad of phlegm. One more deep breath and a pink tinge blushed his ear lobes and lips. He coughed again, but not so violently, and then struggled to sit up. I pushed him back, my eyes warning him to relax. He collapsed on the bed, tears welling up in his eyes.

'He's OK,' I said. 'But tell whoever's smoking out there to move away.' I listened with secret delight as some wretch was given a dressing down. Hell, I thought, this is the way it should be. I'm in charge. For the first time in longer than I could remember I felt good with myself.

In medicine you have to act confident even though your legs are jelly and your body shaking. Patients expect self-assurance and have little faith in the nervous or uncertain doctor. If you check your textbook before giving an answer you'd be better off looking down a microscope where the bugs don't squint back. As I beckoned O'Hara and the translator to one side I pushed my positive image to the front.

'Sefik does not have asthma.' Two sets of eyebrows shot up. 'I'm not going to bore you with a lot of medical jargon but nothing I saw tonight suggests asthma.' This was true but I was going out on a limb, making a snap diagnosis based on minimal information. 'Everything points to stress, worry, tension, whatever word you want to use. Back there all I saw was vocal cord spasm, a recognised response to anxiety. He's not doing it deliberately but that breathlessness is his mind's way of saying "I've had enough, I'm taking time out". Do you understand?'

O'Hara was surprisingly passive, head nodding as he listened. The translator was sombre, no doubt having to factor this information into the bigger picture. He gestured that he grasped my explanation.

'The injection was sterile water, there was no medication in it.' There was a flash of surprise. While I waited for this to sink in I glanced over O'Hara's shoulder into another cell. Trays of food, and good food too, were stacked on a trolley. A makeshift shower was set up. A lot of effort was going into making Sefik comfortable in this hell-hole landing. There was no sign of a sanitation revamp.

'I too have not been sure about this asthma,'

said the interpreter. 'Sefik takes what the American army doctor prescribed but every day he's like this. Tonight was the worst time.'

American army doctor. The clues were slipping and out of the corner of my eye I noticed O'Hara freeze. 'If you can tell me what's going on I can advise how to deal with this.'

'No.' O'Hara physically drew me away. 'I'll explain this to Dr Ryan.' He signalled and I felt strong grips encircle my arms. Minutes later I was on the other side of the J-wing barrier, O'Hara's face squashed close to mine. 'You are bound by the Official Secrets Act, Ryan, and don't forget that. What you just saw and heard goes no further than the back of your brain, understand? I don't want this on the front page of the papers tomorrow with you as the source.'

'Sure Bill, you can trust me.'

The scepticism in his eyes suggested otherwise. 'I'll have a driver take you home.' I was dismissed. But like hell was I going that easy.

'One thing, Bill. Where did you take my girl-friend Lisa? I've looked at CCTV tapes of that night. I saw Noel Dempsey. I saw cars coming and going. And I saw Lisa being driven away. Where is she?'

It was as if I'd exploded a bomb in O'Hara's brain. His features contorted, face went puce and he struggled to speak. He came towards me, hands raised, and I stepped back to fend off any blow. A police officer pushed between us and bear-hugged O'Hara. 'Tell her I was asking for her, won't you?'

Then I quit while I was ahead.

17

I was angry but in control, outraged yet contained. I had to rein in the desire to take Bill O'Hara's head off at the shoulders, strangle Dan Steele in the prison medical room and then go a-huntin' for Ratko and his lying henchman, Roger Nixon. The threat against my family distressed me greatly but I knew any knee-jerk response would be futile. This war would be won by guile rather than brute force, consecutive small victories and not one major offensive. The most stressful violent urge was to seek and destroy Noel Dempsey, the architect, I believed, of most of my misery.

And while I held back, the restraint didn't come easy. For hours after I fled Harmon revenge tortured my senses, making me restless and agitated. I wandered from room to room, clipping imaginary rounds at the enemy. Dan Steele pleaded on bended knees when I forced the muzzle of my Glock 19 against the back of his head. And Ratko, killer Ratko, became putty in my hands as my grip encircled his throat and tightened until his eyes bulged and his lips turned blue, then black, then deathly white. With Roger Nixon I didn't waste time, two quick rounds to the heart (if the bastard had a heart). But Noel Dempsey suffered most. I had him strapped to a chair, toyed with him until he told the truth. One bullet into the right knee. No, no. Stop, please. A second into his left knee. AAAGGGHHH. Then I worked my way up his limbs, watching him wriggle and squirm, scream and plead.

'Where is she? Where is Lisa?' At first he denied all knowledge, of course, begging me to understand. Finally I placed the tip of the barrel between his eyes and gently squeezed the trigger. And then he spilled everything, rambling and cursing and beseeching me not to kill him. I am only a foot soldier, only carrying out orders. Lisa is . . . My imagination wouldn't take me further. *Where* is Lisa? I had one contact in Belgrade I hoped might help shed light on the situation but knew the details could not be discussed by phone. I decided to have a one-to-one meeting with him.

Without sleep I caught a cab to Dublin airport and was in the concourse by five o'clock on the morning of 7 March. I grabbed a seat on the first Aer Lingus flight to Zurich, taking off at six exactly, and arrived at the bustling Swiss aerodrome three hours later. From the same terminal I managed to connect with a Czech Airlines plane direct to Belgrade, leaving in ninety minutes. I rushed around a mall of shops until I found a set of thermal underwear, rainproof hiking trousers and boots and a rainproof, fleece-lined jacket. Putting everything on my credit card (now significantly in the red), I added a ski hat. In a wine store with shutters half open and manned by a yawning assistant I added a bottle of Chateau Margaux '96, in broken German asking her to gift-wrap it.

The weather in Zurich was cold, temperatures around five Celsius, but in Belgrade there had been a freeze for the past three days with heavy snow falls in the surrounding countryside and traffic chaos along the capital's streets. All this I had gleaned from the Internet before leaving my apartment. On board and toying with inflight breakfast I passed the time trying to identify landmarks out of the port window but could only find the Swiss Alps before cloud banks blocked the view.

I was left to my thoughts. And what confused and conflicting notions I had to consider. 'His name is Sefik Barisik and he is from the village of Vukovar in Croatia.' Hours earlier, around twelve thirty, I had finally got the clue I needed. And the translator's accent provided more valuable information. He was Croatian. Therefore Ratko was also Croatian, or at least from that area. Roger Nixon, whoever the hell he really was, could converse in the same language. That I considered most unusual; common criminals rarely know anything other than the mother tongue. Indeed, if Harmon was anything to go by, they hardly even knew that. Lisa Duggan, according to Conor Mason, was attached to the Office of the Prosecutor at the UN in Belgrade. 'She deals with prosecution of human-rights abuses,' Mason's words played rollerball in my brain. 'She's in charge of collecting evidence, identifying witnesses and exhuming mass graves. Then she prepares indictments for tribunal judges.'

They say love is blind but in my case I now knew it was more than that. As a doctor I am trained to be an observer, to look for the signs and clues that clinch diagnoses. The yellowing tinge on skin and sclera reflecting jaundice, cause to be determined. Thickening or pitting or indentations or small haemorrhages of the nails are telltale signs in lung cancer, anaemia or heart-valve infection. Changed personality patterns, paranoia and hearing strange messages are found in schizophrenia. There are highs and appalling low mood swings in manic depression. I had studied textbooks and been lectured until I was near to screaming about observation, observation, observation. 'Listen to the patient,' was a favourite. 'And never stop looking.'

A long time ago this advice was highlighted, but in an embarrassing way when I detected a suspicious skin lesion on the buttock of a girl I was dating. When it was surgically excised and healed she asked me to remove the stitches. We ended up in bed again, her pleading 'check me all over, I'd hate to think you missed anything else'. At least in those days I was thinking straight, functioning as a doctor and able to combine vocation demands and playtime.

But when Lisa Duggan came along my mind went to porridge. I worked as usual; hell, I was practising medicine among a group of hardened criminals and had to stay alert. But it was my everyday observation of life and living that became swamped by lust and passion and then love for this beautiful woman. I didn't challenge her absences, all the time assuming Lisa was trying to right some family wrong, resolve some personal issue she didn't yet feel comfortable sharing. 'Frank, my dad's not well and I have to go down home to see him.' Would you like me to go with you? 'No, Frank, not now. He's too sick. Maybe another time.' Of course, of course. How insensitive of me. Call me when you're back in town. Anyway, this'll give me a chance to catch up on research. 'Oh, Frank, you're wonderful. Kiss me.' I did. 'More.' I did. 'Make love to me, Frank.' I did. Twice.

She announced one Wednesday she was off to London. Again? So soon? This was less than ten days after yet another trip and unusual by her standards. 'Bank business,' she explained, her expression full of frowns and disappointment. 'We're pulling together a deal for a multinational corporation and they want an exchange broker in on it.' Oh, which company? Coquettish look. 'Frank Ryan, you should know better than to ask. I'm not allowed to divulge that sort of information.' Oh sorry, silly me. Can I come with you?

The protests were long and loud and convincing but in the end she relented and we both took a midday flight to Heathrow airport, the express train to Paddington and a taxi to the Langham Hilton, close to Oxford Circus. While Lisa attended her meeting I scoured the area for a dinner venue and stumbled on Edalinas, an Italian restaurant close to Wigmore Street in the fashionable end of town. It had a chic bar, tables on two levels covered by starched white linen cloths. The napkins were generous and thick, the cutlery heavy and shiny clean. Landscape paintings adorned the walls and the staff looked good enough to eat. It was an ideal venue for a romantic evening.

Later I waited outside the offices where we'd planned to meet, surprised to find Lisa sneaking out of a black limousine with tinted windows at the side of the building. She emerged five minutes later through the front door and into my arms. So I challenged her.

She didn't miss a beat. 'I was buying something sexy to wear. Like to have a peek?' She knew how to steer probing questions into lust, so much so I blanked out the black limo. In the back of a cab she crossed her long legs, allowing the skirt to ride up. While I engaged the driver in banter about the next England versus Australia cricket series Lisa wriggled her bottom until the edge of her lace panties showed. In heavy traffic we kissed hungrily. Along side streets she ran tantalising fingers up and down my inner thighs. At a red light she deliberately leaned forward to give directions, offering me a wonderful and arousing view. By the time we alighted I could hardly walk and had to cover my awkwardness with a newspaper.

In the bedroom she slowly unveiled her purchases, teasing and lingering over every stitch as first blouse, then skirt, then bra fell to the floor. I lay on the bed mesmerised and aching, desperate to touch. Now she was in stockings and garters with disgracefully tight panties that hid little. I dragged them off with my teeth. We devoured each other, the passion delayed and played with. I drew her to climax once, twice, three times and took a rest. She climbed onto me and grabbed two more before I could no longer hold back. When I exploded my moan must have been heard in the lobby, three levels below. Certainly the concierge gave us knowing looks when we went out.

That evening in Edalinas we savoured pasta and seafood, a bottle and a half of a deep Sicilian red, full of the flavours of berry and nuts and oak. Tipsy and contented we lurched back to the hotel, arm in arm, stopping every hundred yards to kiss and grope. It was mid-January and bitterly cold yet I hardly felt the chill. My body was warm from food and wine and love. And I told her.

She snuggled up to me in bed, one arm around my chest, her limbs jumping in pre-sleep. 'And I love you too, Dr Ryan.'

I pushed up to take a closer look at the beautiful face resting on my shoulder. 'Do you, Lisa? Are you telling the truth?' She mumbled something and I was desperate to hear. 'Lisa, Lisa. What did you say?'

She kissed me, slow and wet and all tongues. 'I love you, Dr Ryan.'

I didn't touch her for a week, frightened lest anything would change that moment. Lisa Duggan loves me. I love Lisa Duggan. I am the happiest man in the world. I didn't want to lose her. I didn't want to know who owned the black limousine with tinted windows. I found it easier to stifle my suspicions.

Now, as the Czech Airlines plane came in low

the cabin rocked and my ears popped. A crackling intercom advised headrests straightened and seatbelts buckled. What a fool I am. Balls before brain, as my bush mates used to chide. Yet I felt I was closing in on discovery. I believed I could make sense of my nightmare. And I'd find Lisa and we would pick up the pieces and start again. Surely our love affair isn't dead?

BUMP. The tyres hit tarmac and I was in Belgrade. Belgrade on the Balkan Peninsula, the hilly city rising on the banks of the rivers Sava and Danube and the crossing line between east and west Europe. Formerly in the Federal Republic of Yugoslavia, bombed for three months by NATO forces in 1999 and subsequent focal point for the overthrow of the murderous communist regime of Slobodan Milošević. Belgrade, now the civic, historical, romantic and cultural capital of Serbia and Montenegro.

I disembarked into a wind-chill factor of minus ten Celsius, dragged my ski cap down over my ears and hurried past customs. Snow was falling in soft flurries from dark and ominous skies and everyone was hunched into their overcoats. Backpackers struggled with knapsacks, older folk looked anxiously at the outside gloom. Overhead announcements in different languages advised of flight delays and cancellations from as far away as Moscow and Uzbekistan. There were groans and multilingual curses as information racks flicked up new data. The road running along in front of the arrivals hall was a hive of feverish activity with coaches, taxis and cars vying for parking spaces. Cab-drivers stomped their feet and glared in at potential customers. My feet crunched, my face glowed and my eyebrows began to frost over. I was only vaguely aware of the conditions or of fellow travellers, they were no more than backdrop. I had arrived. I was searching. And I wasn't sure what I might find.

The freeze was worse than I feared and the taxi-driver cursed and mumbled and smoked, and snapped when I eased a window half open to escape the fumes. It took an hour, the route choked with abandoned vehicles, police diversions and lorries hugging the middle tracks. Banks of snow lay in heaped piles against hedges and walls, traffic signs blasted with frost. Exhaust fumes rose and then disappeared as fresh flurries attacked the outer suburbs. For six hundred dinars I was finally dropped at the front of Hotel Moskva, at the corner of Terazije and Balkanska Street in the heart of town.

For another fifty dinars I might have got more than the surly and snarled directions but I was closing in on broke and couldn't risk a tip. I had visited the Moskva before, while working with Amnesty, and knew the ground-floor layout. The rooms were comfortable if uninspiring but with good views over the neighbouring streets.

First I made a call to Harmon Penitentiary informing the nurse I wouldn't be in. She told me Dan Steele had been to the dispensary, complaining bitterly about headaches. He'd got sick that morning.

'Should I do anything?'

I passed on a few basic tips, promising to call late tomorrow. Since Steele's symptoms were fake I had a clear conscience, even if I did feel bad at not being able to fully reassure the nurse's concerns.

Next I called Republicko Ministarstvo Unutrasnjih Poslova (Ministry of Internal Affairs of the Republic of Serbia) and asked to speak with Kneza Pasica. There was immediate language confusion and I was incorrectly routed twice before hitting the right number. Kneza answered in Serb, I countered in English.

'Frank Ryan, the Aussie doctor,' he came back and there was genuine warmth in his voice. 'How are you? And what takes you back to Belgrade?'

How many hours have you got to listen? 'Can we meet, Kneza? I'm here for only a day and need advice.'

He didn't pause, didn't need time to think. 'I'll give you directions to our old haunt and see you in an hour. I hope you brought warm clothes, it's below zero on the streets.'

I couldn't hold back the dam of relief. 'Thank you, Kneza. Thank you very much.'

Now there was a silence. Then: 'This advice you need. It must be important.'

The chill took my breath away, even though I was well wrapped in my new purchases. I had never seen or touched snow in Australia and my first delight was in Europe. A few years ago I sat near a roaring fire in a house along the Hungarian–Slovenian border, watching out a window with childlike amazement as the first falls of winter drifted in from Siberia. I stayed there for most of the night, fascinated as the country-side whitened and then disappeared under a blanket of snow. The next morning I had my first snowball fight, built my first snowman and had my first photograph in a blizzard, flakes settling on my fleece protector and melting on my blazing cheeks.

Now, as I trudged through the side streets with my bottle of expensive French wine under an arm I cursed the stuff. Snowploughs and gritters had cleared the main arteries but the back roads were still hazardous and accessed only by foot. Parked cars became hazards, sidewalks impossible to feel. Shop lights glowed, throwing orange and green and blue and red shadows onto the glistening whiteness. At one corner music drifted from a first-floor hairdressing salon, an old Beatles' track. 'Is there anything that you want? Is there anything I can dooooo?'

I was following Kneza's directions. 'Turn left outside the hotel main entrance and walk for two blocks. Then turn left for another block. You will pass a row of shops offering expensive goods for the new rich.' And there it was, a decadence of designer labels in luggage, perfumes, fashion and accessories. 'Follow this row until you come to a side street on the right. Turn into that and continue to the end.' I skidded over one major road, dodging sliding cars and lorries that were unsteady despite the salt and grit surfacing. Horns blared and curses filled the freezing air. Head down and hands firmly jammed into pockets I avoided fellow travellers, not that many had ventured out.

Thirty-five minutes later and along another narrow alley I pushed open the door of a café and entered into heat, light and smoke. The rooms were buzzing, the atmosphere filled with cigarette and pipe-tobacco smoke. The conversation was loud and animated, mainly a young crowd deciding to make the best of a lousy day. Waiters struggled past overflowing tables, trays tipping with drinks and coffees and food. The ambience was pleasing, carefree and lively and I envied the mood. It was as I remembered it the last time, though now the clientele seemed flush with money. There was wine and champagne, cigars and cheroots. I scanned the tables, up one level and to another, but didn't recognise anyone. In luck, a couple vacated a setting nearby and I muscled my way in, ordered a beer and settled back. I was starving, the inflight food had been poor and insubstantial. I realised I hadn't eaten anything significant for over twelve hours and flagged for a menu, giving my order before the waiter could escape. Kneza still hadn't arrived. But I knew he would, he was reliable.

Kneza Pasica was once an activist with the Democratic Opposition of Serbia (DOS), an anti-communist, anti-Slobodan Milošević political party. Deprived of victory in the rigged elections of September 2000, DOS counter-attacked by organising popular demonstrations. Accusing Milošević of 'vote theft', the group called citizens to gather in front of the Yugoslav Federal Assembly on 5 October. DOS then demanded the resignation of the general director, main editor and staff of Radio-Television Serbia, accusing them of distorting events taking place throughout Serbia. Hundreds of thousands attended the rally and at 3.35 that afternoon, a large number broke into the parliament building, among them my friend Pasica.

Then a thirty-year-old lawyer, Pasica became actively involved in politics during the disastrous

Balkan wars. Disenchanted by the ruling regime and appalled by human-rights abuses he joined DOS and began agitating for reforms. He was arrested twice by secret police, imprisoned and beaten. Only the intervention of a local communist mayor and family friend saved him from worse treatment. But Pasica was enraged and even more determined to see change in his native country. He became a close adviser to the UN and Amnesty International, both investigating atrocities committed throughout the Balkans. When Milošević was finally overthrown Pasica rose quickly through the ranks and was soon appointed to a senior position in the Ministry of Internal Affairs.

My last conversation with him was in this very café shortly after that, when I handed over results of forensic digs in graves along the border with Albania. Pasica was preparing his government's response to verdicts at the International War Crimes Tribunal. He had his finger on the pulse of ongoing investigations and I was praying he would share some of his secrets.

He hadn't changed much. Maybe a few pounds heavier, certainly his tightly trimmed moustache was becoming grey, but other than that I recognised the lawyer immediately. He was easing his long body out of several layers of clothes, dark brown eyes darting as he took in the lunch crowd.

'What did you eat?'

I pushed a fork at the remains of steak with fries and vegetables. 'It was good. Plain and not ruined with sauces.' I flagged a waiter. 'Would you like to join me?'

He wet the tip of his moustache with his tongue, flicked over a menu and shook his head. 'No, it's too early in the day. If I have a heavy meal I'll sleep all afternoon.' In the local dialect he ordered coffee and I recognised the language, if not the meaning.

When we were alone again I offered my gift. 'Chateau Margaux, 1996. I know you like this in particular.' The story was that Kneza celebrated the fall of communism with a crate of Margaux, a bottle for every day he'd been kept in prison. Friends claimed he exaggerated the sentence for self-indulgence.

He peeled off the wrapping and inspected the label. 'You have a good memory, Dr Ryan. And thank you.' He put the bottle at his feet. 'It's still a long way to come to present it to me personally. Does DHL not collect from Ireland?'

I shrugged, unsure how to direct the conversation.

'And you've lost weight,' he added. I looked up to see him inspecting me. 'You haven't shaved today, your eyes are avoiding me and there is a haunted look to you that I don't remember.' He paused while a mug of steaming coffee was set on the table. 'What's happening?'

I drained my beer, wiped my lips with a linen napkin and faced forward, desperate to tell my story. 'OK,' I began. 'It started like this.'

It took me nearly forty minutes and he interrupted only once. 'Sefik Barisik? You are sure of the name?' I nodded. 'And from Vukovar? Vukovar in Croatia?' I nodded again.

Throughout my discourse Kneza's expression hadn't changed and I wasn't sure whether he found my predicament hilarious or dangerous. Now as he swirled the dregs of coffee, his face scrunched in concentration. The restaurant was emptying, the lunch crowd having to face the elements once more. A group of three stopped by our table and greeted Kneza and he took time out to talk with them, deliberately not introducing me even though one glanced towards me a few times. When they'd left and he was sure we wouldn't be disturbed Kneza pulled tightly in and leaned across. His moustache bobbed as he spoke.

'When we last met you told me you were returning to Australia, you'd had enough of Europe and our poisoned politics. What happened?'

I considered the question for a moment. 'I'm an adventurer, I like to stay challenged. As soon as I touch down in Sydney I'm going to have to find a regular job and become a proper doctor. I wasn't ready for that and the position in Harmon sounded exciting.'

Kneza's gaze never wandered despite the shifting of tables and chairs beside us. We were amongst the last stragglers and the waiters were hanging around, brushing at clean linen and shining clean glasses and throwing murderous looks in our direction. 'And now you find yourself in a nightmare?'

'Yes.'

'And you love this woman?'

'Yes.'

He groaned and rolled his eyes heavenwards. 'Is there still time to get out?' He was back to his practical self, dismissive of my romantic troubles. 'Could you not cut your losses and go?'

'No. I need to know what happened to Lisa. And I have to protect my family.'

He flagged for the bill, ignoring my protests to share. I was secretly delighted to keep yet another charge from my credit card. In silence we wrapped ourselves tightly against the freeze. In silence Kneza opened the café door, stopped and stared at the almost deserted streets. 'In my office they tell me they are struggling to keep the airport open.' Damn it, I cursed to myself. I can't afford to be stranded here. A heavy gloved hand rested on my shoulder. 'But don't worry, there is always one runway kept clear for emergencies. Milošević was careful to protect the airport, so we must thank him for that at least.' I offered a half-smile of thanks. 'You will be on the first flight out tomorrow, I promise. But now I must put you wise to events you know nothing about.'

18

Kneza's office was on the sixth floor of the Interior
Ministry division. It was a grand, oak-panelled area
with wonderful views over downtown Belgrade. As
I waited for my contact to get organised I stared
out through a picture window at the unusually quiet
streets below. Even though the skies were now clear-
ing, traffic was light and guarded, pedestrians shuffling through banks of snow driven onto footpaths
by ploughs. Cars edged nervously along icy roads
and steam whooshed from underground ducts like
mini geysers. Nearby buildings were frosted and
white lines peppered electricity and telephone
cables.

Inside the Ministry room a flag of the City of
Belgrade hung proudly on one wall, on another the
national emblem. The desk in the centre was
littered with paperwork, a bank of telephone and
fax machines and a PC monitor. Organised chaos,

I decided. Kneza pulled open drawer after drawer until he found an A4 pad and pushed it towards me.

'Write the names you consider important. On the left set out those who are Irish and on the right all foreigners. I'll be gone for about ten minutes and then we talk.'

He buzzed an intercom and a young woman in slacks and floral blouse came in, pen and pad ready. In local dialect Kneza issued instructions and she glanced at me, nodding and murmuring. A few minutes later a tray with bottled water and sealed glass was set in front. My minder smiled and asked me something I couldn't understand. I shrugged; she rolled her eyes and then mimed eating. I shook my head and said 'No thanks'. She came back with an 'It's a pleasure' and I was left in a no man's land of mystery. Can she speak English or not? It didn't matter; I was in neutral territory and didn't believe I'd fallen into another conspiracy.

I poured a glass of water and doodled with a pen engraved with a government logo, wondering whom to include. First was Noel Dempsey and even as I scribbled my temper rose, recalling our last encounter at a windswept aerodrome.

'I know you, don't I?' I was sitting across from him in the narrow confines of a Cessna 340 light aeroplane.

'Not that I'm aware of,' he said, 'and I doubt we mix in the same circles.'

'You rang me about six days ago, didn't you?'

'What are you talking about?'

'Yeah, you did. I recognise your voice. You told me to come to the prison, that some young guy on an assault charge had hanged himself. Come on, you must remember?'

'You're talking shite, Ryan. I've never seen you before in my life.'

'Yes, you have, you bastard. And you pointed a shotgun at me while I lay half-conscious on the ground.'

It was then that I head-butted him in the middle of his face and I've been regretting ever since that I didn't follow through with a few more body blows.

Forcing my mind clear I added Lisa Duggan, again having to keep my concentration. An image flashed, Lisa in shorts and T-shirt playing tennis the previous autumn. On the day I couldn't keep tabs of the score, mesmerised by her body and the ease with which she moved. Around 5–4 to her in the third set she stopped to take a call on her mobile, face frowning as whatever news was relayed. I stood at the net trying to listen in but quickly sensed the call was important and retreated to the baseline. One hour later I dropped her at Americabank, watching as she disappeared into the staff elevator from the underground car park. That evening, when I asked what was so important in the world of finance that she had to go in on a Sunday she deflected the query with her usual evasion.

'Banks, Frank, they do my head in. They want everything ready yesterday. Just because New York and Tokyo are on different time zones they think we should dance to their tune.'

I considered that briefly. New York and Tokyo were still on Sunday time, even if five to nine hours apart from GMT. But I didn't pursue it, deciding there could be some workaholic on the other side of the world demanding attention. Next day she left Dublin and didn't return for a week. By that stage I was very puzzled by her disappearances and excuses. What *was* going on? What family crisis demanded such bizarre behaviour?

Right now I had to park these issues and concentrate. After Lisa I scribbled Bill O'Hara, adding in brackets my understanding of his role in the Irish Justice Department. Then came prison governor Don Campbell, Patrick Halloran the staunchly Republican Justice Minister, and finally Dan Steele, cell-block king and career criminal. I was switching to the other half of the page when I suddenly remembered Conor Mason.

The right-hand side had three names: Ratko, surname unknown; Sefik Barisik (from Vukovar in Croatia), a witness-protection inmate at Harmon

Penitentiary; and then Roger Nixon (? correct name), associated with Ratko and Dan Steele. I leaned back in my chair and stared at the walls, racking my brains for other suspects. In the corridor I heard voices come and go, words I couldn't understand. Somewhere a phone rang and no one answered and I was sorely tempted to find it, if only to stop the annoying tone. Then a flash of importance, the mercenaries killed in Baghdad. Declan Tierney (criminal associate of Dan Steele) and Goran Mujkic (wanted by the International War Crimes Tribunal in the Hague). Their names hit the page just as Kneza came back.

He wasn't alone. Immediately behind him was a sombre-faced man in a sharp suit. He was about six three with close-cropped grey hair and tight lips that closed when he saw me. I made a rough guess at forty to forty-five years of age. Next was a young woman in long skirt and crew-neck sweater. Her reddish brown hair was swept back and held in place with a clasp, exaggerating her wide brow. Despite her youth, probably early thirties, she had a significant weight problem and I could see her straining to hold in her belly as we were introduced. He was Nikica and she Maria, both attached to the state secret service agency. No surnames came and I didn't ask. Anyway, the information I so desperately sought didn't extend to unnecessary data.

Kneza ushered the agents to a corner of the table where they sat forward, their gazes hardly shifting from me. Words were exchanged in Serbian as my list was scanned. Nikica took up the page and pored over it as if he was checking lottery numbers. There weren't that many names for such intense scrutiny, I thought, but obviously he believed differently as his eyes widened and then narrowed and then became neutral. The sheet was copied and one set passed to Maria who studied it for a minute or so. The original was fed into the fax machine, a number dialled and the information transferred to some distant source. Now all three faced me and I noticed Kneza trying to force a smile. It didn't come, looking more like a grimace, and for the first time I realised how much his features had sagged in the years since we'd last met. It's the job, I decided. Whatever he's working at is grinding him down.

Finally he spoke. 'Frank, tell me exactly what you want. Are you looking for the truth? For revenge? For your girlfriend?'

I started to answer but was cut short.

'You talked about your family in Australia and how concerned you are for their safety. Surely you should notify the authorities and let them handle the situation?'

It was a fair question yet one I thought Kneza would have the answer to already. He knew I was dealing with dangerous and vindictive criminals. He knew no one was safe, police protection or not, with such thugs. Hell, if Ratko flew all the way to Australia for a warning photo shoot there was little doubt he'd go back to prove he wasn't fooling. More importantly, I'd held back that I was up to my neck in a plan to spring Dan Steele from jail.

'My priority is my family. I can't sleep at night worrying about what will happen to them.' I waited, expecting this to be translated but no one interrupted. 'Then I want the truth. Too much has happened to me, too much hurt and pain, physical as well as emotional. *And* I want to see Lisa.'

'What if she doesn't want to see you?' Maria stopped me in my tracks. 'Have you considered that?' Her English was perfect.

'Yes, I have,' I lied. If somewhere in the recesses of my mind I had factored that into my thinking it wasn't taking up too much space. I had to see Lisa; I had to hear from her what was going on. And there were dark and unspoken fears that she was in danger, that whatever was involved had become greater than her powers to control. 'Revenge is no longer an issue.' Now I was telling the truth. Earlier I'd turned over motives and options and decided to bottle the blood lust and go for safety. The numbers were stacked against me, the clientele better informed and better armed. Revenge was a negative emotion compared to the protection of my family and finding Lisa.

Kneza said something in Serbian to Maria and she shrugged a reply. Then Nikica joined in and for a few minutes I found my concentration bouncing from one to the other as a discussion raged over my head. Suddenly the fax machine burst into action and soon pages were spewing onto the desk, each one picked up and inspected and then passed from one to the other. I was totally at sea, confused and agitated. What is going on?

'I have been deciding how best to explain this to you,' Kneza said at last and I suddenly realised what it must be like for a patient hanging onto a doctor's word as he inspects test results. Is it good news or bad, will I live or die? Or here, in this government room in the city of Belgrade, will I be told to go back to Australia and start another life? Shake off the dust of Europe and play safe in Adelaide?

'But I cannot think of an easy way.' He folded his arms and fixed on me. 'My colleagues are very interested in your story. It has a direct bearing on their work.' Now what could that be? 'Also, I am unable to answer all questions. Some of what you told me is bizarre and almost incredible.' Here he gave me a hard look but I immediately put him right on any doubts. 'So let me offer you help. As a friend.'

I felt a huge sigh of relief building but subdued my expression. Don't drag this out, Kneza. I'm screaming here, begging even. 'But even as a friend I am restricted in what I can say.' Now his voice was cautious, the words carefully considered. 'We are dealing with important matters, dangerous games played on an international stage. My government, the Irish government and other administrations are actively involved in many of these issues.' He pointed to my scribbles. 'Some of these names mean nothing to us so I can only tell you what is known. Noel Dempsey is a government official, I can say no more.' I'd gained no ground there and Dempsey's role remained a mystery. 'The woman Lisa Duggan did work here in Belgrade at the UN but has not been at her office for some time.'

My spirits sank. The vibes were not good. Does Kneza know more and isn't telling or is he as wise as me? Something shouted he was telling it as it is and to shut up and listen. 'OK. I'll follow that angle myself.'

Now his fingers flicked at the rest of the names. 'On Roger Nixon we can find nothing.' This did not surprise me. I believed the name Roger Nixon was false and the others straightforward. I did wonder why there was no comment about Patrick Halloran, the Irish Justice Minister.

Then Kneza shrugged and waved his hands over the desk as if casting a spell. 'Do I start with the main players, or where it all went wrong for you?'

I considered both options. Anything was better than ignorance and I was desperate for clues, names and identities. I knew what had happened, what I didn't know was why. 'Start with the main players.'

The security team settled back in their chairs. Nikica lit a cigarette and blew the smoke behind him, while Maria took out a pen and pad as if to take notes.

Kneza scanned one of the faxes and began to read me the gist of its contents. 'On 2 February this year, police in Milan went to a room in a fashionable city-centre hotel.' Milan? I was instantly dragged to yet a different country and my mind kicked into overdrive. 'This followed a complaint from a common prostitute that the resident of room 303 had availed of her services for five days in a row but was refusing to pay. The girl also stated that she had been beaten and abused and showed bruises and cuts. To local police this was no more than a routine grievance, the problem widespread in northern Italy since the influx of East European prostitutes. The street girls are usually illegal aliens and risk deportation if they come to the attention of the authorities. Men often use their services and disappear, knowing that little if anything will happen. So this girl's statement was unusual but not surprising. What was surprising was what they discovered.'

As a second fax was scrutinised Kneza pressed

the intercom and spoke to his secretary. Then he continued. 'In 303 they found Dmytro Kazelawk, a forty-five-year-old Ukrainian. He was in bed, naked and almost comatose from a cocaine overdose. Beside him were three young women, also naked and also heavily drugged. The girls were taken for treatment and questioning, the Ukrainian arrested and hospitalised and his room searched. Inside a collection of suitcases investigating officers found one hundred and fifty thousand US dollars in cash and half a million's worth of African diamonds. There was also one kilo of cocaine and a significant cache of documents. These detailed Kazelawk's involvement in oil, timber, gems, narcotics and guns. The papers showed that two weeks before this arrest he chartered an Antov-124 transport plane in Moscow, had it flown to Kyyiv in the Ukraine where it was loaded with tons of small arms, grenade launchers, sniper rifles, night-vision equipment and ammunition. The aircraft's final destination was Sierra Leone. Forged end-user certificates suggested the consignment was pledged to the legitimate forces of Sudan.'

There was a pause while more pages were shuffled. Nikica ground out his cigarette butt, leaving a trail of smoke in the air.

'Kazelawk is a native of Odessa, a trading port on the northern fringes of the Black Sea. He emigrated to Israel in the 1970s before going into the Russian oil business after the collapse of the USSR. Are you following?'

I gulped, my mind reeling. 'What has this to do with me, or Lisa Duggan, or what I was talking to you about?'

'Patience, Frank. As this unravels you will see.' He pressed the intercom and barked an order. 'We will wait for a moment.' Soon a tray with mugs and a pot of steaming coffee was set on the table and distributed. As I waited for the brew to cool I tried to get my thoughts in order. What was unfolding was almost more than I could take in.

'You may be wondering why Kazelawk came up on our security radar?' Kneza asked. Beside him the agents shared out milk and sugar and there was a moment's lapse while personal tastes were sorted.

I shrugged. 'Why is he important?'

'Kazelawk provided guns and ammunition to communist Serb militiamen in the early nineties. He was a personal friend of Goran Babic, a senior official in the Serbian Democratic Party of BiH, and colluded with criminal elements in various militias. He was seen in Bosnia in July 1995, advising on the segregation of Muslim families when the spa town of Srebrenica was overrun. In Srebrenica, over a period of five days, seven thousand men and boys were systematically murdered in fields, schools and warehouses. Kazelawk organised a convoy of heavy machinery to dig mass graves and hide the massacre. For this he was rewarded with cash and diamonds.'

Now a link was forming in my mind and I had a sense of where Kneza was leading me. Another fax page was fingered and explained. 'The official, Goran Babic, is wanted by the War Crimes Tribunal for offences that include genocide, holding UN peacekeepers as hostage, rape, murder, and terrorising and demoralising Bosnian Muslim and Bosnian Croat civilians.'

From a folder I hadn't noticed she was carrying Maria slid a photo across the table. My blood went cold when I saw the image. 'This man you have already met?' Her eyebrows raised and I nodded a weak yes. 'He is Ratko Predojevic, a crook with links to the old Yugoslav secret police and a member of the notorious "Tigers" paramilitary gang. Ratko served the Serb war machine well, killing and terrorising non-Serb populations. He is also wanted for war crimes.'

My mind was teeming with information, none of it good. Ratko, my tormentor, was worse than I believed. 'Is there more?' I asked, hoping there wasn't.

Kneza pulled a face and the agents exchanged looks. 'Yes.'

I set my mug down with both hands to disguise the shake that I felt coursing through my limbs. What's next?

'Both Kazelawk and Predojevic –' Kneza corrected himself: 'or Ratko as you know him – are linked to the gangster Milos Bracchovis. Bracchovis runs drugs and guns through Albania to the rest of Europe. He also provides victims for the sex-slave industry in Kosovo. He has abducted, bought or recruited as many as two thousand women, many of them under-age girls. Sources tell us these unfortunates are tortured, raped, abused and then criminalised. All to satisfy the massive Western presence in the area.'

I wasn't sure I could take much more. My life as a doctor hadn't exposed me to such international criminality. Until I came to Europe. During my time in Kosovo and working with Amnesty International I'd caught a snapshot of war crimes and brutality. However, this new information made me feel physically sick. And I still hadn't heard how I came to be embroiled in the situation, or what Lisa Duggan's role was.

'Now we come to the Irish dimension.' I sat bolt upright.

'Bracchovis has been running guns to conflict zones for years. The man in Harmon Penitentiary you spoke about –' Kneza looked to me for a name and I told him Dan Steele. 'Yes, Steele. He has been providing cover and organising bank accounts in Cyprus, Greece, Turkey and Thailand. He moved from common criminal to arms trader, linking

Ukraine to Africa.' Here he allowed himself a weak smile. 'Much more lucrative.'

Nikica interrupted. 'Steele is at the centre of an international investigation into the global arms trade. He has connections with all the major players and has considerable assets salted away in offshore banks.'

In law-enforcement terms I knew 'considerable assets' meant exactly that, probably millions of US dollars. Why then, I asked myself, did he follow two small-time crooks and murder them when he could be hanging out somewhere and enjoying his ill-gotten gains? 'Nobody got hurt unless they crossed me.' Steele's words echoed in my head. Even though the monster had a fortune stashed he couldn't hold back his lust for revenge. And his desire to escape from Harmon became more than a hunger for freedom. Steele wanted to claim his booty.

Maria spoke. 'The two killed in Baghdad were not security personnel. They were arms dealers negotiating a shipment of artillery and ammunition to Iraqi insurgents. Communication intercepts suggest they were offering to supply enriched uranium stolen from a decommissioned USSR nuclear reactor. The CIA believes there was a plan to explode a dirty bomb in the green zone of the city. If that had happened the consequences would be catastrophic.'

I forced through a question to try and keep my understanding clear. 'What does the witness-protection inmate have to do with this?'

'Sefik Barisik is one of three dispersed to safe custody in centres around Europe. There was an attempt on his life and he was treated at a US military hospital.' That explained the bullet-entry scar under his right clavicle. And how an American doctor came to be involved in diagnosing asthma later. Kneza went on. 'Sefik survived the slaughter of 261 non-Serbs rounded up at the hospital in Vukovar in Croatia. Two men were actively involved in this killing spree, Milos Bracchovis and Ratko Predojevic.'

'And where is Bracchovis now?' I had a vague idea where Ratko was.

'He was arrested at the beginning of February following a gun battle in the hills outside Zagreb. He is in a military compound in Germany. To the world media he is still at large and being hunted but soon he will be brought before the courts. And then Sefik Barisik will be taken from that Irish prison to present his account. Keeping him unharmed until then is an international priority.'

'But if it is known there is a link between Dan Steele and Bracchovis, why put him there? Steele knows everything about him.'

'That I cannot help you with. I can make you

understand your personal nightmare but I cannot reveal classified information just because your lover is missing. There is a bigger picture here. You are embroiled in an intelligence operation linking a number of governments. The successful prosecution of Bracchovis will allow investigators to break up a network spreading from eastern to western Europe and beyond. The thugs involved are active in narco-terrorism, people trafficking, forced prostitution and arms smuggling. This country is under considerable pressure from Washington to bring Bracchovis to trial and secure a conviction. It is considered a test of our resolve to deal with past issues.' Now the group disappeared into another conversation and I was left to my thoughts. This was bigger than my worst fears. I was searching for some mind scheme to put all I'd heard into context when Maria interrupted.

'The Irish Justice Minister, Patrick Halloran. He is considered a strong man?'

Halloran came with a formidable reputation, anti-terrorist, anti-crime, and anti-everything. He'd forced my dismissal as CMO to Harmon after the so-called 'incident' in London. I'd never met him but was aware he kept a close eye on all things criminal.

'Yes,' I said, 'he is a strong man.'

'Many of your problems could be resolved if you spoke with him.'

I offered a wry smile. 'I'll certainly try that first thing.'

As I was being escorted from the building Kneza took me to one side. 'We have a consulate in Dublin. Check there in forty-eight hours. I may have extra information for you.' He glanced around to make sure we weren't being overheard. 'You will be collected from your hotel at five tomorrow morning and put on whatever flight can get out. Hopefully you can then make an onward connection to Dublin.' He shook my hand with a grip that almost broke my knuckles. 'Good luck.' I was left staring at a whiteness that seemed to stretch for ever.

For the first time I seriously wondered if I could win this battle. Once I'd considered it a heavyweight contest, each round an exchange of blows between the Justice Department and myself. Then, with Dan Steele's involvement, I switched to bush tactics, allowing the opposition get the upper hand before I finally ended the conflict with killer punches. Now I wasn't sure about any strategy. The opposition was bigger and more dangerous than I could ever have possibly imagined.

19

When they came for me the next morning I was waiting. For the second night in a row I hadn't slept, tormented by the new and chilling information and equally tormented by the lack of hard intelligence on Lisa. They came in military uniforms and in a convoy of covered army jeeps with snow chains on the wheels for better grip. They came in a foul mood and with angry eyes, each command a grunted and bad-tempered gesture. They drove slowly along ghost roads, deserted and still with only office and street lights suggesting life. There were few shadows in the total white-out, the only other traffic trucks and occasional taxis. Outside it was five degrees below freezing and I huddled into my woollens for comfort.

The first conversation I had was at the Alitalia check-in at Belgrade airport. My destination, I learned, was Rome. The patrol leader, a burly man wearing a long grey overcoat and peaked military cap, barked orders so loudly the exhausted young woman behind the counter jumped with fright. As I was checked in I found myself among a red-faced, sweating and angry scrum trying to flee the city. Most had been stranded for twenty-four hours, others coming up on forty-eight. Tension was running high and tempers were flaring. Small children wailed from lack of sleep and food while their agitated parents tried to claim a flight out. Italy was as good a destination as anywhere. Rome was clear with normal air traffic. For the majority the Eternal City would be no more than a set-down point to their final destinations.

Thirty minutes later, after I was hurried through immigration channels and onto the aircraft like a celebrity, the cabin crew couldn't hide their dismay. Two days' beard, hair dishevelled, haunted face and bleary eyes. Crumpled clothes. That was the down-and-out-looking VIP they got.

The take-off was delayed an hour as snow-ploughs fought overnight drifts and men in thick jackets sprayed de-icing fluid on the wings. When the jet finally lifted just after eight the daylight was poor with fresh falls blanketing the countryside.

Aeroplane journeys are good for thinking. You can't watch television and channel hop. You can't go for a walk or a drive or distract yourself in any usual way. So on the morning of 8 March as I sat in the first-class section of the Alitalia 707 I nursed coffee and croissants and stared at the countryside below. Mountain ranges loomed large, hills and valleys no more than soft white undulations in the vast plains of central Europe. Above, in a sky so blue you almost wanted to touch it, an orange sun burned brightly. In better times I might have enjoyed these views. But these were not good times and I was preoccupied.

I was no wiser about Noel Dempsey.

'*Un altro caffè, signore?*' A cabin steward bustled. I was the sole premier passenger and behind me the plane was full. Perhaps Kneza had arranged this for my safety. 'Yes, please.' My fine bone-china cup was topped up, a half eaten croissant cleared.

And I was no wiser about Lisa. *Except*, why did Maria, the secret-service agent, challenge me? I have to see Lisa, I'd said. 'What if she doesn't want to see you?' Maria knew something. Maybe not a lot but enough. Why would Lisa *not* want to see me? Now old conversations flooded my mind. 'Marry me, Lisa. Marry me and I promise you I'll make you the unhappiest woman in the world.' Words I'd sworn I'd never use with any woman until I was at least forty.

'Is that a proposal, Dr Ryan?'

'If it is will you say yes?'

321

'No.'

'Why not?'

'Because it's too risky, Frank. It's too risky.'

The plane was enveloped in a bank of clouds, the terrain below no more than a misting memory. What was too risky? Was it too risky in love and some uncertainty about our relationship? Or too risky because of her work at the UN? I cursed myself now for not questioning her words at the time.

Now a different puzzle surfaced, triggered by another comment from Maria. 'The Irish Justice Minister, Patrick Halloran. He is considered a strong man?'

'Yes, he is a strong man.'

'Many of your problems could be resolved if you spoke with him.'

No chance. Halloran forced through my sacking at cabinet level and wouldn't give me the time of day. He considered me dirt, a lowlife in the Harmon Penitentiary food chain. There wasn't a hope in hell he'd explain anything to me. We hit an air pocket and my stomach lurched. I heard ohs and ahs from behind and then an intercom warning in three languages to refasten seatbelts until the turbulence cleared. I glanced at the right wing, watching it tilt in the air currents. I didn't care if we crashed. I didn't care if I never saw tomorrow. I was tired of fighting, tired of the deceit

322

and treachery. Maybe it *was* time to go home. I closed my mind and tried to doze.

Somewhere behind a child screamed and I jumped in the seat, my legs jerking, my eyes desperate to stay shut. I needed sleep, my body cried out for rest. Instead, Ratko's murderous image blocked any peace. 'Ratko Predojevic is a crook with links to the old Yugoslav secret police and a member of the notorious "Tigers" paramilitary gang . . . He is also wanted for war crimes.' Ratko was worse than my worst nightmare. 'Ratko Predojevic and Milos Bracchovis were actively involved in the slaughter of two hundred and sixty-one non-Serbs rounded up at the hospital in Vukovar in Croatia.' That was the link to the witness-protection inmate at Harmon. 'Bracchovis has been running guns to conflict zones for years . . . the man in Harmon Penitentiary . . . Dan Steele . . . has been providing cover and organising bank accounts . . . He moved from common criminal to arms trader, linking Ukraine to Africa . . . Steele is at the centre of an international investigation into the global arms trade.'

Now I knew everything about Dan Steele. But I also had a new and dangerous enemy to think about: Milos Bracchovis. 'Bracchovis runs drugs and guns through Albania to the rest of Europe. He also provides victims for the sex-slave industry in Kosovo.' Bracchovis was in jail, hidden from the world in a military compound and awaiting trial. Like Dan Steele, Bracchovis would undoubtedly have outside helpers plotting to seek and kill the main witnesses. And one of them, Sefik Barisik, was under my care at Harmon Penitentiary.

Not for the first time I wondered how I'd become embroiled in an international conspiracy involving secretive government agencies. But the answer was clear – through Lisa Duggan. My lover had unwittingly dragged me into an investigation she was pursuing through the UN. A thought jolted me and I struggled to sit up. Or is she working elsewhere and using the UN as a front? After all, I thought, she did use Americabank as a cover. She even seduced innocent colleagues into concealing her true activities. No matter which way I looked at the situation I kept running in circles, dangerous and razor-sharp circles.

I glanced up to find the cabin steward staring at me anxiously. '*Sta bene?*' His eyes searched for an English offering. 'You are well, sir?'

I forced a smile and tried to make myself look less like a madman. 'Yes, thanks. I've just had a bad run recently.' Whether that was understood I couldn't decide as he backed away, suspicious glances darting. I ran a hand through my hair. I need a haircut, that's a priority. I remembered the muscle ache that had dragged on after my beating and moved both arms in an arc, silently pleased nothing twinged. At least my body was healing, if not my mind. Second priority, check if Conor Mason has sourced the extra hardware. And then talk with Dan Steele. I had moved on from protector to avenger, I now knew too much about Steele and his international criminality. I wanted to destroy him and his network.

At a crowded Rome airport I managed to get a trim while I waited for an Aer Lingus flight to Dublin. The barber, a bald and podgy man with podgy fingers, tried to engage me in conversation and show off his English but I was not in the mood to indulge him and he lapsed into a grumpy silence. For thirty euros he shaved my stubble and washed and cut my hair and by the time he dusted me off and threw me out I was sorry I hadn't been more polite. But I was too distracted by events and found it difficult to be civil to anyone. And that included the elderly man who sat beside me on the flight to Ireland and who was determined to tell me everything about his tour of the Vatican. Somewhere over France I told him to 'shut the fuck up' and he immediately transferred to another seat. I was left to myself, inspecting yet another bank of clouds. I noticed green-uniformed staff checking every ten minutes. More suspicious eyes and doubtful frowns. Watch it, Ryan, you'll get a reputation.

At the arrivals terminal in Dublin airport I called Conor Mason. He was guarded in his replies and I hoped that was because he didn't want to be overheard. One minute later I received a text.

GOODS ARRIVED. COLLECT 2NITE.
WILL CALL @ 10.

I checked my watch. It was now five thirty. I caught a cab to my apartment and showered and changed my clothes. Amongst a pile of junk mail was a letter from my bank manager advising that I had exceeded my overdraft limit. 'Perhaps you would make an appointment to discuss this?' I made a quick call to the branch and lied that my next pay cheque would leave me significantly in credit. It wouldn't and I was damned if I knew what would. I briefly considered doing out-of-hours medical work to supplement my income and gain some cash. But I dismissed that notion. I had to stay on track and avoid diversions, no matter how pressing. I withdrew one hundred euros from an ATM and grabbed a fish supper from a nearby takeaway, washing down the battered cod and vinegar-soaked chips with a Pepsi. It was a far cry from romantic dinners at expensive Italian restaurants with Lisa. Hunger still gnawed at my belly and I munched on chocolate while I sheltered from a steady drizzle that soaked the streets and rainbow-rippled neon signs. I felt cold, lonely and abandoned.

Before I started the late shift at the medical facility of Harmon Penitentiary I was updated on the situation by my nurse. There was the usual litany of minor and possibly major issues, cuts and abrasions, aches and pains. We sifted through the list, deciding on immediate, can wait and too trivial for consideration. With an air of unexaggerated innocence I asked about J-wing and any problems there? I was met with a blank stare. J-wing is empty, I was told. J-wing has been empty for weeks. J-wing is having a sanitation upgrade. My nurse was ignorant of the real position and offered nothing to suggest that my witness-protection patient needed attention. Either he'd been moved while I was away (unlikely) or had improved. One way or another I'd find out eventually.

In the mean time, there was the daily grind of prison health and I wasn't surprised to find Dan Steele fourth in line waiting to see me. The first three patients had relatively minor ailments, or minor compared to their usual pressing problems. Number one had noticed his urine becoming darker and his eyes were very obviously jaundiced. He had Hepatitis B and C from sharing infected needles for shooting up and I assumed his liver function

327

had deteriorated. I ordered fresh bloods to update his status. The second inmate had infected sores on his legs from trying out new veins to inject. The third had severe back pain and stood during the consultation.

'How did it start?'

He was a small man in his thirties with little body fat. He had a wide forehead with narrow, suspicious eyes that searched my desk for something to steal. 'I heard something crack. I couldn't get up.' He threw a hand towards his lumbar area and offered a wince. His face scrunched in discomfort, his brow furrowed and he leaned heavily onto the chair in front.

I inspected him closely. Men with his body mass and build don't usually develop sudden and un-explained back problems. According to the medical records I had sight of he was fit and active and boxed regularly. His demeanour screamed fake, the agony exaggerated, and the frown too deep and prolonged. There was no pain in his eyes, only hopeful expectation. And possible larceny.

'Maybe we should get an X-ray?' I suggested and his face lit up. That was all he wanted, a day out from prison where he could see female flesh at close quarters and probably eat one decent meal. It was a frequent and easily recognised problem at the clinic. Was the complaint real or contrived? Physical examination was almost always unremarkable and the patients well versed in the correct signs and symptoms of spinal disease. They knew how to fake anything from epilepsy to heart attacks.

Tonight I decided not to make a fuss and went straight for an X-ray. I could slip this and Dan Steele's request in with a group of three already decided on. That would offer a better chance of the radiological requests being accepted and also make it easier for the governor to arrange security. My job was to force the issue with enough significant clinical details. If the inmates were sick enough the authorities had to run with the treating doctor's decisions. Usually, if a group of prisoners needed X-rays a radiologist would have been ordered to spend a day at the jail using the on-site machine. But the apparatus was still damaged and back at the medical-supply company awaiting spare parts. And the man who'd sabotaged it in the first place was now settling into the seat opposite.

'Where the fuck have you been? You disappeared off my radar again.' It was three days since I'd made my pact with Steele and I was surprised at how ill he'd managed to make himself appear in that time. Even in the poor light his pugilist's nose looked more prominent against sunken cheeks. His lips seemed thinner, his skin pale and unhealthy. I turned a swivel lamp to get a better view. The snake tattoo sagged on his turkey neck and the nicotine staining on his fingers was deeper and longer than before, now reaching his knuckles. The V-shaped scar that ran from left ear to chin was taut, a sign that he was agitated and uptight. Join the club.

'Here and there,' I offered. 'Met a few people, learned a few things.' I leaned into my chair and kept eye contact. 'Your friends Ratko and Nixon offered nothing but threats against my family so I had to go further to hear the truth.' This was a dangerous game I was playing. How much should I say? How much should I hold back?

'And what'd you hear?' He was clenching and unclenching his fists.

'I know about Sierra Leone and Ukraine.' I watched for a reaction. There was none, he sat stony faced, his eyes searching mine. 'And I now know everything about Ratko. Nixon's proving more difficult; I just can't get a handle on him. English accent but with a good command of languages. That's not your usual company.'

'Gerry is ex-British army,' Steele cut through, immediately giving me the real first name of Roger Nixon. 'He speaks about five languages and knows his way around every hot spot in Europe and Africa. Gerry would slit your throat quick as look at you.'

'I'm sure he would. But not if I take him out

first.' It was bravado but I had to let Steele feel that his cronies didn't intimidate me.

He snorted his disgust. 'Go fuck yourself, doc. You don't fool me.'

I leaned forward on the desk. 'This is no game we're playing, is it? When you threatened my folks you changed the ground rules.'

My anger didn't faze him. 'Now you know not to double-cross me,' he said. 'If I don't get you I'll get someone close enough. And by the time I'm finished you'll even wish I had got you.' That was no idle warning, as I knew from his past record.

I pretended not to be intimidated. 'What if I say no? Huh? What if I back off now and haul in the Australian police for protection?'

A ghost sneer flickered. 'You'll do what I tell you.'

'We'll both do what we each tell one another,' I came back.

Steele shrugged, as if he was indulging a difficult child. 'Whatever.'

I rested my hands behind my head and tried to force an air of confidence. 'I was called to J-wing two nights ago.'

'I know.' Harmon Penitentiary held no secrets.

'I have chapter and verse on the inmate holed up there.'

'And?'

'There's a connection, isn't there?'

'Not something I'd follow if I were you, doc. I was hoping to keep you away from this for a while longer. You're entering dangerous territory.'

'Dangerous to me or you?'

'Both of us. Stay away or you'll get sucked into something you won't come out of.'

'Like what?'

'Like a bullet in the back of the head while you're writing prescriptions or a knife between the ribs when you're climbing into bed. Anything can happen. It's a risky world out there. Don't make it more difficult.'

I sensed Steele wasn't going to allow further discussion. But now he knew that I knew. Now he knew I wasn't sitting idly at home twiddling my thumbs. I decided the mind games were over, it was time to push the agenda further. 'Today I'm going to call the nurse in while I go through the motions of a full physical.'

He nodded.

'You're going to say the headaches are much the same but no worse than the last day. I don't want you to exaggerate or start moaning. Just tell it like I say.'

His eyes told me he was following every word.

I made careful notes in his file. 'I heard you got sick yesterday.'

'I did,' the growl was as deep as the grave, 'and I've been starving myself.'

That explained the dramatic increase in cigarette consumption; he was smoking to dull his hunger. 'Start eating again, small amounts and don't bolt the food down.'

'Have you tasted the food here? Nobody bolts it down.'

I allowed a half-smile. The kitchens at Harmon weren't likely to win awards, unless the number of rats caught there could be considered a world record. 'It doesn't matter, start eating. Make yourself sick tomorrow morning and make sure that it's noticed and recorded.'

'Done.'

I checked my time. Steele had been with me eleven minutes. I knew Bill O'Hara monitored these visits and they could be interpreted two ways. Steele was genuinely unwell and required the extra attention. That's what I was hoping they'd accept. Or Steele and I were plotting something. That's what I believed they'd be thinking. It was cat and mouse, neither side declaring a hand and both watching the other closely. I pressed on.

'I'm putting in formal requests for X-rays for you and four others. In your case I really should be going for an MRI scan . . .' I waved his questioning look away, 'but to get that you would need to be seen by at least three other doctors. You'd be rumbled immediately. By going for something simple I can swing the request. The rest is up to you.'

'You're talking sense now, doc. I'll see you're looked after when this is over.'

I put down my pen and faced the murderer. 'I don't want anything to do with you ever again. If you pull this off, then disappear. Don't make contact with me, don't come looking for me and don't set foot in the southern hemisphere. If I see you I'll kill you.'

'You're taking this too personally. Think of it as another job.'

'Fuck off.'

'My needs coincide with your needs. We can solve two problems at the same time.'

I pretended to add more details to his file, as much to give myself time to think as to calm the desire to reach out and strangle the bastard. 'Before we go any further I need more information.'

'Like?'

'Who is Noel Dempsey?'

Steele grinned, too smugly for my liking. 'He's my ace card. When I'm in that van and on my way to the City Hospital I'll make sure you hear. But not until then.'

'Then my commitment ends now.'

'No, it doesn't. You haven't asked about Lisa Duggan.'

This was like a fist in the face and I grabbed the desk to control the rage surging through my body. Steele had avoided answering my questions about Lisa when first challenged.

'You're still looking for her, aren't you?' He was goading me.

I eased myself back and fixed on him. There was no mistaking the triumphant look. Gotcha by the balls.

'Where is she?'

'In Dublin.'

My heart took off like a jet fighter. 'Where in Dublin?'

Steele's gleeful expression deepened. 'Ask your stooges at Justice. They know.'

I snapped. His gloating was more than I could take. Days of mental anguish and sleepless nights collapsed my control and I lunged across the desk and grabbed him by the throat. 'Where is she, you bastard? Don't fuck with me. Where is she?'

Maybe it was lack of strength from five days with little food but Steele couldn't prise my choking fingers from his neck. His face went puce, his lips twisted and suddenly turned purple. His eyes went a sudden and dramatic red and started to water. My rage surged like a torrent unleashed and I couldn't stop myself. I tightened my grip, delighting in the bulging eyes and contorted features. Pinpoint blood spots burst like a rash on his skin.

'Where is she?' I was beyond control, shouting and rocking his head back and forward as his nails dug into my hands, trying desperately to free the strangling grasp. Suddenly I felt a vice-like grab on my testicles. A dull and sickening ache filled my gut as Steele twisted and turned his handful until I pulled away, panting and gasping. Steele coughed violently and drew lungfuls of air into his chest, spluttering and wheezing and clinging to the desk for support. There was froth on his lips and his tongue was protruding and he spat out, then coughed and took a deep breath and then spat out again. I fell back into the chair, exhausted and drained and shocked by my crazed fury. Now I knew my breaking point, now I knew my mind could take no more. The deceit and treachery, half-truths and downright lies had caught up with me. I was beyond being pushed to everyone's agenda. I had started to fight back.

Steele clutched at his throat, his breaths still rasping, his eyes still bulging but now full of murder. 'You . . . you . . . you fucking bastard. You'll pay for that, I swear you will.' There were deep indentations and welts on his neck, his face red and bloated and vicious. I didn't care. I half wished I had killed him, ending one part of the torment I'd been subjected to. Yet that wouldn't have resolved the bigger issues. My family would have been targeted as reprisal; I would have lost Lisa forever. And I would have ended up among the very criminals I was employed to look after. As I fixed on the killer's cruel stare I believed I was preparing for the final showdown. It was me against Steele and his homicidal cronies and me against shadowy government agencies using me as a pawn.

'We'll both pay for our actions.' My fury was still white hot but now contained. 'We'll both get what's coming to us.'

20

20

By eight thirty that evening I had composed myself
sufficiently to make a telephone call. 'Hi. My Name
is Dr Frank Ryan and I'm CMO to Harmon
Penitentiary. I'd like to arrange X-rays for a group
of inmates, please. The clinical details were faxed
ten minutes ago.' I was through to the after-hours
booking service at the City Hospital. My query drew
a deathly silence at the other end of the line. Then:
'Can you hold a moment, Dr Ryan? I need to talk
to the duty radiologist.'

'Sure.'

I wasn't expecting this to be easy. On Dublin's
Northside, a little over three miles from the prison,
the City Hospital was the Justice Department's only
medical services provider. However, for security
reasons staff there were none too enamoured with
processing convicts. And with good cause. In the
past there had been desperate and often violent

escape bids through the facility. One HIV-positive inmate with Hepatitis C threatened to bite anyone who got in his way as he crawled down a drain-pipe from the cardiology unit. Unfortunately for him, he fell two levels and cracked a leg, thus frus-trating the getaway and wrecking any hope of sympathy from the medics. There had been other breaks for freedom through the dermatology divi-sion (female detainee presenting with an angry and painful rash brought on by deliberate scouring with sandpaper and then bleach), ophthalmology (tiny metal object in right eye, carefully lodged there by a cellmate), haematology (anaemia, deliberate from blood letting while in the shower), orthopaedics (severe back pain that so incapacitated the convict he was stretchered into the clinic, but ten minutes later this same semi-invalid was seen sprinting through the car park in a vain attempt to outpace pursuing warders). The radiology department had been abused recently and it was understandable that investigation requests would be greeted with little enthusiasm.

The receptionist returned, her voice suggesting horror. 'Did you say a *group* of prisoners?'

'Yeah. Five, to be exact. I decided to collect them in a bunch rather than string this out over days. One security detail for five is cheaper than a separate squad for each offender. We can have them in and out of your department within an hour. None of the

339

requests is complicated.' Earlier I'd typed the convict names and prison IDs and added individual medical histories.

'One moment.' While the unfortunate girl tried to track down the on-call doctor I was offered a string quartet. Ignoring the music, I went over the immediate consequences of the Dan Steele incident. After the fracas I forced Steele onto the examination couch, lying to the startled warder who'd heard the commotion and hurried in, baton drawn and can of Mace ready.

'I was waiting for the panic alarm. You OK?'

Presenting myself as calm as my adrenalin-soaked system allowed I told him Steele 'had almost collapsed'. Steele 'showed features of a grand mal epileptic attack'. Steele 'shook uncontrollably, shouted and had difficulty breathing'. There wasn't much deceit in that description. I had offered 'immediate help, protecting his airway and laying him in the recovery position'. This was a pack of lies but the warder bought the deal, even asking whether I wanted an ambulance. No, I said, the crisis is over. I'll take it from here.

Then, good doctor that I am, I called the nurse and relayed the same story, sharing whispered fears that Steele might have a brain tumour. I told her I was going to arrange a skull X-ray to rule out bony damage. (Another untruth: 'He says he was in a fight recently and crashed his head against iron bars.

He could have a skull fracture. If the films are clear I'll have to push for an MRI scan.')

My nurse was a middle-aged lady who'd returned to duties after many years' absence while she reared her family. Her clinical skills were second to none but she was intimidated by the prison and its inmates and rarely challenged complaints. She deferred to my judgement in matters of responsibility and was obviously pleased to have the high-profile murderer removed from her care.

Throughout the false explanations and muttered exchanges Steele scowled at me from a distance. Propped up on an elbow on the couch he massaged his neck, firing threatening glances when no one was looking. But his conduct didn't intimidate, the game was up as far as I was concerned and the final days of the nightmare closing in. In Belgrade I'd told Kneza my motivation was safety for family and girlfriend. But the stomach-churning facts I'd learned about Dan Steele and his criminal associates changed everything. I now wanted to destroy them all. Also, by attacking him I had put my life on the line. Details of this were probably already with his outside cronies. However, I knew there'd be no move on me until he escaped. Then he'd hunt with all the murderous help he could muster. And if he couldn't find me he'd put a contract on my family. It was a no-win situation unless I delivered a killer blow to him and his organisation.

'Dr Ryan, it's Terry Killop here,' a male voice cut through my troubled thoughts. Deep brogue, rich tones. 'I'm head of the radiology division at the City.'

'I'm sorry to disturb you this late,' I began, 'but I couldn't get through during office hours.' Another lie in what was becoming a litany.

The pleasantries ended there. 'I'm sure you're aware of the difficulties we've had with some of your charges?' said Killop.

'Indeed I am. Nobody's more tuned in to these problems than me but at the same time I am accountable for their health and can't work in the dark.'

'I appreciate that, Dr Ryan—'

'Call me Frank.'

'—but I have responsibility for the employees here. In the past my unit has been used for escape bids. One prisoner arranged for accomplices to attack the staff as a diversion. Another criminal cleared the ground floor with CS gas. Now, that behaviour doesn't help me recruit and retain highly qualified and experienced radiographers. They'll get the same pay but a damn sight better conditions in any of the other hospitals in this city.' The deep brogue had changed to a complaining growl. I had nothing but sympathy for Killop's plight; hell, if I was in a similar situation I'd be protesting just as strongly. And in truth I was setting up an appointment for Dan Steele in the full knowledge that he was planning a breakout. Indeed, considering how much I knew about Steele and his henchmen my plan was reckless in the extreme. But equally I knew my requests would succeed, no matter how much the doctor argued. The City Hospital was contracted by the state to provide facilities to Harmon Penitentiary.

'It's impossible to practise good medicine without investigation access,' I said. 'I have five men with significant symptoms and enough clinical findings to justify further evaluation. I can't walk away from them and they certainly can't go looking for a second opinion somewhere else.' Wild and dangerous as my strategy was I was still determined to see it through.

There was a long pause and I could almost hear Killop turning over the situation in his head. 'Dr Ryan, what guarantees can you give that there won't be any trouble?'

It was still the formal Dr Ryan. 'None. I'm health officer, not the security chief.'

There was another awkward moment with heavy breathing and now I sensed suppressed anger. 'Call them out,' he snapped.

I ruffled paper as if checking notes. 'One lumbar-sacral spines film—'

'Reason?'

'There should be a fax in fr—'

'I'm looking at it right this minute. I want to

343

hear from you why this man needs a lumbar-sacral spines X-ray.'

I sighed, as if annoyed my judgement was being questioned. 'Low back pain for eight months, recent acute exacerbation with left sciatic nerve irritation. Restricted movement and reduced ankle reflex. This is a preliminary film before I ask for a more detailed analysis.'

Pause. 'OK, I'll take him. Next.'

'Two inmates with coughs unresponsive to standard therapies. Both are heavy smokers and one had an episode of haemoptysis. There could be pulmonary lesions here.'

'Humph, I suppose you're right. I'll allow them. Next.' He wasn't accommodating with much grace.

'Follow-up right tib and fib for patient who sustained a compound fracture ten months ago. He still complains of ache and has a significant limp. I'm not convinced there's anything wrong but have to make sure I'm on solid ground before I challenge him. Criminals are just as litigious as the general population. Miss a diagnosis or mess up a treatment and they call in their lawyers just like everyone else.'

'OK, I'll allow it. Last one now, why a skull X-ray?'

This was the formal request for Dan Steele.

'You've read the notes I sent?'

Killop called out my own words. '"Headaches for some time. Recent vomiting and worsening of symptoms with bending and stooping. Blunt trauma to right temporal area three weeks ago. Please arrange AP and lateral films of skull, query bone fracture. If X-ray negative and symptoms persist this man will need an MRI scan to rule out intra-cranial pathology."' I'd made it up, mixing and matching symptoms to add a level of doubt about diagnosis with just enough suspicion to justify radiological assessment.

'You're considering a brain tumour, aren't you?'

'It is a concern,' I agreed, suitably sombre.

'Why not go for an MRI scan?'

Oh, that would be great. I'll hang on until you get a free slot. That's what my response should have been if I was genuine. 'I'd like to rule out a fracture first,' is what I said.

'You're the doctor,' Killop came back. 'He's your patient.'

Damn sure he is. That's my main problem. 'Yeah,' was all I could offer.

'Give me a minute. I need to access the unit booking system.'

'Sure. Take as long as you need.' I believed I'd swung it, however begrudgingly. Now there was much to plan. As soon as I had a date and time I would pass this information to the prison governor. He in turn would probably relay the facts to Bill

O'Hara at the Justice Department. What happened then was anyone's guess but I assumed there would be a significant security troop arranged, both en route and at the hospital. Also, since the Irish government was aware of Dan Steele's international criminality, advance preparations would be made to prevent any escape. One way or another it was shaping up for a showdown.

'Can you bring them in first thing on the eleventh?'

My heart jumped at the sudden realisation that this was going through. Today was 8 March. In three days' time I would set in train a chain of events with explosive and far-reaching consequences. I considered the options quickly. 'No, that's too early in the morning. There's rush hour to consider and I don't want them delayed.'

The radiologist grunted something unintelligible and I heard a PC keyboard being hammered. 'How about ten thirty? I can clear the department twenty minutes beforehand to allow a clean run at this and have them out by twelve.'

'That sounds good. Go ahead and make the arrangements.' I felt my legs wobble. The implications were sinking deeper. 'Thanks for your help.'

Now came the backlash. 'If this hospital wasn't getting significant grants to look after those scum I wouldn't have them about the place.' Killop's control was slipping. 'Or you for that matter.'

'I'll certainly keep that in mind.'

'I want the governor to send me a detailed security strategy for these men.' He was on a run now, his self-righteous streak in full flow. 'I will not have my division intimidated or my staff cowed.'

'I'm not sure that's possible. The Justice Department tends to keep security plans tight to the chest. But I'll pass on your concerns.'

'If anything happens, Dr Ryan, I will hold you personally responsible.' The line went dead leaving me staring at the receiver. All hell will break out, I thought. And I will be responsible.

I made my way towards the prison exit along the usual route. First I signed off with the protection warder, both of us acknowledging the number of inmates who'd presented themselves for attention and that the same names had returned to their cells. Before I was allowed further he rang the blocks to double-check that the patients had been restored to prisoner status and hadn't wandered off to another wing. Why I had to hang around I never understood but it was tradition and one I wasn't going to argue with. Finally cleared, I walked the hundred or so yards along landings and spiral staircases, my path blocked by solid steel doors that opened when I flashed my ID. For some reason the short journey was unusually delayed, bolts taking longer to turn than I remembered, the duty officers staring suspiciously.

Do they know something? Maybe my nurse wasn't fooled by the Dan Steele charade and reported her concerns? Maybe I'm going to be detained and questioned before I leave? I kept a calm exterior even though my insides were far from quiet. My guts knotted and my forehead beaded with sweat.

I gripped my Gladstone tightly, its worn leather offering inner strength. The black bag had been passed on to me as a gift from a bush doctor out of New South Wales. He'd worked the outback for years, delivering babies, pulling teeth, stitching wounds and mending broken bones. Most of his career he'd practised by instinct, relying on blood tests and X-rays only when pushed. Forceps deliveries, heart attacks, asthma attacks, panic attacks, brain haemorrhages, stomach haemorrhages, kidney stones, gall stones, biliary colic. He'd seen and dealt with most everything and hadn't been sued once, a record in modern times. And that included setting fractures, excising skin cancers and restoring shoulder dislocations without anaesthetic. Rumour had it he even drained a sub-dural haematoma with a DIY Black & Decker drill (after sterilising the bit with boiling water and alcohol). He retired close to where my folks now lived and when he learned I was going abroad he offered his Gladstone. It was worn and battered with the grip frayed and restitched with binding twine. Inside, the lining was clean with only an occasional stain from liquid medicines. Otherwise it was a bag of character and had seen much action. Now as I entered the warren of underground corridors leading to the staff door I wondered what new adventures it might experience.

My thoughts were interrupted by another delay at the last exit, the security more than usual for the time of night. 'Any problems?' I asked idly while the bolts and locks were freed.

'Not that I know of, Dr Ryan.' The officer inspected the night sky, one hand out for rain. 'Not that I know of.' Yet he slammed the door with some force.

It was now closing on nine o'clock and I had arranged to meet Conor Mason, my journalist contact, at ten. That left an hour for research. The lights that flooded the perimeter walls of the prison caught misty droplets blowing in a slight wind. The background hum of city traffic was like a constant drone; rarely did it let up until after two in the morning, only to kick-start again at five. Dublin was a twenty-four-hour city with shift work the norm to allow employees to get to their desks when productive rather than during standard office times. This meant a fairly continuous stream of traffic heading to and from the dormitory suburbs north, south and west of the downtown areas.

My Saab rested in the prison forecourt like a wet rat, forlorn and solitary. The engine growled with pleasure as I turned the ignition and edged through another two barriers that were stubbornly slow to lift. I was pulling onto the main road when I noticed Bill O'Hara escorting the Croatian translator towards the buildings. I stopped and kept both men in sight. They were almost joined at the head so close was the conversation. The Croatian's hands flailed in the air and after about ten yards he stopped and there was a short but heated exchange. At one point O'Hara put both hands on the other man's shoulders to calm him but the gesture was angrily shrugged off. Then they disappeared round a corner and out of sight. Now what the hell was that all about? Conor Mason said the minder got in and out through a back entrance reserved for the governor and used fire escapes to avoid direct contact with most of the warders. Tonight he was storming through the front entrance, in full view of everyone. That was definitely odd.

The image of Bill O'Hara arguing with the Croatian minder intrigued. Was witness-protection detainee, Sefik Barisik, in trouble again? Was O'Hara blocking medical intervention? I forced this from my mind (too many distractions) and circled the dark and damp streets surrounding the prison, checking for vulnerable ambush points. Dan Steele knew the locale and would have a detailed idea already set out for his getaway. By his own words he claimed he would wait until he was in the City Hospital ('I have contacts in the City who make things happen') but I had to prepare for every eventuality. Ratko and his gang could attack the detention van anywhere along the three-mile trip.

I drove the journey twice, scanning buildings and houses and roadworks, intersections and junctions. I skirted narrow tracks and side alleys, my eyes straining to see likely target zones. Teenagers in packs gathered underneath lights, chewing the fat and sharing beer and joints. I could see glowing butts passed and hear giggly laughter. The glare from television sets lit up most front rooms. At an occasional doorway neighbours exchanged gossip, their stares taking in everything that moved. Harmon was located in an old part of the city with a half-circle of restored red-brick labourers' cottages directly across from the main entrance. Many unmarried warders stayed at this rent-subsidised accommodation and offered their services in emergencies or sick leave. The overtime rates were more than generous.

A major one-way artery carrying traffic from the northern fringes ran alongside the perimeter walls before dividing into two choked lanes about a mile closer to the city. There was a maze of feeder lanes, many of them culs-de-sac and clogged with on-street parking. I stopped at a petrol station five hundred yards away and laboured over topping up the tank, checking tyre pressures and oil levels. All the time I searched the quarter, noting shadows and recesses, shops and dwellings.

I climbed back into my Saab and stared out of the misted windows, deep in thought. The drizzle had eased leaving behind it a gentle breeze which carried dampness through the night sky. The area was quiet with only an occasional pedestrian. Most activity came from a nearby public house showing English premier-league soccer. Tonight Liverpool FC was at home to some Turkish side and the match was still being relayed. I could hear occasional cheers interspersed with moans. Strains of 'you'll never walk alone' reached my ears. I wished I were somewhere warm and carefree like the bar, mixing with friends and enjoying life instead of planning to kill before I was killed.

There was a sudden roar and a red-shirted fan ran out from the pub and began a mad dance in the street. Two others joined him and there was some whooping and celebrating. Either Liverpool FC had scored or someone had won the lottery. Minutes later the bar began to empty and I gunned the engine alive to edge away from the noisy crowd. A sudden rap on the window lifted me out of my skin and instinctively I ducked my head. When I turned I found the service-station cashier staring in at me. In his left hand he held a credit card, pointing to the card and then me. The panic surge eased and I smiled weakly, patting my pocket where I usually kept my Visa card. I wound down the window and muttered my thanks.

'I've been shouting at you for the past five minutes,' he rebuked me. 'You in another world?'

I forced a grin. 'Kind of,' I admitted. Then behind me someone blared a car horn and I grabbed the Visa card and sped off.

Thirty minutes later I decided the most likely fault line between Harmon Penitentiary and the City Hospital was at an intersection where traffic peeled onto a motorway connection. Lights here had a short transmission and progress was notoriously slow as converging lanes fed long tailbacks onto the same junction. Thinking like a criminal I plotted how to free Steele and saw a number of advantages to positioning an assault here. The prison van could be rammed while stalled in a line and the doors burst open using a small explosive charge. Steele could be released while the area was cleared using CS gas or similar deterrent. Any rescue party would come prepared with face masks, detonators and small arms. Steele could then be spirited by motorcycle along the single corridor that fast tracked to the ring-road motorway circling the city. Within thirty minutes he could be in a safe house and bedded down. Probably the squad would keep him there for a number of days before attempting another move. The junction had other strategic bonuses. The gang could deploy their attack vehicles along the designated common facilities, maybe install decoy cars the night before and move them out nearer the time. One vehicle would leave a coveted site while another waited to take the vacancy.

If the attack were attempted closer it would fail because of the significant security presence surrounding the jail. Practice drills ensured rapid responses to disturbances in the immediate neighbourhood. Any further along and traffic congestion would make escape well-nigh impossible. My conclusion was that any en-route ambush would erupt at this intersection. Where I would settle all scores my own way.

If this prediction were wrong that left the City Hospital but I wasn't convinced Steele would wait until he reached the facility. Also, there was considerable congestion in the wards and corridors, too much movement of vehicles and ambulances. There was a significant risk of confusion and interference. No, I decided, they'd go for a roadside confrontation.

*

Now I had to make my own preparations. The suspect intersection was overlooked on two sides by offices, on another by a group of shops and the final corner was open space with building works. Red-on-blue hoarding fringed the plot and there was a single work entrance. Behind the fencing a tall yellow crane moved blocks and girders around, its lifts and pulleys now silent but raucous at full tilt. In three days' time, as the prison convoy edged its way out from Harmon Penitentiary, the building site would be busy and noisy, creating the ideal background for muffled explosions and possible gunfire. I scanned the offices, noting exits, fire escapes and potential sniper positions. It took me another half-hour but I finally spotted a nook at the front of the second block that overlooked the road junction and surrounding streets. It was ideal. All I needed was the hardware. Even though it was closing in on eleven I contacted Conor Mason. His mobile rang out twice and I swore loudly and slapped the steering wheel. Dammit, man, we agreed to meet tonight.

I knew immediately that it was gunfire. There was the distinct spit of an automatic sub-machine gun. One burst, and then silence, then another sustained salvo. I jumped out of the Saab and stared wildly in all directions. Then came the screech of tyres, angry shouts, and another round of bullets filled the night air. Now there were screams, more voices, agitated and urgent. A small explosion muffled my ears and seconds later an enormous orange fireball sought the darkness.

I ran back along the road towards Harmon Penitentiary, my heart pounding and my legs not carrying me fast enough. A black Mercedes with tinted windows scorched past, horn blaring and swerving wildly on the road. It forced a laundry van up onto the pavement. In the distance alarm klaxons started up, the wailing demanding attention. The prison compound was flooded with light and ahead I could see armed officers taking up defensive positions while others sprayed foam onto the burning wreck of a car. The inferno was askew to the side of the road, its tyres now alight and flaming. Then I heard a howl that made my blood run cold and stopped me in my tracks. I stood and stared, my body trembling, my mind numb from shock.

21

UN OFFICIAL ASSASSINATED.

The media feasted on the brutal murder of the Croatian minder. One of the broadsheets identified him as a UN investigator while a major tabloid opted for a more secretive role.

HIT SQUAD TARGETS UN SPOOK.

The British *Guardian* newspaper posted the most accurate account I read. Quoting 'inside sources' it headlined:

CROATIAN POLICE OFFICER BRUTALLY SLAIN.

No report, in TV, radio or print, could get any closer to the story and all asked the burning question: What was a Croatian police officer (or spook, or UN official) doing in Dublin? Then an association with Harmon Penitentiary surfaced and journalists began probing deeper. To kill off speculation, Justice Minister Patrick Halloran called a press conference that was broadcast live on national television and fed direct to Sky News in London. I'd seen Halloran before, once a fleeting glimpse in the Justice Department offices but mainly through public appearances. He was a tall man in his early sixties with a shock of grey hair that he had a habit of repeatedly sweeping back from his forehead. He was broad shouldered with large hands used to good effect when pounding the podium at briefings. His face was sallow and wrinkled with age spots, his eyes bright and suspicious and constantly challenging. He dressed severely in dark suits and sombre ties, always with a starched white shirt. He carried his reputation as a tough negotiator like a shield, brandishing it at the slightest insult. Press meetings often ended in rancour, Halloran storming off when he decided the questions had gone too far.

I watched his performance in a bar along the quays near the Four Courts, Dublin's legal centre. The pub was busy with a lunch-time crowd drawn by its excellent range of sandwiches and soups, ideal fare to break up a working day.

On screen Halloran gave nothing away, relaying that the Croatian executive was in Dublin as part of Ireland's ongoing UN role. There were, he reminded the audience, Irish army and policemen actively involved in peacekeeping duties in the Balkans. The victim was coordinator to a contingent stationed along the border with Serbia. There were no leads 'as yet' as to why he was assassinated, Halloran claimed. The Irish government had set up a special team of investigators to bring the killers to justice and were already following significant leads. He would not be drawn on this, citing 'security reasons'. It was simplistic in the extreme, he chided, to link the assassination with anyone at Harmon Penitentiary. It was nothing more than coincidence that the attack took place less than fifty yards from its main entrance.

Rather than field potentially embarrassing queries Halloran quit the briefing after ten minutes, leaving reporters scrambling to file reports.

I knew he was lying.

I knew the victim was the interpreter and protector of fifty-one-year-old Sefik Barisik, survivor of a massacre at Vukovar in Croatia and one of three key witnesses in the forthcoming war-crimes trial of Milos Bracchovis. And I believed that Bracchovis, international gun-runner, narco-terrorist, pimp and killer, was probably behind the assassination. And I also knew a gang closely linked to Bracchovis was conspiring to spring Dan Steele from Harmon Penitentiary. With my help.

I finished my ploughman's platter, finger-tipping crumbs from the plate. I could have eaten the same again but had to reign in my hunger. My bank account didn't allow for double midday breaks. I moved to a quiet corner and dialled up Conor Mason's mobile phone, the fifth call this morning. No reply. Against surroundings of laughter and guffaws from fellow diners I listened to the tones ring out to voicemail. As before, I left a message.

'Hi Conor, Frank here. I've been trying to reach you since last night. Do you have the goods and when can we meet?' Then I contacted his workplace and was rerouted twice before finding a voice.

'Crime desk, Roisin speaking. Can I help you?' Female, young sounding and tapping on a keyboard while she spoke. The pounding of her fingers just about drowned out a background clamour of office shouts.

'Yes. Is Conor Mason there?'

'One moment.' I sensed a hand cupping the mouthpiece and then a call to someone.

'No.' She wasn't giving much away.

'Any idea where I might find him? I've arranged a meeting and can't track him down.'

My voice was so casual and unconcerned it even surprised me. But I was far from relaxed in my thinking. Where the hell is he? Has anything happened to him?

'I'm putting you on hold while I find his editor.' The line switched to music, then she came back abruptly. 'Can I have a name, please?'

I didn't have time to consider evasion. 'Frank Ryan.'

'OK.' Music. I flagged a barman and ordered another coffee, idly inspecting the crowd. There were as many young women as men and they seemed to be better dressed, one or two even in pinstripe suits. I decided it was a group of legal eagles discussing briefs or whatever it is that legal eagles discuss. Probably how best to sue doctors. The televised news briefing had ended and the screen was flickering with images of another suicide bombing in Israel. Wailing faces, fists pounding chests, bloodstained clothes and rag-doll bodies. Ambulances scorching through a crowded marketplace, narrowly missing the stunned survivors. Apart from myself, as far as I could see nobody in the packed room was paying the slightest attention. Terrorist outrage fatigue.

'You're looking for Conor Mason?' Now I had a male voice, much older and tired with a hint of a midlands accent.

'Yeah. We arranged a meeting last night but I couldn't get through to him. I was hoping he might be at his desk today.'

'So was I. Conor left at lunch-time yesterday and hasn't been back. I've already called his land-line and mobile phone but got no reply.'

I had a sickening feeling in my stomach. 'Oh,' was all I could say.

'I sent a courier to his apartment with a bunch of files about an hour ago. No one answered. He doesn't usually take off like this. Have you any idea where he might be?'

I had a mountain of ideas but none I would share. 'No, sorry. I don't know him that well.'

The crime-desk editor wasn't satisfied with this anaemic answer. 'What was the meeting about?'

'Nothing important,' I lied. Deceit was becoming second nature to me. 'Just a social drink and chat.'

'Right, a social meeting.' He obviously didn't believe me. 'Are you by any chance CMO to Harmon Penitentiary?'

Dammit. Mason must have spilled my name as background source. 'Yeah, that's me.' This time I couldn't force my voice to sound unconcerned.

'Do you have any idea who was behind that assassination last night?'

His brazenness took my breath away. 'Nah,' I laughed. 'I'm as wise as the Justice Minister and he doesn't seem too clued in.'

There was a cynical grunt from the other end of the line. 'Never is.'

Now came an awkward silence. 'So what do we do?' I finally pushed.

'We wait, Dr Ryan. We wait. Conor was following something big and I suspect he's gone underground to get more information. He'll surface sometime, he always does.'

'Has he done this before?' The sickening feeling that was ruining my digestion lifted momentarily.

'A few times. But he always warned me in advance. We'll sit it out. He's a grown man and has the right to hide if he wants.'

'Sure. Maybe he got lucky with some girl.'

'That might be lucky for him but I wouldn't exactly describe it as lucky for her.' There was a sense of humour in the voice but I wasn't lifted by his quip. Mason's no-show was worrying me. He moved in dangerous circles and was very uptight about the fallout from his reporting of the Harmon riots.

'Jesus, I'll be a nervous wreck by the time this is finished,' he'd said when we were startled during one of our car-park meetings. Then, after I'd told him about Ratko and his photographic threat against my family, he was really taken aback. 'This is much bigger than I thought.'

Had Mason got lucky in love or unlucky in life? Was he tucked up in bed with some girl-friend or lying in a ditch with a bullet in the head? Instinct didn't allow room for chance. I felt nervous cramps in my belly and an urge to use the lavatory.

'If he comes in maybe you'd tell him I called.'

'Will do. And if you hear anything interesting we could use about that hellhole prison I'll pay you handsomely for the information.'

'We could help each other, couldn't we?' I was trying hard to sound money hungry.

'We could indeed, Dr Ryan. We could indeed.'

I considered the conversation as I quit the bar, inspecting the heavy cloud cover for signs of rain. The editor knew who I was and my role as CMO to Harmon Penitentiary. However, his shameless fishing for background material suggested he wasn't aware of the relationship I'd established with his crime correspondent. That reassured me somewhat. I waited at the kerbside, container lorries skimming my toes and spraying my trousers with wheel splash. It was a damp and cold day and along the river Liffey seagulls swooped and dived, their raucous screeches rising above the traffic drone. There was a smell of roasted hops from the Guinness brewery further along the waterway.

Slumped against a lamppost a down-and-out begged. His knees were drawn in to his belly, he held out a dirty tweed cap in one hand and badly scribbled note in the other. It stated that he hadn't eaten for days. Well-heeled pedestrians ignored him and street urchins taunted from a distance. I inspected the gaunt and haggard features, unshaven and grime streaked, the bedraggled hair. He didn't deserve that existence, no more than I deserved the nightmare I was going through. Even though I was close to bankruptcy I fished in my pocket and separated euro notes, peeling off a ten bill and stuffing it into his filthy grasp. He glanced up, startled and uncertain, as if he'd been mugged rather than tipped. For a moment there was a flicker of thanks, his sunken eyes glinting as the amount was considered. Then, as fast as the note disappeared, the shutters came down over his expression and the pleading look was restored. It followed me all the way to the car.

Inside the Saab I pondered the situation. My last contact with Conor Mason was the previous night, after my return from Belgrade. Then the conversation was brief and guarded but a text followed:

GOODS ARRIVED. COLLECT 2NITE.
WILL CALL @ 10.

This was the sniper rifle I'd ordered, my specifications of an M-76 very precise. If I was to stay ahead of Ratko and his ex-British army henchman I really needed this extra firepower. I had worked out where I would position myself for the presumed ambush of Dan Steele's convoy, reckoning I could pick off both attackers and escapers from the vantage position. Now, with Mason AWOL, I had to factor in a contingency plan.

As my brain slipped through the gears I went back over the media coverage of Harmon Penitentiary. HARMON HELL. WE TELL THE SHOCKING TRUTH. This was the first of Conor Mason's exclusives, from inside information provided by me. DRUGS, AIDS AND NOT ENOUGH DOCS. An account of addiction and the abysmal health system in which I was named as sole CMO. Then came RIOT DEATHS OUTRAGE: MUSLIM PRISONER TARGETED, followed by HARMON CMO QUITS. Other papers had followed the Harmon issues, but not with the same enthusiasm and their reports were mid-section rather than grabbing the front pages. Mason and I had discussed the government's response to the revelations and we both believed an attempt would be made to silence us. But there was no official censorship of any significance, apart from one shot across the bows by Bill O'Hara the night I treated the witness-protection detainee. 'You are bound by the Official Secrets Act, Ryan, and don't forget that. What you just saw and heard goes no further than the back of your brain, understand? I don't want this on the front page of the papers tomorrow with you as the source.'

It was more a caution than a lock-you-up-and-throw-away-the-key warning.

I mentally sifted the reports I'd read and heard since and it gradually dawned on me that the intense interest in Harmon had disappeared. Prisoners and prison issues were no longer sexy to journalists covering such conflicts as terrorist cells, suicide bombings and the beheading of Western hostages in Middle East trouble spots. Domestically, a fresh round of revelations on crooked politicians was grabbing attention. In an atmosphere of significant public outrage Harmon was of little consequence. The world had enough killers, bombers, terrorists, rapists and arsonists on the loose. Those behind bars were out of sight and out of mind.

Had the government got to Mason, I wondered? Had the government got to other journalists as well? Was reporting on the prison off limits while the witness-protection programme continued?

Fifty yards ahead a petrol tanker had almost jack-knifed and was blocking both lanes of the road. Horns blared and drivers climbed out of their cars, gesticulating and protesting. I watched as different attempts were made to right the cab under the disapproving stare of a traffic cop, then glanced at my watch. It was coming up on three o'clock. I parked Conor Mason in my mind, deciding I'd come back to him later. From a side pocket I dragged out a scrunched-up piece of paper and read the address and number that I'd taken from the Dublin telephone directory. One quick call and I was soon edging past the tanker, now half corrected and freeing up one lane.

Forty minutes later I stood at the bottom of a flight of granite steps at a terrace Georgian building in a leafy southside square. A brass plate on wrought-iron railings at the front told the world this was the Consulate of Serbia and Montenegro.

I presented myself at reception and a young man in a sharp suit asked me to wait. Five minutes later I was ushered into a high-ceilinged room, sparsely furnished with only a large rectangular desk, three chairs and the national flag hanging from a pole. A large picture window looked out onto a garden, shielded by partly drawn curtains.

The consul was a tall and bald man with the air of an undertaker, sombre and slow voiced. He stood and I didn't sit, anxious to press ahead.

'You are Dr Frank Ryan?'

'Yes.'

'Do you have any identification?'

I was out and back inside three minutes, breathless and agitated and flourishing a driving licence. The consul inspected it closely, eyes flicking from my face to the certificate photograph. Apparently satisfied he shook my hand, his grip surprisingly limp.

'Whom did you speak with in Belgrade?' Perfect English.

'Kneza Pasica,' I replied, my body language screaming hurry up. 'He's attached to the Ministry of Internal Affairs.'

'Yes.'

'He said he might have something for me today and suggested I check in with the consulate.'

'Yes.'

'And do you have something for me?'

He shrugged a 'perhaps' and I almost grabbed him by the lapels and shook him.

'Help me out here, sir,' I pleaded. 'I'm double-parked and you know how easy it is to get clamped in this city. Do you have something for me or not?'

'I do.'

'Could I have it?'

'Yes.'

Oh, for Chrissake, what game are you playing?

'Could I have it now?'

'Yes. I have it here in this drawer.'

Minutes later I walked as slowly from the Georgian building as my excited body would allow. Under my left arm was a yellow padded bag which the consul had dragged from a sealed diplomatic pouch in my presence.

I sat in the car and stared at the package on the passenger seat, heart racing and mouth dry. Passers-by became blurred images, street traffic no more than shadows. I forced my imagination quiet and stared ahead, gripping the steering wheel tightly. My hands shook as I turned the keys in the ignition, the engine growled as I touched off the accelerator. I waited until a line of traffic passed, then did a U-turn and headed for my apartment.

I drove slowly, the secrets within the package burning into my imagination and distracting concentration. At one set of lights I was so preoccupied I nearly rear-ended a courier van and jerked forward as my feet slammed the brakes. Relax, Ryan. Control yourself. But my pleadings fell on deaf ears. I was already mentally far ahead. Had Kneza uncovered some file that would unravel more of my torment? Would I finally learn what Lisa Duggan was involved in? Would I grasp at last why I was lured from my apartment and beaten unconscious? Why I was taken to an English jail and interrogated under sedation? Who Noel Dempsey really was and what his role in my affairs had become? I had so many questions, so many unanswered and tortured issues to resolve. And I had less than forty-eight hours to solve the riddle before I fanned the fires of hell.

I took the stairs to my flat two at a time, banging the front door in frustration while I waited for the time-delay mechanism to free the lock. Why didn't the Justice Department disconnect that when they were removing everything else, I fumed. Minutes later I sat at the kitchen table and stared at the yellow padded bag. Feeling at the bulk I sensed documents inside and with a steak knife slit the top open. Out slid a sheaf of pages, held together by a large clip. On the top was a scribbled message from Kneza on his official Ministry of Internal Affairs notepaper.

> Dear Frank,
> This may help you some more. I still think it would be wise to stay out of these matters.
> Go back to Australia. It's a nice country.
> Good luck.
> Kneza Pasica.

Go back to Australia. That idea was suddenly very consoling and attractive. Get up this minute, Frank Ryan, and pack your bags. Book one of those cheap flights over the Internet and get the hell away from Ireland with its accursed politics, treachery and double-crossing. Go while you still can. But the typescript I stared at intrigued me and I couldn't stop myself reading. By the third line any thoughts of fleeing had disappeared.

The first sheet explained the contents: transcript of interviews and video recordings. Material sourced from news organisations and United Nations inspection reports. This document prepared by Lisa Duggan, Office of the Prosecutor (UN) investigating war crimes in the former Yugoslavia.

*

I had a sense of finality, that at last I would uncover Lisa Duggan's real role in life.

Introduction: undocumented reports of brutality, torture and massacres in and around the villages and areas known as Ljubovija, Pobudja, Konjevic Polje, Potcari and Kasaba in the former Yugoslavia (July and August 1995) persist. The Office of the Prosecutor (UN) decided to investigate this further, especially when fresh information came to light. One name is mentioned repeatedly as both ordering and being actively involved in the atrocities. News bureaux archive film is used to explain the background to the events. The whole is recorded in VCR format.

(1) Short clip © BBC News (July 11th 1995)

10:01:29 Milan Djukic, general in Bosnian Serb Army (BSA), Srebrenica, talks to soldiers. 'On to Potocari, on to Potocari, Bratunac. Don't stop. Let's go.'

10:01:46 BSA soldier talking to General Milan Djukic: '11th July, I'll remember this day.'

10:01:50 Srebrenica streets littered with belongings of Muslims who fled.

10:01:54 Corpses, Srebrenica.

(2) Video film © Office of the Prosecutor UN

United Nations investigator Lisa Duggan talking to Fatima Martic Ahmetovic. According to Fatima, on July 13th 1995 her cousins, both men in their late 30s, went on foot to try to reach Bosnian government territory, but never made it to the other side. Her husband and male brothers were abducted in Potocari.

UN investigator Lisa Duggan: 'I am with the United Nations investigation team. I must hear your own words. Please tell me what happened.'

Shows ID and camera pans to document. Personal details clearly marked.

Set-up: Fatima with her only remaining child (girl). Camera shows interview taking place.

10:02:19 I/V Fatima Martic: 'We never thought that Srebrenica could fall. The United Nations soldiers said "protected, protected", come on . . . but nothing of that was protected. Nothing.'

10:02:37 'I lived on the front line and when everyone went to sleep at night we went to work, while they weren't shooting, until dawn. We women worked by night so that we would be able to have something to feed our children . . . When they took my husband away he said, "Hide the boys, just hide the boys. They are taking the boys." He was right. They came for the boys that night and I never saw any of them again.'

10:02:59 LD: 'How many boys did you have? I'm sorry but I have to ask. How many boys were in your family? Three? Did I get that right, three?' To camera: 'Three.' Three fingers held up.

10:03:04 LD to camera: 'Approximately 15,000 people fled on foot through the woods trying to reach Bosnian Government territory. Thousands of those captured in ambushes by Bosnian Serb soldiers have never been seen again. US Intelligence has aerial photographs pointing to the existence of mass graves in this area.'

Moving road shots: woods outside Srebrenica, Pobudja area. Ruined houses.

10:04:12 Set-up: Three men who escaped through woods looking at map with UN investigator Lisa Duggan. One man, Pero Mrksic, speaks.

10:04:25 I/V Pero Mrksic: 'The most difficult the next night was in the place Pobudja here, and the crossing of the road at Konjevic Polje. We had the most problems here because of the crossing. They waited for us there; because they knew we could only cross at this point . . . they wanted to personally kill as many of us as possible, to make us disappear . . . Kasaba. That is this place, Kasaba, not far from Konjevic Polje. There is a playing field there, for sports. Here I saw them take maybe 300 to 350 people that day. All day they took people to that field and that night, in the evening, trucks came, and started to massively take them away, without their equipment, they stripped them there, prepared them, as if they were going to help them get to free territory. From there they went in the other direction towards Zvornik and Karakaj.'

UN investigator LD shows Pero Mrksic a selection of photographs. 'Do you recognise any of these men? Is there one or more than one who did these things?'

Pero Mrksic sifts through photographs. 'This man, yes. Him. He was in charge. He gave the orders and followed the soldiers.'

LD: 'Did he do anything else?'

Pero Mrksic: 'Yes. I saw him shoot the wounded in the back of the head. They were alive because I saw a lot of blood and heard cries. Many were already dead but many were also still alive. He made sure.'

UN investigator LD to camera, holds photograph up. Camera closes in.

The phone rang and I stood up to answer and then stopped. I was engrossed and didn't want any interruption. I had caller ID on the set and would ring back when ready. I quickly poured a coffee and tore open a packet of biscuits and began munching. My eyes sought the next lines.

(3) Short film clip © ITN (London)

10:06:22 Prisoners walking along dirt track. (The boy shown has been identified as a 16-year-old called Mirko Gruban who escaped, hiding among a woman's belongings on a bus while his captors were distracted getting water from a spring. His testimony is on record at the UN.)

(4) © Office of the Prosecutor United Nations

10:06:35 Voiceover: 'Prisoners were taken into this agricultural warehouse in Kravic where survivors report that mass executions took place.'

10:06:38 UN investigator LD interviews woman (not identified): 'They knew what awaited them there. I also thought, knew, that something awaited them, that they'd be killed. They were praying to God that they would only be killed, I heard people whispering that they hoped that they would be killed, that they wouldn't be made to suffer.'

(5) Short film clip © SKY News (Aug 4th 1995)

10:06:43 Agricultural warehouse.

10:06:49 Personal belongings (glasses and wallet) on grass outside.

10:06:54 Bullet holes in outside walls.

10:07:06 Bullet holes inside warehouse.

10:07:10 Bloodstains on inside walls.

(6) © Office of the Prosecutor United Nations

UN investigator LD speaking to camera: 'Thousands of civilians fled to the area surrounding the Dutch UN compound at Potocari, about 4km north of Srebrenica, to await evacuation. When Bosnian Serb soldiers arrived, they divided them and took mostly men to an unknown destination. Some corpses, including nine who were shot in the back of the head, were documented in the area by Dutch UNPRO-FOR [United Nations Protection Force] soldiers.'

10:08:56 White building – former slaughter-house.

10:09:23 UN signpost.

10:09:33 Warehouse.

10:09:43 UN watchtower.

(7) Short film clip © BBC News (July 29th 1995)

10:09:56 Pan to woman's shoe.

10:10:06 Woman cleaning shoes in stream. Former slaughterhouse in background.

10:10:18 Wrecked cars and buses.

10:12:06 Women and children walking towards buses.

(8) © Office of the Prosecutor United Nations

Camera shows Milina Meakic, 35yr old, whose father and three brothers were taken by Bosnian Serb soldiers from Potocari. Milina reports seeing 20 bodies lying in a field with their throats cut.

I/V UN investigator LD with Milina Meakic: 'We were all together at Potocari. My father worked at UNPROFOR [United Nations Protection Force] as a translator. He was highly regarded and often the UNPROFOR soldiers came to our house with food and stayed to eat. My father believed if anything happened they [UNPROFOR] would protect us. They would stop anyone from taking our house. So when they came my father waited here, at this house. He knew immediately they were not real soldiers. "These are militiamen," he shouted to us. "Stay here, do not move. I will be back immediately." My father told me he was going to UNPROFOR so that UNPROFOR could help us, that they would save us, that Serbs wouldn't be able to do anything if UNPROFOR came down. He went further on, maybe one hundred yards from the front gate, and two Chetniks came up to him, grabbed him and took him away. Then they came to the house and took my brothers. They were screaming with terror and my mother pleaded with the men to stop, to leave the boys. "They are only children," she said. One of the Chetniks hit my mother with his fist and broke her jaw.'

UN investigator LD: 'Have you seen your father or brothers since?'

Milina Meakic: 'No.'

10:13:40 'And there was one building, I saw them lead one of my father's cousins; how they took him also, they took him into that building. Before, in peace, it was a slaughterhouse for cattle and that's where they took the men now. They took that cousin of my father and behind him followed another Chetnik with a big knife. And before that they had collected many men at that building and took them towards Bratunac.'

UN investigator LD: 'How many men? Do you know how many men there were in that group?'

'I would guess at a hundred, maybe more or maybe a little less. I was hiding so I did not see everything clearly. But I heard the screams and shouts and the gunfire. One man escaped out a back window and ran towards us. He was shouting.'

UN investigator LD: 'What did he shout? Can you remember what he was saying?'

'He said they were slitting the men's throats. He said they lined them up facing each other and started at one end and kept killing. The men in the opposite row who tried to escape were shot. It was terrible. He was crying and banging his hands on the ground and wailing at the heavens. Then he grabbed a rock, it was a big rock, and ran back into the building. I heard him roaring and there were shots and he stopped roaring. Shortly the commander came out and he was covered in blood and he was laughing and joking.'

UN investigator LD: 'Would you recognise this man again? If I showed you photographs do you think you would be able to pick him out?'

Milina Meakic: 'Yes, his face I will never forget.'

UN investigator LD shows Milina Meakic a selection of photographs. 'Is the man you spoke of in any of these?'

Milina Meakic: 'That is him.' Holds photograph. 'That is the man who came outside covered in blood.'

UN investigator LD: 'The photograph Milina Meakic holds is of Milos Bracchovis.'

Oh, my God, not Bracchovis. Lisa was after the most dangerous of all criminals and the man behind the assassination last night. She was putting her life on the line going after him. Now I began to understand the secrecy, the sudden trips away and façade as a banker. Lisa Duggan needed a cloak of camouflage to protect her against the tentacles of this master criminal and war-crimes killer.

The telephone rang again but I hadn't the stomach to answer, the information I was reading shocked and distressed me too much. How could Lisa have been involved in this sort of inquiry and not let it slip to me? The phone kept ringing, whoever was calling was persistent. But it was the land-line and Conor Mason knew not to use that. I ignored the shrill tones.

I slumped back in the chair, mentally drained and emotionally exhausted. Images of my days and nights with Lisa flooded my thinking and I choked back tears. Now I realised her bizarre behaviour was her way of protecting herself and her work. Her superiors probably insisted she keep a low profile considering the killer she was investigating. And Bracchovis would have known the UN was after him, would have known who Lisa Duggan was and her role in the chase. And Bracchovis was killing any witness brave enough to testify against him. He must have Lisa in his sights as well.

I turned to the final page of the transcript and found a grainy photo image, presumably downloaded from a computer file. The man in the shot looked short, almost insignificant. He had small features, a squat nose, chisel chin and thin lips. His head was turned slightly to the left making it difficult to see his eyes. But there was one distinguishing feature: underneath a receding hairline was a birthmark, like a large blobbed ink stain. Beside, a name was scrawled in pencil: Milos Bracchovis.

I suddenly felt cold and started shivering.

The phone rang again and I let it ring for maybe a minute. It stopped and then started up again immediately. In frustration I stormed to the bedroom and picked up the receiver.

'Yes?' I snapped. Then my heart almost stopped.

'Hi, Conor, Frank here. I've been trying to reach

you since last night. Do you have the goods and when can we meet?' It was my own voice, as recorded on Conor Mason's mobile phone.

'Who's there?' I roared. 'Who's calling?'

There was silence. Then a sudden gunshot and a gurgled moan. The line went dead.

22

Sleep, if only I could sleep. I'd lost track of the last time I'd slept soundly. Was it drug induced while in the UK prison, or even earlier again, before the night of 12 February when I was attacked and abducted from my apartment?

When Lisa stayed over we'd curl up into one another's arms, naked and sexually sated. I'd draw my knees up slightly and create a lap into which she'd ease her bottom. Then I'd drape an arm around her body and cup a breast and allow my mind to drift, smelling the scent off her hair (Oatmeal and Honey) and perfume from her neck (Dolce & Gabbana). Happier days. Delicious nights. When she turned I turned and her hands would stray to my loins and hold me. Even in sleep we were hot for each other, fingers stroking, lips brushing in drowsy aroused kisses. If I woke first, which was more often than not, I stared at the young woman beside me, convinced no one could be as lucky as me. Lisa Duggan was physically beautiful. She had long limbs, a slim and curved figure with pert breasts that made for a pleasant handful. Her ash-blonde hair, even when bedraggled and splayed on the pillow, was inviting. I ached to touch and kiss and regularly did just that, one particular morning disturbing her with a soft and gentle wetness.

'Mmm, hi, Frank,' she murmured. 'That was nice. How long have you been awake?'

I fudged the answer. 'A minute, maybe two.'

She wiped the bleariness from her eyes and sat up, searching for the time. 'It's too early. Go back to sleep.' She burrowed into the pillow and snuggled down for comfort. I watched until she stirred again and the day began, that time with a mock fight, pillows flying and both of us ending up on the floor.

Lisa was also intelligent and lively, much brighter than me I concluded after months of arguments and conversations. And she had a wicked sense of humour. 'Two Aussies walked out of a pub,' she once teased.

'Oh, yeah?'

She bit on her knuckles, face impish with exaggerated innocence. 'It could happen.'

It was only an excuse for another round of arm wrestling and groping.

She educated me, dragging me round art galleries and to theatres where I tried to appear interested and engaged instead of bored and indifferent. I'm sure I suffered bone damage from the repeated digs in the ribs. But I was secretly pleased to learn more of her world and came to enjoy Irish art. The delicate landscapes of Roderic O'Connor, Paul Henry and John Lavery were her favourites while I found the swirling strokes and dark hues of Jack B. Yeats more appealing. She was saving to buy a Basil Blackshaw canvas, a rural scene with dogs, but I surprised her with a vibrant and scowling Knuttel. (Is it any wonder my bank manager sent me warning letters?) Lisa enjoyed modern Irish playwrights while I preferred *Mamma Mia* or *Chicago*, brash and loud musicals. We were miles apart in tastes but not in our company. We liked being with one another, pined when we were apart. Or at least I did and she told me she did. I believed her and in that period I did sleep soundly, contented in love and life.

Now my nights were lost to horror and violent images, lost to the loss of Lisa and where she was and how I could find her again. And tonight, the ninth night leading into the early hours of the tenth day of March, my peace was further distressed by that late telephone call and sound of a handgun being discharged. And a gurgled moan. They were warning me. Ratko and his thug colleague Nixon had let me know what they were capable of doing. They'd murdered the Croatian minder and I felt sure they'd also killed Conor Mason. Everything was shifting into place and they were preparing the final ground rules. By my reckoning, anyone involved in taking Milos Bracchovis to trial was under threat of death. That included the other witness-protection inmates scattered throughout Europe and my patient, Sefik Barisik, in Harmon Penitentiary.

I sat up in bed, duvet drawn to chin against the cold. Lights off and in the gloom I stared at the walls, searching for explanations and trying to plot strategies. Tomorrow, 11 March, would be the most dangerous day of my life. And considering what I'd come through in the previous four weeks this thought troubled me greatly. By noon I could be dead, my torment perhaps brought to a brutal end. But I was too young to die, barely closing in on my thirty-first birthday and surely with many good years ahead. I had a future, where I didn't know but somewhere better than this accursed city. In what seemed like another existence I had turned down an offer of a highly paid position with the Defence Ministry in London, looking after soldiers on the front line in Iraq. I would have been far away from battle zones, stationed safely in an international medical community in Jordan. However, my conscience hadn't allowed me to take up this post.

So instead of Jordan I opted for Dublin and the Irish Justice Department. Now, as my feet sought a warm spot under the covers, I cursed that decision. I could be bedded down in a better climate with no personal security issues instead of holed up and waiting for a shoot-out on the cold and wet streets around Harmon Penitentiary. But then again, I would not have met Lisa Duggan. Girls like that come along once in a lifetime; a love so smitten and besotted would not be easy to find again. If I had an ounce of strength left in my body by tomorrow afternoon I was determined to find her. I would speak with her and tell her I loved her and wanted to be with her for ever.

'There is no life for me without you, Lisa.' I would say that and more, so she understood the depth of my feelings.

I recalled a drowsy whisper in a London hotel bed. 'I love you, Dr Ryan.'

We *could* still make it happen. I had to see her again, whatever the outcome, I had to hear from her lips if our relationship was sound. From those deep, lush and so kissable lips I wanted the language tumbling free. I love you, Frank. I love you and want to be with you. No matter where you go or what you do I will be at your side. In my mind I could see her sitting in some room in the Justice Department, possibly across the same table where Bill O'Hara had lectured me. She'd look me in the eyes and I would see only tenderness and care, perhaps tempered by the fear that our affair was too damaged. And I'd listen with beating heart and dry mouth, frantic to hear what I wanted to hear. Desperate to salvage my life and my lover and move on. To leave Dublin with its hateful prison and demented and dangerous inmates. Yes, as soon as Lisa told me she loved me I would find happiness again. And I would share that delight with her and with our future children. Against the darkened backdrop of my apartment I saw a little blonde-haired, blue-eyed girl laughing and running along some outback track. I was chasing her, hiding behind wizened gum trees and jumping out, boo, whenever she came looking for her dad.

The last time I glanced at the digital clock it was 2.28 a.m. The next I looked it was 6.05 a.m. In between I must have dozed off and was thankful for that at least. Then I heard car doors slamming and voices outside and for a moment wondered whether I was dreaming. The voices became louder and I was out of the bed and at the window. Have they come for me again? It was still dark, the usual grey dawn that rolled across Dublin's skyline not yet showing. Headlights flooded the forecourt and

I could see shapes. There was no obvious urgency and now two heads were together, hands exchanging something.

I ran to the apartment door and listened, urging my breathing quiet. There was movement downstairs, of that I was certain. But as far as I could detect no one had come upstairs. I darted back to the bedroom and felt along the mattress until I touched off the slit I'd cut into the padding. Then I forced my hand between layers of down and feathers until I had the Glock pistol. Seconds later I pulled out a box of ammunition and in the dark loaded a full clip. Then I hurried back to the door, gun clasped in both hands, safety catch off. If they burst in I wasn't going to be taken without a fight. Now there were loud voices from the ground-floor hallway, no attempt to hide any presence. I went to the window and risked a squint. Still the headlights burned, still shapes stirred.

I grabbed a towel and darted to the front hallway, perspiration freely trickling down my neck even though it was cold and I was naked. I dried my sweaty palms, not daring to risk losing a firm grip on the handgun. I ran the cloth across my brow, an ear pressed against wood. All activity was one level below, of that I was sure. But it was possible one or two or even three had sneaked up and were positioned outside this very minute. I used the spyhole. Darkness. What the hell's going on?

I needed to empty my bladder but couldn't risk losing my vantage position. Dammit, if they came for me and I was having a leak I wouldn't stand a chance. Gunned down, pecker in hand. Just my bloody luck. I held the towel at groin height and bunched it tightly, then felt relief as warm urine left my body and was absorbed. Still I kept an ear trained for scuffling or scraping that might suggest an imminent attack. I felt a trickle of pee run down my legs and pool at my feet but I dared not move. And I was pleased; if anyone burst though the door they'd slip on the fluid. I pressed on my abdomen to encourage the last drops and let them fall.

My mouth was dry, my breathing erratic, my hands shaking and my teeth chattering. I switched the Glock to stop my fingers spasming and retreated, both hands directing the pistol at chest height. Still the locks on the door remained un-challenged. I heard car engines growl and knelt at the glass in time to see two SUVs reverse and turn, then drive out of the complex. Minutes later the forecourt was empty and gloomy with only the hint of breaking daylight.

I dragged a chair from the kitchen, perched it to one side of the window and stood on it. By squinting downwards I could see light from the apartment below, a narrow glow in one small corner. I hurriedly threw on a dressing gown and was back at the front door, listening so intently

I'm sure I'd have heard a mouse scuttle. Nothing. I turned the locks slowly, cursing at every click. Then I counted out the time-release mechanism and stood still, afraid of what I might see if I opened. Don't let it end like this. I yanked at the door and rolled backwards into the apartment, skidding on my own urine. I felt the dressing gown become suddenly wet and smelt pee. The door stayed ajar, the darkness outside both scary and yet strangely inviting. I turned to one side, both hands gripping the Glock and my body half bent so I could see and shoot.

I held my breath until I felt my lungs burst. Zilch. No sound, no rustling, no light, no movement. I exhaled in short, stabbing bursts, and then worm wriggled forward and waited. Sweat plopped, fear and apprehension oozing from every pore. Now I counted to seventy. Still no hint of an ambush. I could stand the tension no longer and determined to go and take whatever came my way. Prayers formed in my mind but remained unsaid. Lisa, pouting and teasing, that image suddenly flashed and disappeared. I moved to a squat, eyes squinting around the corners. Then I heard a noise, I was sure a gun was being cocked. I leapt, a roar filling my throat and my left hand flailing as my right held onto the Glock, trigger finger pressing. I landed on my knees on the hard surface of the first-floor corridor and twisted to see. Nothing. No one. No gun. No knives or switchblades, no Mace or fists, no boots or coshes. Only my fevered imagination and the reek of urine.

Winded and aching, terrified and yet relieved, I chanced the stairs. When I risked a glance there was light coming from the street-level apartment. And when I finally listened in I recognised the accents. The eastern European cleaners were back.

'Hi, Dad, how's it goin', mate?'

There was a surprised pause at the other end of the line. Then, 'That you, Frank?'

'Yeah, sure is. Larger than life as usual.'

'Well, I'll be damned. How're you, son?'

'Bonzer.'

It was an old exchange, one that Dad and I used a lot when things were going well. I was calling home to say hello. Or possibly a last goodbye.

'So what's happenin' over there? Your mam and I got all your e-mails and we've been followin' the shenanigans in Dublin in the papers. Isn't it time you shifted somewhere safe? Jeez, you can't spend all your days there. Don't you miss the sun?'

'Damn straight I do. And a whole lot more as well. How's Mam?'

'She's good, real good. The move here has worked out well. She's a changed woman, I can tell you. It's taken years off her.'

'Great.'

We talked for a bit, Dad filling me in on local gossip and how my sisters were getting on. It was great to hear an Aussie accent for a change.

'Sue's got a lot more strength in her leg since you saw her last. You'll be real pleased at the progress. When're you headin' this way?'

Good question. After tomorrow will I still be standing, let alone heading anywhere?

'Dunno yet. Maybe at the end of the month I might take a break and come home for a spell.'

'That'd be great, Frank. Your mam'll be chuffed to hear that.'

'Don't say anything yet, I haven't made arrangements.'

Now there was a soft chuckle. 'Is it that girl you've been goin' on about? What's her name?'

'Lisa, Lisa Duggan.'

'Yeah, Lisa. You still holdin' hands with her?'

Another good question. 'Still going strong,' I lied. 'Still hanging in there.'

Now Dad snorted. 'Your mam says she'll keep her hooks on you. Handsome kid like you could get any bit of skirt he wanted. You a doctor an' all.'

'Well, maybe I'm passed the any-bit-of-skirt stage.'

'Don't say that, Frank.'

'I'm almost thirty-one.'

'Really? Where do the years go? Still, Sue's got a friend your mam's nursin' in the background.'

'Oh, and who would that be?'

'Carol Belmont. You remember the Belmonts, don't you? They own a station over Bordertown way. Big spread stretchin' into Victoria. Nice folks too. Carol's workin' in Adelaide now . . .' There was a pause and I could hear Dad's voice echo on the line. 'Teachin', that's what she's at. Couldn't recall for a moment there. She's a language teacher in Campbelltown High School. You could be in with a shout.'

Despite my problems I couldn't help but grin. Since I'd left Australia my parents had been matchmaking at every opportunity. There wasn't an available woman from Broken Hill to Victor Harbour they hadn't made enquiries about. 'Is she blonde or brunette?'

A short laugh ricocheted. 'Dark haired, like her mam. Good-looker too and her mam's still pretty fresh.'

Pretty fresh was the ultimate compliment as far as women went. Nicole Kidman was pretty fresh, as were Cate Blanchett and Meg Ryan. Catherine Zeta Jones was not pretty fresh. Too much bosom.

'I prefer blondes.'

'She can dye her hair, that's not a problem. You wait'll you see her though, maybe you won't want to change anythin'.'

'I'll keep that in mind. Tell Mam and the gang I said hello and I miss them big time.'

'Can I say you might be visitin' soon?'

I forced the lump from my throat, bottled the image of me walking up the front paddock, smelling eucalyptus leaves and hearing screeching cockatoos. Bright, dazzling sunshine, warm ground underfoot. Into the welcoming and loving arms of my family. Hi, Mam, I'm back. 'Yeah, tell them the news. I'll be home sometime at the end of the month.'

I hung up, even though I could still hear Dad crowing with delight.

By nine o'clock I'd showered and dressed and cleaned up the mess in the hallway, tossing disinfectant along the floor to take the smell away. I sat at the breakfast table, listening to the local news and praying there wouldn't be an item on Conor Mason's body being discovered. I ate three bowls of Weetabix soaked in cold milk and munched through six slices of toast and marmalade. I was starving, yet my insides were churning with tension. Too much was happening and I felt I was losing control, that the string pullers were tugging like hell and I was dancing yet again to their tunes. Why had the foreign cleaners returned? I wanted to challenge them about the night of 12 February, when I was abducted. Do you know where Lisa Duggan is? But I realised I would get nowhere; they were probably on the Justice Department payroll. So I sat and ate and wondered. I heard doors open and close downstairs, voices and shouts.

For some reason I started packing. I had an uncontrollable urge to put my affairs in order and began folding belongings into three suitcases. I remembered how women coming up to labour were driven to clean the family nest and knew also how suicide plotters often cancelled credit cards and paper rounds, paid bills and then tidied the house before taking a final overdose. I wondered whether my brain was telling me something that rational thought refused to allow. Frank Ryan, you will not see the dawn of 12 March. Don't leave a mess. Consider your position and sort things. Do it now, Frank, before it's too late. It took an hour and by then I had the bags ready, leaving out only toiletries. The urine-soaked dressing gown went into a garbage bag, even though it was a Christmas present from Lisa. Considering how much I treasured any item she'd ever given me, that decision troubled.

I crawled through another of Dublin's traffic nightmares, stuck in tailbacks and jumping lights. It was almost a national custom to ignore the Highway Code. By eleven o'clock the cloud cover had lifted and a weak sun was shining. There was a hint of spring in the air and I noticed buds straining to open on trees while crocuses and daffodils brightened median strips. It was warm enough to have my side window down, an elbow resting on the sill. I wore trousers, shirt and tie with casual jacket and carried my Gladstone bag on the seat beside. For the past week or so I'd almost been oblivious to the daily lives of Dublin and its citizens, my mind otherwise preoccupied. Now I realised winter overcoats weren't so common, lightweight windcheaters taking over. Faces were up and smiling, not burrowed into the chin and red raw from biting winds. There was an air of optimism, but I couldn't share it.

I parked in the prison compound, circling the zone for about five minutes before finding a space. That was unusual as the lot was rarely more than three-quarters full at any time. I glanced around, spotting a cluster of black-tinted SUVs with searchlight mountings. Now what the hell are they doing here? My ID unlocked the same doors as before and I sauntered as casually as I could muster along the corridors and spiral steel stair-wells. A group of workmen in blue overalls was welding iron bars along a fire escape, another crowd repairing locks close to the canteen. A radio was tuned to a music station and an aroma of burnt coffee was in the air. Round another corner I smelt today's lunch, bacon, cabbage and potatoes, and decided I'd eat out. I was broke but I wasn't desperate. The lingering and clinging prison whiff seemed stronger than ever and I held a handkerchief to my face as I took a second flight of razor-meshed stairs and waited at the final steel gate.

'This place stinks,' I complained to the guard at the medical rooms.

'Too many criminals,' he explained as he handed me a list of patients. 'The courts are getting tough on street violence and we're getting more lock-ups every day. It's four to a cell at the moment.'

If that continues, I thought, there'll be another riot.

'Is the nurse here?'

'Nah, she called in sick. Won't be back for a week.' I wondered whether he deliberately avoided my questioning glance but let it ride.

My opening chores included prescribing methadone for regular inmates and a few new faces. Wizened, gnarled, scarred, tattooed, jaundiced, defeated and addicted, they came in a bunch for the heroin substitute and I went through the motion of listening, inspecting and examining. I wasn't up to the usual litany of lies and tricks, the familiar denials of narcotic abuse inside the jail.

'I'm doing very well on the methadone programme, Dr Ryan. With any luck I'll go clean soon.' I'd heard that line and its variations so many times and knew it was bullshit. Today every needle track I scrutinised, be it on arm, leg, neck or groin, showed recent activity. Where a vein was accessible it was speared and heroin injected. The methadone was usually shared out along the landings or traded for stronger hits. In one notorious wing, lifers saved it up for good-looking young offenders. The kids were then plied with the drug and most grabbed the opportunity to dull their senses. When completely stoned they were buggered without resistance. The resulting injuries were often severe and difficult to treat. And no one ever made a formal complaint. Today I was hoping I would be spared a fresh glut of this savagery.

Forty minutes into the surgery Dan Steele sat opposite me and I immediately sensed he was uptight. The scar that ran from his left ear to his chin was straight and quivering, his lips tight and drawn. The nicotine staining was deeper, his nails chewed to the quick. Chain-smoking had discoloured his eyebrows and tinted his skin. Where I'd almost strangled him the nail indentations were still visible but the blood spots had faded.

'What's wrong?' I asked.

'Everything.' He glanced over his shoulder to make sure the door was tightly shut, and then drew himself close to the desk. 'They're shifting guys all over the place. C-wing was raided while we were in the exercise yard. D- and E-wings were turned over around the same time. J-wing is clear and ready for use.'

My eyebrows shot up. J-wing was where the witness-protection candidate was being kept.

'Have they moved the detainee?'

'I don't know.'

'Fuck off, Steele. You know everything that happens in this place.'

'I used to, now I'm not so sure any more.' There was an urgency and uncertainty to the growl I hadn't heard before. 'Nobody's passing anything to me. And that's not good. I pay serious money for information.' He stood and took three steps backwards, left ear cocked to the outside. I could hear the mumble of conversation, an occasional laugh and shout. He was back. 'Are we on track for tomorrow?' No surprises here, Steele already knew the X-ray date. I decided his hospital contact was keeping him informed.

'Yes. You're in a group of five leaving around ten, arriving at the City Hospital by ten thirty. The plan is to have everyone screened and out by twelve. That allows time to make a move.' It was three miles from the prison to the medical facility but I knew the roads would be relatively traffic free. Up to the tailback junction where I anticipated all hell would break loose.

Now Steele sat forward, studying me closely. 'And where will you be, doc?' His eyes had narrowed to suspicious slits.

'Getting ready to quit,' I lied. 'By midnight tomorrow I plan to be on a flight to Singapore, en route to Sydney. I'll be on the beach when you're trying to stay ahead of the posse.'

There was a strained silence, each of us weighing the other up. Finally Steele broke the ice. 'I don't trust you.'

'And I don't trust you. So where does that leave us?'

'Don't double-cross me, doc. I won't say that again, but remember it.' Suddenly the urgency and uncertainty had gone. He was back in killer mode. 'If this screws up I'll come after you and your family. I swear to Christ I'll kill every fucking one of them.' His face was contorted in rage and hatred and I had a feel for the final hours of the two drug couriers he'd killed. But I didn't flinch. I was past being scared.

'If anything happens tomorrow you won't be able to do a thing about it.' Steele made to interrupt but I kept going. 'Nor will Ratko and Gerry whatever-his-name-is. We'll all be dead.'

That caught the convict short and I noticed him startle. 'Waddye mean?'

'If there is a screw-up it won't be by me. Your men could make a bad call or get trigger-happy and start shooting. Anything could go wrong and you know it.'

'I work with professionals, doc. When Gerry organises something it goes to plan. He doesn't do mistakes.' Steele couldn't disguise the boast.

Now I knew who'd be masterminding the break-out. Gerry was ex-British army so would bring military training and expertise to the strategy. Maybe it would run smoothly, maybe there wouldn't be casualties. But since I knew the villains involved, any reassurances were in my mind only. The same gang would stop at nothing to achieve their ends. I decided it was time to end my involvement.

'You want to get out of here and I've arranged it,' I said. 'That means my side of the deal is over. Now I want explanations.'

'Explanations,' Steele repeated.

'Exactly. My sources released details of your involvement with Milos Bracchovis. He's a real Dan Steele crony, isn't he? Mass murderer, gun-runner, drug baron and pimp. You mix in all the right circles.'

If this was news to Steele he didn't show it. He chewed on the inside of his cheek, eyes boring into me. Finally he shrugged. 'That's no big deal, doc. When I'm on the outside I'll be a very rich man. And if all goes to plan some could trickle down to you.'

'I told you, I don't want anything to do with you after this. What I need is information.'

'Like what?'

'Did you have Conor Mason killed?' It was a trawling exercise.

Steele's face scrunched with surprise, real or imagined I couldn't decide. 'No. Maybe I shoulda a long time ago but I didn't. Why?'

'He's missing.' I didn't want to offer Steele more than basic information.

'So? He hangs out with a twisted crowd who get annoyed if things go wrong. Maybe he got on somebody's nerves once too often.'

That was possible, but why contact me? 'You're telling me you know nothing of his whereabouts?'

Steele snorted in disgust. 'I don't care a toss of his whereabouts. He's a piece of shit.'

I knew when Dan Steele was offering information and when he was going to clam. Right now he was a clam and I decided to sideline queries on Mason. Whatever had happened would surface eventually. I pushed my luck on another pressing issue.

'Who is Noel Dempsey and what does he do?'

A smile flickered and then died on Steele's lips. Now there was only a sneer. 'You'll get nothing on Dempsey until I'm out of here. For your own safety.'

I was half expecting that. 'What about Lisa Duggan?'

Steele rested his hands on the desk and inspected his palms. His scar went taut, his features suddenly dark and ominous. In the corridor a telephone rang and I could just about make out a voice answering.

'Come on, I don't have all day. We'll be interrupted. What do you know about Lisa Duggan?'

He stood up, shrugged and looked right past me. There was something strange about his manner and I pushed back from the desk. Then a memory flashed, a friend calling to the homestead. He was an elderly farmer from ten miles east who ran a spread of sheep and horses. Tall, weather-beaten face, big gnarled hands. A good man and a good neighbour, he'd stood exactly as Dan Steele was standing now. On that day he'd nervously passed his bushman's hat from hand to hand, eyes fixed on the slate floor. He was bringing bad news; there'd been a death in the family. Suddenly I didn't want to hear Steele's answer, recoiled at the words spilling from the man's lips. No, no. Oh, God, no.

'I'm real sorry you had to hear this from me, doc. She's dead.'

23

'I read the files on every long-term inmate to familiarise myself with the individual, background and crime. Not long after I started here I realised the majority of urban offenders came from soulless concrete estates or tower blocks with broken elevators, leaking roofs and shoddy plumbing. I've walked the stairs in these places and you wouldn't keep a dog in them. There's a clinging smell of grease and cooking oil, of poverty and decay. The corridors are strewn with dirty nappies, used syringes and rubbish. Behind some battered and scratched doors you can hear screeching babies and angry shouts from drunken and drugged parents. Postmen refuse to deliver mail, the police only visit in numbers. Decent residents are terrorised by out-of-control teenagers who in turn are intimidated by gangs. Drug abuse is widespread: heroin, amphetamines, crack cocaine, cannabis, you name it and they've got it. It's a breeding ground for criminality.'

A long time ago, on my second day as CMO to Harmon Penitentiary, governor Campbell gave me a tour, accompanied by warders carrying batons, cans of Mace and loops of keys. The atmosphere was poisoned with hostile expressions and intimidating frowns. Convicts glared from behind barred landings, scowling at the small troop invading their privacy. Eye contact was brief and furtive, expressions surly and threatening. Anywhere I looked the conversations were hushed and secretive, hands shielding mouths, eyes averted. My first impression was of mutual hatred and loathing, prisoners to guards, guards to prisoners. That day the floors stank more than usual after an attack on cleaning staff and a subsequent wildcat strike. Washing and sluicing were suspended, aerosol air fresheners deployed to dull the stench. Combined with the heavy-handed protection this was unsettling, but no more than that. In truth, at the time I considered the jail a challenge, its medical, psychological and criminal pathology both repulsive and strangely fascinating. The governor opened up to me, more than I was expecting, a discourse that at times was rambling and bitter. But his words stuck in my memory.

'My therapist blames Harmon for my marriage problems. Much of the police evidence is very disturbing. Murder, rape, torture, rape and murder, torture and then rape and then murder: it's all in these wings. This is my

tenth year as governor and I hoped I'd be battle hard-ened by now. But I'm not; I'm worn out and depressed. The convicts and their aggressive behaviour still get to me. I go home grumpy and irritable, snapping at the children and behaving like an anti-Christ. I drink too much and take Prozac to get through the day.'

I was surprised at the man's candour but said nothing.

'One killer in J-wing butchered two young women while spaced out on drink and drugs. The crime-scene photographs are appalling: teenage girls cut up and left to the rats. Those images still give me nightmares. Every time I see this murderer I want to hurt him, and hurt him badly. But the courts decide the penalty and it is not my role to dispense further justice. Instead I make his sentence safe and secure, check that he's fed and washed, adequately housed and protected, offered every medical facility if he becomes unwell.'

That gave me something to think about.

'I used to look at the outside walls and think how massive they are. Now I don't think they're big enough. Sometimes I believe I can even smell the evil lifting off the cell blocks. Harmon Penitentiary is a hell on earth. If you stay long enough it ruins you.'

I was sure he was exaggerating.

'Lying and cheating and killing is the law of the landings and taints everyone. Don't become one of them.'

Alone in my apartment I sat at the kitchen table watching the second hand on my watch tick towards midnight and begin the day of 11 March. In front of me was a half-eaten bag of chips, a discarded beef burger, an empty can of Pepsi and a Glock 19 handgun. I'd bought the food earlier, after wandering aimlessly along the streets and lanes of downtown Dublin. I scanned restaurant windows, inspected public houses and cafés, staring in like some child at a toyshop. Lisa couldn't be dead. Dan Steele was lying. Governor Campbell had warned me most prisoners were pathological liars and immediately after Steele's brutal revelation I begged him for information. He pleaded ignorance.

'I heard it from a source.'

Who?

'Can't say.'

How did she die?

'Dunno, he didn't tell me much.'

When did she die?

'You're losin' it, doc. This isn't my territory, I'm only passing information.'

Then he left me to my distress and my desperate search. I was sure I'd find her, even if with another man and holding hands I didn't care. Just let her be alive. I trawled our old haunts along Grafton Street, the city's premier shopping area. Then I trudged alleyways and side lanes in case she'd gone somewhere different. I knew in my soul the exercise was futile, my actions irrational and hopeless. Yet I couldn't stop my legs, couldn't stop my mind, couldn't stop myself. So for hours I covered square miles of territory before exhaustion, dampness and the night chill took their toll.

Crushed and distraught I drove home, stopping at a chipper to buy enough food to keep me going until morning. And even though my mind told me I must be starving my belly couldn't keep the food down. Twice I gagged and twice I had to gulp Pepsi to hold on to the few bites I'd swallowed. Around eleven I started pacing the floor, talking to myself, arguing and complaining. I was beyond grief, too far gone to understand the proper order of things. Save your energy. Sit down and don't wear yourself out. Sleep. But no matter how much guidance I offered, my seething and tormented brain would not relent. I was agitated and uneasy, anxious for the day ahead. So I collected my handgun, stripped and oiled and reassembled it like a master craftsman. Then I prepared ten bullets, cleaning each one with a rag and kissing the tip before loading. And all the time governor Campbell's monologue played in my head, every phrase now assuming sinister portent.

'You have to see life through their eyes, Dr Ryan. Every contact with the outside world is an opportunity for gain. News, gossip, information, plans and *precautions. Some of the most ingenious heists are hatched behind these walls and carried out by others, the leader getting his cut on release. At some stage you'll be targeted. The doctor before you didn't realise how deeply he'd sunk until it was too late.'*

Now in bed and tossing restlessly, I recognised I'd slid to the bottom. I'd entered into a conspiracy with Dan Steele, Harmon's most notorious resident. Then I'd spiralled further into anarchy, engaging with Ratko Predojevic and some ex-British army thug, all friends of mass murderer Milos Bracchovis. His photo image flashed and I thought how small and insignificant he was. After all I'd heard and read about him, especially the killings and butchery, I was expecting an ogre but instead found a dwarf. However, Bracchovis wasn't so physically insignificant that he couldn't terrorise and murder. And pimp. And run guns and drugs. He was a small man with a big, scheming and deviant mind.

Sleep wouldn't come and at 1 a.m. I was back at the kitchen table, plotting and thinking. I took up my Gladstone bag and inspected it closely. It was like a lady's handbag, barrel-shaped worn black leather with frayed grip; inside, the basics of medical necessities. There was a recess for ampoules of adrenalin and atropine to support an ailing heart, anti-emetics for nausea, antibiotics for infection, anti-psychotics for psychiatric emergencies and finally, painkillers. In a sealed pouch rested a bottle of glucose for diabetic crises. Separately I stored needles and syringes, soothing skin ointments, asthma inhalers, steroids and hypnotics. Breaking every code I'd learned in medicine I took a sleeping tablet, first calculating how much rest I'd get. More than anything I needed to be alert later today. Then I felt along the inner lining, noticing how easy it was to free the cloth. Seconds later all the contents were up-ended and I was gently teasing at the stitching. Within minutes I secured the fully loaded Glock onto the bottom, then replaced the material. Back went the drugs, needles and syringes. I reached inside and teased the cloth-covered pistol until I had it stable and accessible. I was ready. Drowsy and desperate to close my eyes, but ready. I collapsed into bed.

I woke at 7.35 a.m., disorientated and fearful. For maybe five minutes I tried to focus on my surroundings, understand place and time. I sat on the side of the bed, taking deep breaths and rocking my head in my hands. One half of me didn't want to recall yesterday's events, wanted to block Dan Steele's words about Lisa: 'I'm real sorry you had to hear this from me, doc. She's dead.' Finally the rational side kicked in and I staggered to the shower and turned the water to cold and stood there shivering. Slowly I eased the thermostat warmer and spent a long time soaping and lathering my body, then rinsing my skin clean. I brushed my teeth vigorously to rid the bitter taste of the sleeping tablet, eyes averted from the mirror. I didn't dare inspect myself; frightened of the gaunt and tortured reflection looking back. Then I dressed, dragging fresh clothes from the packed suitcases.

And all the time I felt I couldn't go through with the battle ahead. Too many innocent bystanders might get hurt; Steele might succeed and get away, leaving me no wiser and severely compromised. Twice I reached for the telephone and twice my fingers halted inches away. A shrill inner voice warned: Steele will come after you and your family. You have to go through with this, there's no choice. But conscience and common sense forced through: put an end to the madness and allow the police to deal with this. At last I caved in, feeling a surge of relief as I picked up the phone to call Bill O'Hara at the Justice Department.

I had the words ready: 'Hi, Bill. I want you to postpone the convoy organised for today. Dan Steele and four others are being transferred to the City Hospital for X-rays but he's going on false pretences. I'll explain later, just pull the plug.'

That's what I'd rehearsed. But the line was dead. I jabbed at the receiver cradle, certain a dialling tone would break through. Nothing. I stared at the handset in disbelief. They've cut the phone off. They've taken away my main line of communication. I was still astounded at the sheer audacity of the government when I heard my front door being opened.

'Dr Ryan?' There were three already inside when I rushed to the hallway. Three bulky individuals in black tracksuits, black trainers and wearing black gloves. Determined faces, no-nonsense body language.

'How the hell did you get in here?' I was outraged but scared. They'd bypassed the time delay lock.

A bunch of keys was waved. 'Justice Department. This is one of their properties.'

'It's still my personal residence.' The anger was fading as fast as the colour on my face. The intruders didn't look as though they had come for a discussion on privacy rights.

'Our instructions are to take you to the prison.' They surrounded me, edging me towards the door.

'Could you get my Gladstone bag, please?' I stopped just in time.

Three sets of eyes exchanged suspicious looks. 'It contains my emergency drugs,' I explained. 'I'd hate to turn up with no treatments.'

The Gladstone was snapped open, the contents briefly inspected, and then thrust into my offered grasp. It felt like a warm gun in my hand.

I forced a smile. 'OK, I'm ready.'

I was squashed into a squad car, one of the escort taking the driver's seat while the other two sat on either side of me in the rear. Another car waited in the forecourt and when we drove past it I saw the foreign cleaners staring out at me.

'Occasionally I plant undercover policemen in the cell blocks when I suspect something big is being hatched. Murder, riots, drug deals especially.'

Not one word was spoken throughout the journey. The radio was silent, the windows closed even though it was oppressively warm. My Gladstone rested on my lap and I held it tightly, determined no one would take it. Dublin's streets were busy; traffic stop-starting and every forward gain an achievement. After about thirty minutes the roads became easier, the delays less intrusive and the squad car picked up speed. Overhead cotton-wool clouds played hide-and-seek with the sun; brightness sparred with shadows. It might turn out to be a pleasant afternoon. For some.

I glanced at my watch. It was closing on nine o'clock. Ahead in Harmon Penitentiary five men were preparing for the day. For four it meant no more than a break from the stifling and cramped conditions of a prison cell, a chance to see ordinary people leading ordinary lives. But for Dan Steele it marked the crunch point in his break-out plan. Would Ratko and Gerry swing the ambush? In an hour or so would the killers be on the run? There was still time for me to call a halt, quietly inform Bill O'Hara of the scheming. I'd be a hero. But an old feeling stirred inside, an uneasy and disquieting notion. You're being driven to someone else's agenda. I squinted out the rear window. The other car was on our tail.

About ten minutes' driving time from the prison we passed the office blocks at the corner of the junction where I expected the escape to be sprung. The tailbacks were as usual, the lights still offering little time to get through. On the opposite side of the road, over red-on-blue hoarding I could see the giant crane manoeuvring steel girders crossways. The noise of the building works penetrated our closed cocoon. Then I squinted up to where I had planned to direct my firing line, the sniper position so inviting yet so elusive. What now? My guts knotted.

We swung into Harmon Penitentiary through a side gate reserved for service vehicles and came to a halt. In a parking lot I recognised the black-tinted SUVs with searchlight mountings, now with driver doors open and exhausts chugging. There was a clutch of armed policemen speaking into tiny microphones clipped to their jackets. Their attention was focused on a steel door in a significant granite wall fifty yards inside the perimeter.

'Dr Ryan?'

One of the escorts faced me.

'Yes.'

'They want you at the front entrance. Let's go.'

I could have been driven right up to the front entrance. Why the circuitous route?

'Who wants me?'

He didn't answer.

I followed. As I kept pace with my guide I had a sense of being watched, and turned. Two warders, men that I recognised, were staring at me and as our eyes met they immediately inspected the ground. My guts tightened again. I stopped and waited, deliberately delaying, but felt a dig in the ribs and found another black-suited attendant at my side.

'Keep moving.'

'What the hell's going on?' I asked.

He ignored the question, gripping an elbow and hurrying me.

The gate was opened, the thick plate swung inwards and I entered a cobblestone courtyard surrounded by razor wire. Overhead, the cloud cover broke and warm spring sunshine flooded the area, throwing shadows and momentarily dazzling. I shielded my eyes and when I focused, ahead was Patrick Halloran, the Minister for Justice. His tall frame stood out in a scrum of eight people, shock of grey hair hanging over his forehead as usual. It was perplexing to see the Justice Minister at the jail, strange to see him in anything but dark suit and tie. This morning he was in navy trousers and beige roll-neck sweater, as if on the way to a golf course. He was talking to Bill O'Hara, his chief civil servant, the two head to head. The rest were warders and police officers of various ranks. The governor, Don Campbell, wasn't there.

'Wait here, Dr Ryan.' Like a schoolboy I was parked in a corner while the gate behind was secured. I inspected the surroundings. The annexe was one wall away from the main prison entrance. On the other side I could hear voices, barked orders, engines revving.

Halloran detached himself and made his way past without so much as a nod. Out of the corner of an eye I spotted Bill O'Hara glance in my direction but when I turned he turned. I pulled my jacket lapels close to my throat. I felt cold and clenched my teeth to stop them chattering.

'I vary routines or planned excursions to catch the

prisoners off guard. I have to stay one step ahead all the time.'

The noise level on the other side of the wall dropped significantly. A police officer with mobile phone at his ear came towards me.

'This way, Dr Ryan.'

I followed.

We stopped at a wooden gate strengthened with rivets and studs. I heard keys turning locks, first one, then another and then a third. The bolts moved with deep clunks, mortises grinding and clicking with effort. The barrier was swung open and now I was ushered towards the front of Harmon Penitentiary, its massive gates slightly ajar. Ahead, two black Ford transit vans were parked side by side, rear doors drawn apart. The front cabs were screened by bullet-proof glass and when I looked closer I realised the bodywork was made of reinforced steel. The frame rested heavily on unusually wide wheels, the tyres squeezing to hold the load. There were no markings to identify ownership and it was impossible to distinguish one van from the other.

As I waited, a door within a much larger and heavier door opened and governor Campbell poked his head out, searched until he found me and waved.

'Confuse them as often as possible. Vary the routine, change schedules at the last minute.'

My group of patients was waiting inside, handcuffed to each other and in a line that was secured to six prison officers. Dan Steele was in the middle. He looked pale and drawn, his grey hair dishevelled and falling over his brow. A hand kept reaching to push it away but the chains restricted his movement. I could see his legs shaking underneath his denims. By contrast the other prisoners were smiling and jaunty as if off to a day at the races.

Campbell stood in front of them, a clipboard in hand. He turned to me.

'Are these the men for the hospital?'

'Yes.'

He unclipped paperwork and handed each prisoner a single sheet. Except for Dan Steele.

'Change of plan. The X-ray machine was repaired yesterday. I can get films taken here this morning. Return to your cells and you'll be called when needed.'

There were gasps, then an immediate outcry.

'Fuck off.'

'Ah, for fuck's sake.'

'Ah, Jaysus, I was lookin' forward to a day outta this kip.'

'Wankers.'

But within minutes the quartet was being forced to their cells, complaining and stalling and sniping. Dan Steele was left on his own, handcuffed and suspicious. This was not going to plan. Our eyes met briefly and I offered a shrug. I don't know either. At that point I ditched all ideas of revealing the getaway. There was something afoot.

I sneaked a glance at my watch. 9.55 a.m. If we were actually heading for the City Hospital we had to leave within the next five minutes. From behind came the shuffle of feet and now four police officers showed. They were dressed in dark fatigues, wearing combat helmets and holding bulletproof shields. Sheltered between them was Sefik Barisik, the witness-protection detainee. He faced forward, both hands resting on the shoulders of the officer in front. I could just about hear a subdued mumble and realised he was praying.

Suddenly the area was flooded with policemen in body armour and helmets with visors down. In the blur I saw Uzi sub-machine guns, holstered pistols and stun grenades clipped to waistbands. I gripped the Gladstone, frantically wondering how my Glock 19 would protect me. There was serious hardware on display.

Six officers crowded around Dan Steele and he started shouting.

'Leave me alone, ye bastards.'

I saw a gloved hand grip the back of his head while another clamped his face. His shouts became muffled curses. Seconds later I was shoved forward.

'What the hell . . .'

'Keep going, Dr Ryan. We've got to get you to the City Hospital by ten thirty.' I tried to wriggle to find the voice but when I turned all I saw were perspex visors. Then I recognised an accent.

'At the count, everyone move.' It was Noel Dempsey; there was no mistaking the nasal twang. I struggled to find him.

'Dempsey, you bastard,' I screamed over the crowd. 'Where is Lisa Duggan? What have you done to her?'

I managed to break free and saw Dempsey at the entrance. He was in denims and blue open-neck shirt, a heavy-duty gun slung over his left shoulder. He ignored me; his attention was focused on the transit vans. I squinted in that direction and saw Sefik Barisik, his face white and lips trembling. He looked like a man preparing for his own funeral.

'Counting now.' Strong grasps tightened on my arms. Rough hands, stinking of nicotine, smothered my protests.

'Ten, nine, eight, seven, six, five, four . . .'

There was silence, broken only by the background drone of Dublin city traffic. Somewhere an ambulance siren wailed. I struggled to breathe.

'Go.'

Under an umbrella of bulletproof shields Sefik Barisik was bundled from inside the prison to the back of one of the transit vans. Two blurred shapes followed.

Less than a yard away there was an angry struggle and muffled curses. Seconds later, Dan Steele was forced into the second transit. Without my feet touching the ground I was thrown after him and landed in a heap on the floor, winded and confused. As I scrambled to get up I heard scuffling and vicious swearing and the jangle of chains. A heavy hand pushed me down and I couldn't see past a blob of black uniforms.

'Get off me.' Dan Steele was raging. Boots clumped on the bodywork, I heard locks clicking, the distinct thud of punches hitting bone, a winded groan, then a slap, strangled curses and now moaning. Finally, the hand on my head pulled away and when I turned Noel Dempsey was staring straight at me.

Then the doors were slammed shut.

I felt the engine rumble, jolted slightly as the carrier shifted. I dragged myself to a half-squat, frantically trying to take in the situation. From the roof inside a single light glowed, breaking the gloom. Dan Steele was lying on the floor, wrists and ankles chained together. His face was red, his left eye swelling. There was a graze on his lower lip oozing fresh blood. His eyes darted from side to side, disbelief and panic screaming. I was pitched forward as we bumped over a ramp and scrambled to the only window, a narrow rectangle behind the front cab. Over the driver's shoulder I could see we were edging out through the prison entrance. In front was a black SUV with search-light mountings and ahead again was the other transit. At the main road we paused before one half of the convoy swung left towards the City Hospital. Our driver turned right. As we gathered speed I spotted a row of squad cars, blue strobes flashing.

'What's happening?' Dan Steele shouted. 'What the fuck's going on, tell me?'

I slid onto the floor, my heart racing and my breathing laboured. My hands were shaking and I forced my fingers flat.

'I don't know, I really don't know.'

'I always keep my cards close to my chest.'

Neither of us spoke for maybe a minute, possibly two. My mind was racing. The transit was heading in the opposite track to what I'd expected. The attack site I'd decided on was immediately written off. Did Steele's cronies know what was going on? Had they a back-up strategy? I wanted to interrogate Steele but when I looked across he was frozen in his own thoughts. He had dragged himself into a sitting position, back against the bodywork, staring stony faced ahead. He was straining at the chains on his wrists, twisting and untwisting and mumbling a mixture of oaths and prayers. Suddenly he didn't seem so dangerous any more, the hard-man façade vulnerable and cracking.

'There are many ways to skin a cat, Dr Ryan, and many ways to run a prison. Convicts don't believe in regulations so I make my own rules to suit needs. Nobody knows of them, of course. Not even the inmates. And they think they know everything.'

'They're taking us in a different direction.'

Steele didn't respond; his head was down, his lips moving silently.

I went back to the window in time to see the transit veer off the road and into a side street.

'Where are we?' Now Steele was looking over.

'I don't know.'

'What can you see?'

I squinted. The driver's shoulders moved with the steering wheel and I had to go on tiptoe to see past. 'A church, a row of houses, a small shopping mall.' The buildings flew by as the accelerator was pressed. At a tight corner I lurched as the van swung sharply.

When I looked again the black SUV had disappeared.

Then the carrier edged to the side of the road and stopped.

Steele struggled to get up. 'What's happening?'

I could see ahead clearly. It was a narrow street with the usual city traffic. Cars were jammed up on pavements, people about their daily business. Not the sort of area I'd pick for a confrontation. 'I don't know.'

'What can you see?'

'Shut up, I'm trying to find out.'

The driver disappeared from the cab and seconds later a much bulkier form was at the wheel. 'Oh, Jesus,' I muttered.

'What?' Steele shouted. 'What the fuck's wrong?' He'd managed to haul himself upright.

'They've switched drivers.' I darted from side to side, frantic with apprehension. 'And the new guy's in body armour. I can't even see the back of his neck.'

Steele didn't speak. He was trying to find a grip to steady himself. The engine growled to life again and the van took off, this time much slower.

I crouched onto my hunkers, my brain scrambling to make sense. Dan Steele was swaying to the movement of the transit, his chained hands splayed against the panelling. He spread his ankles as wide as the restraints allowed.

'We're fucked, doc. We're totally fucked.'

I didn't know how true that was but decided to prepare for all eventualities. I opened the Gladstone and pushed my shaking fingers through the jumble of drugs, needles and syringes. I teased the Glock free and into my grip. I released the safety catch. Keeping the gun inside I pulled the bag across my belly. Then I slid to the floor.

Now was the time to hold Steele accountable for my unanswered questions. What happened to Lisa? What does Noel Dempsey work at? What is this conspiracy about? 'Steele, I want some straight answers . . .'

Seconds later a crash almost lifted me out of my skin. Through the reinforced panelling I heard a muffled curse, then frantic shouts. The van swerved violently to one side, throwing Steele off balance. I forced my legs wide for support and pushed backwards. I heard gunfire. A single burst followed by a second salvo. The transit hummed as bullet after bullet pinged off the metal. There was a grating of gears, the vehicle bounced, swerved, bounced again, then shuddered to a halt. There was silence. Dan Steele looked up from the corner where his body had been thrown. He started wriggling towards me. Now came thumping on the outside, the carrier was being pummelled. My heart raced as I followed the sounds. I couldn't control my bladder and felt warm urine soak my trousers.

There was another burst of gunfire and the panelling pinged again.

'They've come for me.' Even in the gloom I saw the glint in Steele's eyes. 'They're here.'

Now came a loud thump on the back doors, followed by three bangs, as if fists were pounding. With each bang my stomach lurched.

Steele pushed closer, screaming at me. 'Get down.'

I ducked just in time.

The explosion sent a rush of noise to my ears and I heard ringing and zinging. There was a bright flash that momentarily blinded and I blinked furiously. When I managed to see properly the rear doors were hanging off their hinges and the road behind was visible.

'Go, go, go,' Steele was struggling to break free. 'Get out of here, it could explode.'

I started forward, tripping over myself, and crashed to the floor. Steele was already at the edge, both feet swung sideways, his chains rattling against the panelling. I heard shouts, strange words. Steele shouted back. Suddenly Ratko Predojevic was there, no mistaking the stocky and swarthy frame, the vicious brown eyes dancing with the excitement of the moment. He flourished a pistol in his left hand.

'Gemme outta here,' Steele roared. He held both

arms up to show his chains. 'I can't fucking move. Gemme out.'

I was behind him, my hand still inside the Gladstone and holding the Glock. When Ratko saw me his expression changed. There was a flicker of triumph. Without warning he pointed his revolver at Steele and fired four quick rounds into the convict's chest. I fell backwards at the gunfire, felt warm blood splatter my neck. When I twisted, Ratko was aiming straight at me. I swung the Gladstone in a half-circle, pressing the trigger in rapid succession, and squirmed sideways. Bullets pinged inside the van, zinging off the bodywork. I pulled the Glock out of the bag and took aim again. Ratko was still standing but stunned. His face was contorted in pain and disbelief. His shooting hand dropped and he began to buckle. I finished him with two quick rounds to the head.

From nearby came screams and shouts, angry voices and curses. I jumped onto the road and crouched low, gun in hand. Where is Nixon, Ratko's sidekick? A motorbike engine was gunned alive and the roar came towards me. I slid to the ground and swung the Glock wildly, frantic to find any attacker. Then I heard a fresh volley of bullets and felt a sting in my left leg. I grabbed at the wound, a scream filling my throat. Again the air filled with gunfire and I felt one, then another bullet thud into me. My chest went numb, my breathing immediately laboured. I swallowed and tasted my own blood. A searing pain coursed through my other leg and when I tried to move it didn't respond. I coughed and spat out blood, copious and frothy. My lungs rasped and bubbled and I collapsed onto my back, fighting to get air, fighting to live. I looked up at the sky but the brightness had gone, replaced by a strange darkness.

24

Whoooosh, humphhhhhh. Whoooosh, humphhhhhh. Whoooosh, humphhhhhh.

I came around to the sound of a ventilator.

I kept my eyes closed, my brain befuddled and
disconnected.

I wasn't breathing, a tube down my windpipe
was doing it for me. I gagged at the irritating sensation in my throat, tried desperately to chew and
spit out.

Whoooosh, humphhhhhh. Whoooosh, humph-
hhhh. Whoooosh, humphhhhhh.

I wanted to scream but couldn't. Finally, I
forced my eyes open and closed them immediately,
dazzled by halogen lights burning down on me. I
tried moving but it took too much effort. Soon I
realised I was on my back and restrained by wide
straps.

I wasn't in much pain, just a slight discomfort

in both legs and a rasping, grating ache to the right of my chest. I slowly tried the muscles in the fingers of my left hand. They moved. Now I made a tight grip in the other hand and eased the tension. It moved too.

I was exhausted.

I shut down my brain and tried to slip into the ether from which I'd come.

I was alive.

I didn't want to be.

Whoooosh, humphhhhhh. Whoooosh, humphhhhhh. Whoooosh, humphhhhhh.

The ventilator bellows continued.

Just the flick of an electrical circuit and they could be turned off and I would find peace. It wasn't going to happen.

Why are they keeping me alive? I willed back the pleasant state of unconsciousness.

'Frank, can you hear me?' A male voice came at me from the left.

My eyes flickered and I saw dazzling rainbows.

'If you can hear me, Mr Ryan . . .'

'It's Dr Ryan.' Now there was a female to my right, a voice I didn't recognise but which sounded Filipino. 'He's a doctor.' A soft hand squeezed my right hand.

'Sorry, I forgot that. Dr Ryan, if you can hear me, open your eyes and try and keep them open.'

I tried but the lids felt a ton weight. I struggled

to speak but couldn't. The tube was still down my throat.

My hand was squeezed again, encouraging and cajoling. 'Frank, please try.' The Filipina sounded concerned but with my eyes shut I couldn't see her eyes.

I summoned all my strength and forced my lids open a fraction. I had to be cautious, I was expecting to be dazzled but the halogens were gone. I looked up and saw a white ceiling, and then a blurred face appeared in my line of vision.

'He's conscious, he's opened his eyes.' The male sounded relieved. 'Well done. Now, Dr Ryan, please listen carefully. I'm going to ask questions with a yes or no answer. To tell me "yes" blink once, to tell me "no" blink twice.'

The instructions slowly filtered into my brain. Too slowly.

'Can you hear me? Blink once for yes and twice for no.'

I didn't respond.

'Can you see? It's one blink for yes, two for no.'

Can I see? I stared ahead; the ceiling was coming closer and then retreating. A face, vague and indistinct, returned.

'Can you see?' Now the voice was impatient. 'Blink once for yes and twice for no.' I closed my eyes and kept them shut.

There was a silence, then mutterings I couldn't

hear clearly. My hand was squeezed again. 'I'll come back in half an hour, Frank. Don't go away.' There was a slight giggle, then the sound of stifled laughter.

Whooooosh, humphhhhhh. Whooooosh, humphhhhhh. Whooooosh, humphhhhhh.

I retreated to whatever void I was in.

'I'm taking the tube out now, Frank. Just try and relax, it won't hurt. I know your chest is very sore but take a breath when I say.'

By now I knew there was a significant medical team attending me. Two trauma surgeons, two registrars, a rota of nurses, junior doctors, physiotherapists, radiologists and people with frowning faces who did nothing but look and walk away. What I didn't know was where I was or how long I'd been here.

Now all I could hear was the hiss of gas from a mask strapped to my face. At regular intervals my lips were moistened with ice cubes. I could move my arms only a little, the IV lines in both restricted full flexion. My right leg was encased in plaster. There was a drain in my chest, just underneath the right clavicle, and it hurt like hell. Almost as troublesome, I had an itch on the tip of my nose I was desperate to scratch. I was blinking yes or no at every question posed but hadn't spoken a word.

Listening to conversations I knew this worried them.
I was sure I could speak; I just had nothing to say.
They didn't know that.

I didn't want to be alive. Why all the effort?
After everything that had happened they still
wanted me to live.

This was torture.

I pretended sleep most of the time. I found that
the only way to cope.

Next time the doctors and staff came around I
heard one say, 'His neurological signs are normal.
He's just not saying anything.'

On the eighth day I found that I was in a single-
bed unit of the intensive care facility at the City
Hospital. Apparently I'd been unconscious for the
immediate forty-eight hours after being dragged
off the streets.

'Frank, Frank. Can you hear me? It's Dad. I'm
right here beside you.'

On the ninth day I heard my father's voice.

I was propped up in bed, resting on a bank of
pillows. The chest drain had been removed, the pain
while they did that made me collapse and there
were anxious moments. Anxious to the medical
team as I heard frantic shouts and suddenly the bed
was tilted so my head was lower than my legs. An
oxygen mask was strapped to my face again and my

IV lines stung as new drugs were injected. I wanted to die but they were determined I wouldn't.

'What's happenin' here? How's he doin'?' There was no mistaking the Aussie accent. Outback tinged with educated Adelaide. The anguish in Dad's voice I hadn't heard since the night Sue had her accident and it distressed me.

'Two trauma surgeons worked on him after he was admitted.' One of the medical team explained my state. 'He was in the operating theatre twice in twelve hours on the first day and on the critical list for some time after. A bullet collapsed his right lung and he bled a lot into the chest cavity. Another bullet shattered the large bone in his right thigh. He had a significant flesh wound in the left leg and lost a lot of blood from that too. For a while we thought he'd sustained brain damage. What with his blood pressure dangerously low for so long we were concerned he'd been deprived of oxygen. He just didn't respond and it was touch and go. To be brutally honest, we didn't think he'd pull through.'

There was a silence so charged I could almost feel it.

Then: 'Do you know what went on that day?'

'No, I'm only concerned with the medical side of things. The police are saying little other than there was a gun battle. It's all hush-hush. There hasn't been a single report in the press. But he's getting VIP treatment. The Minister for Justice called yesterday to see how he's getting on.'

'Halloran? Patrick Halloran, is that the guy?'

'Yes.'

'He's a real nice bloke. I met him m'self and he went out of his way to show how much they're doin' for Frank. It was his suggestion to fly me over here at the government's expense.'

Now that made me take notice and I struggled to sit higher. I felt a searing pain in my chest and sweat poured from my skin. I suddenly felt weak and nauseous, and groaned.

'Frank, Frank, are you all right? Oh, Christ. Nurse, nurse, can you come quickly?' My poor father, he was sobbing. Then I passed out.

When I finally opened up I spoke only to Dad. I didn't trust anyone else and while I wasn't up to offering suspicious glares or challenging questions, they knew by my lack of response that I wouldn't cooperate. I didn't give a damn. I felt wretched, weak and in pain. ('We've stopped the morphine pump. From now on you're on oral analgesics.') My belly felt swollen and I was constipated. Griping gut cramps caught me sharp. My sleep pattern was out of kilter; I dozed most of the day and stared into the gloom each night. I had a lot of time to think but my brain was too addled to cope with logic and memory loss. I was still in a room to myself with no TV or radio for company. Just my father keeping a lonely and worrying bedside vigil.

'I reckon it was within an hour of you gettin' shot we were called. Policeman came to the door. It was past midnight and we were asleep. Your mam was frantic and your sisters cried the night through. It was a real worryin' time, I can tell you.'

I could only cope with snatches of conversation, Dad speaking while I nodded I understood or fell asleep mid-sentence. I said very little, the effort and pain and distress too draining. I wished I'd died but watching my father's anguish made me rethink that selfish notion. Now I wanted to know what did happen that day but no one was prepared to go down that route and Dad was being stonewalled. It was classic Justice Department tactics. They had outwitted me at every turn. I cursed a lot, silent but deep. If only I had the strength I'd pull their accursed house down. But I hadn't the strength, so I held my tongue.

'It was the next day Mr Halloran called me. Said how sorry he was with all the bad news and what, but at least you were alive and in the best hospital and bein' looked after by top surgeons. Then he offered to fly me to Dublin at the government's expense and put me up in a five-star hotel for as long as I wanted to stay. I thought that was real generous.'

The bastard, was all I thought. The scheming, devious and lying bastard; ingratiating himself with my poor deluded father and making himself out to be kind and generous. What an act, what a class bloody act.

'He says they're still tryin' to figure out everythin'. I spoke with one of the top cops and he promised he'd get to the bottom of the case and tell me personally whatever came out. They've all been very helpful, Frank. Why are you lookin' at me like that?'

It was difficult enough for my father; I could see the fear and dread in his face any time I found the strength to say a word. I didn't want to make life any more unbearable. So I kept my counsel.

On the tenth night I got into difficulties.

'How are you feeling, Frank?' One of the junior doctors was frowning at me.

'Hot.' I had to say something, I felt so awful. For the past twelve hours I'd been rambling, sometimes sense, most times nonsense.

'Yeah, you're spiking a temperature. It's a hundred and three. You feeling jittery?'

I'd been experiencing a rush of new sensations.

439

I was hot one minute, then cold the next. There was a strange feeling as if someone was walking frost fingertips up and down my back. My teeth were chattering and my hands and feet felt like ice. I started shivering, so violently the bed frame rattled.

'He's having a rigor,' I heard someone say as I burrowed deeper into the clothes.

'OK, do a blood culture and FBC and try and get a urine sample for microbiology. We'd better get a portable chest X-ray.'

I shook like a leaf, my body attacked by wave after wave of shudders.

I started to hallucinate. I was back home on the station during the shearing season. I could hear sheep bleating in nearby paddocks, the barking of dogs and the pounding of hooves against parched earth. I could see a dustbowl, high and thick and blocking the sun. I felt sweat trickle down my neck and back. It was hot and sticky and I longed for the shade of the front porch and a cold beer. I was on horseback and dug my heels into the mare's flanks, urging her forward. Now there was a cool breeze on my face and I galloped flat strap across creeks and slate trails, shouting and delighting in the freedom. Yet I was still parched with an intense thirst. I stopped at a well at the back of the property and pumped fresh water, then tied my mount and made sure she was drinking. I sat under the cover of a windmill and poured a bucketful of cold water over my head, shivering as it splashed my shoulders and my belly. I gulped at the rivulets spilling over my face.

Suddenly the water changed and I tasted someone's mouth, felt the delicious and arousing glow of warm lips kissing my lips. I smelt perfume, Dolce & Gabbana, and wrinkled my nose as wisps of hair brushed my skin. I heard a young woman's voice.

'Oh, Frank, what have they done to you?' The kisses moved to my cheeks and neck and then slowly and lovingly moist lips met each closed eyelid, lingering and wetting. 'Oh, my God, Frank, how can I ever forgive myself? What have they done? How could they let this happen?'

I wanted to wake up and reach out. I knew it was Lisa, I knew her smells and strokes, remembered her accent. But I was frightened to open my eyes; scared it was nothing but a dream. So I said nothing, just eased myself into the warm glow of my lover's caresses.

A door opened and now I heard sobbing, deep and plaintive cries of grief. Then my father's subdued but consoling voice. 'He'll be OK, he's a strong kid. He's had bigger knocks than this in the bush on his damned trail bike.

I know he'll pull through. Go on home, I'll keep in touch.'

And for the first time in longer than I could remember I fell into a deep and relaxed sleep. Lisa was back. The nightmare was over.

25

Six months later.

Balgawroo was the small town in South Australia
my folks moved to when they quit the outback.
And it was here, in the new family dwelling, that
I completed my rehabilitation. After Dublin it
dazzled, a grey-versus-blue challenge that was no
contest at all. Every morning I woke up I saw azure
skies broken only by an occasional cloud. I enjoyed
hours of warm sunshine and delighted in hearing
cockatoos screeching and crows fffarking. Even
dogs barking in the neighbour's back yard gave me
a lift. These were the familiar and reassuring
sounds of Australia, of home and safety. When I
looked out my bedroom window I saw gum trees,
bottlebrush and rolling hills planted with grape
vines. It made me feel good.

★　★　★

The prolonged drought broke during the winter months of July and August with wonderful waves of drizzle followed by downpours. The red clay held firm, trying desperately to suck up every drop of moisture. The countryside changed from arid brown to lush green within a week. Some nights I lay awake listening to rain drilling off the tin roof, gurgling down drainpipes and sloshing onto the ground.

Dad was delighted. 'It's good rain too, Frank. Not the stair-rod type that washes topsoil away. It's good and steady and regular and that nourishes the earth.'

The house was a modern version of the traditional outback residence with local brownstone walls, slate floors and corrugated roof and veranda. The front garden, where Mam grew her flowers, was a mix of native Australian and sun-loving European species. In the back there was a tennis court and small swimming pool. The pool was a blessing; I swam for two hours daily to keep my legs pumping and air coursing through my lungs. Every evening when the temperature dropped I jogged. The route was always the same: out the front door and turn left to Second Street and along side tracks until I reached Main Street, one mile further ahead. I hurried past Delange Real Estate, Cowper Bakery, McKenna Hardware ('Hiya, Frank. How's the leg holdin' up?' from the owner), then ran by the other shops and pub and petrol station. I usually took a break underneath the shade of the bridge, inspecting the river level and trying to calculate how much rainfall there'd been further north. The pace wasn't over-stretching and I stopped when pain kicked in. Even in the warmth of a South Australian spring my bones ached. And there were dawns I awoke gasping, as if my right lung had collapsed again.

Most times I slept well. In the morning I eased myself out of bed and limbered up for about fifteen minutes. The local physiotherapist left a set of exercises to rebuild the weakened muscles around the shattered right thighbone and I followed them religiously. Stretch and relax, stretch and relax. I passed the time gazing out at the road that ran alongside the house.

At midday I lay on the bed for a breathing workout. Deep inspiration caught me on the side where a bullet passed one inch from a major artery. Any lower and I wouldn't have survived. Most times I pushed myself beyond the point of discomfort, my mind turning over again and again the newspaper clipping sent to me at the end of April.

Hostages freed.
Exclusive by our foreign correspondent.

Three Irish hostages kidnapped by a criminal gang in Kosovo were released into UN custody today. Justice Minister Patrick Halloran arrived in the Serbian capital Belgrade to greet the captives and pledged his government's resolve to continue international peacekeeping duties.

The trio, law-enforcement officers based in Pristina, was snatched at gunpoint on 6 February. Within 24 hours a fax arrived at the UN War Crimes Tribunal at The Hague, demanding the release of Milos Bracchovis in exchange for their safe release. Bracchovis is a notorious hoodlum involved in narco-terrorism, gun running and prostitution. He is currently in a military prison in Germany awaiting trial for atrocities committed in the Balkans in the mid-1990s.

The Irish government, in consultation with the UN, forced an immediate media blackout. An elite task force headed by Noel Dempsey was dispatched to the area. Forty-two-year-old Dempsey, a veteran in crisis management, was given total freedom on strategy. In an unprecedented liaison with the underworld, Dempsey established links with known felons and bargained with them for contacts and influence.

'My brief,' explained Dempsey during a private interview in Belgrade, 'was to get the hostages home safely. And by whatever means. British and American military commanders offered little help. Their response was: "This is not within our security remit. But Bracchovis is and he will not be set free." So I had to bend the rules.'

First he recruited Dan Steele, an inmate at Dublin's infamous Harmon Penitentiary. Steele was offered freedom by way of an elaborate escape plan in exchange for information on Bracchovis.

'I had to think like the kidnappers,' Dempsey said. 'I wasn't dealing with religious fanatics or political terrorists. Intelligence suggested Ratko Predojevic, a thug from the old Yugoslav secret police days, was holding the hostages and this was confirmed by Steele's contacts. Predojevic had a history of kidnappings and killings, of extracting large ransoms by abducting UN employees. He also had a well-tested plan for prisoner exchange. At this point I needed to drag the conflict out as long as possible and lure him from his hiding place.'

It worked. Predojevic was promised the release of Bracchovis. He was also offered Dan Steele as a bonus part of the deal. In a dangerous game of trickery, lying and downright treachery, Dempsey pitted one criminal against the other.

'Bracchovis was told what was on offer and told Predojevic to grab it. Almost as much as his freedom Bracchovis wanted Steele dead. The Dublin mobster had stolen over US $1 million plus a considerable booty of conflict diamonds. This plunder was the result of years of collaboration between the two hoodlums. But Steele double-crossed Bracchovis and made off with most of the takings, dispersing it in offshore bank accounts. Now his head was being offered on a plate.'

For Milos Bracchovis this was a golden opportunity to settle a major grievance. Dan Steele wanted freedom and a chance to lead the good life. Ratko Predojevic went along with the escape bid, believing it part of the overall deal to get Bracchovis out of custody.

Dempsey will only outline so much of his master plan. There is no mention of shadowy underworld figures and clandestine meetings, nor the names of everyone he manipulated to his own needs, saying only that the final result justified his tactics.

What can now be revealed is that Dan Steele was shot dead by Ratko Predojevic, the man he believed had come to free him. Also known is that a co-conspirator called Gerry Barnes (alias

Roger Nixon) acted as a double agent. Barnes, an ex-SAS paratrooper turned mercenary, passed false information to Bracchovis and in turn relayed the intelligence he gathered about the kidnappers' whereabouts. In a dramatic final conflict two fronts erupted on the same day. In Dublin on 11 March the escape from Harmon Penitentiary was foiled in a shoot-out along side streets. During the skirmish prison CMO Dr Frank Ryan was injured by friendly fire and almost died. He was rushed to the City Hospital and spent days on a life-support machine. Dr Ryan is now recovering at a secret location.

Again, on 11 March, near the village of Veldea along the Croat–Serb border, an army undercover unit stormed a remote farmhouse and freed the captives. In the subsequent gun battle seven henchmen loyal to Bracchovis were killed or captured. Noel Dempsey flew to Belgrade that night to formally receive the Irish hostages. 'It was such a joyful reunion,' he told me. 'They'd been beaten and starved and kept chained to one another in a single bedroom. They believed they would be murdered and were in a state of near collapse when discovered. Their release marks a significant chapter in international peacekeeping duties. Now the world knows how highly the Irish government regards the safety of its citizens, soldiers and police officers. There is no price that won't be paid to protect that value.'

Milos Bracchovis goes to trial at the beginning of May and informed sources say the evidence against him is both terrifying and overwhelming. He is expected to spend the rest of his life behind bars.

Belgrade 14 March

By now I knew the report by heart, could recite it verbatim if put to the task. Of course the account barely touched on the real events, the other players and bit-part stooges were air-brushed out: Bill O'Hara at the Justice Department and prison governor Don Campbell each acted out their roles to perfection.

The cleaners in the ground-floor apartment were government spies employed to keep tabs on Lisa. Her affair with me was repeatedly raised at cabinet briefings, my background checked for suspicious intent.

Sefik Barisik, the witness-protection inmate, was planted in Harmon Penitentiary as a warning to Dan Steele. His presence was a constant reminder to Steele of the vendetta between him and Bracchovis. Cooperate or else.

Bracchovis ordered the murder of the Croatian minder, a signal to the Irish government and the

UN that he could strike where and whenever he wanted. Get me out or the hostages die.

I was abducted, beaten and interrogated under sedation to find out how much I knew of Lisa's UN work and whether I was a security risk. I was humiliated, deceived, duped and lied to as it suited. Then I was deliberately twisted and turned, moved like a pawn to fit in with Dempsey's secretive scheming. I was, as I suspected all along, being driven to someone else's agenda. With so many double agents, any counter-attack was doomed to fail. Especially since my sole confidante Conor Mason was feeding this to the government. The journalist switched sides, agreeing to Justice Department control when he realised that he was dealing with a bigger agenda than he could handle.

'I know when to play the opposition to stay alive,' he'd once boasted.

I should have known he was too flaky to trust. Last I heard he was still working as an investigative correspondent.

I couldn't begin to grasp the rest of the manoeuvring, the deception and half-truths, the deliberate scare tactics. The late-night telephone call with a shot being fired and gurgled moan was designed to intimidate. Right down to Dan Steele's awful lie that Lisa was dead and Dempsey's attempt to silence me for ever in a 'friendly fire' exchange. All these were agreed devices to force the main strategy through and minimise any subsequent fallout.

To me, Dempsey's boast that there was no price the Irish government wouldn't pay to protect its citizens rang hollow. He didn't say there was no law that same administration wouldn't break either.

In the end the covert operation was a stunning success. Dempsey did what he was asked, delivering the hostages up safely; taking out any troublemakers, pulping all resistance. He carried no prisoners and made sure the media heard and reported only what he wanted. I was shipped out as soon as the medical team felt it safe to move me, first to France, then on to Australia via Hong Kong.

Nowhere in the exclusive account, among the syco-phantic words about bravery, cunning and clever-ness, is there a mention of the lives lost or careers wrecked. Of a mind tormented, a body battered, a spirit crushed. Or of a love affair destroyed.

Noel Dempsey killed my relationship with Lisa Duggan. In a plan as calculated and ruthless as his strategy to free the hostages he transferred Lisa to New York and out of the UN. She was put in protec-tive custody, assigned a new career and identity. We tried to meet up but physical exhaustion on my part and security concerns on her side frustrated every effort. Dempsey claimed the UN work had compromised her safety and refused unaccompanied travel. Then even accompanied travel was blocked as another alert surfaced. Milos Bracchovis had threatened her and no one was taking this lightly. Experience in Dublin showed that even from a prison cell Bracchovis could arrange a hit where and whenever he wanted.

Lisa was moved again, this time to Chicago. Another new career, another new identity. We spoke a lot by phone, both of us bottling our emotions, both pledging our affection. But after a while I sensed she was drifting, the distance between us more than just miles. She was beginning to sound frightened and apprehensive. Two trips were booked and cancelled within as many weeks, a third discussed but never arranged. Clicks on the line warned us our exchanges were being monitored and the terms of endearment hardened to casual gossip.

How are you?

Do you miss me?

What's the weather like there?

Can we meet?

Why not?

You'll have to come to me, Lisa. I'm not strong enough for a long-haul flight.

OK, we'll talk again in a couple of days.

But in a couple of days it was Noel Dempsey

who answered the phone, his nasal twang so sickeningly familiar.

She said she'd call one Wednesday and I waited in all day. Nothing. Nothing again until four days later and a detached and vague Lisa Duggan was talking about an opportunity back at the UN, this time based in Johannesburg. It would be a human-rights post, tracking abuses in neighbouring countries. The work, she told me, would be challenging and exciting. She forgot to tell me (neglected to tell me, didn't want to tell me) that she loved me before she hung up. The next time she rang I declined to speak, my heart broken, my morale rock bottom. I knew it was over between us.

Now, so many months on from the night of 12 February, I still feel betrayed. Used. Tricked and deceived. Bitter and forgotten. And I can't rid my thoughts of Lisa's words and her kisses in that hospital recovery unit.

Ambush

Paul Carson

Murder Cuts Both Ways . . .

Scott Nolan wants vengeance. One wintry Dublin morning a hit man took out not only his medical career and rising profile as a campaigner against drug abuse but also his beautiful wife, Laura.

Fuelled by guilt, grief and revenge, Scott enters into an uneasy alliance with Laura's brother, Detective Mark Higgins. Together they embark on a highly controversial covert mission to track down the killer. Using secret US army interrogation compounds and breaking almost every law in the land, the duo finally close in on their target.

As *Ambush* moves towards its violent climax, Paul Carson takes the reader on a white-knuckle ride of treachery, double-crossing and murder in this incredibly powerful thriller.

arrow books

**Order further Paul Carson titles
from your local bookshop, or have them delivered
direct to your door by Bookpost**